BY MY OWN HANDS

BY MY OWN HANDS
Jude Idada

CREOTERNITY BOOKS
A DIVISION OF CREOTERNITY INC.
CANADA

Order this book online at www.amazon.com
or at any other international amazon website.

© Copyright 2014 Jude Idada.
All rights reserved. No part of this publication may be
reproduced, stored in a retrieval system, or transmitted, in any
form or by any means, electronic, mechanical, photocopying,
recording, or otherwise, without the written prior permission
of the author.

Cover and Book design by Daniel Choi.

Printed in the United States of America.
ISBN: 1501080563 (sc)
LCCN: 2014917907
CreateSpace Independent Publishing Platform, North Charleston, SC.

A Creoternity Books Publication.
www.creoternity.com

Book sales also available through other participating online stores and book stores.

This title is also available as an ebook.

To You For Being There.

1

Annabelle Sciorra wiped the tears that ran like meandering streams down her cheeks. She stifled a sob, closed her eyes, and kicked the chair from beneath her feet. For a fraction of a second, she froze in mid-air then came down with a swoosh. Her fall broke when the nylon rope went taut, cutting deep into her neck.

She held her breath and waited for the inevitable. She counted silently and relaxed. She could feel her body getting heavier; her lungs had begun to burn. When she got to the number thirteen, in the darkness of her resigned mind, an image suddenly appeared. It was her daughter, dressed in the silk white chiffon dress that fell just below her knees, which she had worn to her first holy communion. She was smiling, a smile that revealed her missing baby teeth and one that shone the light of hope. Then her lips moved and the words came out in a whisper, sprinkled with all the droppings of childlike innocence.

"Mummy... please don't leave me."

A thousand alarm bells exploded in Annabelle's ears and her

eyes flew open, mouth ajar in a silent scream as her hands flew to her neck, clawing desperately at the strangulating rope.

For a fraction of a second, she kicked her legs in all directions, and then focused them on the legs of the upturned chair that sat a few unfortunate metres from her. She stretched out the tip of her left white shoe in a bid to gain a foothold. It couldn't reach it. She heaved and rocked harder towards it but her shoe came up a couple of inches short, the effort forcing her to swing in the opposite direction.

A grunt escaped her tightly constricted windpipe as she desperately sucked in air; her neck, crisscrossed by fingernail marks that left it a mass of thinly bleeding lines. Her eyes rolled in their sockets, cheeks glistened with tears, pale tongue shot out from parched lips as her body jerked spasmodically.

On one end, the taut rope pulled heavily on the metal hook of the ceiling fan while at the other end it fought against the struggling body of Annabelle. Slowly, her flailing lower limbs reduced their momentum, her fighting upper limbs decreased their struggle, and in less than two minutes she became still, hanging like a marionette at rest from the end of the green nylon rope.

She was clad in her white Balenciaga wedding gown.

Andrew Sciorra's breath came out in short loud groans as he repeatedly pounded into the mass of feminine flesh that lay wet, moaning beneath him. Sweat glistened on his surprisingly muscular body as he strove successfully to satisfy the young, lustful flesh. He was sixty-two; she was only twenty-one.

They were ensconced in her posh three bedroom condominium on Queens Quay in downtown Toronto. The title deed was in his name. She was the fifth and longest lasting tenant; the rest had all been female.

She screamed out his name as she reached the crest for the

second time. At that moment the beeper of his pager went off. He stopped in mid-stroke, bile rising up angrily in his throat. Instantly, he was tempted to continue, deciding to ignore the insistent beep, but he knew better. The pager was for emergencies only and just two people had the number; his personal assistant and himself.

He tried to roll over but the bucking machine beneath him held on tightly, she increased her grinding movements in the same instant, artfully clinching her lower lips and the muscles hidden within her, which sensuously gripped and coaxed a much-needed release from him. As the pleasure increased, he pushed the immediacy of the beeper behind, resolving to return the call after he crested, and then moved furiously in unison with the woman beneath him as he ecstatically rode along towards the horizon of his own release.

Therese Sciorra fought desperately to maintain control of her already rising temper as she watched Timothy Vinelatter shouting and as though on cue, throw his glass of Henessey at the far wall. It shattered and sprayed its contents on the large oil paintings that hung on the wall. This was him acting out his usual tirade. She stood up and walked over to the large French windows that occupied the entire west wall of the room, leaving the thirty-eight-year-old millionaire sitting agitated on the tan leather sofa.

As she gazed at the flowing traffic, which looked like an army of tiny ants snaking their way along Bay Street twenty floors below, her thoughts drifted away from the scene she was witnessing and wandered to the cause of their latest quarrel.

Five days ago, he had once again accused her of infidelity, saying that she was having an affair with his closest friend. She could not understand why he was so insecure, seeing phantoms whenever she got an inch too close to any man. In her mind's eyes she still could see him as the dashing, young, millionaire sailor with the laissez faire air she met four years ago while holidaying with her family in the tiny holiday resort of Ibiza that lies in the Balearic Islands off the southernmost tip of Spain. As their relationship grew more serious in the last two years, he had become an overly possessive monster. Because of him, she hardly kept friends. Apart from her parents, her social life was nearly nonexistent; to him all that mattered and should was HIM and him alone. She knew it was not the best for her; she knew she had to leave, but she had neither the will nor courage to. Deep down in her heart she knew that she loved him like she had never loved anyone or anything before.

She turned around; her anger dissipating as she looked at his handsomely chiselled face. She hated seeing him so flustered with anger. Her heart beat increased as she walked back to him, knelt before him, put her arms around his waist, her face on his chest,

"I am sorry."

"You better fucking be."

"I won't pick his calls again... I promise... I'll only talk to him, when and where you want me to... is that okay?"

He stared at her, face as stiff as Grecian marble, then he abruptly smiled in response and at that moment her cell phone began to ring. She disengaged and made to pick it up. He pushed it away from her reach, shook his head, and then slowly began to remove her clothing.

The phone kept on ringing.

"Oh my God!" It came out like the whisper of air escaping a burst tire. Andrew Sciorra's face was a mask of shock as he listened to the voice at the other end of the phone. His left hand twitched uncontrollably; his face rapidly drained of colour.

The dozing mass at his side sensed his panicky movements,

woke up, and lifted her shaggily-haired head from the bed, her eyes was still dreamily set.

"Hey, what's wrong?" she asked groggily.

As though in a daze, he got up from the bed with rapid movements and began donning his clothes. She sat up on the bed, legs crossed in the lotus position, and watched him incredulously as he hurried into his charcoal grey dress pants.

"Andy, why are…?"

Before the words came out, he had disappeared out of the door; his silk boxer shorts and tie lay strewn on the floor.

Therese Sciorra's voice rose in an eerie scream as she watched her mother's body being wheeled out of the house. She made to dart towards it, but was held back by the strong arms of Phillip Neri, her father's personal assistant. He manoeuvred her quickly through the crowd of police that had thronged the stately mansion and now scrounged the grounds searching for evidence. He deftly moved her into the silver phantom Rolls Royce that stood at the opposite side of the driveway.

"No… No… Mummy!" she broke out again in a soul-numbing wail as she disappeared into the silent womb of the car.

Therese tried struggling with the restraining Phillip, her body bucking in a bid to spill out of the car.

"Therese, get a hold of yourself!" Phillip shouted in a stern voice.

Through her furious haze, his words finally got to her. As her hysteria quietened, she collapsed onto his chest, her eyes bleeding out tears, her body heaving in its wake.

"It will be okay… she is in a better place." Phillip said reassuringly to her as he repeatedly stroked her tangled blond hair. His shirt was soaked with her hot, salty tears.

The blood-red Porsche 911 Turbo S Cabriolet screeched to a halt in the centre of the road. The door shot open, and Andrew flew out. His eyes were a riot as they took in the scene in front of his house. The crowd went into slow motion as they took in the man that stood there staring; unbuttoned shirt flaring in the slight breeze, ruffled hair, bloodshot eyes darting in all directions. An acknowledgement of recognition silently flowed around. The flashing beacons of the ambulance attracted Andrew's attention. He walked towards it in a daze. As he edged closer, he broke into a staggering jog. The sight of the yellow body bag that was being lifted into the rear compartment sent choked sobs to his throat. He struggled against blurring vision as his chest tightened into a knot; he didn't see the uniformed duo that were making towards him as he broke from his staggering jog into a full throttle. They stopped him a few feet from the open doors.

"Mr Sciorra..." The taller, red-haired one spoke.

"Annabelle..." It was an unbelieving whisper.

He pushed through the standing duo, reaching the gurney in an instant. A uniformed crowd slowly gathered around them.

"Mr Sciorra, I am sorry, but we cannot allow you get to the corpse." The uniformed brunette edged in front of him, her hands placed in comfort on the upper bulge of his arms. Her voice seemed to knock him back to the present; he focused on her, a look of dawning realisation appeared in shock-filled pupils. He opened his parched lips and a hoarse voice escaped.

"She is my wife... I want to see my wife."

Silently, the officers turned him around and gently led him away. He followed them obediently. After a few steps, he turned his head and looked above his escorts towards the doors of the ambulance that were now being closed, and then turned round to face the moving blaring corpse cart. The escorts stood around him, each one standing at alert as they collectively shared in his grief.

As the corpse cart disappeared, something distinctly snapped in Andrew. He opened his quivering mouth in a pained gesture but no sound issued forth, save for the liquid drops of anguish that made their way down his face.

Even at that moment, across the seas in Lagos, Nigeria, two people sat in sorrowful contemplation; one the father, the other the son. The former, Ibude Eweka; the latter, Nosa. They spoke in hushed tones although they were alone in the sprawling mansion.

The lamp on the bedside table partially illuminated the face of the father as he sat on the leather cushion at the foot of the bed, staring at his son, who was making a gargantuan effort in keeping his heavy eyelids from shutting.

"Are you sleepy?" he asked for the umpteenth time.

"No, Dad," he lied, shifting his position on the bed in a bid to clear his sleep filled head.

His father sighed as his eyes took on a faraway look. Nosa noticed and once again made an effort to comfort him.

"Dad, you have to rest. I know how you feel. I feel the same way too, but this is not the way of solving it."

"Then what is the way?" There was a hint of sarcasm in the words.

"I don't know, but tomorrow when the lawyer gets back to us, we will know what to do."

Ibude looked back at him; a short laugh escaped his seated form in visible mockery.

"What's funny, Dad?" He spoke defensively; his father's recent quirky behaviour had begun to irritate him.

"Nothing... It is just that..." his voice trailed off.

Nosa waited for his father to finish his sentence and didn't realise the moment he finally fell asleep.

He sprang awake, body bathed in sweat, mind rolling in panic. His room was enveloped in darkness. Nosa strained his eyes and ears, listening for what he wasn't sure he heard or saw. After a few minutes, he reached over and switched on the bedside lamp, his heart still hammering in his chest.

He squinted as his eyes slowly adjusted to the light as he desperately tried to comprehend what had awakened him in such a panic. He looked around the room as he searched for a reason, then his eyes played to the leather sofa at the foot of the bed. Instantaneously, he remembered. His father! He was out of the room before he even realised it, his feet drumming on the carpeted floors as he ran towards his father's bedroom, his very being trembling in fearful dread.

Therese lay huddled on the settee, her head resting on Timothy's lap. Her eyes were bloodshot; his were not, although a deep sadness hung like worn draperies over his face. Andrew sat slouched, wrapped with a blanket on the La-Z-Boy, looking at the far wall in a vacant stare. Phillip walked back and forth, ten steps in opposite directions; he was deep in thought. The family room was quiet. It had taken Timothy five hours to hear the news; actually, he had left Therese asleep at his apartment to attend a business meeting at the Metro Convention Centre, when Phillip had finally gotten through to her on her phone. He hadn't seen the near-crazy Therese run amok as she fled towards her home neither did he see the morbid scene at the house. It was during the last hour of the meeting that a sobbing Therese had dropped the news over his cellular phone. He stayed until the end of the meeting, had dinner with an elderly business partner at the Sutton Place before he drove to the Sciorra residence. He had been with her ever since then.

"What do we do now?" Timothy's baritone filled the room.

"I am thinking." It came out after a prolonged delay; Phillip had never hidden his dislike for Timothy.

"We can't afford to waste valuable time thinking, this place will soon be teeming with sympathisers once word gets out." He had stressed on the word "we".

Phillip stopped and turned to him. His face a mask of seething rage, he couldn't understand what Therese saw in the barracuda that passed off for a man.

"Do you have any ideas?" His voice didn't betray his anger.

"Yeah, I have a couple of friends at the Metro and Peel region police, I could send word to them to make sure nothing gets out about the contents of the suicide note." Once again he stressed on the word "suicide."

"I have already done that and more," There was no sign of triumph in his words.

He remained silent for a short while, then said, "Good, then we should start working on Mr. Sciorra's press statement."

"There would be no press statement... at least for now." Phillip's irritation was beginning to break through the thin veneer of pretence.

"There has to be... the press will go to town when they find out about Andrew's whereabouts while Mrs Sciorra was busy..."

Phillip looked towards the seated Andrew, concern written all over his face before he shot Timothy a caustic look. This time his voice didn't hide the venom of his disgust.

"Mr. Vinelatter... Please."

Phillip's tone cut like a whip. Timothy swallowed the rest of his words.

They stared at each other in silent battle and then, pulling his wits together, Timothy acted as though celebrating his triumph by stroking the hair of the now-sleeping Therese, a smile plastered on his face as he held the gaze of Phillip, whose anger was flaring hot.

Andrew kept staring into nothingness, oblivious of all that was happening around him.

Nosa didn't burst into his father's room, but stopped in front of the polished obeche wood. He quietened his panting breath, said an inaudible prayer as snippets of his dream came crashing back into his memory, snippets which in themselves made no sense but yet somehow echoed something foreboding. He shook his head clear and then respectfully knocked. He waited for the usual reply. There was none. He knocked again, a little louder. He waited. No reply. He knocked more loudly this time, panic rising. This time there was a reply. The door responded to the furious pounding and slowly swung open. It had been ajar all the while.

He didn't know why fear tightened his guts as he took the first step into the room but an eerie feeling descended on him, a feeling that made adrenaline pump into his veins. He stepped fully into the darkness. Once in, he reached for the switch on the right wall, flicked it on and the room could see.

His father's bed was empty.

Angela Di Canio, the late Annabelle's female aide, sat downstairs by the telephone in the sitting room answering calls. Two private guards sat in the inner lounge of the entrance to the house. One uniformed cop stood in front of the police tape that cordoned off Andrew's study, another stood outside the main entrance, while the remaining three stood at the main gate of the residence keeping the gathering crowd of newsmen away from the scene.

The Sciorras were one of the five wealthiest families in Canada, building a fortune in the diamond trade through half a century of tireless toil, a business that started with Mario Sciorra, a jeweller of distinct expertise and of Italian extraction who had immigrated to Canada in the early 1950s. He had died in the mid 80s alongside his equally celebrated wife in an airplane crash over the Andes at the age of sixty, leaving a multimillion dollar business to his only son, Andrew. He in turn had multiplied his inheritance in countless folds over the years, in addition to establishing a reputation as an intercontinental Casanova.

Andrew had surprised the upper-class world when at the age of forty he married the shy, conservative Catholic lawyer daughter of the then Italian ambassador to Canada. He was truthful when he said in countless circles that she was the first person he genuinely loved. A daughter came the next year after a horrendous life-threatening pregnancy; he named her after his late mother. He had once again surprised the sceptics when he remained extremely loyal and faithful to his scintillating wife and thus became the quintessential family man. The picture shattered two years later when as a result of two consecutive miscarriages the doctors had given the Sciorra's a choice between a hysterectomy or a more-than-likely fatal pregnancy. They had regretfully chosen the former.

In two weeks Andrew had returned to his old ways.

Nosa had walked the length of the gardens; the flowers were in full bloom, giving the sprawling compound a psychedelic look as the green and white finery of the Queen of the Night plant enveloped the moon lit darkness with its alluring scented appeal. This garden was his father's first love, the product of his undying attention. Little wonder it had been the first place Nosa had thought he would be.

He made his way across the driveway towards the entrance of the house, an owl hooted loudly and a raven answered in return. He looked up just in time to see the raven rise in its full majesty and fly into the dark of the night. The thought about it being a bad omen if a raven perches on a house before dawn crossed his mind but unconsciously he pushed it away as a faint sound attracted his attention.

It was a humming sound coming from the three-car garage

that stood some metres to his left. He hesitated for a moment then listened carefully. When the persistent hum became distinct from the surrounding early morning sounds, he cautiously walked towards the direction. The line of white light he could see seeping out through the chinks of the chain door puzzled him. He was sure he had put off the lights when he parked his Audi in the garage the night before. He went into alarm mode as he mentally checked the facts in rhythm to his hurried footsteps.

His dad was already in so he had locked up. The guards did not hold any of the keys as a result of the security measure his father had put in place three years ago, when his mother had been killed in an armed robbery attack on Christmas Eve. It had occurred in the same garage, where she had run for cover, it being the safest and most fortified part of the house. One of the guards had been led there at gunpoint to open the doors. His mother stood no chance.

The new security procedure was one that allowed the door to be biometrically opened by nuclear family members only; all they had to do was place their open palms on the black opaque console that jutted out midway from the right hand corner of the armoured door. It was on that console that Nosa placed his palm.

The door slowly slid open and he was rapidly surrounded by noxious fumes. He staggered back, instantly wracked with coughs. He called out to the guards who sat in their post at the front gates. Nosa waved his hands in front of him to clear a view into the fume filled garage. Through his racing thoughts he struggled hard to understand how fire had engulfed the garage.

The guards arrived at Nosa's side, each one shouting at the top of their voices. All he could hear were the words "Fire extinguisher!" He answered in the affirmative as soon as he realised that they were asking him if there was one in the garage. No sooner had he said this than one of them ran into the garage, his arms clearing the fumes away from his sight. It took the fumes about two minutes to escape into the cool early morning air. The light in the garage spewed out. He could see the guard searching for the source of the fire, extinguisher in hand. As the fumes continually dispersed, the interior of the garage became partially visible and from the place he stood he could see that the Lexus sedan also had its interior filled with fumes. He shouted to the guard and pointed in that direction. The burly guard nodded in response and moved towards the car, circling it from the far left, looking for signs of flames.

Just then from where he stood outside the garage, stomach feeling nauseous, he saw something jutting from the rear of the car, over the trunk and onto the roof. His heart froze in his chest. He walked towards the car unconsciously, beads of sweat appearing on his forehead, his stomach filled with dread.

As Nosa stopped by the window of the driver's seat he gaped in horror at the sight that beheld him; his father buckled in on the driver's seat, his head hanging low on his chest. The blue garden hose snaked from the exhaust pipe to the right window belching out fumes. He didn't need anyone to tell him his father was dead.

One by one, sympathisers with their heads bowed slowly marched into the confines of the Sciorra residence. These were the people who could not be kept away by a simple phone call. They were the names that appeared on North America's who's who; the transcontinental bourgeoisie. Most of them had been here on more beatific occasions, but now they were here to mourn the very hostess that had often made them feel like royalty.

Once inside the Tudor style mansion that sat on Dunvegan Avenue in the high brow residential area of Forest Hill, they were greeted by Phillip Neri, who led them into the post- modernist furnished sitting room, where Andrew sat in mute stupor and Therese played the mourning hostess.

They all stayed an average of thirty gruesome minutes, excusing themselves after they inadvertently ran short of words. Andrew's silence and unfocused look was disquieting, Therese put on her cheerfulness and her small talk was comforting, but her extremely sad blue eyes told a different story. It was too much for anyone, especially when the story about the hanging body clad in a wedding dress replaced the life size portrait of the dazzlingly beautiful Annabelle that hung on the south wall, beneath which lay an opened book, a gold pen and a wreath of white tulips.

The house was a mourning bustle of family relatives. At the core of the gloomy scene was an immobile group of three men, discussing something in hush tones. All dressed in black. Nosa was one of the three.

"It is against tradition," the grey haired man said, ending in his usual slow cadence.

"I know, but at least, there should be a compromise in this case," Nosa argued stubbornly.

"Suicide is suicide, our custom abhors it," the other man said, sternness evident in his voice.

"So what do you want me to do?" Nosa looked him straight in the face; he couldn't believe that his father's only brother was taking an opposite stance to him.

"This is what we have been saying. We have to first do some cleansing rituals to the house, and then to you, since you were the one who found the body..."

"I am not performing any rituals." His voice rose slightly as he cut his uncle off. They both looked at him, their eyes burning with sorrowful angst.

"I mean I am a Christian, and..."

"We are all Christians." His uncle's voice had a bitter taste to it.

Again, silence prevailed. The sarcasm had registered.

"Look, no one is trying to force you to do anything against your wishes or beliefs, but believe me, what we are facing here is above any one of us." The grey haired man had his right hand on Nosa's shoulder. He continued, "Your father has committed a taboo. I mean the land itself will reject him if we bury him without those rituals. Have you read Chinua Achebe's *Things Fall Apart*?"

"Yes." Nosa was obviously becoming impatient.

"Remember that Okonkwo's corpse had to be dumped in the evil forest after he took his life." His words were caked with condemnation.

"Uncle, we are in the twenty-first century for Christ's sake! We can't allow some dumb old pagan tradition rule our lives. I mean you are a medical doctor, so am I. We can convince the old folks in the village to see reason." His temper was having free reign.

"That thing you call a dumb old pagan tradition is your identity, you can never run away from it."

"It will only be my identity if I accept it as such. Uncle, culture itself is dynamic, if it wasn't, the Egyptians would be embalming their dead and the Ugep people would still be cannibals." Nosa's voice had taken a pleading tone, his temper nose diving.

"Let us save ourselves all the hassle; the plain fact is that your father will not be buried if we do not perform those rituals." His uncle had a look of stubborn determination. A silence followed during which Nosa's shifting eyes and rising heartbeat signalled he was also about to make his own decision.

"Fine, in that case I will bury him myself," Nosa said.

The shaved jaws of the two men dropped. Their eyes flew wide open in shock. Nosa watched them defiantly. Their tempers were bulging with swollen veins. He could hear their pulses thumping rapidly within them.

"You can't be serious." His uncle tried vainly to hide his alarm.

"Try me." Nosa's eyes were made of cold steel. "Excuse me, I have a funeral to arrange." With that he turned and walked away.

Two mouths hung agape, as the four eyes above them stared in shock.

The funeral was low-key. Spring accompanied the small crowd as they escorted the body. Fourteen people stood by as the steel casket was lowered into the grave in the Sciorra family lot at the Mount Pleasant cemetery in Toronto.

Their eyes were misted. Lips quivering but silent as they watched the last earthly remains of Annabelle Sciorra take their place alongside her father and mother-in-law. There was a collective disdain for Andrew, who painted a picture of pure, hopeless grief, as he stood with a blank stare in his black double-breasted Armani suit. Therese stood by his right side, fashionably dressed in a chic black Vivienne Westwood skirt suit, a black halo hat and wide brim sunglasses, arm wrapped around the waist of Timothy Vinelatter who had his handsome face set in a smirk. Phillip Neri stood by Andrew's left, separating him from Annabelle's sister who was bristling with sorrowful rage, mumbling inaudibly to no one in particular. It was a sad end to that joy-streaked summer afternoon, some two plus decades ago, when Andrew Sciorra had taken as his wife, the art worthy beautiful Annabelle Medici.

Only Nosa's close friends and those of his nuclear family witnessed him bury his father. His bloodshot eyes were cleverly hidden behind Gucci sunglasses as he performed the last rites at the graveside in Ikoyi cemetery. His face was set in a benign smile, belying the fact that his soul was in turmoil.

It had been a battle to get a Catholic priest to officiate over the burial. His father, who had been a knight of the Augustine order and the major financial contributor to the building of the parish, was refused a Catholic burial because of what the Bishop had explained as "a crime against God, the church, and himself."

Nosa had to resort to seeking the services of a Pentecostal revivalist pastor, who had accepted the onerous task without having previously known him or the departed. Wisely, the Pastor had given a short exhortation on condemnation and judgement at the graveside, evidently a jab at the extended family and the Catholic Church, who in his words "had cast the first stone even though they were not without sin."

Even as the proceedings went on, many people stood in the blazing midday sun, wondering where the other son of the deceased was; the word was around that it was as a result of a calamitous action of the "nowhere to be seen" first son that the deceased had taken his life.

"You Godforsaken, double crossing, cheating, miserable son of a swamp rat!" With those words, the perfectly manicured long fingernails of Annabelle's sister racked jagged lines across Andrew's face.

The unexpectedness of the action caught everyone off guard. Phillip was the first person to break free from the group paralysis and make for the darting bundle of fury; he caught her in mid-air, taking the brunt of her kicking legs. With amazing strength and gentlemanly comportment he made his way from the drawing room where the tempered funeral reception was being held, while holding tight to the shrieking woman.

"You will burn in hell, Andrew Sciorra!" she shrieked, "Annabelle's spirit will not rest until you join her, you miserable whore lover." She shrieked again.

"Let go of me!... let go of me!" She was becoming more hysterical, as Phillip struggled to get her up the grand staircase. Therese, awash with shame ran to his aid.

"Auntie M, please... for God's sake, stop!" Her cry was desperate.

Like magic, her aunt immediately went docile. Then after a break of a few seconds she broke out in quiet sobs, crumbling in Phillips arms.

"Phillip, it's okay, you can put her down." Therese had been showing such strength and control since the morning after the death. Phillip did as he was told.

"Oh Therese... Oh my baby," the handsomely proportioned maudlin woman said as she moved towards Therese, enveloping her in a motherly hug.

"How could this happen...? How could he do this to her?" Her words were wet with tears.

"It's okay. It's all right... Let's go upstairs, we are already creating a scene," she said this in reference to the small crowd that was gravitating towards them. Slowly, they made their way up the winding staircase, leaving Phillip and the whispering crowd staring after them. At the first landing, her aunt stopped and looked up at the family portrait that hung high up on the wall. The smiling trio of Andrew, Annabelle and Therese returned her stare. The picture had been taken the day Therese graduated from the Osgoode Law School.

"He killed her... Therese, you know that the bastardo finally killed her?" Therese was silent.

In her mind's eye, she could see the scene of her mother crying into her aunt's breast as the news of her father's latest and seemingly permanent concubines made the rounds of their social circles. Even then as she watched the two sisters, from the corridor of their summer residence in the French Riviera,

Therese could feel the clinging wetness of her mother's soul deep embarrassment and could smell the suffocating stench of her father's shameless trysts. It was at that moment that Therese had first felt the passion of the blossoming hatred she had for her father.

The note her mother left behind had made it worse.

"There is really nothing we can do." The family lawyer sat talking with Nosa. They were both ensconced in his father's personal living room, family mementoes plastered on the walls and perching on every available space.

"You mean it's all gone?"

"Apart from the cars, everything else." the lawyer's head was bent low.

"I can't believe it," Nosa said. His statement lacked conviction.

"I believe your father understood the gravity of the situation."

"Whooh!... So the bastard sold everything... How could he?" The question seemed rhetorical. "I mean..." Nosa stopped and then as if realising what was staring him in the face, he gasped out, "We are finished."

The lawyer was quiet.

After a prolonged silence, Nosa spoke "How long do we have?"

"The buyers want to take possession of the houses in two weeks."

"What about the factory?"

"Well, as I told your Dad, that is a no win situation."

"But he said that he was settling out of court with the bankers."

"Yes, that was why he had intended selling the land in Abuja..."

"And what about that one?" Nosa was impatient.

"It was the first to go and then others followed; the way I see it, the bank is taking the factory and the business..." He broke for a short while and then continued, "I hope you now understand why your Dad did what he did?"

"Yeah... I do."

"I collected his letter back from the police." The lawyer brought out the embossed paper from his inner jacket and handed it over. Nosa took it and although he had found it himself, he began reading it again.

The lawyer watched the bowed head of his friend's son. From his vantage position he could feel the young man's aching heart. He wished he could do more than all he had already done, but lost for ideas he had no choice but allow his own heart, ache in accompaniment to that of the grief stricken young man. Just out of medical school and seized by such grief.

Without shifting his eyes from the paper, which was vibrating in his hands, Nosa spoke, "Any word about my brother?"

"Nothing... it is like he has vanished into thin air. I was surprised that even your dad's obituary didn't drag him out... Sometimes, it is so hard to believe that he actually did it." The pain was evident in the lawyer's eyes "Well, the police are still searching." The lawyer sounded as though he also needed some consolation himself.

He let his eyes bore into Nosa, who sat there staring at the letter, emotions rioting.

"I know how you feel... Believe me, I do... if there is anything you need or in case you want to talk through it all... I will always be here for you" The last words were meant as a reassurance from a man who single-handedly bankrolled his father's funeral.

Nosa quietly listened; shoulders hunched, head bowed, hands shaking, tears flowing.

2

"I am the king of my country." Osasu's sexy baritone drawled out. The faint smile that hung on his face had a subliminal quality to it that gave him the look of a schooled predator. His burnished brown eyes glowed like amber as he held the gaze of the blue eyes that stared back at him in a swoon. In the arena of skirt chasing, he was a maestro.

The snow fell heavily like dollops of wet confetti, as it danced in the wind that billowed outside, but the accompanying chill was barely discernible inside the sardine packed nightclub on Richmond Street West in downtown Toronto. The music boomed out from the surrounding Bose speakers and like drunken fiends the revellers glowing under psychedelic lights grooved to the beat; man to woman, woman to woman, man to man, black, White, Latino, Asian, sweating, hollering as the day slowly woke up.

The smile that glided across Angela's face as she stared at Osasu was barely noticeable. She listened in mercurial attention to the honeyed words that poured from his lips. Even then her heart was drumming out the rhythm of infatuation. Angela's muscle of life had been doing this since the night she met Osasu at the Sharks sports bar at the north eastern corner of Islington and Steeles.

On that chilly winter night, while returning from work, she had slipped in to get a couple of margaritas and had been surprised by the crowd at the bar. She pushed through bodies that stood gyrating as they celebrated a goal that had just been scored by the Maple leafs, which was being shown on one of the super sized high definition televisions that hugged the northern walls. It had been while she was pushing through that a firm hand grabbed her arm, she had stopped for a moment, willing out a bristling rage from the core of her being, her rising fury fuelled by the presumption that it was one of the drunken louts that passed as men who had laid hands on her.

How dare they touch her! She wheeled about, slamming her fragile shoulders into muscled biceps and was stopped in mid-motion by the arresting good looks of Osasu. They stared at each other for a moment. Brown eyes boring into blue eyes, he smiled; she unconsciously smiled back. It was when he spoke that her heart started beating in that peculiar rhythm. That was five weeks ago. It had been beating ever since.

A stop to get a couple of margaritas had quickly metamorphosed into a whirlwind romance. All it had taken was one electrifying look and she was soaring high on the wings of Cupid. Who would have believed that Angela, who had been brought up with the conviction that all things Italian were Kosher; that God was a Catholic and therefore Italian; that the way to heaven was paved with the stones that ran along the Appian way; that there was a good Italian boy for every Italian girl; would fall helplessly in love with a black African. Angela herself was amazed at the turn of events and tired of questioning her heart, she had abandoned herself to this ebony Adonis of a man that sat smiling in front of her.

Osasu stood up, rising to the full majesty of his six foot five inches frame and walked towards the door. Angela followed him, stopping at the cloakroom to pick up her leather jacket, she knew that when Osasu went quiet in this fashion, it was a sign that testosterone was soaring through his veins. She could also feel the blood coagulating in her lower lips. She took a deep breath, zipped up her jacket, braced herself for the pleasurable ordeal that lay ahead of her, and hurried after Osasu into the freezing Toronto night.

Osasu watched the smoke from his joint of marijuana swirl up in the air. As it dissipated, he slightly opened his darkly pink lips and more smoke slipped out. He gazed at it again, this time it rose up in the air in the shape of an amorphous circle. He smiled, bright pink tongue flicking at his upper lip.

He turned his head sideways to look at the sleeping mane by his side. He watched it move slightly and then settle back in innocent slumber.

"Angela," he whispered.

"Mmmm," she replied, her voice drugged with sleep. She stayed motionless for a short while and then turned to face him. Her eyelids fluttered open and the blue of her eyes shone. She was the first woman he had met that still looked arrestingly beautiful after just waking from sleep.

"How's your boss?"

"Oooh Saz," she moaned in fake annoyance. *Saz* was the name she called him.

"Sorry love, was just concerned, don't want you losing your job."

"You're so sweet." She raised her head an inch and pecked him on his lips. "Just the same, catatonic is the word, says nothing, does nothing. He just stares and stares." Her voice took up a faraway tone.

"And Therese?"

"Hey boy! You sure are catching on fast, you even know her name?" Laughter sang behind her voice. He smiled. She continued, rising up and placing her head on his chest. Face to face. "What about her?"

"How is she putting up?"

"Pretty good I'll say, better than expected to be honest, that's when you think of how close she was to her mother." She went quiet for a while. Her eyes glazed. A deep heavy blanket of sorrow slid over her. Then words slowly tumbled out; "I loved Annabelle Sciorra... She treated me like her own... Sometimes I just feel you men are all bastards."

"Yeah sometimes I think we are," Osasu concluded, staring into the relaxed peace of her eyes.

Osasu was the first son of Ibude Eweka. He it was whose infamous action had driven his father to suicide.

His striking good looks were a direct inheritance from his mother. His tall athletic frame was handed down by his father. No one could say from whom he had inherited his cold steel heart or the cunning that ordered his day. But one thing was certain, he had lived without any outward complaint under the shadow of his excitingly brilliant younger brother; Nosa.

There was a difference of two years between the two brothers. But where Nosa had finished medical school at the age of twenty-four, Osasu had barely managed to stagger through high school. As the former's sharp intelligence was celebrated, the latter's acumen for street smarts went unnoticed. Little wonder Osasu had continually plotted out a strategy to steal what he believed was his rightful inheritance; his father's wealth in its entirety.

Ibude Eweka on his part had been burdened by Osasu's lack

of scholarly expertise. He had first noticed it when Nosa had memorised the complete alphabets a year before his elder brother. At the time, his wife had shrugged it off, saying that people learnt at their own pace, but when at the age of seven, he still couldn't master the alphabets, they had been alarmed. It was at that time they began their trips to doctors and behavioural therapists. Some said dyslexia, others disputed it. Some said Attention Deficit Disorder, others disputed it. One had even said that Osasu was a classic case of a natural born moron, it had taken the pleas of his wife to stop Ibude from smashing in the doctor's face.

And when they had begun to tire, Osasu had surprised them all. One Monday morning as they sat at the breakfast table, he had calmly reached over his bowl of corn-flakes cereal, picked up his father's Daily Times newspaper, and in a confident and calm voice began to read loudly. For the first few seconds Ibude and his wife didn't notice the feat that was being performed as they discussed their plans for the day. It was Nosa sitting askance from his brother, sweetened milk forming a moustache on his bewildered face, who had brought their attention to it when he shouted:

"Osasu is reading!"

Silence dropped like a lead ball on the table. His father and mother stared with shocked eyes at the scene that was unfolding before them. Sitting there with back ramrod straight was their first son dressed in a navy blue cotton T-shirt, reading audibly from a newspaper. That had been the beginning of the wonders that Osasu had wrought.

For the next six years, Osasu's mental acumen developed at a frightening pace as he climbed through the school ladder. An infectious charismatic aura surrounded him as his features grew into a striking handsomeness that was further complimented by his growing height, athletic abilities, and his way with words. At the time it seemed like all his mother's friends playfully referred to him as their daughters' husband and his father's friends jokingly claimed that he was the true replica of his father, Ibude. Osasu took all the compliments in his youthful stride as each added day seemed to reveal him in another light. On his fourteenth birthday, Osasu simply switched off.

His abrupt stagnation baffled everyone who knew him. It was like someone had died. The scholarly fire that burned in his eyes lost their fierceness and was replaced with the dull glow of dying embers. His voracious reading of the written word was replaced by an allergy to books. His grades at school nosedived. His lengthy intellectual discourses with his parents tapered off. His bubbly nature was replaced by a cold calm that stared daggers from his brown hazelnut eyes. Avarice slowly claimed control of Osasu's soul as his fascination shifted to the dark shadows that peopled the streets. It was like he had disappeared into a psychological vortex within which he could no longer be reached.

As Osasu's silence deepened so did his star dim and right before his eyes, Nosa stepped into his shoes. Osasu's shoes unfortunately proved to be too small for Nosa and as fate willed it, Nosa unconsciously assumed the position of first son of the Eweka family. Osasu on his part seemed to be relieved of the responsibilities that came with that position and drifted away emotionally from his family.

There actually were two Osasu's; the morbidly quiet one at home and the raucous one in the teeming streets of Lagos Island; the dull one at school and the cunning one in the betting parlours of Akala, Mushin; the shy one who shunned girls at the Catholic Church at Falomo and the debonair one chasing the skirts along Allen Avenue; the recluse that avoided confrontations at the sports field at school and the rugged hero of more than a dozen fisticuffs in the backwaters of Ajegunle known as "Land of Settlement."

No one knew of the double lifestyle he lived since he was an authority unto himself. He had worn his parents out through the countless battles they waged in a bid to draw him out of his shell and monitor his movements. All his father asked was that he finish high school and Osasu in his silent way lumbered towards that goal. He realised long ago that having a high school diploma was in his best interests. Osasu only did things that were in his best interests.

He didn't even show up to take his place on the rostrum as his classmates, face plastered with smiles, bright purple gowns hanging from their shoulders, orange tassels dangling from the cap on their heads, walked in a file to receive their handshakes and certificates from the dirty-black, stout, and vulture-headed Minister of Education.

He wasn't there as the others received hugs from their ecstatic parents because at that same time his parents and Nosa kept embarrassed, straight faces while surrounded by the evident celebrations around them, Osasu was nearly fifty miles away threatening a local timber merchant to pay his monthly dues. The last thing his father would have imagined was that his seventeen-year-old son was a feared "Area father" in the inner slums of Lagos Island.

Therese Sciorra brushed aside the strand of black hair that dangled across her fore head. She didn't bother to wipe the tears that strolled down her cheeks as she watched the home video of her eighteenth birthday. She looked at her mother as she pirouetted across the dance floor in pure happiness. So full of life and now dead. Finished. Gone.

"Mum." The word escaped in a whisper.

She had repeated that word unconsciously for the past week at unforeseen moments. It had been a month and a half since her mother was buried and it seemed that the reality of her death had finally begun to sink in. She wrapped her sweater-clad arms around herself in a hug coated with grief. She didn't hear the door silently swing open neither did she see Angela stand in the doorway, staring at her.

Angela watched the scene playing out on the large screen plasma television. It was as if Annabelle had come to life. As though her spirit would leap out of the screen and materialise before them. She looked at Andrew laughing into the camera as it panned across him. She watched the sprightly teenagers dancing. She watched Phillip sharing a word with a group of black suited gentlemen; ever loyal Phillip. Phillip who had been there from the get-go. Phillip who had hired her. Just then she heard a sob escape the seated Therese. Angela's compassion overflowed and she glided into the room, taking a seat beside Therese. For a while, the crying lady didn't look at her late mother's personal assistant and then in a spontaneous motion she laid her head on Angela's shoulder, her tears soaking into the cotton material. Angela reached over and pulled her closer. Another sob escaped from Therese.

"Was it enough for her to leave me?"

"Sometimes some things cannot be explained," Angela replied without realising she was speaking, a habit of soliloquy that had dogged her since she began babbling as a dangly ten month old. There was quiet for a while. Therese broke the silence:

"But she always said she loved me."

"I know she did,"

"It's so painful. So unfair. I can't even imagine how sad she must have been."

"Sadder than we can ever imagine," Angela replied.

She didn't notice the tears that had begun to run down her reddening cheeks as she watched the mother and comforted the daughter.

Phillip Neri gently swabbed at the pool of saliva that was accumulating at the left edge of Andrew Sciorra's mouth. He placed the soiled handkerchief on the crystal-topped side stool and leaned back on the leather chair. His eyes played on his boss, who sat there in his Fuschia coloured terry robe, hair in disarray, unlit eyes staring directly in front of him. Andrew's lips were silent. A silence that he hadn't broken since the day he watched the ambulance drive away from the house, his wife stone cold within it.

"Andrew," Phillip's voice was full of concern. His boss didn't acknowledge his name. "You can't keep on like this." There was silence. Phillip leaned forward, the top of his starched linen shirt opened to reveal a dark hirsute chest.

"It's going onto two months." He stressed the word "two," as though the mention of time would jolt Andrew out of his stupor. Silence.

"This might sound cold but you've got to get a hold of yourself." Silence. A wait of five minutes. More silence.

"She is gone, Andrew... Gone... Nothing we can do can bring her back," A brief pause, "We just can't afford to lose you too." Phillip took a deep breath and continued, "If you can't do it for the business or for life itself, please do it for Therese, she needs you now much more than ever before."

Andrew's gaze did not falter as silence again descended on them. And then like a scene shot in slow motion, a single teardrop made its way down Andrew's face. Phillip noticed it. He was comforted by the thought that Andrew had heard him or he hoped that he had. He patted Andrew's limp ashen white hand in understanding and leaned back on his chair, resuming his watch.

Timothy Vinelatter stood up as the two gentlemen made their way towards his table at Sotto Sotto in downtown Toronto. One was a Senior Vice President at the Royale Bank of Canada, the other was a top flight corporate lawyer who was one of the principal partners in Barnum, Mackenzie & Depardieu, the largest and most successful Law firm in Canada. The trio were gathering for an unscheduled meeting to discuss a multi-million dollar business deal.

After exchanging pleasantries, they sat down and immediately proceeded to discuss the issue that had forced them to gather on such short notice.

"All hell is breaking loose," The banker began in a whisper.

"How bad is it?" Timothy's palms were sweaty.

The banker had his arms crossed across his chest in resignation; "Very bad, they are threatening to pull the plug."

They fell silent. Their eyes trained at Timothy as though he had a magic wand. A miracle formula. Timothy on his part had his eyes lowered, his fingers rapping on the table. His mind racing. They watched him in apprehension.

"What are the chances they'll carry out their threats?" Timothy asked without looking up.

"They will carry out their threats."

Timothy looked up. The confidence in the lawyer's voice was unmistakable.

"Why are you so sure?" Timothy had no reverence for the gray hair that sat like a halo on the lawyer's head. His voice was filled with scorn. He hated it when people stood up to him.

"Because I spoke to their lawyers and they have given us twenty-four hours to come up with the approval or we are toast." The lawyer kept his wizened eyes trained on him. The dislike was mutual.

"We have eight more hours," the lawyer continued, certain that it would drive a steel peg through the heart of the impetuous young man.

"Eight hours?!" Timothy's voice attracted the startled stares of other dinners. He ignored them and continued as his rising anger found a voice.

"Why didn't anyone call me?"

"I called you repeatedly and you didn't pick up." The lawyer's voice was calm.

Anger spewed out of Timothy's eyes; "You should have left a message, sent a text or something."

"I did."

"No, you didn't."

"Then how come you are here?"

"All the message I got said was that we had to meet here for ten this morning."

"Because?" His voice took on its more familiar cross-examining tone.

"You left a long message; I didn't listen to the entire ramble."

"You should have." The lawyer had taken the implied insult lying low.

They fell silent again. The other dinners returned to their plates. The waiters resumed their rounds.

"What do we do?" asked the banker who had been quiet during the tirade of words. His mind preoccupied by the millions the bank stood to lose.

Timothy looked at the banker. He wanted to laugh out loud at the sight he presented; blond hair matted to his head, hand shaking slightly, head perched forward like a praying mantis. How the fear of losing millions can transform these Bay Street gnomes into quivering nutcrackers, Timothy mused, but instead he spoke softly.

"I will have to speak with someone."

"Who will that be, if I may ask?" The lawyer spoke up and without looking at him, Timothy replied:

"Therese Sciorra."

The lawyer smiled to himself. As usual whenever the rich playboy ran into trouble he dutifully turned to Therese. He knew that no door could remain locked in the face of the might of the Sciorra's. The fact that Timothy Vinelatter rode the highway to the heart of Therese Sciorra was counted in the financial circles as good credit.

Nosa Eweka was lost in thought as he drove along the Third Mainland Bridge that married Lagos Island to the mainland. He kept on ruminating on the information he had just gleaned from one of his cousins who knew a friend of his brother, Osasu.

His brother was in the cold climes of Canada. It had jumped at him. As regards the exact city, they had no idea. He flogged himself mercilessly with accusatory thoughts. Why hadn't he figured it out? His mother had been born in Canada to Nigerian parents who were amongst the first Africans to go there for undergraduate studies. Her being born there had given her Canadian citizenship, but she had never assumed it and thus it had faded out of the collective memory of the family. Osasu had remembered as he always did. He must have claimed his right to Canadian citizenship, courtesy of his mother. Nosa asked himself again, did he do it before or after she died? Did she know he was doing it? He quickly chided himself; it was very unlike his mother to keep secrets from him or his father. He looked at the cars that wheezed past him, melting into the Thursday night. How come his brother had turned out so different? What evil had taken hold of the brother he so loved and turned him to a stranger he didn't only loathe but feared. He closed his eyes to prevent the image of his father sitting dead behind the steering wheel from jumping into his mind.

He opened his eyes with a start when a horn blared behind him. He straightened the wheel, putting the car back on its lane. Then the questions resumed. How come they hadn't noticed the signs as Osasu hatched his plans? Was he guilty of basking in the adulation that his parents showered on him while his elder brother was ignored? Was his brother actually ignored?

Didn't his parents try all they could for his brother? Who actually was Osasu?

Nosa stepped on the gas pedal sending the metallic black Audi darting over the shimmering blue aquamarine waters of the Lagos lagoon, cutting through the warm night as it sped towards Victoria Island where he was staying with family friends; his father's house having already been repossessed by creditors.

He blinked his heavy eyelids repeatedly as he stared at the eyesight of the headlights that illuminated his way. He needed to sleep. To wake up and find out that it was all a dream. To see his very self sitting with his parents cheering Osasu on as he led the pack who were running down the home stretch of the 200 metres school race.

All Nosa could do was wish while his mind unconsciously cried out for closure.

The cold bit savagely into Osasu's exposed face as he walked briskly across the car park of the Albion mall in Etobicoke. He was dressed warmly in a tanned leather jacket with mink trimmings, black head warmer, black leather gloves, insulated black denims and black shin length boots; all from the House of Gucci. He cut the picture of a cover page model stepping out of an issue of GQ as his tall erect frame, steam rising from his mouth as he exhaled, made his way towards the mall entrance.

He walked down the main hallway of the mall, took off his head warmer and gloves, brushed off the specks of snow that clung to his jacket. Eyes followed him, furtive glances that announced admiration. He didn't pay any attention to them as he made his way towards the perfumery that was nestled next to the cinema that played Indian movies to the sizeable East Asian community that peopled the Greater Toronto Area.

His face lit up in an electrifying smile when he saw the owner of the perfumery standing in front of the shop conversing with a pot bellied man. And as usual he didn't walk to them but went straight to the counter and waited, allowing his eyes caress the perfume bottles that hugged the shelves of the shop.

"My friend!" the bald headed Lebanese called out walking towards Osasu, arms outstretched. Osasu turned and received the hug. They exchanged a hearty laugh.

"I see business is doing good for you."

"With customers like you how can I complain?"

"Got my stuff?"

"If Ali can't get it, who can?" he asked jokingly walking behind the counter and disappearing into the inner room. He came out in five minutes.

"Here, just as you ordered." He placed a gold coloured box in front of Osasu.

Osasu's face hardened, his eyes narrowed. He picked up the box, untied the silver ribbon that bound it and lifted the cover. Ali watched him as he looked at the content of the box.

"Beautiful," was all Osasu said. Ali's face broke out in an ear to ear grin.

"Aaaah, I knew you like. Ali treats good customers perfect!" He leaned forward, a deft movement that meant that he was expecting payment.

Osasu reached into his jacket, pulled out a wad of crisp hundred dollar bills and peeled out fifty notes. He handed it over and waited while it was counted. Ali smiled, tucking the money into the pocket of his trousers. They exchanged smiles and Osasu departed.

"Things always have a way of working out." He chuckled to himself as he walked down the hallway heading back to his car.

He couldn't wait to see Angela's reaction when he gave her the contents of the box. It was ironic how everything seemed to be falling into place. Four months ago he had been wondering how he was going to consolidate his finances and establish a life of luxury in Canada. The amount of money he had brought with him from Nigeria could definitely not tide him over for more than a year. He had been in that mental quagmire when he met Angela in the sports bar that night. At the time, he had looked at her as a one-night stand and when she had told him that she was a personal assistant to Annabelle Sciorra it hadn't meant a thing to him. The only thought that occupied his mind that night was raw animal sex with the Italian beauty that stood before him. But then as usual, no information that seeped into his ears or eyes was wasted. So, when he got home that night, he had typed in Angela's name into the Google search engine on the Internet. A habit he had picked up when he arrived in Canada since feeling like a fig leaf in the endless snow waste of Inuit land had left him no choice but find leaves of his ilk. Now he googled everything.

That night her name had brought up nothing. He was about to log out when he remembered the name Annabelle Sciorra, so, he typed that in, clicked search and struck gold. He couldn't believe what he was reading. Every word he read spelt wealth. Every sentence power. And as usual his mind began to work at a furious speed. He was hunched over his keyboard, typing and clicking, smiling at the computer screen for the next six hours. Osasu was not one to let opportunities slip by.

His strategy was going according to plan. He had Angela where he wanted her; a pawn in his quest for wealth. The content of the box that sat in the lower pocket of his jacket would reinforce his hold on her. He was sure of that. All he had to do was be patient. Bide his time and when the moment comes. He will strike. He could already smell the stashes of dollars that awaited him. But for the moment, he was playing the waiting game.

Angela Di Canio pushed her shopping cart down the beverage

aisle of the Dominion store at Yonge and Shepherd in North York, a bustling multi-cultural but mainly Asian neighbourhood of Toronto. She looked shyly at a pregnant lithe Korean woman that walked towards her holding gingerly to the arm of a lean muscled black man. The woman was giggling happily to something he had said. She moved the cart to the left in order to make way for them. The woman smiled at her as a token of gratitude. Angela returned the smile and in another beat she stole a glance at the left hand of the woman; gold band beneath a glittering stone. She looked at that of the man; another band. They were married. A sigh escaped her lips.

Why didn't she have the same guts as that woman? The courage to take Osasu home to her parents and introduce him as her fiancé. She couldn't pin point the exact moment he had ascended from the level of a casual fling, to a bad habit, onto a constant lover, and now a fiancé. Osasu hadn't proposed to her but in her heart she knew that he was the one for her. A gentleman at heart. A voice to die for. A nuclear bomb in bed and every other place. Sparkling intellect. To her he was the best thing to have ever stepped out of Africa.

Her heart was already pounding as her mind was clouded with thoughts of Osasu. She smiled to herself as she picked up a can of Maxwell House instant coffee, because although he didn't know it, he was the one thing that she could lay down her life for. Ironically, she had a reputation of going into relationships with her eyes open and keeping them the same way all through. Little wonder that amongst her friends she held the record of having never had her heart-broken. And although he hadn't asked for it, she had put her heart, soul, and body on a silver platter and given it to Osasu.

She looked at her wristwatch and hurried towards the frozen food section. It was an hour and a half before their rendezvous. She had so much to tell him and as usual he always listened.

The doorbell rang loudly. Phillip who was coming down the

winding Italian marble staircase made for the front door. The house was now empty of the policemen and private security guards that he had hired after Annabelle's death. Now it was just Andrew, Stephan the resident butler, and Therese who stayed in the expansive mansion, while Angela, Andrew's day nurse, Maria, his night time nurse, Harriet, and Phillip came in daily. This was apart from the regular guards that sat at the security lounge, which was to the left of the main gates to the stately mansion.

He opened the door. Sunlight streamed in, blinding him for an instant. He squinted and looked at the person who stood there on the steps. She looked back at him, her face set in a sad smile. She was wearing a severe black suit, cut in a style that accentuated her hourglass figure. Her hair was done in a bun. Her eyes hidden behind dark sunglasses that stretched from an inch above her eyebrow to the half way length of her prominent cheekbones. She was about the same height as he was; six feet two inches. She was beautiful. She was Andrew's concubine.

Phillip was visibly shocked. He looked behind her; on the opposite end of the driveway to the right was her trademark silver Jaguar XJS with the personalised license plates that sang *BUN 2B YLD*. He looked back at her for a second time as though he needed to be sure he wasn't dreaming. Then he hurriedly stepped out and shut the door behind him.

"What are you doing here?" Phillip's voice couldn't hide his shock even though it came out as a whisper. "I thought I told you to stay in the shadows until Andrew comes out of the cold?" he continued not giving her the time to respond.

"I was doing as you said until I received the phone call." Her face still hung sadly.

"What call?" Phillip was befuddled, the crease between his brow very visible. She looked down at her red painted toe nails that stuck out of her black platforms. Her hands balled into embarrassed fists.

"I didn't call you." A faint trace of anger had begun to surface.

"Therese did."

"What?!"

"Last night… she said I should meet her here today." Her tone was matter of fact, her resolve had returned.

Phillip was speechless. His mind was crowding with thoughts. How did Therese get her number? He knew that most people were aware of the fact that Andrew Sciorra had extramarital affairs although Andrew had made it a point of duty to keep it away from his family, since that way the possibility of the paths of his family and his numerous kept women crossing would be kept to the barest minimum. He didn't even make public appearances with his concubines; no paparazzi had ever succeeded in capturing him with one on picture. Pity the rumour machine still wagged. Pity Annabelle couldn't live with the stories that made the rounds. The whispers that went on behind her back were like a cancer that ate at her soul. Some women were just not created to live with the shame of having a husband who kept a regular concubine or concubines, to them it was like polygamy and the idea of sharing the one they loved was anathema to them, like liquid fire burning into their moribund souls.

"She left my name at the gate." She looked up and continued.

Phillip took a deep breath. So Therese had known about her all the while. An uneasy feeling enveloped him. He could have sworn that he really knew Therese, but now he wasn't so sure. Did she also condemn him for being an active conspirator with her father? He hoped she understood that he was just doing his job.

"Is she in?" The lady was already getting restless as she watched the normally in control Phillip visibly disintegrating.

He focused on her, put on the toga of self-control and with a voice stripped of all emotions spoke, "Miss Sciorra should be ready to see you."

He turned, opened the polished thick oak door that had the bronze head of a roaring lion on it, and stepped aside. She walked past him; her perfume assailing him as he followed her into the house. He shut the door behind him, and at the click of the lock, she stopped and began staring at the larger than life portrait of the Sciorra family that greeted every visitor that stepped into the luxurious confines of the house. Her sunglasses successfully hid her emotions.

"Phillip, I will take it from here." Therese's voice drifted down the winding staircase.

They both turned in surprise. Therese looked down at them. She was wearing a kimono, her jet-black hair falling down over her shoulders. Her azure blue eyes shifted to Phillip. His gaze held hers as he tried to decode her feelings. Therese was a blank wall, totally inscrutable. She smiled; an unspoken gesture that said she was aware of his intentions.

Phillip lowered his head and walked away, heading towards the east wing of the house that housed the study where Andrew silently sat.

Therese returned her gaze to the tastefully dressed lady. They both stood staring at each other for a short while. Each one sizing up the other then Therese began walking down the stairs. Her gaze unwavering. The well-defined jaw line of the beautiful lady stiffened as she prepared herself for what lay ahead.

Phillip walked into the study. It was dimly lit; the table lamp with the Mandarin shade giving it the only light. Andrew sat on the recliner by the large window. He was wearing a thick sweater although the room was warm. He was staring out of the window through a chink in the drawn blinds.

Phillip signalled to the nurse who was sitting by the door to excuse him. She stood up, gave him a slight smile and left. He walked to Andrew and stood above him. He looked through the chink in the window blind in order to see what it was that so held Andrew's attention. All he saw was the gardener tending the carnations that lay outside the beautifully landscaped front yard of the study. He turned back to Andrew and squatted by his side. He looked into his faraway bluish green eyes. It was a wonder how such one way intimacy had developed between them.

Phillip wasn't sure if he should tell Andrew what had happened. Will Andrew want to know that one of his amorous liaisons was right at that moment meeting with his daughter under this same roof?

He looked at the face that faced the window. He could see the pained lines that stretched from the edges of the eyes. The doctors had said that Andrew would come out of the catatonic state that had firmly held him in its grip for the better of six months. They had called it a fugue; a psychological flight from reality that the human mind takes when it is rudely shocked. They called it a healing process. Andrews's mind was recovering at its own pace. But then it had started this flight in late autumn, the night Annabelle died and now it was the middle of summer and still the plane hadn't landed. They were all worried. He patted Andrew's hand as he straightened up.

Phillip knew that Andrew could hear things and was aware of his surroundings; he knew that Andrew didn't suffer from amnesia; the doctors had assured him concerning that, so Phillip had decided not to tell Andrew about the events unfolding in the house, he couldn't afford to sow fear in his comatose mind. Let him heal, he said to himself as he walked to the door. When he heals, all will be revealed. Phillip's heart was heavy as he forced himself to focus on something other than the silent Andrew.

"What in heaven's name is Therese up to?" he wondered to

himself. In the same moment he opened the door; his mind once again descending into a riot.

As Phillip stepped out of the study he nearly bumped into Angela. He apologised and she continued on her way, walking down the hallway with a spring in her steps, yellow bright patterned dress breezing along with her. Lately he had been wondering why Angela was so gay. The normally reticent girl had become a vivacious bunny, acting like she had won the lottery. What troubled him was the fact that everyone was still carrying themselves like they were mourning, not only for Annabelle but for Andrew, and Angela who had been the closest to Annabelle amongst the staff just acted like the summer weather predicated. He kept his eyes on her as she disappeared around the corner. Then he looked towards his left as he resumed his thoughts of Therese and the bombshell that had rung the bell that morning.

3

Timothy took another sip from his glass of Bourbon. He looked at the vintage African wall clock that hung on the opposite wall. It was an ancient clock housed in the open mouth of a Cheetah, the expert taxidermy giving it a life-like appearance. He had picked it up on one of his Safaris in Kenya. The word from the Indian Sikh who sold it to him was that the clock had hung in the living room of the first British Governor General of the country, Sir Arthur Hardinge. He went on to explain that it had been stolen by a cook from the kikuyu tribal extraction and had resurfaced forty-one years later in the hut of a tribal chief in the eastern farmlands of the country during a British armed operation against the Mau Mau revolutionaries and their leader Dedan Kimathi. Every word was a lie from the pit of hell.

Timothy had bought it for two hundred and twenty American dollars without haggling. The Sikh smiled broadly as he counted the money. Timothy on his part had not believed a word of the man's story. He just loved the look of the clock.

Silver face on which were bronze Roman numerals around which circulated bronze arms, the whole encased in that fearsome opened jaw, steely ferocious eyes staring from above the smooth finery of speckled white fur. The soft tick tock that emanated from it proved that it was not battery operated. Timothy repeated the Sikh's story to all that admired the clock omitting the fact that he thought it was a lie. The last offer he had for the clock was twelve thousand five hundred dollars. He set his mind to selling it when the asking price got to fifteen thousand dollars.

The clock read fifty minutes past midday. He reclined further into the large white leather cushion, his thoughts revolving around the phone call he was expecting. Two more minutes. He took another sip, relaxed, and allowed the soothing strains of Piotr Tchaikovsky's Violin Concerto in D major massage his tensed muscles. The phone rang. He reached over with his left hand, picked up the phone, eyes still closed.

He spoke. He listened. He asked. He listened. He spoke. He hung up and smiled.

The deal was completed. He had just made thirty five million dollars. The banker was happy. The lawyer was ecstatic. The multi-million dollar property development on the large expanse of mountainous, snow filled land in Whistler, the famous city noted for its ski resort in British Columbia was sealed. The high end residential project was for the Winter Olympics which was to take place in a couple of years, and that call confirmed that the provincial government was paying in their share of the financing. This meant that secondary investors, made up of a hedge fund company and a building consortium would buy out their stake in the initial development. Timothy and his friends were now richer for it.

It had been four months since he spoke to the grieving Therese about his little problem. He had explained his situation and without asking for her help, she had volunteered. A couple of calls. The longest being the one to Phillip, who advised Therese to stem the flow of her generosity.

How Timothy hated Phillip. He couldn't wait to put him in his place. Phillip on the other hand knew that Timothy couldn't wait to officially make Andrew Sciorra his father-in-law. Deep down he knew Timothy wasn't doing it for love, but he was helpless in preventing the machinations that Timothy was painstakingly putting into place. How does one tell a woman in love that the one she loved was only in love with her fortune? Wasn't there a song that said loving eyes never see?

As usual Therese didn't listen to Phillip. The fifty million she had transferred to Timothy's account had cemented the deal. That meant over a hundred percent in profit. Knowing Therese she wouldn't ask for the repayment of the loan. Knowing him he wouldn't offer. He simply couldn't wait for their marriage.

Timothy took a long swallow of the bourbon and emptied the glass.

Nosa stood under the blazing sun outside the Canadian High Commission in Victoria Island, Lagos. His starched button down stripped white shirt was clinging to his sweat soaked torso as he repeatedly mopped his face with his wet handkerchief. He had been there for the past nine hours trying to get the security personnel to see reason with him. They had repeatedly told him to come back the next day because as they said "We only attend to the first thirty people on the list". Nosa was number thirty-two. He had arrived at 2.35 a.m. This was the fourth day of coming to the High Commission yet he still hadn't succeeded in being counted amongst the lucky thirty even when he progressively came earlier each day.

He walked back to the gate, resolving to try his luck again. As he approached, the lead security guard turned to face him, waving his black baton in a circular motion, stance akimbo, face hardened, eyes glaring. Nosa noticed his threatening posture and it did not faze him. This was Nigeria, he had a right to be heard. Before he got to the pedestrian gate that protected the entrance to the security post, the guard barked out.

"O boy, you no dey hear wetin we talk?"

"Bros I hear una but una never hear me." Nosa had switched to broken English in a bid to ignite a spark of camaraderie with them.

"We don hear your tori, order na order, vamoose!" The guard finished with his baton pointing in the direction he wanted Nosa to go. Nosa did not move. He tried to smile. It came out wanly. The guard was not impressed. Just then another guard, who was short, stout, and pot-bellied stepped out from the plexi-glassed post and walked out of the gate. He was laughing before he broke into a song in an ear drum jarring falsetto.

"Obey the order."

"Na im be order." The frowning guard was now smiling as he responded with glee.

"If you make a mistake o."

"We go show you pepper o."

The crowd that had been teeming outside the Commission watched them with angst. They were used to the sight of the guards' perennially poking fun at hapless visa applicants. It was common knowledge that these guards who were in themselves Nigerians carried themselves like gods as they dealt with the other Nigerians who came to apply for a Canadian visa. They comported themselves as though they were Canadians. Towering with authority as they conducted their duties in the presence of Nigerians but quivering in their boots when the real Canadian officials were present. A middle aged woman with a wailing baby in her arms spat on the ground and hissed loudly. Such hypocrisy!

As they sang at Nosa in derision, a black Ford Durango carrying diplomatic license plates pulled up at the gates. It was chauffeur driven, with a red haired Caucasian male sitting behind. The guards snapped into official mood. Song freezing in mid-air. The first one saluted shamelessly, the occupant of the car didn't respond. He kept his salute as the gate slid open; comically, the Caucasian yawned in response. The people who were sitting under the shelter that ran along the left side of the outside of the fence burst out laughing, Nosa couldn't help but join them. This drew the ire of the guards who waited for the car to disappear into the compound before they verbally pounced on him.

"Na your papa you dey laugh!" the formerly unsmiling one shouted.

The mention of his father nearly pushed Nosa over the edge but he reined in his anger. He stepped up to the guard and looked him squarely in the eye.

"Wetin you wan do?" the guard asked as he sprayed spittle on Nosa's face.

Nosa brought out his wet handkerchief and wiped his face. He looked at the handkerchief and then at the guard. Nosa's nostrils were flared. His breath quickened. Everyone went quiet; each watching. The other guard broke the sanctity of the moment when he called out to the well-armed policemen, who had been watching the drama from the left side of the gate.

"O.C., e be like say dis man na terrorist o!" Upon saying that, he disappeared behind the gate. On hearing this, one of the gun totting policemen made towards Nosa. The crowd burst out laughing. The pot bellied guard looked at them from behind the gate and smiled.

"Me I no fit die for oyinbo o," he continued, "All dis Bin Ladin's pikins wen dey wear shirt and tie, man must to be careful."

The crowd laughed louder. The policeman joined them. Nosa smiled. The guard who he had been glaring at smiled in return, yellow teeth peeking out from blackened lips. The tension dissipated. Some of the crowd went back to their seats, others into the flashy cars that dotted the streets, while the rest coagulated in groups discussing their chances of securing a visa as the policeman stood listening to Nosa's explanation of his predicament. It was then that the guard heard for the first time that Nosa was a Canadian. He didn't bother to obtain proof as he apologised profusely, laughing stupidly.

How could he have maltreated a Canadian? Maltreating Nigerians was in line with the books, after all they only understood brute force. Animals they all were. He knew that for certain, he was one of them. But Canadians, you treat them like human beings. After all it was only Canada that relocated their High Commission to Accra, Ghana when the brutal regime of General Abacha, the erstwhile dictator of Nigeria, went berserk. Yes Canada, a country known worldwide as a bastion of neutrality. But others will say the same neutrality that allowed them stand aside as fellow Africans in Rwanda chopped themselves to pieces. The same Canada that opens its gates of liberty to the millions of highly skilled professionals around the world that dream of a better life, a life that it provides them in form of taxi cab drivers, cleaners, minimum wage paid servers in fast food restaurants, and back breaking workers in low paying factory jobs. Yes, Canadians you treat them with respect!

Nosa walked into the High Commission twelve hours, thirty-four minutes and twelve seconds after he arrived that day.

Therese sat opposite her on the chaise lounge. There was a convivial air surrounding them that belied the fact that the two women were putting on a facade. It had taken them a little over an hour to thaw, thanks to the double scotch on ice the lady had drunk that helped to calm her nerves. Therese held sway as they finally zeroed down to brass tacks.

"I understand how you must feel about me."
"You have no idea," Therese replied.

"I agree… but I pray you understand that I never meant your mother any harm."

"That's the fifth time you've said that."

The beautiful lady bowed her head, painting a picture of a child caught with her hand in a cookie jar. Therese looked at her father's concubine. She took in her svelte figure; she knew the lady was younger than her but was dressed so maturely. Therese admired the clothing her father's money must have bought. She couldn't take it from her, she was a power dresser. It meant her father had good taste but from the pictures of her own mother at that same age which were standing on the living room mantel piece, this lady would have begged to pay good money for the honour of playing body double to Annabelle in her prime. Therese caught herself just in time. She had promised herself to remain objective.

"I should hate you but I don't."

The lady looked up, her almond shaped eyes rimmed with tears. Therese fell silent as she allowed her words sink in, then she continued.

"Do I blame you? Yes I do." A tear ran down the lady's cheeks. "I blame you because I need someone to blame, I need to make sense of it all," She paused then continued, "I am going to ask you a question and I will appreciate it if you are honest with me."

"I will be."

"Fine… Are you in love with my father?"

The lady paused, lowered her head and replied "No."

"Does he know that?"

"I believe he does."

"Did he ever talk about my mother?"

"Yes."

Therese let out an audible sigh, then spoke, "Negatively or positively?"

She looked squarely at Therese, "Do you want the truth?"

"Yes." It came in a whisper, her heart hammering in her ears.
"Your father loved your mother, he just couldn't forgive her."
"Why?" Therese sounded puzzled.
"Because she couldn't give him an heir." The statement knocked the wind out of Therese. They sat looking at each other. Therese's mouth was slightly open. Her eyes unfocused. Then she blinked and came to life.

"Did he want you to have a son for him?"
"No he didn't. He was fanatical about using protection."
Therese fell quiet again, then she spoke, "Did he talk about me?"
"Yes he did… always." Therese heard her and opened her mouth to speak, when the lady continued.
"You are his life, and when you really look at it for what it truly is, that is what matters. Your father deeply loves you."
Therese stared at her. How could her father have been so close to this stranger? How could she know so much? So it was true that a concubine was not just a vessel of sexual release but also a confidante. A shrink. The last refuge from the internal demons that plague so many men. She stared at the eyes of the stunning woman that sat opposite her and all she saw was naked truth. Therese believed her.

"I need you to do me a favour."
"Anything." The lady straightened up and leaned forward.
"I need my father back."
The lady was puzzled. She stared at Therese; visibly looking for answers. Therese continued. Her voice calm, filled with authority.

"My father hasn't spoken since the day my mother died." There was a gasp from the lady. Her fist clenched tight, showing white knuckles.

"Hasn't Phillip told you?" The lady shook her head in the negative. Therese continued immediately, hiding a trace of her opinion of Phillip from her.

"My parents are my world." Therese blinked twice; a reflection of the fact that Timothy Vinelatter also occupied three quarters of it.

"My mother's death is one death too many. I can't risk losing my father." She paused, lowered her head and continued, "If you can get my father out of his shell; I will let things remain as they were."

"Meaning?" The lady was shifting into business mode. Her iridescent eyes coming to life.

"You will keep the apartment, the car... everything."

"Everything?"

Therese understood what she meant by the last question. She looked up, "That is for my father to decide."

The lady didn't waste time thinking things through. She knew what it meant to lose all the privileges she had acquired under Andrew. Life in a remote town in the prairie lands of Saskatchewan was no woman's idea of heaven. Moreover, she owed this family a lot. All she had wanted when she moved to Toronto was just to raise enough money to pay her way to Hollywood where her dreams of being a movie star was waiting to explode into reality. She hadn't bargained on falling into the bosom of wealth. She hadn't bargained on causing a woman to commit suicide. The Catholic in her fanned the glowing embers of self-guilt that had consumed her since she got the news of the woman wearing her wedding dress hanging from the neck in death. It would take the rest of her life to observe penance. Didn't people go to hell for this? The lady was resolute in her faith.

"When do I meet him?"

Angela opened her mouth in silent disbelief as she stared at the contents of the black velvet box. She reached in, her manicured fingers picking up the ring that sat snugly on satin cushions. The ten carat flawless diamond blinked at her as it caught the rays of the candlelight that flickered on the dinner table. She turned it around, devouring it in mindless wonder. The blinking stone was held by a band of twenty two carats gold, which in itself comprised of a spiral of overlapping hearts.

Angela didn't realise that the ring that invoked such wonderment in her had journeyed across three continents and two seas, over three years in order to get to her. It belonged to a nineteenth century Bavarian duchess who had worn it to her grave. It had entered the black market sixty years ago when a gentile peasant had stumbled upon an unmarked tombstone on the grounds of a particularly arid plot of land in the Free State of Bavaria which lies within the territory of Germany. The farmers' co-operative association he had joined for just under a year had apportioned the hopefully arable plot to him. It had not yielded him any fruits, just regurgitated scorched barley seeds in repayment for the endless time he had spent sowing seeds from a threadbare bag, a bag that came from the same batch of seeds that was distributed by the co-operative which bore a bountiful harvest for the other peasants.

Local lore had been of the opinion that the area had once housed the castle of a very wealthy Duke who had died in one of the wars that ravaged Europe at the time. The castle was no more, just a couple of ancient hewn rocks that dotted the area. The tombstone the peasant saw had the markings of a cross on it, apart from that it was bare. It's positioning was synonymous with the sort of graves that lay in the ancient cemetery that stood across the ravine a couple of miles away.

The peasant had remained silent about it for a fortnight, but curiosity had gotten the better of him. So, he went to the village pub on a particularly starry autumn night and over wooden mugs of Germanic ale he had told his best friend, a burly fellow about his find. His friend, who was more worldly, had wasted no time in realising the value of the find, since he knew that nobility were never buried amongst commoners. So, the fact the grave stood apart was a sign of the inhabitant being of a higher class. So he had pressured the peasant into allowing them dig up the grave, regaling him with stories of the vast amount of ancient wealth that lay unfound in the semi arable earth upon which the village sat and the vast expanse of land that surrounded it, wealth that the earth gave up to a soul whose situation was so precarious that it was deserving of supernatural help. He went on to tell the peasant that the grave had appeared to him because it wanted to save him from a life of poverty and to refuse the help being offered from its mysterious bowels was to invite a curse in its place. The last information was what actually tipped the scale in his favour, since the reticent peasant was himself a superstitious paranoid.

Shovels and pick axes in hand, they had stormed the newly found grave that very night. After an hour of sweat and grime they hit pay dirt. A decayed composite of splinters of wood, yellowed metatarsals, one femur, a quarter jaw bone, a tibia, a complete pair of radius and ulna, moth eaten pieces of clothes and amongst all these residue of death, glittering in the starry night was a most exquisite diamond diadem and the ring. They had knelt down on the mound of excavated soil and praised God. Gingerly, they had extracted the treasures, shovelled back the dirt after throwing the faded tombstone into the grave and disappeared into the night.

The ring was taken by the peasant and the smarter friend had taken the diadem. They both met two days from that night and the friend offered to go up to the city and sell their find, since they both knew that it was of no value in the poverty stricken village in which they lived. The peasant had handed his ring over to him. The friend had left the very next morning; the peasant escorted him to the edge of the village from where he was to hitch a ride from one of the trucks that thundered up the gravel road to the city which was just recovering from the ravages of the First World War.

The peasant had waited through the Second World War. He had waited until his hair turned white. He had waited until the grave consumed his withered body. He never saw wealth neither did he see material comfort. He never saw his friend again.

His friend had met his death from the hands of the Jew who had purchased the treasures. The Jew had met his death in the hands of the SS soldier who had accepted the treasures from him as a payment for an escape from the monstrosity of Nazi Germany. The SS soldier had met his death when the soldiers of Stalin had marched on Berlin and a lowly peasant from Bavaria who had moved to the city to find work in the reconstruction had found the treasures in the pockets of the dead soldier who he was processing for burial on one of the concrete slabs of an abattoir that had been converted to a make shift mortuary. Life and its ironic jokes.

He had kept it to himself, telling no one. For five years he was silent about his find and on a starry autumn night as Germany woke up from its near death he had sold it to a balding Jewish merchant he met by chance in a pub upon the latter's return to Germany from the safe havens of New York, in search of any surviving members of his family.

And so the treasures had begun their journey. Hand to hand they went. Across continents and borders. They were transformed into family heirlooms, residing in the trinket box of the granddaughter of the Jewish merchant who had inherited them from her father. She was single and a recluse. It was from there they were stolen, when her upscale apartment in Mayfair, London was robbed. The police didn't know about it since she was murdered in the robbery. The robbers had sold it to a Lebanese black market jeweller, from whom Ali had bought it when Osasu had asked him to source for him the most captivating ring at the cheapest of prices. Osasu had paid a total of fifteen thousand dollars; a ten thousand dollar deposit and a balance of five thousand. It was an investment he knew would have a huge payback.

No one really knew the true value of the ring, since it had never been professionally appraised. If Osasu was aware of the worth of the ring, he might have simply packed up his plan, said good bye to Angela and auctioned it off at Sotheby's for the same amount of money he was hoping to make from the dark haired beauty. To Osasu the ring was expensive, a worthy investment in a veritable venture, little did he know how expensive or the value its rich history added to it. Sometimes ignorance is not bliss.

Angela looked up at Osasu at the same moment the restaurant began its hourly rotation. They were both having dinner at the 360 degrees restaurant that hugged the top of the CN tower in Downtown Toronto. As she took in his sharply defined features, she placed her left hand over her heart, as though feeling for the size it had swollen up to as it filled up with so much emotion. He should be a movie star she had once remarked to herself after a heavy session of love making. His looks were of the kind that pushed one to the edge of an awe induced cardiac arrest. Who said Adonis was Greek?

She opened her mouth to speak and nothing came out. Her eyes clouded with tears as she looked at the ring that was being so sensuously caressed by her fingers. She looked again at Osasu who was now smiling in that unique way that lit up his surroundings. Just then the music that had enveloped the restaurant changed into a strain of Sade's "No Ordinary Love." Four male waiters who were walking by the table suddenly stopped and went down on one knee. Angela looked at them, taken aback in surprise. Then Osasu stood up and walked to the opposite side of the table and fell into the same posture as the waiters. A hush fell over the other diners, as heads turned to watch the happenings. The music continually serenaded them. Osasu's white shirt which was partially covered by the blackness of his jacket gave him a certain consonance with the waiters that could be taken for chivalry.

He took her right hand, his touch felt like the light stroking of the tail feather of a peacock. He gently took the ring from her hand, a pleasurable languid air surrounding his actions, and then he looked at her, the brown of his pupils dilating as he spoke.

"Angela, in the presence of all things good and true. With the appreciation of all that you have been to me. With the knowledge of the love that we both share. With the fulfilment that you have brought to my life and the satisfaction that I have found in you. I humbly ask you this day. Would you spend the rest of your earthly life with me?"

A tear ran down her left cheek as she stared back at him. A warmth that she had never felt before rose from her innards and crowded the back of her throat. She could taste the sweetness of indescribable joy in her mouth. With the grace of a gazelle she slid off her chair and knelt in front of him. She reached out and ran her fingers around the contours of his face. She gazed at every pore in the skin that covered that face and then she looked into his eyes. He stared back at her soul. What had she done to deserve such perfection?

Lost for words all Angela could do was nod in affirmation. A smiling Osasu slid the ring on the fourth finger of her left hand as the diners burst out in applause. A staccato of cheers rented the air. She fell into his arms in ecstatic tears. He stroked her head in comfort. She raised her head and gently kissed his fleshy slightly dark pink lips. He returned her passion; to him it was a game of chess. He was saying check, with time it will be mate. The applause continued as Toronto carried on with its business hundreds of feet below.

The door silently opened and Therese stepped in. She stood

there for a moment staring silently at the seated Andrew. His hair seemed greyer she thought to herself as she looked at him staring out of the large French windows. She turned to the dark-haired middle aged nurse who sat knitting at the right-hand corner of the room. Therese nodded at her with a slight smile, the nurse returned her smile, placed her knitting pins and pink yarns on the table before she exited the room.

As the nurse stepped out of the room she was startled by the beautiful lady with sad frightened eyes that stood outside the door, a little to the right. The nurse stopped in her steps staring at her with enquiring eyes, the lady looked back at her and then looked into the room, a silent gesture that said she was with Therese. Before the nurse could respond, the door opened wider and Therese's low whisper floated out.

"Please come in."

The lady smiled stiffly at the nurse and walked into the room. The door closed behind her. The nurse walked across the hallway and sat on a chair that faced the door to the study, her mind beginning to map out the beginning paragraphs of the stories she was bound to share with her friends that evening during their usual gossip sessions. Not everyone had such intimate access to the Sciorra's; therefore, in her own social circles, she was heralded as the queen of the ball. Lost in her thoughts, she didn't notice Phillip standing on the first landing of the staircase, his face creased with worry as he stared at the closed doors of the study.

The beautiful lady watched as Therese squatted by the side of her father and gently placed her open hand on his arm.

"Dad, there is someone here to see you."

Andrew paid her no heed and kept staring out of the window. Therese hesitated for a moment and then reduced her voice to an audible whisper.

"Dad, no one is condemning you, all we want is for you to get well..." she stopped, the words choking in her throat.

"I want you back, daddy... please..." the last words faded away.

Therese stayed motionless for a short while then she stood up and stepped aside. She turned to the beautiful lady, who had tears already hanging in her eyes and smiled.

The lady shuffled forward in uncertainty and stopped by Andrew's side. She was surprised at how pale and aged he now looked. His skin that just some months ago shone from a rugged tan now crumpled in a white blotched palate of greenish veins, his robust cheeks were now sunken, a dark circle had grown around his eyes, from her vantage position, the angularity of his face held a morbid connotation of a skeleton, the surreal gaze that emanated from his eyes sent chills down her spine. She stood there at loss for what to do but the gaze of Therese that bored into her back made her slowly fall to her knees and place her open palm on Andrew's arm in the same fashion Therese had earlier done.

She looked at the stubble that peopled his jaw, then at his faraway eyes, and at his cracked, vaguely purple lips before returning back to his glazed eyes which appeared frozen in horror. It was as though he was staring at the gates of hell. She took a deep breath and opened her parched lips.

"Hi Andrew." She stopped abruptly as the words left her mouth. Calling his name sounded sacrilegious all of a sudden. He didn't move. She held her breath again and spoke.

"It's me... your baby... " she halted on those words, fearful of the reaction it would bring forth in Therese.

Therese on her part closed her eyes and steeled her heart as the words hit her ears. She could taste the angry bile in her throat, but she fought to control her emotions, holding tight to the reasoning of her decision to save her father from himself at all costs.

The beautiful lady did not see Therese's reaction so she continued "Andrew, it's me Nicole." Once again he did not flinch.

She waited and then let her words go "I heard the sad news and I came to help you through this difficult time" There was silence. She opened her mouth again to speak at the same time she heard the door shutting quietly, she turned towards the door. It stared back at her. It was firmly shut. Therese was no longer in the dimly lit suddenly cold room.

Understanding crept on her; Therese had left her alone with her father to work her magic. She turned back and stared at the immobile Andrew as the silence deepened around them.

Nosa brought down the cardboard box from the top shelf of the cabinet and placed it on the large wooden table. He carefully opened the folded covers and gingerly brought out the black leather bound file. He opened it and began leafing through the yellow dog eared papers; there were letters his mother had written to his father while she studied for her undergrad degree at McGill University in Montreal. There were other letters his father had written to her interspersed with the phone bills, gas receipts, store coupons and other relics of his mother's stay in Canada that gave the file its bulky look. Nosa smiled to himself; his mother had been so meticulous. He was amazed that Osasu had returned the documents, since he was sure that these were the same ones he had taken to the Canadian High Commission in order to get his passport processed.

Nosa placed the original copy of his and his mother's birth certificate, his parent's marriage certificate, and their death certificates into the file, closed it, placed it on the table, and lifted the box back to its former position on the shelf. He picked up the file and walked back to the door of the store room, before he switched off the light. He turned around and looked at the cramped room, his eyes played to the suitcases that were heaped at the far left corner, the neatly stacked wooden crates close to the wall to his left; these were all that was left of the tireless sweat of his parents. In those suitcases and crates were family memorabilia and the rest of the property he hadn't sold, given away or that were not confiscated by the bailiffs. He stood there for a while looking at his inheritance. He inhaled deeply and sighed audibly before he turned, switched off the light, and walked out of the room.

Now that he had all the documentation he needed, he was looking forward to the meeting with the Consular officer at the Canadian High Commission in Victoria Island, Lagos at nine the next morning. He was focused on getting answers to the questions that had plagued him since he found the body of his father in the car that morning.

Nosa was determined to find Osasu.

Osasu wiped the tears that snaked down his cheeks. He kept his eyes on the face of his mother as she smiled up at him from the picture he held in his hands. There was a deep pain in his chest that felt as though he was having a heart attack, he didn't panic because he knew all too well that it was the painful grip of the grief that had consumed him ever since that fateful night that was constricting his chest.

He stood up and walked over to the window, downtown Toronto stared up at him in all its lighted splendour, he gazed back at it, standing there in his white terry robe and in no time instead of the dazzling neon lights he saw the greenery of the garden at his father's home in Lagos, Nigeria. Instead of the lit windows of the skyscrapers that stood like behemoths in the night, he saw his father crouched over the body of his mother as she lay in a pool of her own blood on the floor of the garage, sobbing loudly as he called out her name. Osasu closed his eyes in an effort to stop the flood of memories and once again the urge to call home seized him.

He had often wondered how his father took it, when the

knowledge of what he had done was revealed to him. Osasu knew that there must have been shock, then rage and after that dissipated, he would have started a search for him and when that turned up nothing, his father would have begun to build up his business again. After all, it was said in Nigerian business circles that Ibude Eweka possessed the Midas touch, a business acumen that was second to none, a knack for making money and spotting investments that yielded bountiful returns. So, trusting his father, his treachery would just have been a minor blip, nothing the old man couldn't take in his stride.

Although he hadn't heard a word from Nigeria since he left clandestinely, he comforted himself with the thought that his father was like the proverbial phoenix, a toughened sense of survival that had weathered many a debacle, therefore, there was no point shedding tears, all he had done was taken what was rightfully his. No harm intended and hopefully there would be no harm done.

Then Osasu began to think of his younger brother Nosa. It was a mixture of the good and the bad, the contentious and the convivial, he smiled as fond memories of them as kids playing on the sand banks of Bar Beach came flooding through. He grimaced as he remembered the constant attention that was showered on Nosa whilst he stewed silently for affection, he wondered how Nosa would take it when he heard that his older brother had upped and left with the family fortune, a fountain of remorse began to swell in his heart and once again with lighting speed he blocked the thought and replaced it with a cold resolve to blot out all memories of his past life. A resolve he had continually made and fervently broken.

He flogged himself mentally as he forced his mind to fall into line. Two and a half years before he left Nigeria, he had made it his business to sever all links to his life on the streets of Lagos. He had killed the Osasu who was known as a street lord and returned to the docility of a life in his father's house. He had needed that volte face as a ruse in order to put his plan in action, not only as a way to win his father's trust, but also to erase all traces that could lead to his present whereabouts. The streets had ears and tongues that wagged at the right price; he knew that for a fact, so he had decided while he planned his filial heist that all that happened in Nigeria must remain in Nigeria. For that to happen, it was a must that he operated in the utmost secrecy, a feat that was not in any way alien to him.

4

Timothy Vinelatter walked briskly down the marble underground hallways of the First Canadian Place on Bay Street in downtown Toronto, an iconic building that stood on the intersection of Bay and King, a location fondly called the "Wall Street" of Canada.

The warmth of the beautiful surroundings hugged him. It was lunch hour so the place was buzzing with men and women primly dressed in dark suits, each hurrying to make the best use of the respite they were having from their arduous task of oiling the financial wheels of the Canadian economy. He was heading to the office of McCulkin & Barnum; a stock broking firm on the twenty seventh floor. In his head were the first steps of his plan to begin a hostile anonymous takeover bid of the Quad Mining Company; one of the crown jewels of the multibillion dollar conglomerate of Andrew Sciorra.

Phillip accosted Therese as she came out of the study. He held her by the arm and gently nudged her towards the drawing room that stood at the far left of the study. To an onlooker it would have looked like an avuncular gesture, but Phillip knew the nurse and her type. He could see her nose uplifted, subtly sniffing like a pig for gossip, so it would have been foolhardy to let his concerns boil over in her presence; he had to put up the charade. Therese on her part obediently played along and walked down the hallway with him.

Once in, Phillip shut the door behind him and turned to her. She stood there staring up at him, her face expressionless.

"Therese, what are you doing?" Phillip blurted out unable to hide his concern.

"What am I doing?" Therese asked as though surprised that he asked the question.

Phillip stalled for a while in a bid to reframe his approach; he let his gaze play to one of the large, highly prized expressionist painting by Edvard Munch that hung on the wall behind her. Holding his gaze, he placed his left hand in the pocket of his pants and used the palm of his right hand to wipe off the thin layer of sweat that had gathered on his fore head. Letting out an audible sigh, he looked squarely at her and spoke.

"I know you blame me for..."

"No, I don't," Therese cut him short.

Phillip was surprised. He let out another sigh and then continued. "You can't bring her to Andrew..."

"Why?" There was a note of authority in her voice.

"It will kill him."

"On the contrary, I think it will save him."

"Therese, for Christ's sake, your mother killed herself because of that woman." Phillip regretted the words as soon as they left his lips.

Therese was quiet. She stood there looking up at Phillip. She had not even bated an eye lid. Phillip cowered beneath her scorching gaze before he bowed his head in remorse.

"I'm sorry, I shouldn't have said that."

"Don't be sorry."

Phillip didn't lift up his head but instead put his other hand into the other pocket of his pants and took up the stance of a guilty British schoolboy; repentant but proud.

"My mother didn't kill herself because of her." Therese broke the silence. "She killed herself because of him."

Phillip looked up at her. They were silent as they drank in each other's thoughts. As if to confirm if he understood what she was saying, she continued,

"My mother killed herself because of my father."

Phillip looked away in shame, not only for himself but for Andrew.

"I appreciate your loyalty and I respect your sense of duty, but I want you to understand that I will not stand aside and allow my father slowly rot away. Let God be the judge, as for me, I will do all that is in my power to ensure that my father outlives his grief."

Phillip allowed his saddened gaze travel back to her. She continued "That lady is the only hope we have of getting through to him. I might be wrong but then, I rather be wrong trying than be wrong not trying, so she will be staying in this house as long as it takes her to bring him out of the cold."

Phillip was taken aback by the fact that Nicole would stay in the house. His mind took a fast pace in thought. Was Therese punishing her father? Was she making him confront his sinful dalliances as a way of playing back her mother's death in his sub conscious? Didn't she realise that Andrew was blaming himself for her death and in blaming himself would be cursing the day he began to cheat on her? Wasn't the presence of Nicole a constant reminder of that? He looked at her, tried to think as she was thinking, then slowly it began to occur to him. Alarm bells began to ring in his head. He could feel his palms begin to sweat, his heart begin to hammer loudly. He knew he had to confirm his fears.

"How did you know about her?" he asked finally.

"What difference does that make?" she retorted.

"I have to be sure that you are doing the right thing."

"And knowing my source will confirm that?" Therese was intrigued.

Phillip nodded. Therese was quiet as she looked up at him. Her eyes narrowing, her nose cringing, her upper lip tightening in a squeeze, it was apparent she smelt a fish, then just as Phillip's heart began to pound louder, she surprised him by smiling broadly.

"Okay, if it will give you peace, I'll let you know, but it is between us, no word leaves this room." She waited for a promise from him. Phillip nodded in agreement.

"Fine... Timothy told me."

The alarm bells rang louder in Phillip's head as her words confirmed his greatest fear.

Angela periodically stole furtive glances at her parents as they sat across the dinner table. Her father was busy chatting noisily with her elder brother while he gobbled up the spaghetti and meatballs that sat like a dunghill on his plate. Her mother was spooning out some asparagus soup into her little niece's bowl. There was a collective din of laughter around the room which wasn't unusual whenever the extended Di Canio family gathered for lunch in her family home built in Tudor fashion in the upscale residences of Thornhill in the Greater Toronto Area.

Angela had been toying with the idea of telling her family about Osasu for the last three weeks, especially after he had given her the diamond ring. To her, he was the person she would spend the rest of her *earthly existence* with but she still had the presence of mind in recognising the stiff albeit vociferous opposition she would receive from her family, so she had bided her time, subtly prodding her parents on every opportunity about their views on interracial marriages. She wasn't too surprised when her father said that God in all his wisdom created the races apart and who was man to put them together? Her mother on her own part went on to explain that it wasn't that they were racists but it was good for the sakes of the preservation of culture.

So, as she sat smugly at the table, she contemplated voicing her opposition to their views but commonsense prevailed. It was safer she fought her battles one person at a time; this bustling crowd of laughing Italians were one person too many. Letting out a deep sigh she reached over for a glass of the Fontodi Chianti Classico that sat on the table in front of her. She swirled the contents of the glass, took a swallow, feeling the richness of the Italian red wine bathe her silent tongue. She placed the glass back on the table and allowed her mind go day dreaming. Soon and very soon, this family will have no choice but celebrate their first interracial marriage, she thought to herself. Of that she was certain.

Nicole slowly stroked Andrew's arm. It was a light caress; the kind he used to like. She watched him intently hoping to see a reaction. There was none. She continued for a while, moving from his arm up to his shoulder, then his neck, and finally to his cheek. He sat there like a living cadaver. She began to get bored so she let her eyes do a round of the study. She admired the leather bound books that were arranged neatly on the shelves that stood against the walls; the leather armchairs that dotted the room in a well laid out pattern which seemed to give it a shape of a star cut in half. Then she looked at the life-size lion that sat at the far corner, illuminated by a single spot light, its mane forming a flaming red halo that made it look frighteningly alive.

Andrew had told her about it as they lay on the hot white sands of their rented private island in the Maldives. It was the story of a safari he went on in Kenya with his parents when he was seventeen. He had told her that the lion had attacked a tourist and his father had shot it point blank with his Musgrave hunting rifle before the guides could move a muscle, saying if not for the quick action of his father who had bought the carcass and had it go through the ritual of taxidermy before bringing it back home to Canada, the Kenyans would have had a lot of explaining to do to the Americans, since the tourist concerned was the wife of the American Secretary of Defence, Lloyd Feinstein. Andrew never failed to idolise his late father at any given opportunity.

As she allowed her eyes play around the room, she continued stroking his cheeks lightly and stopped abruptly when her roving eyes settled on the gold framed picture of Annabelle that hung on the eastern wall. Annabelle's eyes looked at her contemplatively as though wondering what the hell she was doing stroking her husband. Immediately her arm dropped to her side as a wave of embarrassment washed over her. She looked away and slowly got to her feet, straightening her short skirt in the same motion. Seeing that picture had brought the true scenario to her; there she was standing in the home of the woman she had robbed of a husband, the woman she had caused such grief that death was the only palliative.

She felt a tug in her chest, a shift in her spirit that signalled the beginning of overwhelming guilt. Her prairie innocence and sense of moral values that she thought she had gotten rid of in the first months of her arrival in Toronto was rearing its head. At that moment all she saw and smelt was the coldness of death; a death she was beginning to fully realise she had played a huge part in. Previously, she had laid most of the blame on the mental state of Annabelle, claiming to her close friends that Andrew had once whispered to her that his wife at times displayed a dissonance of reasoning and an imbalance of emotions. She knew cheating was wrong. Adultery doubly wrong, but then, that was no excuse for suicide. Now, she realised how truly culpable she was in the death of Annabelle.

She stood there for a moment unsure of what to do and just at that instant there was a knock on the door and before she could turn in response, the polished oak door opened and the nurse stepped in. Protocol stipulated that she wait for a response, state her mission, and enter when asked to but her unbridled desire to catch the ailing Andrew and this steaming beauty in flagrante delicto had overridden any sense of decorum on her part. Sitting outside in front of the study wondering what in heaven's name was happening in the study had been like sitting on hot coals.

Her wizened mind had dictated to her that the flaming beauty was more than a family friend. The concern in Phillip's eyes as he led Therese away was enough to light the flames of her curiosity. She couldn't wait to tell her husband and her band of lonesome nurses what she had seen. To the nurse, what she thought was the same thing as what she saw when she repeated events to her audience of busy-bodies.

Nicole looked at the middle aged nurse standing at the open door, eyes bleeding with nosiness. She smiled at her in a bid to hide her nervousness. The nurse replied with a face set in stone.

"It is time for Mr. Sciorra's medication." The words slipped icily out of the thin lipped woman.

Nicole nodded in understanding and the nurse stepped away from the door, leaving it open in an invitation to leave. Nicole looked at the door and walked regally towards it without giving Andrew a parting look. All she wanted was to get as far away from the house as possible. She didn't have an inkling of the fact that she had taken temporary residence with the Sciorra's in Forest Hill. A decision already made of which she was not a part of, to stay in this house *ad indefinitum*.

As she exited the study, the one thought on her mind was one that spoke of the marvel of Annabelle's beauty. Having seen for the first time a younger-looking picture of the woman Andrew had taken for his wife, Nicole knew that she could not have under any circumstance rivaled the breathtaking aesthetic brilliance of Annabelle. Men were such mysterious animals Nicole mused to herself as the nurse silently shut the door behind her, leaving her standing clueless on the marble floored hallway.

Nosa strutted out of the revolving doors of the Canadian High Commission in Lagos. He had a smile plastered on his face although the heat wave and intense sunlight strove to wipe it off. You never realised how hot the midday weather of Lagos was until you stepped out of an air-conditioned house, he thought to himself as he made for the gate where his former tormentors held sway. He walked with a new found leisurely pace now that his travelling papers had been handed to him.

Since the security guards now knew he was a Canadian, they treated him as royalty, clearing a path for him by threatening to flog the mass of Nigerians that formed a crowd outside the gate, every single one of them desperate on gaining access to the hallowed visa office were their fate was to be decided. The guards saluted him with broad smiles as he made to leave.

"Our very own oga your boys are loyal!" the one with long tribal scarification on both cheeks said.

Nosa responded by handing over to him an envelope he had stacked full of five hundred naira notes earlier in the day. The guard didn't even bother checking the contents, stuffing it into his back pocket with superhuman speed.

The envelope seemed to act upon them like an intoxicant; they shouted louder and rained expletives in staccato at the other perspiring Nigerians who blocked the gate with their pleading bodies.

"Oya comot for road!" the scarified guard began.

"Una no dey hear, na bulala una want?" the second one followed, advancing with giant strides, baton in hand.

The crowd slowly backed away. A stubborn one or two remained. The shorter one gave voice to his vexation.

"I no go comot. No be you say you go allow me enter if I settle?"

"You settle me?" the guard barked at him.

"I don find your broda something already."

"God go punish you. Na who tell you say e be ma broda?" the guard got to the gate and stood akimbo, bulging stomach thrust forward.

"No be una dey do five and six since morning?"

"O boy give dat man one hot slap make e close e dirty mouth dia!" the scarified guard said as he followed suit approaching the gate.

Nosa was immobile as he watched the building commotion. His file clutched close to his chest. He looked back at the imposing building behind him. The tinted windows betrayed nothing. He returned his gaze to the gate.

"I settle you na. Tell your broda make e give us chance enter."

"Na your papa you settle. Thunder fire you!" the scarified guard cursed, his five fingers spread out in front of his outstretched hand.

"Waka to your papa too!" the man retorted instantly, imitating the same five finger gesture.

"If I reach dia you go see pepper, born bastard like you!" the scarified guard began opening the gate. The other guard looked over at the gun totting police men who were sitting under the mango tree in the compound.

"O.C. abeg come help us teach dis fuckin useless barawos something," he called to them. One of them stood up, dusted the seat of his black pants, picked his rifle, and jogged towards the gate. The two men stole a glance at him and instead of backing off, they gripped the gates tighter.

"Oya make una clear from that gate before I open fire!" the policeman announced.

"Na so e easy?" the taller man responded with a laugh. Some of the people who had earlier cleared away from the gate started returning.

"Oya stand dia!" he cocked his rifle and aimed at the gate.

The people who had started walking towards the gate, seeing the pointed rifle quickly retraced their steps. Some of the women picked up their children and ran across the street, some others ducked into their cars. The two men remained standing at the gate. Nosa slowly backed up; he looked back at the building. Nothing.

"I go count up to three and if you no disappear, una own don finish bi dat. One..." the policeman called out. The other policemen under the tree looked on. The two guards gleefully watched the events.

"Dem no born you to fire!" the shorter man teased.

"Two..."

"Dis one na Canadian embassy o! No bi check point, if you shoot us, yawa go gas big time. Oya fire if you get liver."

"I say if I count three, I go fire una... I say one..."

The two men began to laugh.

"Una think say e dey joke?" the scarified guard looked at them incredulously.

"Make e fire, we dey here dey wait am," the shorter man crossed his arms on his chest defiantly.

"I say two!" the policeman called out, spreading his leg wider as though to steady himself.

A woman standing across the road shouted at the two men.

"Na hia una wan die? Una no get family? Dis olopa people no get sense o! Dem no dey send o! Abeg make una comot for gate make dem do dia business, so we fit see road do our own business! Na beg I dey use beg una o."

The men did not acknowledge her entreaties. Other people began chiming in, pleading with the men to leave the gate. Nosa stood there watching. So did the policeman and guards. Finally, the two men looked at each other and as though sending unspoken signals to each of them, they backed down and turned away from the gates. The shorter one shouted at the guards as he walked away.

"Una lucky, I for show una say na he-goat dem dey take cook ogufe."

"Three!" the policeman suddenly called out.

Silence. He lowered his rifle and looked at the gate; the two men were now standing on the street away from the gate, staring back at him.

"Where dem dey?" the policeman asked with clueless pretence.

"Dem don waka," the shorter guard replied implying they had walked away.

"Ah, na God save dem, the kind bullet I don aim for dia belle, na die!" he wiped his face as though the encounter had been very strenuous.

Everyone burst out laughing. It was infectious; the guards smiled. Nosa stifled a giggle. The two men on the road seemed to take offence.

"See mugu! Olopa Oshi! Ole buruku! You no fit fire, na sake of say we wan collect visa na im we waka o, make you no dey fool unaselves, we for show una ta ton today, make una no try, this tie wen we wear all na efizzy, na correct agbero we be, go Eko go ask for Jelili..." the shorter man kept on as he walked to and fro on the street.

The policeman turned to Nosa. Butt of his rifle on the ground, hand holding his rifle by the barrel.

"Oga, you go find me something o, dis work wen I do for you e no easy o."

Nosa looked at the guard he had handed the envelope to. The

guard shrugged his shoulder and spoke.

"Oga, abeg gi am something, as you see dem so, dem never pay dem salary for like tiri monts."

"Six months and two weeks." The policeman corrected.

Nosa pulled out his wallet, removed two five hundred naira bills and handed it over to the policeman. He took it from him and bowed respectfully.

"God go bless you, Oga, the thing wen you dey find go Canada, na dash dem go dash you, na Western Union you go take turn your family to Orobo special..." He chimed on and on with more blessings as he walked back to the tree until he was out of earshot.

The guards opened the gate for Nosa. As he walked towards it, they both saluted in unison.

"Safe journey back to Canada sir," the scarified one spoke as he maintained the salutation. Open palm at an angle to his head.

"Thank you," Nosa mumbled the words and stepped out of the compound. He could feel eyes stabbing into his back as he walked towards his black Audi that was parked a short distance away. Everyone watched him, some enviously, others angrily, while the rest watched for the sakes of watching.

He looked back at the compound and glimpsed as the people walked back towards the gates, each one hurriedly walking to take up their position of vigil. He turned back to the direction he was headed and wondered how such events could happen so openly at the gates to the High Commission of a developed country like Canada and no one in the High Commission itself intervened. Threats, near riots, dehumanising punishment, bribes, puerile insults, scams, yet the representatives of one of G7 nations kept a deafening silence? Maybe the sanctity of the morality of the sacred grounds of the High Commission was all that mattered to them, their reasoning being the dictum, 'what exists outside those gates is the business of Nigeria, we must respect their sovereignty.' But then, he wondered what wisdom there was in respecting the rights to unleash mayhem on one's own citizens by fellow citizens, even when intervention would have taken minimal effort and sent the loudest, most forceful message, 'Canada will stand for what is right no matter the circumstances'. He shook his head, Utopia existed only in Neverland. On Earth, it was selfishness first, altruism last, no matter how neutral and *United-Nationish* the individual or country pretended to be. After all, wasn't it rumoured that a hefty bribe could get you a Canadian visa, a heftier one, a landed immigrant visa, and the heftiest one the dark blue passport? Under the table business had no conscience or suffered no prejudice, whether in the offices of the high and mighty in the continent of Africa or the other six sister continents.

Bribes, he was guilty of that, but then, the behaviour of the guards and policeman were in itself inexcusable. Nosa walked on and silently chewed on questions as regards the wisdom of what he had done. He couldn't place a finger on why he had given them the money even though he understood that there were things that came naturally when you grew up in a system of backhand subtleties in forms of bribes and nepotism; traits that had unconsciously become you in the entirety even though you voiced your opposition to them in many a public arena. These traits were a symbol of survival. Brushing aside the silent questions, he hugged the leather folder that contained his travelling documents tighter, the pick pockets who did brisk business were notoriously known for the magic they performed; one lighting quick movement and they could rob a nun off her habit.

Finally, he got to his car, entered, and sat down for a moment to gather his frayed nerves. It had been a long, arduous journey getting all he needed for his next step of action. He slotted his key into the ignition, turned it, and the engine came to life.

As he drove away, he couldn't help but remember the young,

handsome boy of about nineteen or twenty years of age who had burst into tears in the visa office when the consular officer had refused him a visa. As he sobbed, Nosa could see in his face the look that signified the hopelessness of a cornered animal.

He wondered to himself as he slowed down his Audi at a potholed junction what lay in store for the boy now that his hopes had been dashed; more attempts to leave a country that didn't give a hoot about its citizens? A determination to start a life in Nigeria no matter how impossible a future here was, or a slowly metamorphosis into a monster of the kind his brother Osasu had become?

There were no answers, so Nosa changed gears and drove down Kofo Abayomi Street. He slowed down respectfully in front of the Brigade of Guards' offices; a ritual that was sine qua non in order not to draw the ire of the gun-toting soldiers who stood guard in front of it. Militarisation was in the popular psyche of Nigeria and its citizens were socialised to operate successfully within its rigidity. Nosa waited for a respectable moment before he slowly accelerated, face forward, not giving into the temptation of a sideways glance into the military forte. Clearing the imposing green gates and now at a safe distance, he changed gears once again and sped off towards his maternal uncle's house where he had taken temporary residence.

Their sinister ploy was sealed with a firm handshake before they parted ways with the assurance that under no circumstances will his identity be revealed. Peter McCulkin was the link between Timothy and Maggie Lan, an incredibly brilliant economist, venture capitalist, and sales woman. Although he linked them, Maggie Lan didn't know who Timothy was; all she knew from Peter was that a high net worth individual was interested in her services and needed her as a face of an aggressive takeover bid. Maggie was a financial mercenary and had no scruples jumping on board. She and Peter went far back and they both had made huge sums of money through using the services of one another. She trusted Peter; Peter trusted Timothy. Timothy trusted no one.

Maggie had registered a holding company in Canada with a board of directors comprising acquaintances she had made during a one week conference she had attended in Vancouver. She had charmed them with her sparkling intellect, extremely good looks, and bright personality. They were all very rich men with enough money to gamble on promising ventures. These acquaintances had acquired insignificant shares when they listened to her yarn about an offshore company that was interested in doing big business in Canada and needed partners of good repute to purchase shares in the venture.

She had shown them the twenty-five page prospectus Timothy had prepared three weeks earlier and they were blown away by the literature, statistics, graphs, charts, and dazzling images that jumped out from the pages. She had claimed to be a representative of this company and whispered to them that the offshore company was going to acquire a blue chip company in Canada as its first course of business and once the acquisition sailed through they would be open to sell their shares in the company back to the offshore company for a handsome profit. These men lived and swore by profit; to them, working around laws and regulations was an everyday practise, so her proposition met no opposition, especially as she dangled her curvaceous body as bait to the lecherous men. Profit and a beautiful woman of exotic leanings, what more could they ask for?

This offshore company was set up by Timothy and based in the Bahamas; he had a team of four young, experienced, and extremely brilliant Bahamians running the business. Actually, he had an executive search agency handle the recruiting so that there was no contact between himself and his staff. He also had Peter McCulkin, the principal partner of the stock broking firm, handle all the business with the search agency. To the staff in the Bahamas, Peter McCulkin was the boss; they had never heard of a Timothy Vinelatter. This was exactly as he wanted it.

Timothy had set up his scheme in such a way that the offshore company held controlling shares in the holding company and Peter represented it on the board. In fact, the offshore company was registered under Peter's name so there would be no raised eyebrows, thus Timothy's name was conveniently missing from the roll call of the company. In his plans, it was this holding company that was to launch the takeover bid of the Quad mining company and when that was successful, he would formerly acquire the offshore company in the Bahamas and in one strike he would dissolve the board of the holding company by the virtue of his controlling shares. Through this, he would have opened the doors to an avalanche of riches.

At present, the offshore company had a paid up capital of fifty million dollars provided by Timothy in the form of soft loans that could not be traced back to him. The holding company had a paid up capital of ten million dollars, eighty five percent of which was provided by the offshore company. He was putting a lot into the plot. He was putting a lot of something that looked and smelt like trust, but was not actually trust in Peter McCulkin. That kind of trust was exactly all that mattered. Especially when Timothy had solid evidence to prove that Peter was responsible for the gory death of a missing seven-year-old boy in Martha's Vineyard eighteen summers ago and a predilection of taking trips to Thailand to satisfy his peculiar taste.

The last Forbes magazine financial analysis of Quad mining company had forecast that profits would increase by twenty-five percent in the next three years if production stats were to remain the same, that meant a profit of about one hundred and eighty million dollars in that time span. He knew that the present value of the company was around one and a half billion dollars. To acquire it was going to be by sheer miracle, a miracle that occasioned massive devaluation of the company, a miracle that stood nearly impossible to occur, but then, in the business of miracles, Timothy was a maverick. He knew something that no one else knew, save for a now dead geologist. A geologist he had been having a discrete, steamy relationship with. A geologist who hid his homosexuality from the wickedly judgemental world, especially one that knew he was the son of a respected evangelical bishop and that he was married to a darn beautiful lady with whom he shared three children. A geologist who was going to use his new found secret knowledge as a bargaining chip with his employers for a pay raise and appointment as Chief Geologist. A geologist who had confided in Timothy who he truly believed was not just fucking him, but was in love with him. A geologist who had to die for the secret he had innocently shared with Timothy; the one person that he unfortunately didn't know needed it more than him. This secret was the surest bet of bringing forth the miracle Timothy so desperately needed, and he was ready to shed blood for it.

Timothy smiled to himself as he waited for the elevator; his heart was racing with excitement as the thought of the machinery he had set in motion consumed his mind. There was a lot of money to be made, but first he will need money to make that money. He knew where to go although it was apparent he couldn't get what he would need from there alone. But then, little drops of water make a mighty ocean, he mused to himself before he brought out his Iridium cell phone and called a name into it. The phone began auto dialling, there was silence for a brief moment before a ringing tone could be heard. It rang thrice after which a voice came on.

"Hi darling." It was Therese.

Osasu looked at the white sheet of paper that lay on the table in front of him. He studied the scrawls of signatures that were scattered all around it. He smiled to himself because he was now satisfied that he had finally mastered the signature of the American whose cheque lay open at the edge of the table.

He had bought it off an acquaintance who worked at the Sheraton Hotel and Towers on Queen Street West in Downtown Toronto. The acquaintance was a twenty-two year old Somali lady who worked as a chambermaid at the hotel. Her modus operandi was searching the pockets and suitcases of guests when she got into their rooms to do the daily cleaning. She was smart for if she saw a credit card, she didn't steal it but instead copied down the numbers, both the ones in front and at the back. Then she made a sketch of the signature. If she saw a chequebook, she tore out a sleeve underneath the top most one, right from the stem, that way she left no evidence of it being missing. Then she searched for a sample of the signature, checking receipts, signed documents, and going as far as striking up relationships with the waiters at the hotel bar and restaurants where she knew the owners of the cheques might go for late drinks or dinners. She was diligent, methodical, and daring. She never took money or jewellery or clothes. She had never been caught.

Osasu was her most ardent customer. They met at the food court at College Park every week on Thursday morning during which time they exchanged goods. Most of the money Osasu gave her went via Western Union to her family who were living at the Kebribeyah refugee camp in Ethiopia. Most of the goods she gave Osasu were expertly cashed through channels he had created.

In a swift motion, he signed the cheque and the end product was like a photocopy of the original. He then wrote on it the figures; four thousand five hundred and two dollars. It was a risk because he didn't know the actual amount in the account, but then, nothing ventured, nothing gained he had often reasoned. In four hours, the cheque was presented and cashed at the Cash Mart outlet at Albion and Islington by a blond white girl he had met at the Jane and Finch mall that afternoon. He had made out a fake driver's license with her picture right there in the trunk of his car, then he paid the pre-agreed upon fee of a hundred grams bag of skyrocket for taking the risk of getting the money. Skyrocket was the street name of a kind of weed that was made by soaking the marijuana leaves in a vat of cocaine, table salt, bicarbonate of soda, and diesel. The word amongst its users was that it made one touch the edges of the universe.

If she had been caught, there would have been no way of getting him in handcuffs for Osasu would have melted into the surrounding human traffic in an instant. In order to save his hide, his eyes watched those doors with the focus of an eagle. All these were partially in preparation for the mother of all heists he was planning to pull when he finally had Angela where he wanted her.

Phillip excused Therese from the room and walked out into the hallway, shutting the door after him. She had asked for privacy to answer her cell phone. His head was aching slightly, a sign that the stress had begun to get to him; actually, he needed space to think, time to sort out his thoughts and start making contingency plans. His gut feeling screamed at him that Timothy was up to something sinister and he knew that for the sake of Andrew and all that was good and true, he had to stop him in his tracks.

He looked across the hallway and saw Nicole standing outside the study staring up at the staircase. He pushed his present concerns aside and quickly walked towards her. As his clicking feet hurried towards her, he tried to knock up a plan of action and in that instant he realised what he had to do.

Nicole felt the eyes that approached her from her left hand side. She turned in that direction and saw Phillip in his perennial white cotton shirt marching towards her. His face was set in a frown and his hands were clenched in fists. She knew that he was in one of his foul moods. She had never liked him. To her, he was like a pit bull. Not in looks, but in mannerism, the kind of dog that looked at everyone who came close to its master as an enemy. A dog that could lay down its life without a second thought for the one it felt enamoured to. There was no gain saying that Phillip detested Andrews's concubines and she knew that as Andrews's numero uno, he loathed her the most. She placed a shy smile on her face as he walked closer.

"Follow me," was all Phillip said, walking past her without a break in his stride. She was surprised, but like a programmed Stepford wife, she followed him, watching the square of his shoulders, wondering where they were going to and what lay in store for her.

Phillip tried to hasten his steps without making it apparent that he wanted her out of the hallway before anyone saw them both. He knew that he had always instilled fear in her although she always put on that calm facade that seemed to say that she was in full control. Maybe it wasn't fear but hatred he thought to himself as he walked on, despising himself for looking out for his boss, detesting the fact that he was the one who made sure that they all remained in their places by reminding Andrew to treat them as what they truly were; female hustlers ready to sell not only their bodies but their souls to the highest bidder. Whatever it was, fear or hate, he knew he had to use it to his advantage, but first he had to get her to a place where he could be with her alone. He needed the privacy in order to work on her in a way that would bring forth the results he wanted.

Nicole followed him around a corner, her mind still in a state of wonderment. They both didn't see Therese as she stood outside the door of the drawing room watching them.

5

Nosa sat opposite his late father's lawyer in the dining room of his palatial residence in Victoria Garden City; a residential estate on the Lekki Peninsula in Lagos. An epicurean meal lay before them in expensive, finely decorated Chinese porcelain bowls from which Nosa had filled his plate with a mound of pounded yam and two servings of egusi soup. The lawyer watched him tear into a thick, juicy chunk of bush meat and smiled. It was nice seeing the young man start to live life again.

"So what airline are you flying?" he asked.

"British Airways," Nosa replied in between mouthfuls.

They both continued eating silently. The table was empty save for both of them. The lawyer's family was at that moment holidaying in Paris.

The lawyer drank from his glass of freshly squeezed orange juice and looked up at the giant chandelier that hung above them. He kept his eyes focused on twinkling lights before he leaned back on his chair and shifted his gaze to Nosa.

"Where will you be staying?"

"My cousin has a friend who will put me up for a month or two."

"You realise you won't be able to practise medicine there?"

"Not immediately."

"And what will you do for a living until you can?"

"Anything and everything."

The lawyer smiled and took another sip from his orange juice. Nosa on his part washed his hand in the bowl of water that sat on the table before he downed his glass of water.

"Any word from your brother?"

The mention of Osasu seemed to immediately bring a portentous tension into the room. Nosa fell silent for the briefest of moments before he replied.

"No." He had informed the lawyer some time ago that Osasu was somewhere in Canada.

"It's a very big country."

Nosa looked directly at him. There was a certain coldness in his eyes that transformed him from the jocular fellow he usually was to the focused hunter he was slowly becoming.

"I will find him." It came out with finality.

Silence fell again like thick fog. This time there was no more eating to keep them occupied, so Nosa looked away at the large oil painting of a nude village maiden with a gourd of water on her head that adorned the wall opposite him. He liked the brazenness of the painting. He loved the female physique in all its glory, a pity that he hadn't been able to keep a committed relationship for more than two months. Not because he was a philanderer, but because his profession had always been number one. Very few women could live with that fact. Maybe one day he would re-prioritise he mused to himself, but for now there was too much to do.

The lawyer stretched his arm across the table towards Nosa. In his hand was a white envelope. Nosa tore his eyes from the painting and looked at him; there was a glint of incomprehension as Nosa lowered his eyes to the envelope.

"Just a little something to tide you over," the lawyer softly spoke before he retracted his arm, leaving the envelope in front of Nosa.

Nosa lifted the envelope and opened it. He saw the crisp edges of several hundred dollar bills. He kept his eyes fixed on it. A warm pleasant feeling crowded his chest. His eyes misted over and then he looked up at the lawyer.

"My father found a true friend in you," A tear slid down Nosa's cheek. "Thank you." He finished in a voice choked with emotion.

The lawyer reached across the table with his right arm and clasped Nosa's hand. There was a moment between them; unspoken words with a very clear message. Nosa smiled at the now sombre lawyer in that unique way that always reminded the lawyer of his father.

"Your father will be proud of you."

Nosa lowered his head to hide the tears that were now rapidly making their way down his face.

"Good luck, son."

To Nosa, those words sounded like a negation of the saying that blood is thicker than water; there was no blood between him and the lawyer, yet the love was just as genuine if not more, and for the first time since his father died, Nosa allowed himself to cry in the presence of another person.

Phillip opened the door and walked into the dark room. Nicole stopped outside the door and peered into the darkness. She felt a wave of uneasiness creep upon her. She looked away at the deserted corridor and up the short staircase that stood at the end of it. They had walked down that entire length, right down into the lower levels of the house up this carpeted, windowless corridor with oil pastels on the wall, each hanging at the junction of several locked doors of silent rooms. Nicole knew that they were now underground. That fact made her all the more worried.

The rooms which lay along the corridor had originally been designed as servant quarters when the house was built in the late nineteenth century, but the series of renovations the house had enjoyed since that time had converted them to guest rooms. They had housed guests who hadn't made the A-list of the Sciorra's. Some relatives had also stayed in them from time to time, but overtime they had mostly stayed unoccupied. Phillip knew that this was the place where he could find the privacy he needed.

Nicole heard a faint click and turned back to the room. It was now bathed in bright light, showing off the giant four poster bed that sat at the center of the room. The room itself was expansive. Apart from the bed, there was a commode hewn from polished acacia wood leaning against the right wall upon which was a large painting of a Nordic landscape. There was a door which Nicole guessed led into the bathroom. At the opposite end were a closet, a single leather armchair, and a table in an alcove in the wall. There was a phone and TV set on top of the table. Phillip was leaning against the table, staring at her. She slowly walked in.

"Please shut the door." There was unmistakeable authority in his voice. Nicole did as told. Then they stood facing one another.

"I will cut to the chase," Phillip spoke.

Nicole quietly looked on.

"You have to leave this house."

She remained silent.

He continued, "You will tell Miss Sciorra that you cannot do what she wants you to do."

"I... can't..." she stammered, as she gave life to her words.

"Why?" Phillip crossed his arms across his chest, peering at her as though she were an errant child and he the all knowing parent.

"If I walk away, I will lose everything."

"Do you know that you're going to be locked up in this house until you get Andrew out of his fugue?"

"No... that is not what Therese said." There was a faint hint of panic in her voice.

"Well, there is a lot going on around here that you know nothing about." He squared his shoulders and continued, "Some of us folks are players while others are pawns... you are a pawn."

Nicole looked on with her lips pursed. She had no idea where he was heading to, but then her razor sharp mind had begun to draw up inferences. Quickly, questions began to pop up in her eyes. Phillip could not only see them, he could read them.

"Therese is also a pawn," he answered the first one.

"Andrew is a pawn," he answered the second one.

"I'm a player," he answered the third.

Nicole lowered her head, frightened at the accuracy with which he had read her thoughts. Phillip smiled and walked towards her. He stood in front of her and held her by the shoulder. Nicole flushed instantly in discomfort for she had never been this close to him, never assumed a position of seeming intimacy with him before.

"Nicole..." His voice was a bare whisper. She looked up at him. She saw the blue of his eyes and was marvelled at the transparency of it, the depth it seemed to conjure. She felt herself sinking into it.

"If you do what Therese wants, you will destroy Andrew." It came out plain and simple. Nicole heard it clearly and it woke her from her swoon instantly.

"She wants to save him..." she countered.

"So she thinks."

"What are you getting at?" Control had begun to seep into her voice.

Phillip looked at her for a short while, and then he lowered his arms and walked back to the table. He leaned on it and crossed his arms across his chest once again.

"There is another player." Nicole was quiet as she watched him with questioning eyes. He continued, "I am not sure of his plan, but one thing I am certain of is that he is up to no good." A deep hush fell on them as he finished speaking.

Phillip could feel it. He could feel her emotions shifting. He was banking on his belief that although Nicole was all for the money and comfort her relationship with Andrew provided, she will not consciously play a part in seeing him destroyed. He took the dive.

"We have to stop him." She was quiet as the words came out of Phillip. There was an accentuation of the "we."

"We have to save Andrew." Phillip locked his eyes on her.

They stared at each other. An electric current was building between them. Phillip felt his energy flowing into her. Nicole felt the aura of his truth. She tasted his conviction on the tip of her tongue. She began to see the truth of his reasoning when a knock sounded on the door. They both turned towards it. They were quiet. There was silence, and then the knock came again. Phillip rose up from the table and silently made his way towards the door. He was stopped dead in his tracks when he heard the voice.

"Phillip."

It was the icy cold voice of Therese Sciorra.

Angela let down the window of her black Mini and felt the wind slap pleasurably on her face as she drove north along the Highway 400 heading towards Canada Wonderland; a large theme park operated by the Paramount Entertainment conglomerate that progressively came to life in the short hot summer that blasted Canada during the months of May to early October. She loved the carefree air that summer brought in its Pandora box. She loved the excesses it wrought amongst the weather frozen people of the northern hemispheres. To her it was like being born again, especially when you spent it with someone like Osasu. She looked at the empty expanse of land that stood to her left and was tempted to shout out his name.

As the name dropped into her mind, she unconsciously stepped on the gas pedal, sending the car shooting to 120 mph. Such was the eagerness she had to see him. They were going to spend the whole day riding the scary contraptions in the park and she knew that it will all be interspersed with bouts of making out in peculiar places and positions, but all that she was looking forward to was just the time to spend with the man she loved without the faintest worry in the world.

She looked at the diamond ring on her finger as it gripped the steering. She smiled at it and it winked back at her. The dazzling lights that bounced off it were a sight to behold, pity that she could only wear it when not at home or at work. Her generously-proportioned female cousins would keel over in jealousy if they could see it, she laughed to herself. How she wished she didn't have to play hide and seek. How she wished she could share her joy with the family she loved.

She remembered when Osasu had looked at her with those his hypnotic eyes after a hot bout of lovemaking and asked her what she could do for him. At the time she had replied that she would do anything in the world. At that time it was just the rush of lust and the early seeds of love that made her flippant. But now as she drove along like a speed demon, she knew with every ounce of her being that she would truly do anything for Osasu Eweka.

Little did she know that what he will ask of her will shake the very foundations of her existence.

Phillip Neri was an avowed bachelor. He was the sort of guy the bureaucracies of the world called an establishment man. He was born in the early sixties in Little Italy, the neighbourhood between College and Grace Streets in midtown Toronto, to middle class parents who were immigrants from Turkey. Unlike their neighbours who were mostly Italians, his parents were from Istanbul and were not only illiterate but Armenian, so people looked down on them not only in the neighbourhood but among the Turkish community in Toronto.

As an only child, Phillip was the vortex around which his parent's revolved. Though his father worked as a day labourer in the several construction sites that dotted the area and his mother was a seamstress in the downtown Toronto hosiery industry, they made it a matter of spirituality to ensure that he had an unfettered access to quality education. His father wanted to save him the shame of his heritage so he changed his last name from Kouyoumdjian to Neri after his favourite actor Franco Nero. Thus Phillip grew up with the name Neri and put smiles on his parents face when he came home like clockwork with straight A's. He attended the University of Toronto, where he studied Political science and graduated top of his class. He had intended going to Law School but cut it short when his father took ill. Phillip needed a job to cater for his medical bills and the upkeep of his aging mother, so he put his dream of becoming the Prime Minister of Canada on the back burner and took on the responsibility of family provider and protector. A position he was willing to hold until the family finances were back in order and his father had recovered. He was twenty-four years old at the time.

It was while searching for a good paying job along King Street West that he ran into the affluent playboy; Andrew Sciorra. It was a cold February morning and Phillip was hurrying along the snow filled street in a bid to arrive early for a job interview. He was dressed in a black double breasted suit, white starched cotton shirt, black oxford tie, and polished black brogues. His hair slicked back conservatively. He was an apostle of the school that preached the gospel of first-impressions-speak-loudest. He didn't notice the Ford mustang that came speeding down the street and was about to cross the street when a sheet of wet sludge that had accumulated from the melting snow came splashing on him.

He stood there in a daze and watched the car continue on its way, and then stop at the red light that stood at the intersection of King and Bay Streets. He looked at himself and was enraged by the mess that was now his impeccable clothing. He realised with horror that he could no longer attend the interview in such a state and before he could quantify his anger, he was already sprinting down the street towards the car that stood waiting for the lights to say go at the intersection.

Andrew Sciorra was behind the wheel. He was also dressed impeccably and was on his way to a breakfast meeting with a group of South African miners who were shopping for equity investors for a new diamond mine in the Transvaal. Andrew's father had sent him to test their waters. He was running late and was surprised at the raging Phillip who opened the car door and began raining insults on him.

Through the loud voice and burning eyes, Andrew had realised that he was responsible for the sludge that dripped off Phillip's clothes. He had apologised profusely and it seemed that his apologies had made Phillip a lot angrier. As the traffic lights turned green, he heard Phillip talk about a job he was going to lose as a result of his drenched clothes and without thinking Andrew had offered him a job.

Phillip had looked at him in incredulity and was just about raising his voice again, when the cars behind started blaring their horns. Andrew who was becoming uncomfortable and who now feared that a cop would appear and charge them for traffic obstruction told Phillip to hop into the car and discuss the terms of employment while he drove to his meeting.

Phillip got into the car with reservation, wondering at the time if this obviously wealthy-looking man was a joke or an angel from heaven. He proved to be the latter.

Nearly twenty-five years later, through all the highs and lows of life on a fast lane, the man Andrew hired right on the street of Toronto had not only turned out to be an ace employee but had proven to be his most loyal friend.

Timothy leaned against the head board of the queen size bed and threw the wad of ten hundred dollar bills at the naked Indian girl.

"Get the fuck out of here!" He threw the words at her with scorn.

She quickly picked up her clothes and began wearing them, careful to keep her eyes away from him. He had seemed really nice and suave when she had appeared at the door of his motel room in the Highway 410 and Bovaird corridor in the city of Brampton earlier that evening. He had even sounded better when he had called her that afternoon, saying that he had seen her number in the classifieds section of the eye weekly magazine. But now three hours later, she knew that voices could be deceptive. She had large welts on her pert buttocks and well-toned back to prove it. The guy was a closet pervert. The cavity in her nether regions which felt like it was ablaze with a thousand eternal fires could testify to that. At least he paid good money, she said under her breath as she gingerly walked towards the door, grimacing at every foot step, her hair in disarray, her lips bruised. She didn't say a word to him before she disappeared into the night, slamming the motel door loudly behind her.

Timothy smiled and switched on the colour television that sat on a table in front of the bed. He flicked channels until he got to CNN and then settled to watch a re-run of Larry King

Live. As he listened to the voice droning on, his mind strayed to his well oiled plan. He was impressed that all was going according to the book, every piece falling into place one after the other. One day soon, Larry King himself might have him as a guest on his show, asking him in that fatherly voice of his, what the secret of his success was and as would be expected, Timothy knew he would surely lie. Hitler had once said, that if one must lie, one must tell such a great lie that it would shake the very foundations of the listener because only then would you be able to steal the souls one needs to go places. As usual Timothy had garnished the quotation for his own justification.

He looked at his platinum Rolex chronograph that lay on the bedside table beneath the cheap lamp; ten minutes past midnight. He had forty five more minutes before leaving the anonymity of the motel room. He bunched the second pillow underneath his head and began counting his millions in tune to the voice of Larry King.

Timothy Vinelatter was born on the morning Pope John Paul II was named Cardinal. His mother had named him after the Pope's real name; Karol. His father had given him the name Timothy after a friend whom he had lost in the Second World War on the beaches of Normandy. He was an only child, and grew up as a rambunctious, dark haired, naturally tanned kid in the upscale Toronto neighbourhood of Rosedale.

His father was a well known and respected lawyer while his mother was a notable and much sought after neurosurgeon. The latter was born to immigrant parents from Ireland, the former to immigrant parents from Poland. They were staunch Catholics and had built a fortune from careful prospecting in the global stock markets. Thus Timothy had enjoyed the pampered life of the rich, attending the exclusive Upper Canada College; an all male day and boarding school for the children of the super rich that was founded in 1829 and tucked into the ultra exclusive residential neighbourhood of Avenue road and St Clair Avenue in Toronto. It counted amongst its alumni several past Canadian Prime Ministers, Supreme Court Justices, Captains of industry, and the jet set class from the global arena. Timothy enrolled at the school in junior kindergarten and left as a sturdy eighteen year old who was extremely adventurous, dangerously daring, and frighteningly ambitious. His tutors all remembered him to be uncannily wise beyond his years.

Following in his father's footsteps, he went on to Harvard university where he had proven that even the rich had brains, graduating magna cum laude in Economics and International Finance in three years and without a breather, flown to the London School of Economics for graduate school, finishing top of his MBA class. His father who had believed that he himself was a Jedi in his mastery of the stock markets marvelled at the genius of his son when he had proven his mettle by investing the fifty thousand dollar graduation present he had received from his parents upon the completion of his studies at Harvard. Timothy had invested in a trust that pooled together angel funds for the dot com companies that pervaded the market in the nineties and in the span of four years had made nearly sixteen million dollars.

His mother on the other hand, who believed that the value of money was in the good causes it could accomplish, was a trifle bit concerned about her son's evident, unabashed lust for money. In hushed tones she had discussed it with her husband, who on the contrary believed that it was a trait that should be encouraged; the innocent man had no idea that the trait he so admired was just the tip of an iceberg that would wreck the lives of all who crossed the boy's path whether positively or negatively.

He didn't realise that his son had no moral compass. He didn't believe when his wife had said, one night while they lay in bed after a tedious day, that she had looked into her son's eyes as he watched her sign a cheque for one of her umpteenth charities and all she had seen was the reflection of unbridled ruthlessness, a sense that he believed she was wasting money. As usual his father didn't raise an eyebrow, just like he had done when Timothy stopped attending Sunday mass at the age of fourteen. Just like then, much to the chagrin of his mother, his father attributed it to the rebelliousness of youth.

There were other times this scene had played out before, like when his father didn't complain when a neighbour accused him of seducing that neighbour's wife. Instead, he had raged at the cuckolded man for his nerve in accusing a sixteen-year old boy of seducing a forty-one year old woman. But it was his mother who had believed the poor man when she saw the emerald ring his wife sometimes wore in the top drawer of the mahogany commode in her son's room.

At the time, although she suspected that her son was in it for money or power, she had pushed it out of mind as she bristled from the idea that her son whom they had given all that money could buy will stoop so low as to becoming a gigolo. She was a wise woman and it was from her that he had inherited his street smarts, but then, as it runs in the blood of all mothers, her love for her son stopped her from acknowledging the truth that their son had become an apostle of Mammon.

His father had died in the bliss of ignorance as he sat in the offices of Ernest Mooring & Son's, an embattled firm he was representing in a lawsuit in New York. He didn't see the large American Airlines jumbo jet as it slammed into the south tower of the World Trade Center in which he was. He died on impact. His wife followed a year later from heartbreak. Timothy who was now a six foot four inches chiselled man with high cheekbones, bluish grey eyes, and a thick mat of dark hair that gave him a certain Mediterranean handsomeness surprisingly mourned them deeply for they had been the only people he had ever loved.

After a year of deep misery, he stood up from the ashes and sailed to Ibiza for a rejuvenating vacation, secure in the fact that he had inherited his parents' fortunes, their life insurance pay outs, and a share of the funds set aside for the victims of the 9/11 disaster.

It was during this trip that he met Therese. He had sold her his story in the most dramatic of ways, shed some tears, and charmed himself into not only her life, but that of her desperately sad mother and effervescent father, who were vacationing with her at the highly prized beach front resort of Cote d'Azur. At the time he had viewed his steaming affair with Therese as another conquest of the feminine flesh, but as he got to know the family, the dormant fire of Mammon began to rekindle and before he even realised it, he had begun to look at this new relationship as a passport to the next level. While his heart and lips professed emotional lies, his mind fashioned out business schemes.

Nosa looked at the twin grave stones that stood before him. He read the words that were carved into the polished marble as a slight breeze blew across his face, leaving his collar unfurled in its wake.

He remained there in a squatting position in front of the tombs of his parents in the concrete city that was the Ikoyi cemetery in Obalende Lagos. The din of honking buses, call and respond cries of hawkers, expletives of pedestrians, and motorists serenaded him as he stared at the engraved stones.

He was dry-eyed and curiously uneasy. He looked away at the rows of tombs to his left and fought the urge to cry. He knew that he had to stay focused, to think objectively, but then, these were his parents, the vortex of his world, the two people who made all that he had become possible. It hurt deeply when he realised that they had not reaped the fruit of their labour. They would not be there to see him ascend the dizzying heights of a successful career as a cardio-thoracic surgeon. More depressing was the mode of their death. One by the evil barrel of a thieving gun and the other by the noxious fumes of a car's exhaust pipe, both transcending into the celestial through the actions, both directly and indirectly, of men whose very nature was steeped in evil. The thought that one of these men was his own brother, their son, flesh and blood sent a fiery rage coursing through his veins. He closed his eyes to stem it. He believed it was disrespectful to lose his composure in the sacred concrete city.

Actually, the space on which he was standing was a family plot. His late father had purchased it for the sakes of continuity and eternal bonding, thus the two tomb stones were surrounded by a semi large expanse of green grass from which various weeds stuck out. He knew that if his father's wishes were to be met, then the corpses of he, Osasu and the others that they would bring into this earth would one day rest there, but now he wondered if that could ever happen for he had no idea what he would do when he found Osasu. All he knew for now was that he needed answers and as it concerned restitution and forgiveness, he had searched hard over the last months for the possibility. He had asked himself in the loneliness of those dark nights if he could summon up those capabilities, to forgive and to forget, but try as he had done, a tiny voice in the center of his mind kept whispering "You cannot."

And now as he stooped in front of the tombs, he believed it.

He looked at the wreath of flowers he had placed on the tombs when he first arrived, then he stretched his right arm and stroked the face of the marble tombstone of his mother, he ran his fingers over her name which was hewn into the hard surface, and then he did the same thing to that of his father before whispering some heartfelt words.

"I'm leaving tomorrow for Canada. I'm going to find Osasu. I need you to be with me just as you always have. I need you to lead me to him. I promise you that I'll make him pay for what he did." Then he went quiet and looked down at the concrete between his feet as he quietly asked himself "would they really be a party to vendetta?"

"I feel so lost... so unsure... I don't know what I'll do when I find him... I have prayed but there are no answers...the truth is that... hate is consuming me... I am afraid my hating Osasu will destroy me... and if it does then he has won." When he looked up his eyes were misty but his cheeks were dry.

"Please... tell me what to do." He kept looking at the tombstone of his father and remained motionless as though he expected the granite slab to speak. It was at that moment that the sun dipped in the west and the din of traffic along the main road that had heralded rush hour and formed a constant background sound for the last hour eerily faded away. All that remained was Nosa, the two tombs, and silence.

Five minutes passed although it seemed to Nosa like it was five hours and he still stooped there motionless. He didn't even feel the cramp that had begun to build in his left leg. Suddenly, a slight breeze blew across him and he was suffused with an eerie feeling of peace; a deep settling of his troubled spirit that in human terms could be accepted as fulfilment. A latent satisfaction, the sort that is not exhibited in a laugh or smile but in the form of twin eyes that glow with love. He felt his pulse slow down. A lightness of body and in that instant his mind became crystal clear. He knew what he had to do.

"Thank you," he whispered happily before he stood up, blew them a kiss, and disappeared into the conviviality of the rawness and the excitingly bubbly reverie of the Lagos evening.

Phillip went pale when he heard Therese's voice. He looked at the door with such intensity it was as if he was willing her to disappear. Nicole watched him, she could feel the dreadful feeling that oozed from him; she knew the feeling for she had felt it before. Its name was fear. The same kind of fear she felt when she had received the call from Phillip that sad night and was told that Annabelle had hung herself and it was in the best interest of her and the Sciorra family that she kept her doors and mouth closed to the press.

"Phillip, are you in there?" Her voice came out again.

The silence that came after that was so deep Nicole felt herself sinking into it, and like an outstretched arm yanking out a drowning man from certain death, Phillip's strangely controlled voice yanked her out of it.

"Yes, I am." Phillip's voice was an octave higher than a whisper. Therese heard it.

"I will like a word with you, if you have the time." There was evident bait in it.

Nicole could see the opening for Phillip to come out of the implicating scenario unscathed. She hoped Phillip would grab it. He was a lot wiser, so he did not.

"Of course!" His voice came out upbeat before he swung the door open.

Therese stood there staring at him, her face set in a frozen frame of half surprise, half anger. She was smart and she realised that in that one move Phillip had made, he had exonerated himself. Now any excuse he put forward would pass the litmus test.

"Please come in," Phillip offered, "Nicole and myself were just ironing out some technicalities."

Therese remained standing for a while, out of the view of Nicole, and then she breezed in, her shoulder squared in all the glory of her authority. Once in, she swung her face in the direction of Nicole and then incinerated her with her scorching gaze. Nicole, who knew the score, smiled in response. Therese was taken aback by the seeming normality of both Phillip and Nicole. She had not bargained for this.

When she turned back to Phillip, he was standing there, arms crossed on his chest, a slight smirk on his face. The energy level in the room was now in his favour.

"I hope I'm not barging into anything?" Therese was now gathering back her wits.

"Not at all, we were just rounding off," Phillip replied.

"Strange place for a meeting," Therese let it slip and her spirits dampened immediately. To her it was a faux pas. Phillip smiled.

"Now that Nicole will be staying here, I believe we should be showing her the accommodations we have arranged and smoothening out the rough edges, you know, letting her know what the score is," Phillip lectured on.

"But…" Therese attempted to counter him but he sailed on;

"And then, it seems that the walls in the hallway have ears, especially when Nurse Maria is holding sway… so I took the honour upon myself to show Nicole her room and ensure that we all are on the same page." He finished with a smile hanging from his lips.

Therese was silent. Nicole watched on, impressed by Phillip's manoeuvrability.

"Don't you think it was a good idea?" Phillip asked with a feigned look of concern.

"Yes… it was… time is of the essence." She dragged the words before she looked over at Nicole. Nicole smiled again. Therese cringed and looked back at Phillip. She wasn't sure if she was to be concerned. Earlier on when she saw the duo walking down the hallway, her antennae had risen. She was sure Phillip was working at cross purposes to her, trying to thwart her plans, intent on her father remaining in his living coma for reasons she had not the slightest idea of. She followed them believing that if she caught them in the treacherous act, then she had solid proof to justify her claims and enough evidence to inform her decision.

She was now the de facto head of her family and had the reins of authority in her hands. Barely half an hour ago, she was certain that Phillip Neri, whom she had known for the most part of her life, would be the first of her father's staff she was going to let go. Honourably of course, she had reminded herself, as she walked down the hallway earlier on, because whatever it was he was up to, he still had served the family tirelessly over the years and deserved to be rewarded for that.

But now that she had heard what he said, she immediately began to have a rethink. Therese had watched him as he spoke, she held his eyes, watched his lips move. She knew what the truth looked and sounded like and standing there in front of Phillip, she came to accept that she was wrong. She had jumped into conclusions. Was she overreaching herself? she asked herself silently. Searching for enemies in the wall paper? Unconsciously persecuting Phillip for the sins of her father? She looked at him and heard him speak again.

"You said you had something to discuss with me?" Phillip asked, his voice bringing her back to the present.

She looked at him and blinked twice, trying to comprehend his question. Phillip realised that she was lost and spoke again.

"Nicole, can you give us a minute?" His eyes smiled.

Nicole nodded and made to leave, her mind wondering why no one had asked for her opinion before making decisions. Did she want or not want to stay at the Sciorra's residence while they all fought to save the life of Andrew? Such a simple question, yet so difficult to ask. Phillip was right, she was a pawn.

"No," Therese stopped her with the word. "You both can finish up with the arrangements." She moved towards the door, her face suddenly looking weary, "Phillip, what I have to discuss can wait."

Once at the door, she turned to Nicole and smiled, "Thank you for helping us out," and then she nodded at Phillip and walked out of the room. Her footsteps were silent as she walked down the underground lushly carpeted corridor.

When Phillip turned back to Nicole, he found her smiling shyly. He knew that Therese's compliment had gone down well with her, yet on his part, he felt mightily relieved that his hand was not caught in the cookie jar. But then, he knew that he had to change plans.

He was smart enough to realise that whoever was pulling the strings behind the scene would hear about what had just occurred from Therese and he knew that that person was smart enough to realise that all Phillip had said was a lie. If that happened, then the dynamics of the game would change. His instinct told him that before now, he was just being simply tolerated. He knew that after that night, he would be the enemy. His brow furrowed at the thought, for at that moment he felt that all eyes were on him. He was right.

Timothy stepped hard on the gas pedal and his metallic red Porsche obeyed; speeding wildly down the Don Valley Parkway. He looked to his left and could see the deep ravine that runs between Castle Frank and Broadview neighbourhoods and a faint feeling of fear seeped into him. What if he lost control of this sleek hurtling machine and plummeted down that yawning grave? He thought to himself and quickly he tapped lightly on the brakes and once again the car obeyed.

He was heading to the Sciorra residence to check up on Andrew and Therese. It had been three days since he visited although he had repeatedly called over the phone. He smiled, his eyes taking in the other slow moving cars the Porsche had overtaken, his mind satisfied that Therese had followed his instructions.

Timothy had struck up a relationship with the bar man at the Cosmopolitan Yacht club at Toronto Island. It was an exclusive all male club founded by a group of American businessmen in the late nineteenth century. These adventure-toughened merchants had come up north to take advantage of the flourishing fur trade. It had grown to be a haven of the filthy rich and the well-connected. Membership was highly sought and near impossible to get since it admitted three new members each year. Membership could be inherited as long as the status of wealth and relevance was maintained by the heir and also as long as the heir was male. Timothy had inherited his membership, so had Andrew.

The club stood at the southernmost tip of the Island and was shielded from the view of the shore line that ran along Queens Quay in Toronto mainland by a thick expanse of woods; large fern trees that rose towards the windy skies. It was because of its hidden nature that the founders had chosen that location.

A huge, white sixty-room Victorian mansion occupied a better part of the compound. In addition to this, there were five tennis courts, two Olympic size swimming pools, one of them was indoor and was used during the winter months; a fully equipped gymnasium, a large outdoor restaurant that served cuisines from all over the world, and then there was the harbour that ran alongside the eastern front around which state of the art yachts were moored. The entire expanse was steeped in wealth and class. On these grounds, respect did not come only as a result of the size of your bank account but by the influence your name carried in the hallowed offices of the high and mighty. Andrew Sciorra strode the grounds and people made way. His name was gold. Timothy, though a member, was regarded as a minion. He had a dying ambition to change all that.

By keeping his ears and eyes open, Timothy was slowly climbing the ladder of power as evidenced by the slight nod of recognition he received from the captains of industry when he walked by. He knew for certain that very few of the men brought their wives here for any of the festive occasions or for any reason whatsoever; it was common knowledge that the private, well furnished rooms had housed many a concubine for amorous trysts. One of those concubines was that of Andrew Sciorra.

Timothy had gleaned the information from the sandy-haired, middle-aged bar tender and had proceeded to watch out for her. He had been dazzled by her beauty when he saw her lounging by the indoor pool and had opened up a conversation. At the time she hadn't revealed who she was with, but had handed him her card. It had just her name and phone number. There was no address, no occupation. It was this card that Timothy had handed over to Therese. If all worked out as planned, the presence of Nicole in the house would push Andrew over the edge. It would drive him insane with guilt, make him behave abnormally. So much so that he would be committed to a psychiatric ward for expert care. That was where Timothy wanted him. He even had a doctor waiting for him; the medication to be prescribed was also ready.

He prayed that Therese would smell no rat and continue dancing to his discordant tune. Her voice had sounded tense over the phone five minutes ago, and although she had not said anything out of the ordinary, Timothy could sense something was amiss. He had wasted no time in jumping into his car and heading for her house. He knew that he could leave nothing to chance. Only fools do that, he muttered beneath his breath.

The one thing Timothy prided himself in was his wisdom although the world would have termed it unscrupulous cunning.

Angela slipped her right hand into Osasu's large hand. She could feel the familiar softness of his palm and briefly luxuriated in the sweetness that it evoked. He held her hand tight and smiled at her and at that moment the speed breaks were released and their seats came plummeting down.

She felt her heart leap into her head and the pit of her stomach expand into monstrous proportions as the pull of the Earth's gravity sucked her with such ferocity that she actually thought that the fright will kill her. She closed her eyes tightly and screamed loudly as they descended, air rushing into her mouth.

They had just ridden the drop zone; the ride that was famed as one of the scariest in the repertoire of Paramount Canada's wonderland. Angela loosened the harness and staggered away from the ride, gasping as she fought to regain her breath and silence her thumping heart. She could hear Osasu laughing and whistling loudly behind her. In her dazed state she could still afford a smile, happy that he was having fun. Osasu hugged her from behind and planted a light caress-like kiss behind her ear on the exact spot that always set her on fire. She felt the warmth spread around her body. She dissolved into him.

In two hours she was back at his apartment, spread-eagled on his bed, her pubic hair glistening with the orgasmic tears her lower lips had just shed. Osasu was lying by her side, his body covered in sweat, his breath puffing loudly. She turned over and snuggled up to him. Her right hand caressed his taut, erect right nipple and her right leg hugged him across his stomach. She still felt herself tingling.

"What will I do without you?" she whispered.

Osasu turned his head in her direction and smiled, and then he raised his head and planted a kiss on her forehead. She closed her eyes and savoured the sweetness of it.

"I'm going to tell my folks about us," she spoke without opening her eyes. "It's high time." Her face was set in a serious mien that accentuated the finality of her decision.

"Are you sure you can take the fall out?" he asked in a calm voice that was peppered with feigned concern.

"What's the worst they can do?" her eyes were now open and boring into him.

"They could disown you," he said in a whisper.

"And?" she left the question in the air.

Osasu was silent for a while, and then he spoke, "Isn't that bad enough?"

She smiled, "Not as bad as losing you."

They stared at each other. A silent moment that spoke volumes and then Osasu leaned over and enveloped her lips in a kiss, his lower muscle rising.

Angela was ready to step over the threshold. She was, without his prodding, falling right into his trap. Strike two, he said to himself as he slid into her for the third time that night.

The traffic crawled at a very slow pace along Falomo Bridge. It was rush hour. Nosa was seated at the rear of his maternal uncle's Mercedes Benz which was idling at the crest of the bridge, standing front fender to rear bumper in the traffic jam colloquially referred to as "Go Slow" by Nigerians.

In the trunk of the car were his suitcases. His younger female cousin sat next to him, while his uncle's long standing driver, Sule, was behind the wheel. There had been an emotional parting at the house some thirty minutes ago; his uncle's wife holding back her tears, his uncle patting him on his back as he made his way to the car. There was no doubt that they had enjoyed his stay with them and would miss his wise cracking jokes and his penchant for writing poetry at will, which he then read aloud much to the admiration of everyone. They had implored him to come back home when he found Osasu and had tirelessly pleaded with him not to do anything rash. He had smiled and kept his lips sealed. A promise not made cannot be broken, he reasoned.

He looked out at the throngs of hawkers that darted between

the cars, each one holding an item for sale. There were some people holding plastic bags of water popularly called "pure water" in large boxes soaked with the melting water from the large chunks of ice blocks that were placed on the bags to cool them. These boxes were heavy and yet the boys and girls ran with it, the strain showing in the veins that bulged on their necks as they shuttled from car to car trying to make quick business. Then there were others who sold leather belts. Others had handkerchiefs, underwear, and towels hanging on wooden racks which they carried high above their heads in accompaniment to a sing song that announced their wares. There were pies that went by the name "Gala" being hawked. Apples that had been imported from South Africa also had their say. Plastic sunglasses and cheap wristwatches from China held sway.

It was a virtual supermarket on walking and running feet; young men and women; children in most cases. Some coming straight from school to the streets in order to sell these goods in an attempt to help their impoverished parents put food on the table and clothes on their backs. Some wishing they could afford to attend any school. Others, university graduates, tired of endless, fruitless applications who had taken their destinies into their hands. They were all there; the nation's poor. Each one stared with eyes that spoke of the harsh realities of life. Their chafed lips testified to the misery of poverty. They looked at the flashy cars. They watched the well-dressed occupants respond to their pleas for a purchase. Some of the more fortunate motorists smiled and bought in miserly quantities, others simply ignored them. Yet there was no trace of hatred in the eyes of the hawkers, maybe envy but not hatred. Those eyes which blinked repeatedly from the stream of sweat that flowed into them were devoid of that peculiar glint that spoke of hope. Their foreheads were creased from endless squinting in the sun. They all seemed in some vague way to have aged as they went about their arduous tasks. Each one ran to beat the other, a battle to the last coin, a jovial fight for survival. It was as though they had accepted their fate.

Nosa sighed and turned to look at his cousin. She was twenty-one, beautiful in all sense of the word, a recent university graduate, a job already in waiting. She had lived a life of ease courtesy of her position as an only child. Her parents were wealthy which meant she resided in the neighbourhood of the rich and the spoilt. Had she ever known pain? He found himself asking. Had she ever woken up with an empty stomach without an idea of where the next meal was coming from? Had she watched with envy and sorrow, kids her age walk into school because their parents could afford it and hers could not? Did she even value the life she had or just looked at it as her God-given right? The questions burned in his throat but didn't find a voice.

He looked away. He was once like her, he commented inwardly, and at that time he never spared a thought for the ordinary guy on the street. Not because he was pompous or self conceited but because it never occurred to him to think of them. He saw them walk around the edge of his everyday life and that was it. They were in their world and he was in his, two destinies walking side by side, no one interfering with the other except in the area of necessity, like providing a service of the kind he watched outside the car window.

They were brought up that way. It was the life they knew. As his father used to say, the hand of the giver will always be on top of the hand of the receiver. In that wise he was taught to give as an accentuation of his social and financial superiority and not because he gave a hoot. So he knew that his cousin was just day dreaming about her own cosy world as she looked outside the window. She definitely wasn't seeing the misery that was walking right before her turquoise grey contact lenses. He didn't blame her. She was a product of her society. A society that had so much and yet gave so little to those who needed it most.

Osasu's name slipped into his mind once more. He was still confounded at Osasu's actions because he would have thought that since they grew up in the lap of luxury, the last thing Osasu should have become was the material monster he now was. Why had he chased money in the most despicable of ways when he had it there for the asking? Why did he have to dance with pigs in order to wear the crown of the high and mighty? Was he looking for something that he inertly craved or did he just need to thump his nose up to the elitist class of society by making a statement that he could make it without being spoon fed? Or was he what the Bible had called a child of perdition; a child who has been condemned from birth, a person who brought sorrow to all who came into contact with them? He shuddered at the thought and quickly pushed his brother out of his mind before he turned to his cousin.

"Promise me something," he started. She turned to him. He continued, "Promise me that you will always appreciate the life that you have and you will in any way possible help out your fellow man." He sounded fatherly. She smiled and spoke.

"Funny you said that because I was just thinking about life ... you know, about your family and how things can take a turn for the worse in a split second." An amused look appeared on Nosa's face. She wasn't done, "And I realise how fortunate I am to have what I have and be who I am because the only thing that separates me from the hawker out there is luck."

His eyes misted over and he was filled with an exhilarating feeling, something of the kind a father feels when he cradles his new born child in his arms. Nosa reached over and hugged her tight. He was filled with gratitude for the moment because it had shown him that the disaster that had visited his family could in so many ways be a source of rejuvenation to a lot of people. They had gone from grace to grass in one night. They who went to bed believing they had everything had woken up with nothing. They had been so totally caught up in the world of the fortunate that they had no inkling that their son was being schooled by the unfortunate in the evil ways of the world. They had learnt in a painful way that earthly glory was fleeting, so if it could happen to them, then it could happen to anyone.

Nosa had flown out of Nigeria that night with a smile of renewed hope for the future lighting his face like a halo and a dull ache of longing for a life fading away lightly thumping in the center of his chest as he stared at the twinkling lights of Lagos from the window of the plane.

6

There was a ringing din in her ears as Timothy went on and on with his soul-numbing harangue. Therese cocked her head in an angle that feigned attentive listening but was actually a position she assumed when she wanted to block all things out and catch a nap in the midst of heated action. She had developed the skill whilst at Branksome Hall; an exclusive all girls private school in downtown Toronto, which boasted the children of the excessively wealthy. Her skill was further accentuated by the fact that she could fall asleep with her eyes open. Annabelle always complained it was the creepiest thing she ever did. Therese loved to frighten the bejesus out of her mother.

"Therese!" Timothy's voice crashed into her peaceful quiet.

"Yes darling." Her voice floated out from her snooze.

"I was asking you a question."

"I know, I'm carefully thinking about my response."

"Well, I'm waiting."

"I think the question is rather confusing, can you rephrase

it?" Her mother also said she inherited effortless lying from her father. Therese never really disputed it.

"If you say so." He took a deep breath as though weighing the enormity of the task of rephrasing his question, then he audibly exhaled, "I was asking if you'll rather have Phillip run the estate since you obviously think he is more than capable?"

Therese fell quiet and looked down at her feet. She knew the response to give, but had to play the part. Timothy watched on. She counted up to ten and then looked up.

"In the absence of my father, no one else will run this estate other than me." It came out matter-of-fact. Simple yet powerful, affirming yet subtle. Timothy paid heed to the underlying message. He knew he had to seize control.

"I am not the enemy."

"I never said you were, love, I was just answering your question."

"And you still think Phillip is right?"

"I am just not sure if I am right."

Timothy walked over to her and crouched in front of her. He took hold of her hands and clasped them within his.

"You are right honey, more right than the word itself." He was careful to keep his voice low and assuring.

"What if she does more harm than good?"

"What if by not doing anything he never recovers?" Timothy answered.

"The doctors say…" Her words hung in her throat as Timothy cut her off.

"The doctors will always say what they have to say, but we are family; you and I and Andrew. We are family. In the final analysis, it is us that have the final say." He had said "we" twice to imprint it on her mind, to let her understand that he was in this for the long haul.

"I truly don't think Phillip is going to or willing or even

thinking about stabbing my dad in the back. It just doesn't make sense."

"I didn't say he wanted to do that."

"Well, that's what you've been alluding to."

"How can you say that, Therese?" His voice rose an octave.

"But isn't that what you meant by the wolves will move in for the kill?" Her voice was a trifle lower; a hint of fear in it.

Timothy realised he had to pull back. He couldn't afford to give Phillip the appearance of a hapless victim while he wore the band of vengeful accuser.

"I didn't mean him. I meant others who know your dad is out of it."

"But Phillip has been by his side for years. If there is anyone my father trusts, it is Phillip."

"Phillip is not your father."

"Of course, I know."

"So he can't make decisions for him like he will make for himself."

"Apparently."

"He won't be able to manoeuvre amongst these wolves. He will make mistakes."

"But I am the one making the decisions."

"Therese, what do you know about running the business?"

"I am learning."

"These people wouldn't wait for you to come up to speed before they pounce."

"How come you know so much about these wolves?" Her eyes were suspicious.

"Because they have always been circling me since my parents died. In fact, all through my life, they've wanted to take a chunk off me. It will happen to you too Therese, and I will never forgive myself if I don't do all I can to protect you."

Therese fell quiet. She looked away from him, desperate for a little space to sort out her thoughts. She loved Timothy with a fierce passion and knew how difficult a person he was to love. Sometimes she hovered on the edge of hate; a desperate urge to break free of him and take her chance with whatever else life had in store for her, but then, she couldn't run away from her feelings, from an unspoken connection she had with him. This time around there was an ominous feeling that she couldn't shake off. An air of foreboding that was so thick, she felt she could bite into it. Through the chasm of her troubled thoughts, she could see the sense of Timothy's words. She turned back to him.

"What do I do?"

"Let Nicole do what she has to do."

"And Phillip?"

Timothy took a minute, weighing his options. He decided that was not the moment to stretch his hands out too much.

"We would have to make him understand that we all need to work towards getting Andrew back by any means necessary."

"And will he co-operate?"

"Yes he will, if you make him understand you can't do it without him."

"And if he does not?"

"We will cross that bridge when we get there." He made sure he left it open ended. A coward lives to fight another day.

Therese looked at him quietly. His face was a picture of deep concern. She could feel his love seeping out of his eyes and then she slowly leaned forward and kissed him lightly on his lips, her fingers running across the side of his face.

"I love you," she whispered.

"I'll always love you," he whispered back.

As they moved closer and kissed deeper, the eyes of the paintings that hung on the somber coloured walls in the drawing room looked down at them in dread. Therese pulled him closer to her as passion heated her loins. Timothy smiled inwardly. Fool me once, shame on me, fool me twice shame on you. He couldn't say he was the guilty party. He knew Phillip was no fool.

Nicole was walking to and fro in the room that lay in the underground levels of the Sciorra residence. She was acting out a routine in which she gently hit her forehead on the brightly painted far wall of the room just inches from the painting of a Nordic landscape before turning around and walking to the opposite wall and hitting her forehead once again on it, but this time she did it four times. Each time she did this routine, she increased the amount of times she hit her head on the second wall but kept the first hit constant. This was the way Nicole acted when she needed to think deeply. Many would have called her Obsessive Compulsive. She called it, getting something to do while I needed to think, anything that was repetitive and progressive.

She was still dressed in the clothes she had worn to the house the day before. It was the early hours of the day and darkness still hung around the morning skies. Her mind raced back to her past, settling on the carefree days of her youth. She searched in the archives of her past for the truest version of her. She dug for the real her. Even as she held onto the trappings of the present, she realised how important the moments that enveloped her were. She understood that whatever decision she took in these hours would shape her life for years to come. She was oscillating between cutting loose from it all and disappearing as Phillip wanted or staying and rescuing the man that had given her so much as Therese wanted. But the major question that burdened her was what she herself wanted.

She did two more repetitions of her ritual and then stopped abruptly. Her right eye was twitching; a natural signal that she has made up her mind on what to do. She exhaled loudly and walked out of the room, shutting the door silently behind her.

Phillip had installed an electric stair lift when it was apparent that Andrew had retrogressed to the point where he could not walk under his own power. It was like the debilitation of Lou Gehrig's disease, the difference being that it existed only in Andrew's mind; a hitherto brilliant mind he had shut firmly to all intrusions of the outside world.

The night nurse and a nursing assistant where transferring Andrew from his motorised wheelchair to the stair lift while Phillip watched on when Nicole rounded the corner and walked towards them. It was the clicking of her high heels on the polished marble floors that got Phillip's attention. He turned to the source and saw Nicole walking towards them, back ramrod straight, a steeling of her frame and a march in her stride that spoke of a drastic change in attitude.

She stopped a respectable distance away and waited for Phillip to walk towards her. He delayed until the nurse and her assistant began escorting the moving stair lift as it made its way up the staircase, Andrew in tow, eyes open, staring sightlessly. Once the trio had disappeared up the staircase, Phillip walked to the standing Nicole.

"Thought you were already in bed," he opened up the conversation.

"In these clothes?" she responded, amusement colouring her words.

"You don't have a change of clothes?" it was an honest question.

"Thought you were the one who said I was being kept here against my will?" she observed with an audible exhalation that signalled she was trying to control herself.

"I was only asking a question." He had noticed her rising irritation.

"I want to speak with you and Therese."

"It is somewhat late in case you didn't notice."

"I want to speak with you and Therese." It came out a little bit louder.

"She is already in bed." His tone was placatory.

"Then wake her up." It came out as an order.

"Hey, hold up, what's come over you?" He took a step towards her, she took one back. He stopped for a brief pause, then continued, "Are you okay?"

"Do I look okay?" Her voice was now frosted.

"I think we have to go sit down and talk this over, like…" Nicole cut him off.

"You, Therese, and I will sit down and talk. So now can you please wake her up?"

Phillip went silent as he gauged her. His eyes hid the fact that he was trying to decode the reason for her sudden drastic change in behaviour.

"What if she doesn't want to come down at this hour?"

"Well, that will be her own decision to make, not yours." A smirk flashed across her face and disappeared. Phillip quietly watched her for a moment before he brought out his cell phone. As he scrolled through the numbers, he spoke to her.

"You can wait in the study."

Nicole turned and walked to the study. Head held high as though she had just won an unnerving battle. Phillip placed the call.

"Hi Therese, sorry for calling this late, but something kind of important just came up," he said in a voice tinged with apology.

Nicole opened the door of the study and stepped inside. She did not close the door after her.

Nosa walked along the aisle of the Boeing 747 British Airways Jetliner. He was in economy class and was headed from the minuscule restroom to his window seat at the tail end of the plane. It was a new experience for him because it was his first. Usually he flew business class or in not too rare occasions, first class. That was in the days when all was sane and wonderful. This was his new reality and Nosa was doing all in his power to blend in.

He got to his seat and noticed the tall guy who was seating in the middle seat wasn't there while the lady in the aisle seat was reading a magazine. The absent middle guy was Ghanaian, the woman was Canadian. He politely smiled at the lady, she returned the smile and stood up. He slid in and took his seat. He buckled in and looked out of the window at the darkness so high up and so safe, actually, so seemingly safe. One false move and the plane could simply drop out of the sky. He killed the thought before it spread its morbid wings.

He looked at the empty chair beside him and silently wondered why the charcoal black guy was continually leaving to visit the restroom. He knew what it meant to have a case of the runs while so high up in the air. He made a mental note to advice the guy against drinking water as he put on the head phones and selected a film from the assortment of on-board entertainment.

Nosa was settling in to sleep when the guy returned. The woman stood up, he slid in and sat down, then started patting his sweaty face with his formerly white but now darkish grey handkerchief. As the woman sat down, Nosa took off his headphones.

"How you feeling?"

"Good," the dark, tall man responded.

"Sure?" There was a crease in Nosa's brow.

"Not too good but I will survive," he said with a smile.

"You should stop drinking water; it will help your stomach settle."

"Nothing will settle my stomach until I am safe in Canada."

The woman sitting at the aisle seat turned to them and smiled. It seemed borne of genuine concern.

"Sometimes the height does this to people. Is this your first time flying?"

He nodded. She smiled and tapped him gently on his hand, which was gripping the armrest tightly.

"You will be fine."

He nodded, closed his eyes, and laid back. Nosa was watching him. He couldn't remember having this kind of reaction the first time he flew. The truth was he couldn't even remember the first time he flew. Wealth didn't always have a long memory.

"So what's taking you fine, young men to Canada?" she asked with admiring eyes.

The tall dark guy didn't respond. His eyes were tightly shut. Nosa looked at him and then back at her before he smiled.

"Actually, I'm returning back home."

"Oh, you live in Canada?"

"Not exactly, I was born there."

Her eyes shone brighter. She leaned forward.

"Good for you, how long have you been gone?"

"All my life."

"Interesting, so where have you been all this time?"

"Nigeria."

"With your parents?"

At the mention of his parents, Nosa felt his defences spring up. Who is this lady asking so many personal questions? He thought to himself. He looked at her deeply. Her eyes were honest. Her smile reassuring. He spoke just as the air hostess clad in the British Airways blue and white walked past.

"I believe they are in heaven."

Nosa heard the breath of the woman catch in a gasp.

"I am so sorry, I had no idea."

"It's okay."

"You have anyone in Canada waiting for you?"

"A friend."

She gave him a comforting smile, reached over, opened her hand bag, and pulled out her card holder. She opened it, removed a black card embossed with gold lettering, then handed it over to Nosa, stretching her hand across the motionless limb of the tall, dark guy whose eyes were still tightly shut.

"Call me if you need anything."

Nosa collected the card and read the inscriptions on it. MARSHA STEVENS, ATTORNEY AT LAW. He looked up at her.

"I might fly coach, but trust me, I make things happen," she said with a mischievous glint in her eyes.

"Thank you," Nosa said with a voice that came out as an emotional whisper. Somehow instead of angels, God loved sending lawyers his way.

Therese breezed into the dimly lit study clad in a checkered flannel robe over light pink silk pyjamas. Her face was shockingly beautiful stripped of make-up. Her mother had begged her to go natural, Timothy had insisted she paint up, Andrew had kept silent lips. Timothy always held sway in all things Therese. Her footsteps were silent, hidden in the pink coloured fur bedroom slippers.

She was not angry.

"Is everything okay, Nicole?" It came out for what it was; honest.

"Not really, can we please sit down?" An answer and a request at the same time. Nicole wanted to hurry before she lost her nerve. They all sat down. She coughed briefly.

"Water?" Therese offered.

"It's okay."

Nicole was sitting at the edge of the chair. Therese and Phillip watched her from the different chairs they were both sitting in.

The large painting of Annabele that adorned the far wall also watched on. Nicole averted her eyes from it. She had enough to deal with than the accusatory eyes of that paragon of beauty.

"We are all ears," Phillip spoke. It was impatient.

"I wanted you both to know that I have decided…" she paused. They both sat up. There was tension.

"I wanted you both to know that I have decided to leave." She closed her eyes when the last words came out.

There was silence for a drawn out moment. Therese was in a place that was heartbeats away from shock. Phillip was hovering on the verge of a smile.

"Why?" It was hoarse and a bare whisper and it came from Therese.

"Because that is what I want to do." A seed of defiance was growing in Nicole's voice.

"But you promised to help me save my father?" Therese still couldn't understand the sudden change.

"I know, but I have changed my mind… I'm sorry."

"Why would you do that?" Therese looked over at the now smiling Phillip as though trying to find some explanation from him. She saw his satiated smile and started joining the dots.

"Because I don't want any more of this… this… this tragedy." the last words came with a heavy sob that disappeared just as soon as it appeared.

Therese kept looking at the smiling Phillip. It was at that moment the rage started building in her.

"Why did you do this?" She was cool, a demeanour that hid her building rage.

"Because I don't want anything more to do with what happened… I am dying, can't someone understand what I am trying to say?" Nicole sprang to her feet in response to the question that wasn't directed at her.

Her response took Therese and Phillip by surprise. They turned to her.

"I wasn't speaking to you, Nicole" Therese tried to calm her, standing up as she spoke. Phillip was still seating as he watched Therese walk towards the agitated Nicole.

"Does it matter?"

"Yes it does."

"I just want to go... I'm sorry for what happened to your mother... and Andrew, but if I knew that things were going to turn out like this I swear I would never have gotten myself into this mess." Tears flowed freely as she spoke hurriedly.

Therese reached out and held her hands.

"I know you mean well and Phillip made you change your mind..."

"No one made me change my mind... I can think for myself... I can decide what I will do and what I won't do." She was stepping away from Therese as she spoke, her voice rising in rhythm with her steps.

Therese didn't move. She stood there watching the now visibly trembling Nicole. Phillip stood up. No one needed to tell him that things were going out of hand. He proceeded to take control.

"Nicole, we don't have to..." Phillips voice was calm.

"I have to leave!" Nicole's scream halted his steps.

The trio all stared at each other in dead silence. Then Therese slowly walked to Nicole, her arm stretched out, her hands open in a sign of peace.

"You have to trust me, Nicole."

"Why the hell would I do that?"

"Because what I am asking of you is a win-win for us all."

"You were going to lock me up in this house, take away my freedom, force me to save Andrew..."

"That is not true."

"And if I can't save him what happens to me?"

"You are free to come and go as you wish," Therese was fighting to keep her voice from wandering into the realm of emotion. She needed to think on her feet and emotions always got in the way of clear reasoning.

"Stop lying for Christ's sake!"

"I am not lying."

"Yes you are... Phillip said so," She turned towards Phillip for affirmation. He stood there tongue tied. Therese didn't bother to look at Phillip. She had already labelled him. She continued walking towards Nicole.

"It doesn't matter what he says, it's what I want that counts."

"What about what I want? Do you give a flying fuck what Nicole wants? Tell me I am just a cheap whore whose feelings don't count..."

"You are here to help, Nicole."

"I am guilty of killing your mother, so what you want me to do is live in her house and drown in the grief that oozes out of these very walls as I stare continuously at my handiwork."

"No, I just want my father back."

"You want vengeance!"

"I have forgiven you, Nicole."

"Why would you do that?"

"Because hating and revenge would do nothing for me." Her voice came across as a barely audible whisper.

Nicole stood there and looked at the approaching Therese. She turned her gaze to Phillip. He was rooted to the spot. His face creased with worry. His mind in full recognition of the mental state of Nicole. He had not anticipated this when he spoke to her about turning down Therese's offer. Nicole turned back to Therese and walked towards her. She took her outstretched hand and squeezed it in understanding.

"I want to help, I really want to take everything back if I could. If it means my dying for your mother to live, I will do it, but I can't live in this house and watch over Andrew. I just can't do it. I'm so so sorry."

"If you would let me speak," Phillip found his voice.

Nicole turned to him, her eyes red from crying.

"We can still take care of you even..."

"I don't want anything from you... I'm going to walk out of that door and call myself a cab. I will go to a friend's, spend the night, and decide what path my life will take. I have messed up big time, but it all ends here. No more of this horrible life for me. I have to clean up my shit."

She walked to the chair she had been sitting on, picked up her purse, and walked to the door. Therese and Phillip wordlessly watched her. She turned at the doorway and looked back at them. They stood staring back at her like two pillars of salt.

"I'm truly sorry."

She turned and walked into the hallway. The clicking of her footsteps echoed from its hollowness and was stopped by the sound of the main door opening, shutting, and then there was silence.

Therese kept looking at the empty doorway. Phillip kept looking at her. She was gathering her thoughts, flogging herself for being a fool and trusting Phillip. He was thinking of his next move because he hadn't envisaged Nicole leaving in this manner. He was focused on Timothy who to him was the true enemy. Little did he know that the lady standing with him in the study was slowly morphing into a bundle of trouble that nothing in his arsenal could deal with.

When Therese finally walked out of the study that morning, she was totally set on doing battle with the one person she had decided was the true enemy of the Sciorras. As she lay on her lush queen-sized four-poster bed and closed her eyes to sleep, her heart boiled with a certain kind of vitriol that was akin to complete hatred for Phillip Neri.

The cards had fallen in favour of Timothy Vinelatter.

The music boomed in the jam packed hall. It was Caribana

weekend and Toronto was caught in the hedonistic revelry of Afro-Caribbean festival fare. The flashing colourful light design schemed across the dancing crowd in haphazard patterns, psychedelic and germane, revealing the curvaceous and the muscular, the lean and the flabby. There was a film of smoke, a mixture of the cosmetic and the personal hanging in the air. Then there was, flowing around the hall in bottles, conical vessels, wine glasses and the like, liquor in all its fiery and intoxicating manifestations.

Angela was one of the throng. She was dancing in close proximity to Osasu. This was her first time actually experiencing the Caribana festivities that exists outside the annual Saturday family friendly parade that ran along the stretching length of the Lakeshore Boulevard.

It was a crowd that represented the colour spectrum, each one bound together by the pulsating music that flowed out of the near ceiling high speakers that peopled the four sound proof walls.

Even as they danced, carried away by the collective narcissism of the moment, Osasu didn't notice the three men standing by the railings of the upper balcony looking down at them. Their gaze was cold and calculating. Their angry memories were filled with flashbacks to horrific scenes of senseless madness on the back streets of the Isale-Eko neighbourhood in Lagos, Nigeria.

The high ceilings of the customs hall at the Pearson International Airport in Toronto gave it a cavernous feel. The people who lined up in front of different booths in the hall were like soldier ants in war phalanxes, prepping to receive orders from the officers in the booth. They stepped up one after the other, brought out their passports, handed it over, answered some questions, then more questions before a stamp on the open passport in some cases, or more questions in others and sometimes a direction to follow another standing officer towards some other room in the back vaults of the hall.

Nosa and Marsha were in one of the lines. The one over which hung the sign; CANADIAN PASSPORT HOLDERS in red letters over a white background, the logo of the iconic maple leaf flag above the letters. They were chatting quietly as the line slowly moved forward.

A couple of lines over was the tall, dark guy. He was standing in one of the lines separated from the line in which were Nosa and Marsha by the section that read OTHER PASSPORT HOLDERS. He seemed to be walking like an automaton, sweat making his dark blue shirt stick to his lanky torso in spite of the air-conditioning in the room. Nosa kept shooting glances at him from time to time. He turned to ask Marsha how long it took for the effects of the flight sickness to ease off. At that moment the tall, dark guy walked in front of one the custom booths and as though in a trance, he raised both arms above his head in a sign of surrender.

Nosa was enthralled for a moment, eyes wide as he watched the events unfold. Marsha noticed and turned towards the direction of his gaze and saw the tall, dark guy being led away by two armed custom officers. She smirked and turned to Nosa.

"It's the usual."

He turned back to her, forcefully tearing his eyes from the disappearing trio.

"Usual?"

"Yeah, you see that nearly every other day."

"Why was he surrendering? What did he do?" Osasu wanted to ask a million questions at once. Marsha cut him off after the second one.

"Political asylum, that's what he wants," it was non-judgemental.

"Like he is running from persecution?" he attempted to clarify.

"It could be that or simply wanting a better life," she surmised.

"You mean you can just show up here, raise up your hands, and ask for a better life?"

Marsha laughed and then shook her head, "Only a fool will do that."

Nosa felt foolish. He fell silent and looked back at the now empty corridor, down which the tall, dark guy had been led. So that was why he was so petrified during the flight? He mused to himself. So frightened that at times Nosa was afraid he had stopped breathing. What could he be running from? Nosa thought.

He remembered an article he had read in The Economist that spoke about the human capital flight from Africa. It was titled *"The New Slavery"* and had raised up a raucous from various quarters. It's position was that unlike the Trans-Atlantic slave trade where Africans were taken against their will to foreign lands, the pervasive and perennial harsh economic realities in Africa had created a new scenario where Africans were willing to bear even the most harrowing experiences in order to find their way to the developed world where they were ready to do the most menial of jobs and live in the most humiliating of locations in order to have a shot at building a new life. And the more these people left Africa, the more she was being robbed of her most precious asset, human capital. They concluded that the continent was doomed to poverty if the trend wasn't arrested and advised that it could only be arrested if corruption in high places was uprooted and if the educated African elite left their high horses and joined the masses in fighting the decadent governance that was the curse of the continent, saying that their silent collusion over time was what had enabled the worst of the people rule over the continent for years. It wasn't an entirely new argument but it was the true accounts and first person interviews that were unsettling for the African elite who had opposing views. To them it was another ploy of neo-colonialists, historical apologists, and die-hard imperialists to shift the blame for the continent's problems from the western world that pillaged its natural resources and stifled its global competitiveness to the Africans themselves who had been fighting against external oppression with their arms tied behind their backs. Nosa remembered his father's opinion when it came to these arguments. We are our own worst enemies, he used to say. The white man cannot enslave us if we do not enslave ourselves first.

"You're next," Marsha's voice intruded into his crowded thoughts.

He turned towards the booth. The Customs officer had a welcoming smile. He looked back at Marsha, nodded, and walked towards the officer, bag slung over his right shoulder, leather folder in his left hand.

"Hello."

The officer kept the smile. Now that he was closer, the smile appeared plastic. Her hair was jet black and streaked with strands of grey. It was tied in a bun on top of her head. Her eyes were crowded by crow's feet; her lips severely thin; her jaw set in a frozen grimace. In her black uniform, she looked like something out of a Tim Burton flick. Nosa silently remarked to himself that she would have been much better off if she didn't smile.

"What brings you to Canada?" she said opening her hands for his passport.

Nosa handed it over wondering why she would have asked that question if he had been in the line that was only for Canadians. He tried to answer with humour.

"I was in the line for Canadians, Ma'am?"

"What brings you to Canada?" she asked again, face set as

though she didn't hear what he said or didn't see that the passport she was leafing through was a Canadian passport. Nosa looked back at Marsha. She was watching and saw the concern on his face.

Her face creased but she did not move. Marsha was too smart and experienced to intervene for someone she had only met on the plane a couple of hours ago, especially after seeing the other gentleman request for political asylum. Nosa realised she wasn't going to help and turned back to the officer. He had to deal with this himself he muttered as he turned back to the turgid officer.

"I am Canadian."

She did not look up at him and kept looking through his passport. She scanned it over an optic machine. Then she looked at the screen in front of her for something that felt like forever, tapping the keys of the computer from time to time. Finally, she spoke.

"Where did you fly in from?"

"Nigeria."

"Where in Nigeria?"

"Lagos."

"Directly?"

"No via London, England."

"Where were you born?"

"Montreal."

"When last were you in the country?"

"Over two decades ago."

She fell silent and started typing more rapidly.

"Any family here in Canada?"

Nosa hesitated for a minute. Then he sighed and gave voice.

"Yes."

"Who?"

"My brother."

"Are you staying with him?"

"No."
"Why?"
"Nothing."
"Who are you staying with?"
"A friend."
"Who is your friend?"
"He is a brother of a friend of mine back home in Nigeria."
"Is he expecting you?"
"Yes."
"If I am to call him *will* he confirm that?"
"Yes he will."
"How much are you bringing into the country?"
"I declared it on my form." He pointed at the form that was in his passport.

She made no attempt to read it and kept her eyes glued on the screen as she waited for his response.

"Five thousand dollars," Nosa said finally.

She tore her eyes from the screen and removed the piece of paper from his passport. She read through it.

"You have checked in bags?"
"Yes."

She scribbled on the paper and placed it back into the passport. Then she looked up at him. Her eyes were cold. Nosa felt an urge to use the washroom.

"Can I see the money?"

He reached into his jacket, brought out an envelope, and handed it over. She collected it, opened the envelope, and brought out the clean, crisp hundred US dollar bills. Just then the traveller at the other booth walked away from the officer who had been attending to him and walked towards the baggage collection area and Marsha walked to the booth and handed over her passport. The officer looked at it briefly, said a word to Marsha; she responded. He smiled and handed her passport back to her. She thanked him, shot Nosa a questioning look, and walked towards the baggage area. Nosa looked at her with a puzzled expression. What luck he had today he muttered to himself before turning to the officer who was closely examining each dollar bill.

"Is there any problem, Ma'am?" he finally asked, trying hard to hide his irritation.

She didn't respond and continued at her slow pace. Then she put the money back in the envelope and put it inside the passport instead of handing it back to Nosa. She returned to the monitor.

"What is your brother's name?"

"Osasu Eweka."

She typed and then stopped. She looked at the screen for a while. Her eye brows furrowed. Nosa held his breath. The thought that Osasu had already entered the black book here was unsettling. She kept looking at the screen.

"Your parents?"

"They are both dead." He used the word "dead" for effect; maybe that will get some sympathy from this living cadaver, he thought to himself.

"What do you do for a living?"

There was a pause. Nosa took her in. Her indifference was galling.

He sighed, "I'm a medical doctor."

"And your brother?"

"He... sort of... makes his way," Nosa didn't know how to answer the question as he stumbled through his words.

"Does he know you are here?"

"No, he does not."

"Why?"

"I don't want him to." Nosa was getting to the edge. His voice had risen a scale higher and anger flashed across his eyes.

She looked up at him, her bony features staring at him, then against all odds, she smiled.

"I know how that is. I haven't spoken to my sister in twelve years. A total bitch in all senses of the word. Sometimes God for all His worth, gives us arseholes as siblings and expects us to somehow love them. Sorry Jose, not for me." She chatted on in a total reversal of mannerisms. Her features softened and her aura changed. It was like a new person had materialised. She handed over the passport with the money in it. Nosa collected it.

"Welcome home." She said in a chirpy voice.

"Thank you." Nosa said in a thin whisper. The shock had stolen the verve in his voice. He walked around the booth and made towards the baggage area, stealing one more look at the customs officer before he got to the escalator.

There was another traveller at the booth. The customs officer was back. Severe as a migraine and cold like a cadaver. A professional mien she put on so naturally to defend the territorial integrity of Canada from all enemies foreign and domestic, guilty and innocent, lucky and unlucky, he remarked to himself as the escalator descended towards the revolving belts of the lower catacombs.

7

The main door of the Sciorra residence swung open and Timothy half ran half walked in. He was uncharacteristically dressed in black jeans, a black golf shirt, and sneakers. His hair was dishevelled and his face flushed red.

He ran up the grand staircase, walked hurriedly along the plush carpeting of the second floor, past the fine vases and expensive paintings, until he got to a dark, wooden door. He didn't bother to knock, instead he grabbed the door knob, twisting and pushing it open. He walked in and shut the door quickly.

Therese sat up on the bed, startled by the sudden entrance.

"What the...?" The words jumped out and froze in her throat when she saw Timothy. "Oh Tim, you scared me."

"Sorry, hon." He walked to the bed and sat on it, enveloping her head in his two hands before placing a kiss on her half-awake lips. "I came as soon as I got your message."

"What time is it?" She looked at her bedside clock. It was housed in ivory and had an antique feel to it. A gift from her mother, bought from the art store at the Le Méridien hotel in

Zanzibar. It flashed out the numbers 6:37 a.m.

"My God, it's so early!" she exclaimed, tiredness evident in her voice.

"You said Nicole left."

"Tim, this could have waited for later. I am dog tired," she moaned, lying back on the bed and snuggling under the feather-filled, hand-stitched duvet.

"You sounded upset over the phone. That's why I hurried over."

"That was then. Right now I just want to sleep..."

"But Andrew needs..."

"My dad is sleeping too. Have you had any sleep?"

"Not much but..."

"Why don't you get out of those clothes and come cuddle me," her voice was girly.

"We have..."

"We have to sleep, darling," She cut him off.

"What about Phillip?" He asked, standing up and taking off his golf shirt.

"I don't know and I don't care," Her words were devoid of emotion.

"Was he there?" He was now taking off his sneakers.

"He watched what he caused." She put the duvet over her head.

Timothy's thoughts were racing. He couldn't afford this part of his plan to fall apart. He needed to put things back on track. He took off his jeans and padded around the bed in his boxer shorts. He lifted the duvet and slid underneath it. He went quiet for a moment as he gathered his thoughts, his eyes roving around the room as though seeking for something to calm his riotous mind.

Her bedroom was expansive and decorated with a mishmash of colours. A different colour for each wall; bright turquoise, banana yellow, charm pink, and cinnabar. The large French windows were covered by deep mauve chiffon curtains; the black window blinds hugged them tightly. A little distance to Timothy's side of the bed was the door to the huge walk in closet, while on Therese's side was the door to the washroom that came complete with top of the range Jacuzzi, reinforced glazed glass shower stall, marble bathtub, roman bidet, and a fully automated electronic toilet by Kohler. The paintings from Rothko and Matisse on the wall was an added touch of class, talk about taking a shit and staring at the etchings of a master painter. The bedroom itself had a small living room to the far side close to the shuttered doors that opened onto the balcony. There was an alcove further to the right where Therese worked, a tinted glass table on which lay an open laptop and several papers, a leather swivel chair in front of it. There were pictures all over the room. Some hanging on the walls, some propped against it, some on the table itself, others on the bedside table. It looked like a gallery dedicated to Annabelle, Andrew, and Timothy. A lot of Timothy. Therese had lived in this room for the most part of her life and as she grew and changed, so did the room. An inanimate space that somehow had imbued the vital life force of its sole inhabitant.

Timothy looked over at Therese. Her face was hidden. He hesitated for a fraction of a second before he spoke "Why would Phillip want her to leave?"

Therese moaned from under the duvet. He turned to the bulge and pulled the duvet away from it.

"Oh Tim! I'm trying to sleep."

"How can you sleep when Andrew needs your help?"

"He is asleep like every other sane person and it's not like I'm abandoning him or something," she whined.

"Without Nicole how can we save him?"

"We will think of some other way, but for now let's sleep."

"Nicole is the only one he was closest to and treated like a wife. He loved her. She will get to him if we give her the chance to. He will respond. He will recognise her." He kept speaking, not realising how hurtful his words were to the now quiet Therese.

"Do you mind?" Her words seemed to call him to order.

He looked down at her and saw the pain in her eyes. He leaned over and kissed her on the lips.

"I'm sorry, hon, I wasn't thinking."

"Can we sleep?"

"Yes, love." He lay back and cradled her in his arms. Arms that rippled with lean muscles. Hours in the ultra modern gym in his penthouse apartment kept him chiselled. She relaxed into him, pushing all thoughts away from her lethargic mind. She truly needed sleep. She needed to forget all the problems that lay waiting for her with the rising sun, delay reality and the hard decisions she knew she had to make.

"I love you," Timothy whispered to her as he stared up at the ceiling thinking of the way to get to Nicole. Wondering what it would take to get her to return to the house. He was so caught up in his thoughts that he didn't realise Therese hadn't responded.

The sparkling clean kettle whistled loudly in Phillip's large sunlight filled spartan kitchen. It whistled and whistled and whistled, each time seemingly louder than the last until the water dried up and the galvanised aluminum turned a bright molten red and just when it appeared the red hue was beginning to smoulder, a supremely tired Phillip dragged his feet in.

With steady nerves, he picked up a kitchen napkin, shuffled to the kettle, calmly lifted it up, and deposited it in the kitchen sink. He opened the tap and there was a welcome hiss as the cold water showered the super-heated, angry metal. He left it running and walked over to the fridge, opened it, and brought out a keg of milk.

Phillip began humming the Frank Sinatra tune *"My Way"* to

himself as he walked back to the island and laid the keg on the marble countertop. He turned around, reached for the wooden cupboard under the island, brought out a glass cup, laid it beside the keg, and filled it up with creamy, frothing milk, sitting down in the same motion.

He watched the running water, rearranging his thoughts in consonance with the speeding colourless liquid before downing the entire contents of the glass in one long gurgle. The clock on the stove blinked out 9.07 a.m. Phillip had woken up an hour earlier, put the kettle on for some tea, walked to the living room, and had promptly fallen asleep.

It was a Saturday morning and he was expecting a visit from a famed psychiatrist. On Phillip's list of priorities, getting Andrew back on his feet ranked at the top and to achieve that, all options were open. Even through his awakening mind, he knew that the war had begun.

Osasu walked to the passenger side of his jet black BMW 3 series. The reflection of the alloy wheels shone in the polished surface of his shoes. He opened the door and the laughing Angela got in. The tree underneath which the car sat had its green leaves alive in joyful abandon, blocking the light from the full moon that hung like a communion wafer in the early morning sky that hung over the King and John axis of the entertainment district in downtown Toronto. The summer weather was progressively getting warmer he thought to himself as he returned to the driver's seat.

He opened the car door and was about to get in when a hoarse voice stepped out of the surrounding shadow that hugged the car.

"So na hia you kon hide?"

Osasu turned towards the shadows. The street light was too far away to give face to the threatening dark. He tensed, muscle on high alert, eyes peering ahead, back towards the car. He remained silent.

"You think say you fit run forever?" The darkness continued.

Angela looked towards the driver's seat and saw Osasu's back through the rolled up window. Wondering what was keeping him, she leaned over and knocked on the window.

Osasu heard the knock but knew that he couldn't risk turning around to respond to it. He also knew that he couldn't afford having Angela see whoever it was the darkness was hiding, so fearless as he was, he took several steps forward and stepped into the surrounding darkness, senses alert like a leopard ready to pounce on an approaching antelope. He had the sense of mind to point his electronic keys towards the car without turning back and lock the car doors.

Angela watched him walk into the dark and heard the click of the doors. For a moment concern flashed across her mind and in succession the thought that he was going to pay for parking at the lot's machine that stood a short distance away. She leaned back, her head resting on the cool tan leather seat. Caribana nights were crazy, she smiled to herself, as the memories of the sensuous undulations in the club they had just left came flooding back.

Osasu's pupils widened as it adjusted to the lack of light. It was dark, but in the darkness he could see the silhouettes of three men standing several arm lengths ahead of him. He knew they were afraid of him, if not they would have stepped out into the open and taken him on; standing in the shadows wasn't for effect, it was for self preservation. He walked towards them. Stealthily like an approaching carnivore.

They stood there as he approached and when he was a couple of feet away. They spoke.

"We still remember Okota."

He froze in his steps once those words hit him.

They stood there watching him in the dark for a moment before they turned and walked towards the lit streets on which other licentious revellers were walking.

It took a couple of minutes for Osasu to find his bearings and return back to the car. His palms were clammy with hot sweat. His back tingled with cold fear. His chest slowly tightened with the pain of the memories that had settled in his mind.

When he entered the safe interior, Angela was fast asleep. She didn't even wake up when the purr of the engine replaced the quiet. He engaged the gear and drove out into the night. His mind was set on cleaning up unfinished business. And to do that, he knew just the person to call.

Nosa walked into the arrival lounge with his luggage in tow. It stretched out for a wide expanse and tapered off into corridors at both ends. There were large electronic boards on which flight details scrolled in lit red lights. You could see through the glass walls, the traffic outside on the road that ran in front of the terminals. Escalators crawled up away from it and down to it at various places. The shops sold an assortment of things, food here, more food there, flower shop nearby, bags a short distance away, a bureau du change further away, another one at the opposite end. This was the ever busy Terminal 3.

His eyes scanned the crowd of people that littered the hall. There were groups of twos and threes, some larger, some smaller. The face he begged to see was supposed to be recognisable even though not familiar. Around him other travellers spilled into the hall. Some were greeted with bouquets of flowers, others with hugs, most with kisses, a select few walked out alone and left the hall unaccompanied. Nosa wondered if he would be among the latter group.

He walked to one of the metal benches and placed his bag on it. His suitcase was still in his hand, wheels firmly on the ground. Once again he scanned. Once again he didn't see anyone. There were South Asians, Caucasians, Hispanics, Blacks and a scattering of people he really couldn't classify. There was also Marsha standing with a tall, white man and two children, a boy and a girl, all beautiful, all laughing.

He had seen the picture of his pick up and had even spoken to him before he boarded the plane in Lagos. All the promises of a prompt reception was going up in funereal smoke. He sighed deeply to himself as he moved onto plan B.

"Nosa?"

He turned and beheld a black man, half his size, shaved head, beady eyes, in clothes that were nearly double his size. Nosa had to hold himself from laughing.

"Tirin Tirin," Nosa confirmed.

"My man!" He surprised Nosa with a full-hearted hug.

He returned it awkwardly, embarrassment colouring his discomfort. They disengaged. Tirin Tirin was a nom de guerre that had completely taken over his real name which was Tayo Ogunde. He was called Tirin Tirin because of his tiny size and his accompanying shrill voice.

"Let me help you with that, brother." Tirin Tirin reached for the bag on the metal bench. Nosa was alarmed as he looked at the bag which was being dragged off the bench.

"Are you sure?" Nosa whispered seeing the humongous size of the bag compared to this tiny specimen of a man.

Tirin Tirin laughed in his shrill way, his miniature head bobbing on top of his neck, before he lifted the bag and placed it squarely on his shoulder.

"Make you no try o!" he exhaled with a flourish in broken English. "Toronto dey wait. Make we delete."

Nosa was finding it hard to follow his slang. Tirin Tirin noticed the disconnect. He laughed once again, head bobbing to the crescendo of his laughter.

"Ah! Na aje butter my coz send come meet me o" His expression was one of pseudo panic. He decided to step down his street Pidgin to something Nosa will get, "Don't worry. Tirin Tirin will take care of you."

Nosa smiled in understanding and followed the bubbling Tirin Tirin as he bounced down the hallway towards the automatic glass exit doors, drawing inquisitive, derogatory, and amused looks from everyone who peopled the hall.

Angela strolled leisurely into the large Finnish style sauna. It was already steaming hot. Through the haze, she could see a figure leaning against the wooden backrest on the furthest wall. The figure sat on the lower bench. The sign on the door had said unoccupied so she was surprised to see someone in the interior. There were two saunas, one for each sex. It was a policy in the Sciorra residence that staff could use all facilities in the sprawling mansion. Annabelle rabidly enforced it. She didn't understand the rationale nor did she agree with the wisdom of class delineation.

She had already hung her towel in the ante-room, so she stood there naked. She walked in the adjacent direction and climbed onto the higher bench that ran along the walls of the room. She kept her eyes on the figure. It didn't move. She settled in and lay her head on the wall.

"How are you doing?" It smoothly flowed out of the hot haze. It was Therese.

"Hi Therese, I didn't know it was you," a surprised Angela spoke sitting up.

"It's okay... I needed the heat and quiet."

"I'm sorry, I could leave."

"No, stay, I could do with your company."

Silence enveloped them, thick like the steaming haze. Angela leaned back and held her knees with her hands, pulling them closer to her chest. Time ticked on. Sometimes it was hard to give one's thoughts voice. This was one of those times.

"How have you been holding up?" The ice finally broke

Angela hesitated before she spoke, "How do you mean?"

"You were close to my mother." Therese gave her more rope.

Silence descended again, stretching the distance between them. It stretched and stretched and finally it snapped and opened a flood gate of emotions.

"I miss her so much." It was a whisper.

"I miss her too." Therese said after a moment wherein she viewed memories of the smiling and sincere images of her Annabelle's face.

"I'm sorry I didn't help her." Angela's voice had a faraway tone to it.

"It was not your fault."

"I saw the signs."

"Hind sight is 20/20 vision..."

"No, this is different."

They fell silent once more. Finally, Therese spoke.

"How different?"

Another hesitation and then a sigh "She said more than once that she just wanted it all to end."

"I heard her say that too."

"Did you also hear her say, 'I just want to kill myself?'"

"No."

"She said that and more."

"Like?"

"She asked me once what I thought about suicide and if I believed the soul of someone who took their life went to hell."

"And what did you say?"

"I said no."

"Really?"

"I don't believe that God will do that to a troubled soul."

"Are you saying this to comfort me?"

"No it's what I believe."

"You don't believe in hell?"

"No."

"Are you kidding me?"

"I believe in love."

"Do you believe in God?"

"I believe that God is love."

"So a God that is love cannot create a hell if I get your thinking correctly."

"Precisely."

"And what does he do with the souls of the damned?"

"He gives them a second chance."

"You mean he gives someone like Hitler a second chance?"

Angela would have nodded in response but she knew it would have been difficult if not near impossible for Therese to see her head take a brief dive, so she spoke. "Yes."

"I thought you were a Catholic."

"I am."

"What I hear is some new age religion."

"It's what I believe."

There was a shuffle as Therese stood up and walked over to the seated Angela. She was as naked as Angela was. The two women stared at each other for a fraction of a second.

"You believe in reincarnation?"

"Yes, I do."

"So my mother has been born somewhere else?"

"In God's time she will or maybe she already has."

"I don't believe in reincarnation or second chances."

"It doesn't matter if you do, what is, is." It came out very softly, full of conviction yet devoid of dogma.

"Why are you so sure?"

"The whole point of existence itself is the reunification of God and mankind. The destiny of souls is being one with God. To do that, we have to be pure, because only purity exists with and in God."

Therese stood there listening. She was not buying what she

was hearing but she was impressed by the depth of thought. In all the time she had watched Angela buzz around her mother or walk alone along the corridors of the Sciorra mansion, she had never for once thought there was more to the lady than what the eyes beheld. Now she realised how wrong she had been. She climbed up to the upper bench and sat by her. She didn't say anything, so Angela continued.

"Life is a school. We come here to learn, develop our souls, earn a promotion to a higher level of enlightenment."

"And there is no punishment for our past deeds?"

"Yes there is."

"So where is the eternal love in that?"

"You are thinking of punishment in human terms," Angela said softly as if to a child in Catechism.

"Then tell me what you see as punishment."

"If you fail an exam and you are asked to repeat it, are you being punished?"

"No."

"Why?"

Therese went quiet as she thought about her answer. She could see lights coming up in her head. Tiny dots blinking into life.

"It's all about getting a second chance to learn."

"Precisely, the goal is to develop, acquire something you don't already have."

"But what about the pain you have visited on someone else? Why should you go scot free while the other person suffered?"

"In learning what it was like to suffer that which you visited on someone else, you truly develop, because through that experience, you discard the desire or capacity that led you to inflict that pain or injustice in the first place."

"I don't get you."

Angela shifted into the lotus position on the bench and faced Therese, she could feel the sweat dripping down her back and inner thighs. There was a lightness of being that was refreshing; an inner exhilaration that suffused her with self confidence. She closed her eyes and exhaled before opening them, lucid blue stared through the haze, and then she spoke. "It is a deep spiritual mystery that even I cannot totally explain, but this is as much as I know. Our destiny is to be one with the ultimate truth, the force of all existence, the eternal consciousness. And this consciousness is what we call God. But we are human, complete with all our mundane desires and earthly temptations, so to ascend to this supreme level of consciousness we have to discard all these earthly attributes of mankind and exist in perfection. We have to look at what it was that held us captive before and find no inclination to be in bondage to it. We have to overcome the worst in ourselves, so that the best in us would flourish. The best in us is in the likeness of God. The best in us is God. That is our destiny, to be what we were created to be, a part of a wondrous whole, a drop of water in an expansive ocean, a unit of consciousness in an all encompassing consciousness, a growing, exploring, discovering, all knowing, all experiencing God."

As she sat there on the upper bench speaking her truth to the listening but circumspect Therese, Angela presented an interesting image of a naked *Bhikkhuni* effusing divine wisdom in a pot of steam.

"Why do we have to be first man before we become God, what is the point?" Therese flowed with her logic. She was not setting any traps just honestly unburdening.

"If I knew the answer to that question I would say that life is like fire and our souls are like steel, and as you know, the test of fire makes fine steel. So we come to life to be men so that it perfects us. But the truth, Therese, is that I don't know." It was an honest response.

"And you agree without knowing?"

"Yes, just like I was born, without asking."

The statement sank deep into Therese, clearing out the cobwebs in her mind, spiralling down into the crevices of her heart, searching for union with her troubled soul. There was silence in the sauna. A heavy quiet that amplified the sound of the hissing liquid on burning coal. When Therese surfaced from the mental whirlpool she had descended into, her mind was as clear as a sunny day yet as multifaceted as a diamond. She looked with renewed eyes at Angela and she spoke.

"So is this the secret knowledge you have had in you that makes you bubble in the midst of deep sorrow?"

"I don't get your meaning." The mundane had begun to take hold of Angela as she was pulled down to the troubles of a life on earth.

"I have been watching you, wondering if you were mourning my mother."

"Why would you wonder?"

"Because it didn't seem like you were."

"Sometimes silence is deeper than words can show and pain without borders exists as grief internalised."

Therese grappled with her words, the syntax, the arrangement, the meaning.

"There is a lot to you that I would never have guessed."

"I am just Angela, normal, plain Angela."

"I listen to you and even though I don't totally get all your new age religion stuff, I can feel your love and hear your wisdom."

"I try."

Therese leaned back on the sweating wooden wall and looked ahead as she slowly swooned in the melancholy of her thoughts.

"I can imagine you not having the same problems that bedevil me."

"Like?"

"knowing what is right or what is wrong."

"We all struggle with that."

"It is hard, very hard, when you get all confused and you can't differentiate between your friends and your enemies, those who want your money and those who genuinely want you, those who are ready to stick a knife in your back and those who will die for you."

"The higher you go, the more you have, the greater your problems. I will be honest, I don't envy you."

Therese looked over at Angela and smiled.

"Most people don't think so. They believe money cures all, solves all, is all, but I envy the peace of the poor."

"Don't get it twisted, the poor have problems too."

"I know, but there are problems and there are problems."

"Would you give up all of these, your inheritance, your comfortable life to live in penury?"

"Not in penury, but just to have enough. I really don't need all these luxuries, these excesses. It is too much load to carry."

"Be careful what you wish for because there are people out there who cannot wait to make your wish come true."

Therese fell silent as she ruminated on Angela's words.

"Do you have any plans for your future?"

"How do you mean?"

"Phillip was wondering if we should let you go, seeing that my mother is no more."

Angela fell silent. She had been dreading this conversation. She had wondered if it would be possible to find a new job like the one she had with Annabelle or one that was as wonderful as it was working with the Sciorras and every time she wondered, she realised how impossible it was to find such joy and fulfilment, but she knew with Annabelle gone there was no future here in the Sciorra residence. She was deeply afraid of being let go, a fear she hadn't shared with anyone including Osasu. But like everything else, your fears will one day confront you.

So she held her breath and waited for Therese to give her, her marching orders.

"I would truly want you to stay, Angela." The words rushed into her ears. Her heart leapt. She turned to Therese, the haze hiding the tears that had instantly sprung to her eyes.

"I would love to stay."

"I want you to be to me what you were to my mother." Therese's voice had a pleading tone to it.

"I would love to be more to you than I was to her." It was heartfelt.

Without hesitation, Therese enveloped her in a hug. There was a sincerity to it that finally made the tears cascade down Angela's face and before they even realised it, they were both sobbing into each other's shoulders, two souls whose blossoming bond was smelted in the catharsis of the steaming heat of an opulent yet lonely sauna.

8

Nicole hugged her shoulders tighter as she stared out of the window at the two squirrels playing hide and seek on the bough of the elm tree in the back yard of her friend's bungalow in the Etobicoke neighbourhood of Kipling and Dundas.

She looked dishevelled. Her eyes bloodshot, black circles around them. Lips bruised from having been bitten constantly in regret or remorse depending on the time of the day. Fingers trembling as they repeatedly grabbed unto her terry robe. Her eyes followed the squirrels as though they were the only things that mattered in the trouble soaked world.

The bigger one with a dark patch on its head seemed to be the more docile. The smaller ferret-like one, white tipped tail bobbing in the air, aggressively chased after it. For a minute they looked like two kids playing in the school yard on a sunny day, the next, two ferociously hungry lionesses fighting over the dismembered carcass of an unfortunate antelope. Now, the attacked perched on the bridge of a branch, head staring back at the attacker, like an invite to continue the chase and the attacker immobile, standing up on its hind limbs, gazed into the eyes that gave the silent invite. Time stopped for a fraction of a second and in that instant, the attacker turned and scurried up the bough into its higher reaches, leaving the attacked wondering what changed the rules of engagement.

Nicole saw the similarities between the playful fight of the squirrels and the recent events in her life. She was the attacker, the one who changed its mind in the thick of the game. Andrew was the attacked, the one that had been chased but now stood motionless as it invited another bout of hide and seek. What was it that the attacker had seen that instilled fear in it? Why did it flee when the attacked dared it to engage on a higher plane?

Even now that Nicole had escaped the apparent hostage-taking at the Sciorras, she couldn't quiet her thumping heart. She had fought for sleep and all she got were nightmare-filled naps. Fevered dreams peopled by a chasing horde of demons screaming for her neck as forfeit for the death of Annabelle. In the dreams she had shouted herself hoarse trying to state her claim of innocence, but the futility of her protestations was evident even as the cries left her mouth. Her feminine charms were her tools of entrapment, a section of the horde screamed back. Men were weak and their frailty of will was what she had exploited, another section stated. If there was no her, there wouldn't have been the adulterous affair, and if the affair didn't exist, there would have been no grief and heartbreak for Annabelle, and if heart break didn't exist then the rope in the study wouldn't have taken leave of the life of a wife so deeply hurt, the rest surmised.

Even as Nicole stood there that day, she was very much aware that she had been condemned by her sleeping dreams and her waking thoughts.

Nosa looked through the wound up windows of Tirin Tirin's silver Lexus at the flashing lights that zipped past them on Highway 401 as they headed towards the Kipling and Finch neighbourhood where Tirin Tirin lived.

There was a certain calm in the air, an indescribable feeling of peace that surrounded him. He gazed further at the red, and at different spots, grey rooftops that were visible above the brick wall that stood protectively along the right side of the highway and wondered what the occupants of the house were doing at that very moment. This was a habit he had carried from childhood; an eye that wandered, a mind that silently prodded and questioned.

This was the first time, he had consciously been to Canada, more less Toronto although he had been to the ancient cosmopolitan cities of London, Paris, and Berlin; the awakening cities of Dubai, Buenos Aires, and Kuala Lumpur; the conservatively traditional fiefdoms of Riyadh, Bombay, and Cairo; the tourist marvels of Istanbul, Cape town, and Amsterdam; the spiritual enclaves of Jerusalem, Yerevan, and Addis Ababa; the commercial hubs of New York, Beijing, and Rio de Janeiro; the relaxing beaches of Negril, Barcelona, and Ibiza; the royal enclaves of Monaco, Morocco, and Oslo; and the far flung islands of Reunion, Falklands, and New Zealand. He couldn't really explain why he had somehow never returned to the land of his birth. As he sat down in that car and listened to the soothing tunes of Luther Vandross float out of the car stereo, he finally understood what many mouths had confessed was the peaceful neutrality of Canada. A spiritual consciousness that was unique in itself and evident to the knowing mind.

He looked out of the windscreen and allowed Osasu crawl back into his thoughts. His brow furrowed as he focused on the one thing he desired above all else; finding Osasu and obtaining closure. Where does he start? The question hung like a visible question mark over an exhausted head.

Tirin Tirin swayed his head from side to side in harmony with the music. He pretended like he was the only one in the car, his diminutive size sitting on the throw pillow that was on the driver's seat while his small and delicate hands gripped the steering wheel. Nosa looked at him and smiled. He could feel the infectious happiness that seeped out of the painfully small guy.

"So how long have you been in Canada?" Nosa asked in a bid to make small talk.

"Visibly or invisibly?" Tirin Tirin answered with a chuckle as he turned to Nosa.

"How do you mean?"

"Well, visibly means the government knows you are here and gives you certain rights, chief of which is making you pay taxes; invisibly means no one knows you are here apart from you, obviously, and those you want to know." His voice took a knowledgeable tone as though of a professor delivering a lecture.

"I see." Nosa quipped but didn't ask further. He wasn't so clueless as not to know the dilemma of immigrants the world over.

"Still want an answer?" Tirin Tirin blurted out while he kept his gaze on the road.

"Yes."

"Invisibly, twelve years, visibly, ten years."

"What?" Nosa couldn't hide his surprise. His mind had already added numbers, subtracted and come to his startling conclusions.

"What is what?" Tirin Tirin was still smiling.

"You must have come here as a teenager."

"I told you; don't let my size deceive you."

"Seriously brother, how could a kid be invisible?"

"If that kid was nineteen and came on a visitor's visa which expired after six months and the kid didn't want to return home, then the kid will have no other option but fly underneath the radar."

"You mean you are pushing fifty?" It came out in disbelief.

"Forever young, my brother, forever young," he ended it with a guffaw, "You should see your face."

"Woow!" was the only word Nosa could manage as he stared at Tirin Tirin.

"I get that a lot, but I put it down to genes, eating right, thinking young, staying happy always no matter what, never getting married, and loads of sex." He finished it with a loud guffaw again.

Nosa watched Tirin Tirin in rising alarm as he nearly doubled over the steering wheel as the laughter coursed through him. He looked at the road and then back at him. Tirin Tirin was now trying to catch his breath and still not looking at the road.

"Please can you look at the road?" Even though alarmed, Nosa was civil.

"It's okay, I got this." Tirin Tirin said sitting up and quietening down. "Bro, you should see your face. Where the hell did they get you from? a monastery?"

"Monastery?" Nosa was clueless.

"Yeap, I said loads of sex and you like went dead for a moment."

"Oh that!" Nosa wasn't a prude, just so well mannered; he would have been right at home in the age of the Victorians.

"Yes that!" Tirin Tirin mimicked him perfectly.

"I am a doctor, trust me, I rarely get shocked."

"Maybe not by the action, but the words get you."

"You think I can't say sex?"

"Not in a clinical way like you just did, more of in a social way."

"Of course I can."

"And fuck?"

"Excuse me?"

"Fuck." Tirin Tirin navigated the car down the Martin grove exit.

"You don't need to..."
"Say fuck..."
"Why would I have..."
"You said sex, now say fuck,"
"Fine, you think I will back down." Nosa leaned back on his seat.
"Say it,"
"Fuck." it was a whisper.
"I didn't hear anything,"
"Fuck." A little louder.
"What did you say?"
"Fuck you, man, I said fuck!" It was loud and mixed with laughter.

Tirin Tirin looked over at him seriously and then burst out laughing louder. Nosa smiled as he basked in the good-naturedness of the small man.

"I like you," Tirin Tirin said as his laughter subdued.

"I don't know if I should say 'Thank you sir' or just 'Thank you.'"

"I see you got jokes too, I like that. We will be good friends."

"I hope so."

"Don't hope, just claim it. Say it like it already is. Don't you read your bible?"

"We will be good friends."

"Perfect!" He said that with a loud slap on Nosa's knees. "Tomorrow evening we go to church."

"Church?"

"Yes church. Don't you go to church?"

Nosa went quiet for a minute as he remembered the injustice the Catholic Church had meted out to him during his father's funeral. He sighed audibly.

"Well, I haven't for a while."

"Oh, you can't and shouldn't fuck up with church, man, trust me. You fuck the chicks, fuck your friends if they fuck with you, but if you want to make it in life, you never ever fuck up with church, you hear me?"

Nosa took a while to take in the small man who now had a serious look on his face, then he slowly nodded.

"Sweet. We will be good, you and me. I haven't had a roommate in a while, but my coz called me and said, 'hey Tirin Tirin, you have to do this for me' and my coz, men, I love that mother fucker, love him so much although he can be a fucker sometimes, I tell you, a fucked up motherfucker, you know him, right? He said you guys are close. You know I'm not just bad mouthing him or something, but he fucks up real bad sometimes but still I fucking love the fucking motherfucker…"

"My lord! You have to chill up on the swear words."

"What the fuck is fucking wrong with you man? it's just words."

"There is power in words."

"Then I should be a fucking millionaire, you know, no one ever beats me in a game of scrabble. I'm like the fucking king of the board, like the Mohammed Ali of words, the Tyson before he got his ass beat out of the lexicon. I can do with words what Pele does with a football, so if fucking words have fucking power, trust me, I will be Napoleon Bonaparte or Alexander the Great…"

There was a tight knot that was already forming in the pit of Nosa's stomach. He hadn't bargained for this. Tirin Tirin was like a jigsaw, too many pieces fitting into a complex whole. He inhaled silently as he calmed his nerves. His world had fallen apart so rapidly that Nosa realised also very quickly how he needed to learn new skills in order to survive an unpredictable world, one of which was tolerance and acceptance. He had stepped out of the preserve of the mighty and cultured into the unpredictability of the real world. He looked over at Tirin Tirin, who was still speaking and gesticulating with his left hand, right hand firmly gripping the steering wheel.

"... but then, you just might be right, you know, Adolf fucking Hitler royally fucked over the Germans with the power of words. He spoke them into retrogression. I mean the fucking evil genius fucking spoke to these normally smart folks and made them like move back into the age of barbarians and do things that he himself didn't have the guts to do. They said Hitler never killed one fucking soul his whole life. I mean even in the First World War, he was a fucking mail delivery man, can you believe that? A fucking coward who understood the power of words, fucking used it to turn the world the fuck upside down." Once again, he turned to Nosa and slapped him on his knee, just as he turned the car into the driveway of a huge tenement building that rose high up towards the sky. "I have fucking learnt something from you, mister fucking doctor, thank you!"

"Thank you too," Nosa laughed.

"We are fucking home," Tirin Tirin giggled as he said the words.

"Thank the fucking lord!" Nosa said loudly. It came from his heart; he was glad they had arrived in one piece.

Tirin Tirin sat there, his brown eyes speckled with star dust, each of them twinkling in playful mischief. He was a leprechaun if there ever was one. A feisty sprite that feasted on pranks in whatever form they presented themselves.

Osasu walked with brisk, purposeful steps towards the door of the restaurant, over which, on the red painted signage, were the words MAMA'S PLACE.

He was wearing a black fedora hat and sunglasses. His v-neck white t-shirt gave a loud display of his chiselled figure; lean and compact, tall and sleek. He moved with the smoothness of a feline; a halo hung around him that spoke of power and ruthlessness. Osasu somehow knew how to switch into different personages as events dictated. This time around, he was in a fix it mode. He opened the door and stepped into the dimly lit interior of the Nigerian restaurant that sat at the south east side of the Jane and Lawrence intersection in the west end of Toronto. It was a neighbourhood that was majorly poor and heavily African yet distinctly Caribbean. A fog of decay hovered over the smattering of stores and raggedy vehicles.

He stood there under the red glow of the lone electric bulb that hung over the doorway, adjusting his eyes to the interior of the restaurant, and allowed the aroma of cooking assail him. He could make out the unseen scents in the air, egusi, ogbono, edikang ikong, and pepper-soup in their beginning stages of cooking. It was times like this that made him yearn for home.

His eyes relaxed, took in more light, and the images went crystal clear, his sunglasses still hugging his face. Plastic tables covered with flowered plastic sheets, plastic chairs empty. Walls on which hung various cheap framed photographs of mass produced pictures of far flung landscapes, a television high up over the bar showing an African home video, loud and ingratiating. He hated coming to places like this, but he knew how important this trip was and wasted no time in driving west from his luxurious downtown digs.

He walked down to the bar and pressed on the bell that sat on the counter. The loud chime sang out and was quickly drowned by a maniacal laughter that rang out from the African home video. Osasu cringed. He despised these videos with such vigour it was a marvel he hadn't already smashed the television set.

A middle-aged black woman dressed in a traditional blouse and wrapper sewn from local adire material sauntered out of the door that stood behind the bar. She was sweating and looked markedly angry. She was a few heartbeats away from being grotesquely obese, mounds of fat spilling out from every visible space. She actually didn't saunter, she instead rolled out, heaving and panting. She didn't recognise Osasu, so she spat out the words.

"What do you want?" it dripped with venom.

"Mayor." That was the only word he said.

She looked him over, as though the evident good looks he had were anathema to her well-being. Her upper lip was crumpled up in disapproval, like she could see through the polished veneer of his exterior into the seediness of his insides.

"Wait there." It was a bark.

She turned and rolled through the door towards the unseen caverns that lay further in, from where the rich aroma of African delicacies galloped, crashing with stomach-growling desire in his olfactory lobes. He wondered if she ever left any of what she cooked for the diners who would evidently come to the restaurant, believing that she greedily consumed all she cooked.

Osasu shook his head. He had never understood how a living and breathing human being would allow themselves get so immensely proportioned. How couldn't one control such base human desires like eating or the need to stuff down the amount and type of foods that caused such physical sins? Fatness to Osasu was one of mankind's cardinal sins; after all, it was akin to sloth.

Before Osasu could manage another thought, she appeared at the door.

"Downstairs, through that door." She pointed to the door at the far left. It had a sign on it that read EMPLOYEES ONLY.

Osasu didn't bother to thank her. He turned and walked towards the door, feeling her eyes boring into his back. He didn't mind, she hadn't shown him courtesy, so he was just returning the disfavour. As he opened the door and disappeared down the staircase, he heard her prolonged hiss reverberate around the restaurant, overpowering the irritating loudness of the African home video.

Once downstairs, he saw another door to the far right, walked to it, and knocked.

"Enter," came a soft voice from within.

He opened the door and walked in.

The room he stepped into was a fully furnished office, complete with computers, printers, fax machines, and the other necessities of the office of a power broker. Sitting behind the large desk was a bespectacled black man, dressed in a black Italian suit, yellow polka dotted tie on sky blue shirt. He oozed class. He smiled broadly when he saw Osasu and stood up, rounding the table in three strides and enveloping him in a big hug.

"Oloye," he said respectfully.

"Ba wo ni?" Osasu affectionately asked after his well being in fluent Yoruba.

"Ko si nkan," he replied as they separated.

They took their seats. Each man smiling broadly as they soaked each other's presence. Mayor opened the small refrigerator which sat close to his desk and brought out a bottle of Remy Martin. He placed it on the table. Osasu shook his head even before Mayor offered.

"Ah I never change o, no shacking when man dey work." Osasu switched into broken English.

"Dis one no be Naija na, Oloye. For Canada man must relax as the money dey count dey go," he replied mixing it with a smile here and a giggle there.

This was Osasu, known in the streets of Lagos as Oloye, feared and respected by those who peopled the underworld. This was also the second time Mayor had met him in Canada and the first time in his office. The first had been at a club downtown, he remembered the shock when he laid his eyes on him. Oloye himself on the streets of Canada. He had bowed and hugged him in respect and they had exchanged numbers. That was several months ago. A chance meeting that dissolved into the lore of happenstance and then silence. No word from Oloye. Actually no one on the streets knew him as Osasu Eweka. No one knew of his other more prosperous and extremely fortunate life.

Mayor didn't know why he had come, but his excessive

smiles were meant to hide the fear that was fluttering around in his stomach. When Oloye paid you a visit, whether in the unpredictable madness of Lagos or the cozy comforts of Toronto, you knew something big was up; the nature of the bigness was what was in question. Many an unfortunate story circulated after several of these kinds of visits.

"I don call you since you see me the last time?" Osasu abruptly changed. The words came out cold. His face took on a meanness that bordered on the primeval.

Mayor was waiting and was still taken aback by the swiftness of the change. He shook his head.

"I hold my side all this time, I no bother nobody, I no flex muscle, but e be like say, una wan yawa to gas. Una wan see my red eye, na who you tell say I dey town?" His eyes were locked on Mayor, watching every movement, every gesture, every emotion that flashed across his face or appeared in his dilated pupils.

"I yarn boys generally, you know, just normal gist."

Osasu kept watching him, searching for the truth in his response.

"I no know say e suppose be secret. If I know, u know say I no go flow, I be your man any day." Mayor continued, desperate to convince Osasu.

"Na you cause this problem, na you go sort am out, if after two weeks the smoke never settle den I go be your problem." The threat was clear.

Mayor sat up and licked his lips thrice in rapid succession.

"Oloye, wetin you wan me to do?"

"Some bastards wen no know who dem dey deal with, dey enter my space, dey talk about Okota."

"Okota?" It came out as a breathless whisper.

Osasu nodded, his eyes still searching, still watching, keen as an eagle. He could see the fear pumping through Mayor.

He felt the satisfaction of knowing that he still held that sway over men like this, the control stretching across miles, over a tumultuous sea.

Okota was something he knew he couldn't run away from and it was something he had refused to allow destroy him.

"You go find where the bastards dey, you go arrange dem, use dem set example, if you do am, you no go see me again, if you no do am, den I go join you with dem and I sure say you remember how I dey deal with people who dey mess me up?"

Mayor slowly nodded, he could hear his heart beating in his ears. He began to blink rapidly as though wishing the images of Osasu's victims to vanish away from his memories.

"Correct guy." was all Osasu said again as he stood up and walked out of the office. He didn't shut the door behind him.

Mayor sat there like one of the Chinese terracotta warriors; immobile. His mind cursing the day he opened his mouth to speak about what he saw at the club that night a long string of months ago.

After a time that seemed to him interminable but in actuality was briefly transient, he unfroze, shook his head, painting a picture of a man clearing his thoughts or vigorously rearranging them. He let out a growl of frustration, like a cornered animal squaring up for a fight of survival and then he opened the bottle of Remy Martin and swallowed a large quantity in one gulp. He exhaled the fire from his throat and chest, then picked up his cell phone and placed a call. All he needed to say when the call was picked up at the other end were the words "Oloye" and a series of unfortunate events began in something close to the speed of delayed sound.

The nurse slowly rolled the wet white cloth around Andrew's elbow. It was warm and Andrew was naked. He sat in the half-filled bathtub and stared at the black marble wall in front of him. She put the arm down and it disappeared into the soapy water. She moved to his back, circular movements done with care; his status and the good money that was being paid demanded that she gave him her full attention and the best of her much in demand skills. Andrew on his part sat there, lost in his own world.

There was a sound at the door of the bathroom and the nurse turned around. Her startled eyes rested on Phillip Neri. He smiled.

"Sorry, I didn't mean to scare you."

"It's okay, Mr Neri. I wasn't expecting anyone."

"I should have knocked."

Her face softened in understanding. The chivalry of Phillip was something that wasn't lost on her; impeccable manners devoid of condescending speech or actions. He was her idea of an ideal man. Pity she was already married to a red-haired, barrel-stomach lout.

"How has your morning been, Sir?" She liked conversing with him.

"Pretty good in light of everything," he responded, a cheerful expression on his face. Then he walked into the washroom and leaned against the opposite wall, arms crossed on his chest.

"Lucky you, I on the other hand have had a crappy morning."

"I'm so sorry."

"You don't need to be sorry. You weren't responsible for it."

She turned to Andrew and tilted his head back as she wiped clean his face. He was nearly limp and subserviently pliable. Phillip watched them.

"What happened?" There was genuine concern in his voice.

"Just stuff, I don't want to spoil your day with my troubles."

She continued cleaning Andrew, passing the wet cloth under his left armpit. It was hairless. She hated hair, so had shaved it, not sparing the hair on his chest. But for the thinning hair on his head, he looked as hairless as a Chinese crested dog.

"You're not going to spoil my day, Harriet, tell me what happened?"

She loved it when he called her name in his deeply smooth voice and secretly looked forward to coming to work every evening to replace the main nurse, Maria; a stiff-lipped, stuck up, broad-hipped woman with a disdain for everyone who reported to her or anyone she reported to. A woman who believed she was an authority to herself. A woman she loathed but respected. She knew there was no one better at doing this job than Maria was and she made sure that she lapped up as much as she could in the one hour in which their shifts overlapped. One thing Harriet wasn't was stupid. One other thing amongst others she was pragmatic. It was that strength that had seen her through a nightmare of a life and a bigger nightmare of a marriage.

"I'm waiting." Phillip rapped on the door of her reflecting mind.

"It is Mr. Vinelatter." It came out very low, tinged with fear.

"Timothy?" Phillip was taken aback.

All she did was nod. Then without any normal transition, she picked up the gold plated shower nozzle and began rinsing Andrew down. A light, warm mist rose from the water around him as the warmer water condensed with the colder air.

"What did he do?" Phillip had uncrossed his arms.

"I don't want any trouble." She stood up, walked across the large spotlessly clean bathroom, and brought out a large terry towel from the closet at the far corner. As she walked back to the bathtub, Andrew, and Phillip, she caught a glimpse of her reflection on the floor to ceiling mirror that adorned one wall of the bathroom. Her fear hung on her like an invisible cloak. When she turned away from the mirror, her gaze slammed into that of Phillip. She could feel his thoughts race from him to her.

They were heated and confused.

"What did Timothy do?" There was authority in Phillip's voice.

She stopped in her tracks and took him in. He was no longer leaning on the wall. His pose was akimbo. His breath came out slowly as though he was trying to calm himself. There was no one who worked in the house who didn't know that there was no love lost between Timothy and Phillip. She inhaled and slowly let the words flow.

"He came around earlier on, while Mr. Sciorra was still asleep, and wanted to see a list of his medication, the time I gave them to him, and the quantity."

"What?"

"I told him you had laid down specific orders that Mr. Sciorra's treatment routine was highly confidential."

"Why will he need that information?" Phillip audibly asked himself although it seemed like it was directed to her.

"I wouldn't know that, sir. Actually, I asked him and he flew off the chain. I have never seen him that angry before"

"Did you give him what he wanted?"

"Of course not!" She was angry that he thought that low of her. "I know my job, my boss, and respect my obligations."

"Thank you." He went quiet and looked down at the floor. His thoughts racing, wondering what his next action will be.

"I told him that the only person who could change orders apart from you was Therese and it would be in writing."

"Good." Phillip said looking up at her.

"Sir, I want you to know that I have a lot of respect for the kind of loyalty you have for Mr. Sciorra. He is very lucky to have someone like you by his side."

Phillip was taken aback. No one had actually ever said those words to him. He looked at the five-foot-five dark-haired woman; her pale skin showing from the neck of her scrubs, her slender frame standing there with inspiring courage.

"I am just doing my job," was all he could manage.

"You are doing more than your job, Mr. Neri. You love Mr. Sciorra like a son loves a father. I am a mother; I know love when I see it." It came out resolute.

There was a moment of silence that passed between them.

"I have to go see Therese." Phillip finally spoke as he turned slowly to the door.

"Go do what is right, Mr. Neri."

He gave her a sideways glance as he walked to the door and nodded. She nodded back and walked to the wheel chair that sat a few states away from the bottom end of the bathtub. She wheeled it towards the bathtub just as Phillip walked out of the bathroom.

"We have to get you out of that bathtub, Mr. Sciorra. Now don't you feel clean and refreshed?" She cooed as she opened the towel and approached Andrew.

Therese opened the Globe and Mail newspaper and flipped to the Arts and Entertainment page. She checked her watch and seeing that she had some time to spare, leaned back on her chair in the high ceiling dining room and began to read. Her breakfast of a bowl of fruit salad topped with Greek yoghurt and sprinkled with granola lay on the table in front of her; it had been picked at sparingly. Timothy was all about painfully thin women.

The door silently opened behind her and Phillip walked in. He shut the door and approached her. This room had hosted many a happy dinner in which Annabelle had held sway. A family picture hung on the wall to his left, happy faces beaming through. There were others of grandparents and some more of pictures of festive occasions in this same room.

"Morning Therese, can I have a moment?" Phillip asked

as he arrived at her side.

She didn't bother to look away from the newspaper; a bad sign. Phillip took note.

"Yes."

"I just came from Andrew's room."

"And?"

"The nurse is pretty upset."

"About?"

Phillip paused for a moment as he took in the sight of her face hidden behind the newspaper, her dismissive attitude intentional. He held his nerve and continued.

"I think you should speak to Mr. Vinelatter." He purposely didn't call him by his first name. There was no need showing familiarity in such a hostile environment.

"About what?"

"There are ground rules the staff need to follow."

"Ground rules?"

Another period of silence. Phillip stood there debating his approach.

"We have to protect Andrew."

"From whom?"

Phillip pulled out a chair and sat down. He could feel the soft cushion depress into a cradle of comfort. He remembered Andrew telling him how his father had bought it from the same furniture craftsman who made the furnishings of the Swedish Royal house of Bernadotte. Wealth has its perks and traps; lavish spending and internal wrangling of dark secrets.

"I have come here to speak to you about your father. I am telling you that Mr. Vinelatter is stepping across a line that has been laid out to protect your father. You are choosing to brush me off for reasons I very well know is your belief that somehow, I am working against the interest of yourself, your father, and this household."

"And how did you come by this insight?" She was still behind

171

the newspaper.

"I really do not care if you choose not to show me any regards, but I will bring it to your attention if anything happens or is about to happen to your father."

"And if I choose not to listen to you?"

"Then I will do whatever is in my power to eliminate the threat."

There was silence as Therese remained behind the newspaper. Then she calmly closed it and laid it on the table. She placed her elbows on the polished mahogany and leaned forward. Her eyes narrowed in concealed contempt, her lips pursed in anger.

"Are you calling Timothy a threat?"

"I am telling you that Mr. Vinelatter has been making certain demands on the staff of this household which I believe, and I hope you also will agree with me, are not his place to make." He leaned forward as he spoke in a firm voice.

"Timothy has the right to..."

"Mr. Vinelatter could not have made those demands if your father was not incapacitated." He cut her short. His gnawing irritation had begun to show.

"You are stepping beyond your boundaries, Mr. Neri."

They fell silent as her words hung heavily in the air. This was the first time in all her life she had addressed Phillip as Mr. Neri. It was not lost on him.

"And you believe Mr. Vinelatter is within his boundaries?" There was palpable sadness in his voice as he sat there watching the lady he had watched grow.

"Timothy is my fiancé, he..."

"Is not your husband." Phillip completed her sentence with his own words.

"You will not tell me how to run my life."

"I am concerned about the well being of your father... and that of his estate... I had hoped you will also share my concerns." There was a solemnity in the delivery of the words.

Therese rose up, every fibre of her being shaking in rage.

"How dare you?" she asked in words that came out as a venomous hiss.

He sat there looking up at her. His face calmly set. Hands crossed on the table in front of him. He remained quiet.

"You sit there insinuating that I do not have the best interests of my father at heart, who the hell do you think you are?"

"Your father always valued my candid and knowledgeable opinions."

"I am not my father!" Therese roared.

"Evidently so." It was calm.

"I have a good mind of firing you, right here, right now."

"I do not serve at your discretion, Miss Sciorra."

"That's it, you are fired!" She slammed her open palm on the table.

"I said I do not serve at your discretion, Miss Sciorra. I can only be relieved of my position by your father or God forbid, upon his passing, after a five year period or earlier if I decide to resign myself."

"You are out of your mind." There was a hint of doubt in her voice.

"I have authenticated papers to prove it."

"You are lying." It was an audible whisper.

"You can call your father's lawyers. They have copies."

Therese fell silent and stood there staring at him, before she slowly sat down. Phillip kept his eyes trained on her.

"Sometimes we do not choose who we love, Therese, but when somehow God in his infinite wisdom gives us signs to bring us back to our senses, we are well advised to heed those signs. Mr. Vinelatter is asking questions he should not be asking and I am asking you, actually I am begging you to intervene and put a stop to his aspirations."

Therese who had been looking at the family picture on the wall as he spoke turned to him, her eyes still narrowed with unspoken questions.

"Aspirations?" It was pregnant with meaning.

"Yes."

"Timothy?"

"Don't tell me you have not, even in the slightest of moments, felt his eyes are focused on something else other than you?"

Once again Therese fell silent. She twiddled her fingers as she struggled with her thoughts. Then with a sigh she looked up at Phillip.

"I will make that call to the lawyers and find out about this document you claim to have, and for your information, the questions Timothy asked were asked on my behalf. I have my eyes on you, Mr. Neri, and do not underestimate me, I might not be like my father but that doesn't mean I am not a lot better than him and if need be, a lot worse."

She held his gaze in hers. No blinking, no movements, just a scorching stare that burrowed deep into Phillip. He gave her what she gave him; energies of the same kind, emotions, and silent threats equal and opposite.

Seeing that he didn't dissolve under her scowl, Therese stood up, picked the newspaper, and marched out of the dining room, slamming the door behind her, leaving the echo resounding in the hallway and the dining room.

Phillip sat there in a subdued mood. Once again things hadn't worked out as well as he planned. He leaned back on the chair, brought out his cell phone, and placed a call to the psychiatrist he had been talking with some days ago in his condominium.

The private detective came out of his dark blue dodge caravan and crossed the street. He looked like an insurance salesman in his black suit and briefcase. His sunglasses hid his eyes as it scanned the street and finally focused on the single story detached home that stood about fifty metres ahead of him. He didn't walk any faster.

When he finally got to the home, he consciously placed his megawatt smile on his face and climbed up the short staircase to the porch. He pressed the bell and waited. No response. He waited two minutes before he pressed it again. This time he heard soft steps approaching from behind the shut door. He braced himself. The footsteps went silent. He knew there was an eye watching him from the eye hole of the door. He smiled wider. The lock turned and the door opened slightly and stopped when the safety lock was fully extended and a face appeared in the crack. It was Nicole.

"Can I help you?" Her voice was hesitant.

"Afternoon ma'am. Nicole, right?" He was still smiling.

"Who is asking?" Her face crumpled in suspicion.

"A client of mine has a proposition for you."

"I am not interested in any propositions."

"You haven't heard what it is."

"Please leave or I will call the cops."

"You can do that if you want to, but then, I will tell them what I should have told you." he still maintained his smile.

Nicole went silent as she watched him through the crack. She could feel her head going light and her eyes go fuzzy. How would she get away from this? She asked herself in her mind. She knew it was the Sciorras. No one else would be after her but them, but still she had to make sure, so she swallowed her dry spittle and spoke.

"Who is your client?"

"It doesn't matter..."

"Yes, it does."

"You don't really have a choice here, Ma'am."

"Who is your client?" She asked, firmer.

"Kawartha lakes, cottage country, two years ago, two girls went partying with five guys from Abu Dhabi, rented an apartment right on the lake, alcohol flowing, lines of cocaine, music, skinny dipping in the lake, lots of sex, kinky sex, something goes wrong. One girl overdoses, they panic, guys are afraid to call the cops because of the stink it will cause back home in the Emirates; after all, they are supposed to be celebrating clearing their finals at the University of Toronto and can't wait to return home. So, the boys take her body in the middle of the night, deep into the woods, dig a grave, and bury it. The next morning, they all drive back to Toronto, each person taking an oath of silence. The five guys return back to Abu Dhabi a week later on an Emirates flight, the girl remains in Toronto and goes back to her normal life, playing dumb when the dead girl's parents and friends begin looking for her friend. Nicole, have you by any sliver of a chance ever heard this story before?"

Nicole stood there staring at him. She was as pale as the patch of an orca. The detective noticed and broadened his smile.

"Can I come in now?" There was confidence in his voice.

Nicole slowly came to life and like an automaton she unlatched the security chain, opened the door wider, and stepped aside. The detective nodded curtly in feigned chivalry and stepped into her life.

Angela opened the shower door which was already fogged by the rising steam of the hot water that was pouring forth in the stall and before she could take a step forward, Osasu's muscled arm shot out of the misty enclosure and slammed into her throat. His grip was vice like and suffocating. He rushed out of the stall, lifting her naked body off the floor in the same motion and careening it towards the marble wall. In that same instant, he stopped, loosened his grip, and caught her before she fell on the ground in a rattling bout of coughs.

"I'm so sorry, I wasn't expecting anyone." He let out the words rapidly, hiding his fury and fear with the effort.

"What the hell?" she asked, the words coming out between

coughs that shook her body.

Osasu was covered in soap suds, wiping them from his face by shaking his head as he attempted to place her gently on her feet.

"Are you okay?"

"Of course I'm not. What is wrong with you?" She coughed once more and pushed him away from her in rising anger, "I was just trying to surprise you."

"You know I would never hurt you." He walked towards her.

The hot water was spilling out of the stall onto the bathroom floor behind them.

"What are you afraid of?"

"Nothing... just was startled that's all."

She gingerly touched her neck and winced in pain. Osasu got to her and tenderly touched her neck before gazing into her eyes.

"Let me go get a balm or something, it looks bruised."

"My God, your strength, it's incredible, never knew you had such power and speed in you. We should get you into like WWE or something, young man." She was already smiling as she allowed him massage her neck, his slender fingers expertly soothing the tensed muscles, "Promise you will make it up to me." She affected a most innocent voice.

"You know I always make it up to you."

She rose higher on her toes and kissed his lips which had some soap suds below them. He returned the kiss. They now spoke between brief kisses.

"I love you."

"I love you too."

"You will never hit me?"

"Never."

She reached below and her hand found his limp member. It felt like a thick rope, the kind of which was used to moor yachts to docks. A glint appeared in her eyes.

"What is this?"
"What do you think it is?"
"A snake?"
"No."

It began getting turgid and slowly lifted her hand by the strength of its swelling muscles. She licked her lower lip before kissing him again.

"A baton?"
"A lighting rod."
"Like a lightsabre?"
"Yes. I am Luke Skywalker."
"Did you attack me because you thought I was Darth Vader?"
"Luke Skywalker is always ready to defend the Jedi Order."

She began to gently push him towards the open shower door from where water was spilling out. He stepped back in rhythm to her kisses and her steps.

"Will you pierce me with that lightsabre?"
"Deeper than you have ever been pierced before."

She moaned as the thought raced through her mind; he was now proudly erect. So large she needed her two hands to hold him. Her wetness was instant.

"I surrender to you, Jedi Master."
"You are now my slave, Sith Lord."
"Yours to command, ready to satisfy your every wish."

Osasu stepped back into the shower stall from which most of the steam had escaped. Angela followed after him; some of the cascading hot water rained on her as she stepped into the stall and shut the door behind her.

As she fell to her knees in the stall and kissed the head of his awesomeness, water flowed all over her. Osasu made a mental note to collect his key from her. He couldn't take chances like this again. The stakes were high. His enemies plenty. But for now, he had to keep her enamoured with him, totally addicted to his feigned love and his perennially-ready, finely tuned body.

9

The aroma that assailed Nosa's nostrils made his stomach churn with hunger. It was delicious as much as it was familiar. An omelette, stacked with diced tomatoes, red hot peppers and onions, seasoned with curry, thyme, loaded with canned sardines, and sprinkled with salt to taste.

He opened his sleepy eyes and was greeted with the sight of the food on a plate beside which were a glass of freshly squeezed orange juice and another plate containing six pieces of toasted bread. He sat up and rubbed his eyes, and then he looked again, it was all there. He reached out and touched the edge of one of the toasted slices of bread. The soft brittleness greeted his finger tip. It was real. He smiled. Tirin Tirin never ceased surprising him.

"Thank you!" he called out before he noticed the door was shut.

In the quiet of the room, he listened attentively and could hear the sound of a television set blaring out beyond the closed door. He lay back on the bed and stared at the ceiling. The whiteness of it was soothing in a strange kind of way, like it portended peace and all its positive attributes. He looked around the room. It is small by the standards of the rooms in his home in Nigeria. He caught himself creating that thought and quickly corrected the grammar, past tense not present; he knew he had to try harder to forget the luxuries of his former life in Nigeria. There was a tiny closet to the far left, a window beyond which was a drop of twenty stories, but which looked out to a sprawling public park. There was enough space around the king-size bed to stretch both arms sideways before touching the wall, but the high ceilings somehow fooled one into believing that the room was bigger than it actually was. He complimented the architectural genius of the Canadians; their knack of spatial management was impressive, making small look big and bigger look massive. He sighed to himself and reigned in his wandering thoughts.

Five days in Canada and he still had no clue where to start his search from. It was as though his life had fallen into a lull, an aimlessness that normally would have been disquieting for someone of his personality type, but instead had become strangely welcomed. The last months had been a whirlwind of roller coaster emotions, high stress-inducing situations, chaos, fear, depression, and debilitating yet invigorating rage.

He had pushed himself so hard to set foot on this soil and find Osasu. That all-consuming desire had kept him going; the vitriol was like burning coal in a chugging locomotive, the vision was like a light tower in a raging sea giving hope to the captain of a sinking ship, one more league, one more yard, one more metre and the shore will be reached. Now that he was here, the adrenaline that had kept him going had all but dissipated, leaving him a weary bag of bones desperate for the comforting solace of rest, a need for solitude, the time to be alone to gather his thoughts and chart a course of action. Yet every time he tried to pull away and speak with his inner man, Tirin Tirin blazed into his fledging circle of peace, pistols firing with the infectiousness of his happy self.

He didn't want to look or sound ungrateful by demanding his space; after all, he was the one that was the intruder, the stranger in a new land, a new apartment, barging into a life that was already going joyfully on its own journey. Tirin Tirin had been much more than he had hoped for. What he thought was a couch to crash on while he got his bearings and made his plans had turned into a sizable room, a queen bed, well cooked food, and unending laughter. Even his offer of money to offset the cost of groceries had been rebuffed with a jocular effort at anger by the diminutive man; the man who had known him for just five days and had never stopped addressing him as "my brother", but still Nosa knew that he was apprehensive of such unconditional show of affection.

Why was Tirin Tirin being so nice? What did he want? What was the catch? Did he know about his life in Nigeria? Was he told about his grief? Will he call in a favour later down the line? If he did, would Nosa be able to repay him? The questions came and came, like bullets flying towards an immobile target. There were no replies, no answers, just a tired mind yearning for rest.

He remembered what his mother once said, "the universe will always bring into your path souls to help you on your journey." She had said everything always worked out for good, but even as he lay on the bed that morning and covered himself with the thick duvet, Nosa couldn't think of the wisdom of the latter of his mother's sayings. What good could the events that had bedevilled his life for the last months have in store? Her death, his father's suicide, Osasu's betrayal, everything he had known and loved gone up in smoke? What good could come out of this?

He needed to find Osasu, find out why, and answer the questions that were clawing at the membranes of his mind, like a toothache that desperately needed rooting out. He turned back to the food. It lay there inviting him to feast upon it; a call to extinguish both the hunger of his stomach and his mind. Once again he sat up, lifted the tray, and placed it on his lap. As he picked up a toast and lifted up the fork, he heard his mother whisper in his ear.

"Nosa, go brush your teeth."

"Why?"

"Because."

"Because what?"

"It's healthy."

"Nothing is healthy."

"Bacteria form in your mouth when you sleep, you need to clean them out and start the day fresh, just like I taught you."

He scooped some egg and placed it on the toast.

"I said nothing is healthy, mom."

"Don't lose faith, Nosa."

"It doesn't make sense, Mom."

"Not now, but in the end, you will understand it all when the time is right."

"Why not now?"

"Because the universe does not work in phrases; don't focus on the commas; just wait for the full stop."

"I am tired, Mom."

"Be strong Nosa, it is never too late to start again."

"I need to find Osasu."

"It is not about Osasu, my son, it is about you."

"But..."

"Go brush your teeth, my son."

He felt her hand touch his shoulder. It was filled with deep love. He dropped the toast on the plate, returned the tray to its perch by the bed, stood up, and walked to the door. The bathroom was along the well-lit, tiled corridor. Nosa had never shared with anyone the fact that he frequently had discussions with his dead mother. Discussions he was now so very used to.

Discussions he didn't know if they were real or not, but yet he embraced as the last vestiges of his life as he once knew it. The last thing he wanted to be labelled as was a lunatic, so he knew better to keep some things that were not easy to explain, let alone understand, to himself. His experience as a medical doctor had taught him that science always stopped at the border of the unexplainable and even though it didn't recognise the existence of the unseen, it surrendered in many ways to its miraculous ways, hence when a doctor said, "it is out of our hands now, we have done all we can do, all you can do now is hope," he actually meant, "we are surrendering to the unseen and inviting it to perform the unexplainable." So come what may, he would welcome the voice and touch of his mother, the only compass he could trust, who will lead him through the miasma that had become his life.

He opened the door of the room and the sound of the television set came flooding in, topped with Tirin Tirin singing a nursery rhyme with a pseudo soprano voice. The picture of the fully mature man trapped in the body of an adolescent belting those tunes made Nosa chuckle as he walked down the corridor, practically tip toeing to the bathroom, intending not to attract attention to himself.

The little man had the biggest heart he had ever known, Nosa mused to himself when he shut the bathroom door behind him and reached for his toothbrush, if only he could be like Tirin Tirin, cast his troubles to the four winds, and embrace with gratitude whatever life threw at him.

"You've done well, my friend." Timothy said the words solemnly as though he was the Catholic Patriarch who would have instead used the word "Son" in place of "Friend."

He finished the call, put down the turquoise cell phone on the tinted glass table, and reached over for the new cell phone he had purchased earlier in the day. It was the pay-as-you-go kind and totally untraceable to him. Things were going as planned. The earlier mess was rapidly sorting itself out, not automatically by some hand of an unseen god, but by his careful manoeuvring. Now came the crucial step; selling the game. He placed a call. There were five rings at the other end before it clicked.

"You've reached the voicemail of..." He cut the call.

He counted up to ten and placed the call again. It rang once more; five times and clicked over to voicemail. He cut it, counted to twenty and placed the call again; five times of ringing and then voicemail. He repeated the routine. It went on for six cycles. He laughed out loud. It was cold and evil, like the deceptive calm before the destructive storm. He then started typing out a text message to the number. Once done, he hit send. The message was just six words; "I HAVE A STORY FOR YOU."

He placed the phone back on the table and sat hunched over it. He was smiling as he counted: one, two, three, four, five, six, seven, eight, nine, ten, ele... The phone rang.

"Touché!" he exclaimed in jest.

He allowed the phone ring out. This time he leaned back and put his hands behind his head, his eyes still focused on the phone, a grin plastered on his face. It rang again. He didn't pick up. It rang again. He didn't pick up. Then it chimed; text message. He sat up and picked the phone. He checked the message. It read; "WHO IS THIS?" Once again he laughed out loud, suddenly went deathly quiet, and redialled the number. This time it rang once and it was picked up.

"Hello." The voice was a bare whisper. It was that of a female.

"I have a story for you." Timothy tried to imitate the voice of Marlon Brando as the Godfather. He got it spot on.

"Who are you?" It was still a whisper.

"Someone who knows a story you would love to know."

"How did you get my number?"

"The same way I got the story."

"Is this story about me?" There was concern in the voice.

"Fortunately, you are not that important." The insult was veiled.

There was a sharp intake of breath. It was so sudden and brief that it could have passed without being heard. Timothy heard it and it gladdened his heart.

"Okay, so who is this story about?"

"Someone very important, very wealthy, very powerful."

There was silence. Timothy knew the voice in the other head was calculating, doing a quick risk analysis, wondering if they should hang up at that particular moment and not take the bait. He knew she would. She did.

"Why me?"

"You are the most powerful editor in all of Canada; what you say, what you write about counts."

"I thought a minute ago you said I was not that important."

"Yes. Importance is like currency, the value is not all the same." There was a stress on the last three words. He knew she would understand his meaning. She did.

He looked at the large painting that hung on the wall opposite his desk. It was an expressionist painting by Ernst Wagner of a distorted face depicting fury, angst, and determination. It was called Zorn, meaning anger in German. It was one of the three paintings ever made by the painter whose real name was Ernst Moshe Rabin. He had changed his name proactively when he befriended a German lady in the early years of the Nazi party. She had given him an insight into the dastardly plans of her brothers of the twisted crucifix. He had become a Nazi, spurning any relation and connection to his parents and siblings who lived in a quaint village in Prussia. At the time, the village Jewish boy who had come to the city in search of his artistic fortunes believed he had come into his own. His paintings and sketches were coveted by the Germans who were beholden to the Aryan beliefs. He strangely enough was caught up in mystical fever and had woken up in the dead of the night one Wednesday and furiously painted the Zorn.

Three months later when he gave it to Adolf Hitler, he had patiently explained its meaning to the rabidly focused and attentively listening Fuhrer; this was a pictorial representation of the fury of the souls with pure Germanic and Aryan blood at the desecration of their land and mankind by the existence of inferior mortals. It depicted the fury and determination to wipe the earth clean of humanoid pollutants and re-establish the true kingdom of God on earth. Ernst Moshe Rabin had no qualms about his capitulation. In truth he had convinced himself that he was never a Jew, instead a pure German of Aryan ilk adopted by Jewish parents. That alone could explain his aversion to agriculture and his inclination to artistic creation unlike his siblings and parents who were like a human extension of the land.

Unfortunately his lie ended in the gas chambers of Auschwitz after the German girl, whose heart he had broken when he left her for a fairer and richer bride, revealed the true identity of the artistic darling of the Nazi party to a bewildered Joseph Goebbels. It was with chagrin that Hitler heard about it while having dinner. He flung the plate, food inclusive, on the wall and fuming in fury, had ordered the immediate death of Ernst Wagner. The painting itself was given to Benito Mussolini during one of his state visits.

The Zorn was looted after the fall and execution of Mussolini by an ambitious and righteously indignant peasant and transferred by the exchange of varying sums of money through various hands until its eventual purchase over decades by Timothy from a private collector. It was the only surviving work of art of Ernst Wagner and resonated with Timothy both in identity, history, and desire. It was like Ernst and Timothy were of the same mind. A determination to acquire and create by any means necessary.

"Do I have any guarantees as regards the authenticity of your story?" the voice broke into his ghoulish gaze of admiration.

"I will give you guarantees."

"Written guarantees?"

"Not written."

"In what form then?"

"Pictures, texts messages, voice mails, that sort of thing."

"You know those can be faked, right?"

"These are not fake."

"How can I be sure?"

"You will know when you see them."

"You sound very certain."

"I wouldn't have called if I wasn't."

"So what do you want for all these?"

"Something you can afford."

"What will that be?"

"I will not discuss that over the phone."

"Why?"

"Because I know I am being recorded."

There was silence. Then a sigh.

"I have to protect my magazine."

"Perfectly understood."

"So when and where do you want to meet?"

"You will meet with a representative of mine."

"Why not you?"

"Because."

There was another bout of silence.

"Fine."

"Good."

"I will not meet with anyone if I do not at least have a name to work with."

"I don't need to give you my name."

"You are not that important; I was referring to the name of the person this story is about." She smiled as she said those words. No one insulted her and got off free. It wasn't by playing Mrs. Nice she rose up to become the Editor-in-Chief of *The Quill*, Canada's premier news magazine.

Timothy heard it loud and clear. She had hit him back. He knew about her. He expected it. He sheathed his sword. Time for business.

"It is about Andrew Sciorra." It came out matter of fact, the added huskiness to erase any trace of his own voice still in effect.

There was silence on the other end of the line.

Nurse Maria was furiously knitting her nearly finished sweater. The study was cool and the window blinds mostly drawn. A shaft of light pierced the dimly lit interior and created a silhouette of Andrew as he sat staring out of the French window.

The door opened and Phillip stepped in. Maria looked up. There was a lady behind him. She was amply proportioned and wore a loose, colourful gown. Her feet were shod in shin-high brown boots. Her hair was in dreadlocks and tied in a turban that was in the Rastafarian colours. Three locks escaped the confines of the turban. Across her shoulder was a large tote bag. Her black skin was unnaturally smooth and glowed with vitality. Her smile was like a vibrating essence. It was as though being happy was second nature to her.

She gave Maria a short bow, her palms clasped, one facing the other, like in a prayer in front of her chest. Maria on her part smiled at her in spite of herself, standing up respectfully in the same moment. The aura around the lady soaked her in suffusion of deep calm and like a mirror reflection, she placed her palms together, face to face, in front of her chest. Phillip watched her. He wasn't surprised. He had seen this effect repeated time and time again.

"Maria is it okay if you give us a moment with Mr. Sciorra?" As usual he was respectful even though he really didn't like Maria compared to his pleasant disposition to the more charming Harriet.

"Oh, not a problem." She was cheerful as she picked up her knitting. She bowed once again at the lady and let herself out of the room. Even as she shut the door behind her, she didn't even realise that the normal thoughts of the potential for juicy gossip didn't pop into her mind, instead she just felt happy, a happiness that somehow was propelling her to hug someone, spread good cheer, and say something nice and encouraging to another soul.

She stood alone on the marbled hallway and looked around; no one to pour her love to. She looked down the hall at the doors that led to the kitchen and pantry and remembered the Chef. She had been very mean to him the other day as she fastidiously supervised the preparation of Mr. Sciorra's meals. She knew the Chef loathed her. She didn't blame him. Most people didn't really like her. She had always taken it as a compliment; a badge of honour. The world was a desperately evil place and good souls didn't always have the good fortune of being easily liked. She had always carried her cross with pride but now she wanted to make peace with the Chef, so she turned and walked hurriedly towards the kitchen. There was a distinctive spring in her steps and a pendulous swing to her hips.

Inside the study, Phillip stood a short distance behind the seated Andrew. The lady on the other hand was kneeling by the side of Andrew, whose left hand was nestled in both her hands. She looked up at him and spoke in a low, soothing voice.

"Andrew, my name is Sibongile Bene, I am a psychologist and a dear friend of Phillip. I have come to give you positive energy. I am here to help you heal yourself, I know you hear me, I know you know I have come in peace and unquestioning love."

She squeezed his hand in comfort and just when she was about taking her hand away, he squeezed hers back in return. It was weak but it was real. His face still stared unblinking out of the window but he was connected with Sibongile through an invisible umbilical cord.

Phillip watched them and saw the smile on her face. He knew something was happening. He could see her singular focus on Andrew. It was direct. It was alive, like an electric current running through both of them. He felt the air in the room change.

"I feel your pain, and I hear you; so much guilt and so much regret. You want to make good, you want to bring back the innocent heart you have lost. I feel you."

A tear ran down Andrew's left cheek. Phillip didn't see it. Sibongile did.

"It is okay. It is only natural to grieve. I am here to help you grieve and then to bring you back to the world of the living. The world where you can truly make amends for the wrongs of your past."

Andrew looked on. Her words assailed his ears. He felt their power.

Meanwhile out in the hallway, the main doors of the house opened and Therese walked in. She shut the doors behind her, bent down, and removed her Manolo Blahnik shoes. Her feet were killing her. It had been a busy day for her. She had done all she had wanted to do except for visiting Andrew's lawyers to ascertain Phillip's claims. She had kept his claims to herself, not even sharing it with Timothy. This was a battle she wanted to fight alone. She wanted to prove to everyone that she was supremely capable of handling the Sciorra fortune. It was thirty-three minutes past four, she was returning earlier than usual; there was no need for lunch, just sleep to quell the headache that was already building up in the left side of her head. She was debating returning Timothy's call as she ascended the grand staircase. Even in that mental debate, her eyes still took in the normality that surrounded her. It was in that scanning motion that her eyes fell on the large family painting that hung on the wall above the staircase. She looked at Annabelle and her heart lurched. Time didn't seem to heal the wound of the loss of her mother. Nothing seemed to reduce the pain. She looked at her wonderfully beautiful mother and wondered if Timothy could ever drive her to do what her mother, in a desperate bid to find peace and silence the groans of emotional turmoil, had done. She wasn't sure. Three months ago, she would have speedily said Timothy would never hurt her, but now, she wasn't so sure. In fact she was no longer sure of anything anymore. She stood there looking at the picture of her mother and after a few seconds, she allowed her eyes settle on Andrew. He stood there smiling like the happiest father and husband in the world. A look and smile that could fool even the most cynical minds. Why didn't she hate him as much as she should? Would forgiving him be a betrayal of her mother? What was she expected to do? Make him pay? She sighed and then looked down at the shut doors of the study that lay several doors below, along the vast hallway.

She should check up on him before she goes to bed, she advised herself. There would be time for vengeance in the future. That thought presupposed that there needed to be vengeance, but then, who was to say who could definitely proclaim guilt or innocence in cases like this? But then, she reminded herself that exacting revenge on her father on behalf of her mother as he hung in this state of living nothingness reeked of cowardice. What is pain if the party that was at the receiving end actually didn't feel pain? How can one punish the dead? That was her quagmire, a mental and emotional debate she found her listless soul caught in.

"I would check up on him," she murmured to herself as she turned around and walked down the staircase towards the study. The large chandelier that hung from the high ceilings reflected the sunlight that streamed from the skylight on the ceiling through its pure cubic zirconia crystals onto Therese's diamond earrings and diamond encrusted gold bracelet.

In the study, Sibongile was still kneeling by Andrew and speaking to him in her comforting, nurturing voice, while Phillip stood loyally behind him, holding his breath in joyful expectation.

The two men were laughing hysterically as they pulled up in front of the McDonald's Restaurant at Jane and Driftwood. It was a daily ritual for them. A nine at night pick up of Cheeseburger combos. It seemed as though they were trying to make up for not eating any cheeseburgers while growing up in Nigeria.

The doors of the black Acura Legend opened and the first man got out. At the same moment, the door of the restaurant opened and a group of teens speaking loudly at the top of their voices came out, just as a boy in a hooded top walked towards them from the opposite direction. The second man was coming out when the boy in the hooded top brought out a sawed-off shotgun and opened fire at the man who was already standing out of the car, tucking in his spotless, white oxford dress shirt. The bullet tore into his chest, lifted him up from the ground, and slammed him into one of the concrete pillars outside the restaurant. He was dead before he hit the ground with a thud.

The group of teens scattered like bees away from the sudden violence, screaming at the top of their voices, while the people in the McDonald's Restaurant ducked for cover. The other man froze in mid-motion as he watched his friend being cut down, but years of living in the back streets of Lagos came into play. He unfroze and jumped back into the car, slamming the door behind him, and started the engine.

As he put the car in reverse the first bullets hit the windscreen and shattered it. He ducked behind the steering wheel and floored the gas pedal. The car lurched back and responded with a swerve to the right in obeisance to his turning the wheel in the same direction. Another bullet took out the front side window and rained glass on him. He was driving blind. He tapped on the brake, pushed the gear into drive, and floored the gas pedal. The car screeched as it raced forward, bullets taking out the rear window, as the hooded boy ran after the fleeing car, releasing more bullets in quick succession. One of them flew through the space in which the rear window had once stood and slammed into the back of the driver's seat. The force pushed the man forward and forced him to turn the car left, making the car careen off its escape path and run into some other parked cars.

The man behind the wheel put the car in reverse but it was too late. The hooded boy had already arrived at the side of the car. They both locked eyes. There was no recognition from the man behind the wheels as he stared at the boy who was bent on taking his life.

"Please." It came out without hope.

The hooded boy squeezed the trigger.

The first bullet hit him in the shoulder, the second in the lower abdomen, the last one ripped apart his head. That singular action extinguished the last thoughts of realisation he had been forming. It was about Osasu. It was about Okota. It was about the foolhardiness of confronting the man everyone called Oloye with the memory of the dastardly deeds of his past. Death stole him before he could comprehend it.

The hooded boy took off running towards Driftwood. A car sat there with its engines running. All he had to do was get to it and he knew he would be safe. This wasn't his first hit. He was nineteen and already had eight under his belt. His job as a hired assassin was proving very rewarding. This hit had paid twenty thousand dollars. Ten-a-piece. He wondered what the two men had done to make spending all that money for their death make any sense to the man who made that call to him two weeks ago, but then, he knew that to succeed in his chosen profession, he had to learn not to ask questions. He was a fast learner.

The light from the electronic tube illuminated the otherwise dark living room.

"...the victims have been identified by the Toronto Police as Tunde Allen and Olumide Ajanaku. At this moment, they have not been able to ascertain the motive for their execution style killing but they have confirmed that the victims were previously known to the police..." The newscaster spoke out in a not-at-all-solemn voice.

Osasu switched off the fifty inches television set and leaned back on the tanned leather couch. He turned his neck to the left and then to the right until he heard a barely audible pop sound. He did the same to his knuckles, pressing them in with the other hand until he heard them crack. A wry smile spread across his face, giving him a ghoulish appearance in the near-darkness of the living room, since the light that snuck in from the slit underneath the visitor's washroom was the only illumination available. Now that Mayor had taken care of the problem, everyone would know better not to mess with him. He also knew that he had to do more to stay vast distances away from the Nigerian community, just maintain contact with his point men and that was it. People who knew about his past shouldn't haunt him again, he remarked to himself. Okota must be kept in the graveyard of the past.

He could vividly remember Okota, that town in the suburbs of Lagos that was a mixture of high-brow residences, bustling commercial spaces, and seedy neighbourhoods which stank with the ingratiating odours of grinding poverty. He remembered the events that happened that sunny day on the main thoroughfare that ran through the town; a street that went by the name Ago Palace Way. Even as he closed his eyes, he could see the blood, he could hear the cries, he could still feel the chaos, his heartbeat increased as the excitement dripped down from his memories.

It was all about a hard fought election; two political parties represented by two wealthy candidates claiming superiority and territorial rights over the larger town of Isolo in which Okota lay, as expected in Nigeria where elections weren't won by the true winner of the ballots but by the party who paid the most bribes and could unleash the most violence.

One of the parties was local, popular, and well-loved by the people, the other was not, but he had limitless funds and unflinching resolve to inflict as much harm as possible on anyone who crossed his way, after all, he had an enforcer bar none. Osasu was that enforcer.

He was recruited all the way from Lagos Island where he traditionally held sway to lead the onslaught on the people of Okota. It was, vote for his candidate or die, simple as that. But protecting the people, were the local thuggery machine of the popular candidate and incumbent representative of the town. They were no match for Osasu and his foot soldiers. While the local thugs were ready to war against the intruders, Osasu and his candidate didn't differentiate between combatants and innocent citizens, after all, it really wasn't the final tally of votes that was going to win the elections but the fraudulently altered result sheet, stamped as authentic by the returning electoral officer, who was already on their payroll. So the violence wasn't really about winning the elections; it was more about claiming territorial rights, cowing the opposition, being the one and only authority on the land.

On that sunny day, the popular politician held a huge rally at an open field which lead to Ago Palace Way. As various shades of people stood on the asphalt surface of the road and impeded the slow-moving traffic, Osasu and his goons attacked. As usual he led the charge, cutting down men, women, and children as they hacked their way towards the raised platform upon which the rudely-shocked politician stood.

People fled in all directions, leaving the wounded, dying, and dead in their wake. In a matter of minutes, it was just the two opposing teams of thugs facing each other while the politician and his trusted aides joined the fleeing masses.

The battle took over an hour, and as it raged there was no sign of the police who had already been bought; and even if they were not, they would have been too afraid to intervene. Firepower for firepower they were no match. By the time it ended, Osasu and the remaining of his thugs stood victorious. Okota had become a ghost town.

His candidate won the elections and things changed in the town. The changes were good for a select few and decidedly bad for the rest of the people. Osasu wasn't concerned with the wisdom or the politics of his actions, all he knew was that his fame grew in bounds and his pocket in the same vein. That was the time his nom de guerre became known in the underworld and backwaters of the entire state of Lagos; Oloye, the smooth talking, impeccable English speaking, multi-lingual retorting, suave mannered, strikingly handsome, fiendishly charismatic, cold, calculating, and nightmarishly brutish king of Lagos.

But that which created his fame was also that which his Achilles heel became. The enemies he wrought by that singular action stretched wide and ran deep. Families remembered his name and cursed him daily, widows held him in bristly contempt, invoking disaster on his head and that of his candidate as often as they remembered their dead husbands and to some, even children, but most importantly, there was a change of guard in the office of the governor of the state; from a governor who embraced the politics of the old to a progressive who envisioned a state that served its people and was a representative of those who voted it into power. In this new dispensation, there was no space for the likes of Osasu and in this age, the freedom that hung in the air enabled the regurgitation of many a painful memory. One of those memories was the macabre event at Okota. Someone had to pay. The politician who had emerged victorious wasted no time in securing himself and reinventing his pedigree, but for that to happen, someone had to bear the blame for the massacre. Osasu was thrown under the rampaging reformative bus and found himself enemy number one of the state. The sacrifice of the person who was the face of old, thuggish Lagos and the death of old Lagos itself was necessary for new Lagos to be born.

Luckily for him, no one had a picture of him. He was a phantom. Cameras weren't common-place on the streets of Lagos, so to take one of him meant you had to get him into one of the few studios that dotted the landscape, something that was close to impossible. You had to, maybe, catch him unawares in one of the owambe parties that was the main stay of Lagos social life, around which a madhouse of freelance pay-per-unsolicited-snapshot photographers buzzed, problem was he never went to any. He was an extrovert with a reclusive streak; a combination that he created to create the mystique that surrounded him. You never saw him when you wanted, only when he wanted. He was everywhere and nowhere. No one could boast of knowing where he lived, only where he held sway; a three story fortress in the winding, jam-packed residential quarters of Isale Eko. He came when no one expected and left when no one suspected. He was like the breeze; you felt it but you never knew from where it came or to where it went to.

So when the streets got hot, and his fortress was raided by the State Armed Robbery Squad, Osasu who had left barely minutes before, in obeisance to a gut instinct, knew better than to hang around and fight for his survival and relevance. He knew it was time to reinvent himself, time to return home and embrace his old world. The ideal moment had arrived when he had to try to rebuild the bridges he had all but destroyed and try once again to secure the love, respect, and acceptance of his father, a father who had wronged him in more ways than one. It was in this manner that Osasu disappeared from the streets of Lagos and began the plans that would see him arrive in the safety of the cold climes of Canada.

As he sat on the couch in the near-darkness of the night, Osasu counted his many blessings, none of which he remotely deserved.

Nosa tried to focus on the forms he was filling as he sat in the cubicle in the well-lit, large hall of the Services Canada building. He looked at the questions that peopled the expertly printed forms, his pen dangled from his hand and instead of writing the answers it requested, all he could think about was the avenue through which he could find Osasu.

He still couldn't totally believe the stories he had heard about his brother. Osasu an Area Father, the thought of which made him inwardly cringe. That act was a total betrayal of everything their parents had done for them. It was like throwing pearls to swine. Even as he thought deeply and tried to make sense of it all, he couldn't understand the why. Why did he repudiate his social class? What was so evil about being wealthy that he had do everything that was anathema to it, even if doing that itself also accrued wealth? It didn't add up.

He remembered the times he called home and asked his mother about Osasu's whereabouts. He could hear her weary sigh and feel the darkness of her deep pain when she said for the umpteenth time that she hadn't seen him. His father echoed his mother's emotional distress on several occasions. They were both at loss as to the change that had come over their first son, the departure of his spirit, and then his absence from the house, yet none of them had the slightest idea that Osasu was a totally different being; sleek and lethal. Nosa wondered what his mother would have thought if she had found out before she died. He dropped his pen and placed his head in his palms.

"Mom," he whispered.

There was no response. Just the humming quiet of the hall in which several heads sat bowed, scribbling away: black, blonde, red, straight, curly, kinky, grey, greying, turbaned, niqabed, and face-capped. A smattering of shaved heads completed the picture.

"Mom, I need your help." he continued.

Still no response.

"Are you there?" he persisted.

He felt her presence even before he heard her voice; peaceful, comforting, and reassuring. He relaxed.

"I am always here."

"What do I do, mom?"

"Focus on yourself."

"But I can't."

"Yes, you can."

"I need to find Osasu."

"You need to find you."

"I am here, mom; what are you talking about?"

"You are not, my Nosa."

"Of course I am."

"No you're not."

"I don't understand."

"You will in due time."

"But what about now?"

"Think positive thoughts, my love."

"I am trying."

"Don't give up; send out goodness into all of creation

and goodness will come your way, like a ricochet, like a boomerang."

"But you sent out goodness too, see how you ended up."

"Life is a mystery, my son."

"But Osasu is out here somewhere, he is... "

"You are here, Nosa."

"He needs to tell me why he did it."

"He will."

"Really?"

"Everything always adds up and works out at the end."

"But how?"

"You will find out, my love. For now, focus on you. Rebuild your life."

"Mom, I want to ask you something,"

"Ask, my dear."

"Do you see Dad?"

There was silence. No response. He lifted his head from his palms.

"Mom?" He looked up and saw two Indian ladies looking at him. Their eyes were questioning. Soliloquy in public was a no-no, he chided himself, forcing an embarrassed smile before he picked up his pen and started filling out the form. They were fast, purposeful strokes, leaving a trail of words that came into life on the tip of his pure gold pen, on which were the initials IE. It didn't stand for Internet Explorer but Ibude Eweka, his father's initial. His father had worked so hard to give him and Osasu so much and all he got back in return was bankruptcy, shame, and death.

Even though Nosa wanted to take his mind off Osasu and focus on filling out his form for his Social Insurance Number, he found his mind dwelling on the day Osasu had returned home after his frequently long periods of absence.

It had been a rainy day, the type that fell in Lagos and filled the bellies of the perpetually-garbage-and-sand-filled gutters, thus flooding the streets and in turn, sending streams of dirty, brown water into the houses of both the selfishly rich and the foolishly poor or even those who hung on the last vestiges of social morality. His father and himself were seating in the living room, discussing the news of a military Hercules C130 plane filled with junior army officers that had crashed into the swamps of Ejinrin killing all souls on board, when the door, which was carved with Edo symbols and royal imagery and stood at the fore of the entrance to the main living room, opened and Osasu walked in.

He was drenched and appeared broken; his eyes blood-red, his lower lips quivering, clothes hugging his body, his well chiselled frame hunched. He stopped for a fraction of time as though trying to decide if he should walk into the silence that had descended on the room. Four eyes stared in surprise and shock at him. His two eyes stared back in indecision.

Osasu took in a deep breath, exhaled, and walked into the room, his feet leaving tiny poodles of water on the Italian marble floor upon which various spots were covered with assorted rugs imported from the entire rug weaving capitals of the world. The living room was massive; high ceiling, draperies that hung from forever, paintings of varying values and quality. He was like an ant walking cautiously towards the ones it had so deeply hurt.

Once he got to his father, Ibude, he fell to his knees and remained there in silence. Nosa remembered looking at him and wondering where he had come from and why he was being so dramatic and before he could formulate other thoughts, Osasu began to cry.

It was deep. It was sorrowful. It was enamouring. No words, just tears, shoulders shaking, lips trembling as they strove to form words, words that never came to life.

Nosa could still see it all in his mind's eye, his father standing up and embracing his weeping brother. It was a sight to behold.

He remembered tears slowly invading his eyes that day as he sat there watching his father hugging his prodigal brother, saying over and over again, in his fatherly baritone, the words

"It's okay, you're back home. That's all that matters; it's okay."

Even as Nosa wrote on the form that sat invitingly in front of him, he found himself wondering if that day, Osasu had been crying in remorse for the things he had done to his family in the past or the things he was planning to do to them in the future. There was no way of knowing if he was crying at all or putting up the emotionally charged show he knew would open the doors of his father's continuously forgiving heart and usher him into the generosity of his good graces.

As he sat there in the hall of the newly initiated, in his whirling mind were answerless questions, disquieting wonderment and the echoes of his barely waning anger.

10

The door to the study opened and the barefooted Therese walked in. She stopped there in that instant, shoes dangling from her right hand, crocodile skin Louis Vuitton hobo handbag hanging from her left shoulder. Her eyes squinted and took in the image of the colourfully-dressed, bohemian-looking black lady squatting beside the chair upon which Andrew sat. She saw Phillip as he turned towards her. He wasn't smiling. She wasn't either.

"Therese." Phillip managed the word. It came out in surprise since he had not expected her to return so early.

Sibongile looked towards the door and saw Therese standing there, the light from the hallway behind her framing her in a picture that appeared at once ghoulish as it looked normal. She could feel the energy oozing out of her; suspicious, confrontational, angry.

"What is this?" Therese spoke coolly.

Phillip walked towards her. He was thinking on his feet. He understood what it must have looked like to her. No one was supposed to see or meet with Andrew without her knowledge and now that they both had hit a rough patch in their relationship, Therese had insisted on adding a caveat that stipulated no access without her express permission.

"I brought in a psychologist to take a look at Andrew."

Sibongile stood up and smiled. She raised her palms to her chest and placed them together in a blessing of peace, then she bowed slightly.

"Who is this?" Therese was not impressed.

"Sibongile Bene..."

"What is she doing here?" Therese cut Phillip off.

"She is the psychologist I..."

"You said so before, I want to know what she is doing with my father." Therese dropped her shoes and walked further into the study. She moved in a manner that signalled that she was ready for a fight.

Sibongile maintained her smile and watched as Therese walked around the chair from the other direction and squatted on her haunches by Andrew.

"Daddy, are you okay?" Her voice dripped with care. There was no response. She stood up and faced Sibongile.

"I am sorry, ma'am, but you will have to leave." Therese was curt.

"Your father needs help." Sibongile's voice was calm.

"I know what my father needs; please leave, Ma'am."

Sibongile looked at her for a moment and then at Andrew. She bent towards him and whispered in his ear.

"I will be praying for you."

She patted Andrew on his shoulder and felt him tremble underneath her touch. No one else noticed it since they were both looking at her; one embarrassed as regards how she was treated and the other bristling with rage regarded her presence.

"Your father needs help; we need to get him out of here,

somewhere where he can truly start to heal. He needs unconditional love, true forgiveness, and deep understanding." Sibongile spoke dauntlessly.

"And you need to leave this house." Therese walked around the chair and headed to the door of the study. Upon getting there she stood by the open door and looked back at Sibongile, who was now staring at the flustered Phillip. She was not embarrassed since Phillip had briefed her on the circumstances of her invite.

"I will see you out." Phillip said to Sibongile and escorted her towards the open door where Therese stood, glaring like an enraged pit bull.

Once at the door, Sibongile once again smiled at Therese and spoke in her usual comforting voice; a voice that dripped with warmth on its sonorous alto tone.

"There is no need for anger; I come in peace and love."

She placed her hand gently on Therese's arm in reassured comfort. Therese flinched but Sibongile didn't take away her hand. Suddenly her face crumbled into a frown; her eyes widened for an instant and then returned to normal.

"There are vultures hovering around you; so much darkness. You have to be careful."

"Who the hell is this woman?!" Therese's voice rose.

"Sibongile, let me see you out." Phillip quickly intervened and gently pried her away and led her into the hallway. Nurse Maria was hurriedly walking towards the study, her nose as usual sniffing out the development of a story that would make fodder for juicy gossip, but once she laid eyes on Sibongile again, it all evaporated and a serene feeling descended on her. They both smiled at each other, exchanged a nod, and walked towards their respective directions, Maria to the study, Sibongile to the main door of the house, Phillip dutifully escorting her, his mind wheeling away.

Once they got to the main door, Phillip opened it and Sibongile stepped out; he followed after her into the warm sunlight of the day.

"I'm so sorry for all that."

"You don't have to be, Phillip; there is a lot to do to help Mr. Sciorra."

"How can we do that if Therese shuts you out of the house?"

"The seen stands no chance against the unseen."

"You mean you can help Andrew without actually being with him?"

"You would have to get him out of this house; you have to bring him to me."

"How will I do that?" Phillip was exasperated

"An opportunity will present itself; you just have to be ready."

"Therese will..."

"We will have to save her too."

"Come on, now you are stretching this too far. I told you I know who is messing up her mind, we don't need..."

"Remember, the unseen is what matters."

"But how would I know when..."

"Just believe. That's all, Phillip, just believe." She smiled, tapped him on his shoulder, and walked away towards the parking lot that stood at the far side of the compound.

Phillip watched her as she got into her yellow, old Volkswagen beetle, backed up, and drove down the driveway towards the guarded gates, then he turned around and walked back into the house, bracing himself for the battle he knew was waiting for him.

Nicole looked at the large, brown envelope in her hand. It contained all her correspondence with Andrew: hand written notes in his cursive handwriting on specially-ordered, gold-embossed stationery, signed birthday and valentine cards, short "I miss you" notes. Andrew had known what chivalry meant.

With her he had dated the old way, treating her like a queen even though he had others whose beds he shared. She inhaled sharply as the reality of what she was about to do hit her once again. As she exhaled, it felt as though her vital life force was leaving her. Andrew didn't deserve this, but she knew that she had no choice. She reached across the table and handed it to the Private Investigator.

"Why are you doing this?" she asked.

"The less you know, the better for you."

"I told Phillip and Therese that I didn't want anything to do with Andrew and this whole mess again."

"I will be in touch with you when we need you." He put the envelope into his briefcase and stood up. "I need a number or a name; what if I want to get in touch with you, like in an emergency?"

"There will be no emergencies."

"You are not God."

"Don't be too sure." He smiled. It had an evil tint to it that sent a chill down Nicole's rigid spine. "You will stay put in this house; no calls to anyone, especially Phillip and Therese. You will be ready to move at a moment's notice."

Nicole smiled to herself. These men didn't realise who they were dealing with.

As though he read her mind, he looked at her with that evil smile still plastered on his face before he turned and headed for the door.

"Don't be smart; we've got eyes on you."

She managed a smile, shook her head, and remained silent as she watched him walk to the door, open it and just as he was about stepping out, his cell phone rang. He brought it out of the holder that was hooked to his belt, looked at the caller display, and took the call.

"Yes," was all he said.

He listened.

"Yes," he repeated.

He nodded.

"I understand," he replied.

He turned around and looked at Nicole.

"She is right here."

Nicole took a step back. There was a coldness in his voice that scared her. Who are these people? She muttered to herself as she looked at the screen door that led to the backyard. She was tempted to make a run for it, damning the evidence they had. Worst case scenario, she would be safer with the police than she would be with these men, who spoke in codes and appeared from nowhere with demands that meant her hurting a man she truly cared for and who she knew, deep down in her heart, cared for her too.

"Done." he concluded and hung up.

"Okay, plans have changed." he said, walking back into the living room.

"What?" She still was apprehensive.

"You are coming with me."

"Where are you taking me to?"

"You really should learn to stop asking questions and just do as you are told." there was a hint of irritation in his voice even though he still had his trademark smile.

"My friend will ask questions; she will want to know where I have gone."

"We will make up a good story and you will leave a note for her."

"She will expect me to leave a number she can reach me at."

"You will call her later on tonight and let her know you are okay."

"What if she..."

"No more questions. Now go get your things." It came out authoritatively.

"But..."

"Don't let me get mad at you." A new smile was now on his face. It was hideous.

She knew better than oppose him. As she turned and walked towards the staircase, she could feel her heart thumping loudly and she cursed herself for having refused to stay in what had now turned out to be the safer confines of the Sciorra residence.

What did Andrew do to these men and what did they truly want her to do? She asked herself in her mental enclave as she ascended the staircase. No one needed to tell her that the envelope of intimate correspondence wasn't the only thing they needed from her.

She slowly began saying The Lord's Prayer as she climbed higher. A miracle was what she needed. A fast one.

Angela walked naked to the refrigerator, opened it, and brought out a bottle of Perrier water. She opened it and poured some of the sparkling liquid into a glass cup, which was shaped in the form of an obelisk; she placed the bottle back in the open refrigerator and shut the door. She turned and caught Osasu looking at her as he leaned against the counter top. He was also naked, his well-defined muscles in beautiful contrast with the whiteness of the tiled walls of the kitchen.

"I see your eyes, young man." She giggled, taking a sip from the glass and walking to the stove upon which was a large, stainless steel All-Clad pot.

"I paid for the view," he replied, his calculating eyes following her.

"How much?"

"Confidential info, thank you very much."

"I own the property."

"Then you should know how much I paid."

"Well, I know someone deposited some money into my account, not sure who, so if you claim you were the one, then you should know how much it was."

She opened the pot and steam rose up into the surrounding air, sending the aroma of the boiling *egusi* soup directly into their nostrils. Angela had wasted no time learning how to prepare every Nigerian dish she could put her finger on, the internet being her primary resource. She was traditional, to love a man and desire to be with him meant you had to be one with him, one with him in every respect, one body, one mind, one spirit, one soul; figuratively and symbolically. She picked up the ladle and stirred it; the assorted meat appeared and disappeared with each round of the rotation of the wooden ladle, *abodi*, *shaki*, roundabout, *okporoko*, *pomo*, cowleg, cowtail, *ogufe*, chicken, and beef taking their turns to the surface and back into the miasma of the delicacy.

"That smells good."

"How much did you pay me, homie, for my prime real estate?" she playfully asked, ignoring his attempt at changing the topic.

"Thought we had moved past that."

"Nope, we move past it when I say so; it is my property." She placed the lid back on the pot and walked towards him making an effort to look as seductive as she could. He smiled as she approached. She got to him, offering him the water; he sipped it from the glass without collecting the glass itself. She placed the glass on the marble counter top by his side and pressed her body against his, planting a kiss on his lips in the same movement.

"I paid you with all my heart and every piece of my soul."

She looked deep into his eyes and smiled. It was a soul baring smile. The smile that said, "This is the conqueror of my heart with whom I am well pleased."

"You always know all the right answers, don't you?"

"When you are meant to be with someone, everything naturally falls in place."

"Are you meant for me, Saz?"

"What do you think?"

"Very Nigerian to answer a question with a question?"

"I am Nigerian." he replied

"I am Italian," she countered as she removed the shiny black hair that fell over the creamy-white, flawless skin of her face with a flick of her beautifully-manicured, slender fingers.

"Tell me something I don't know."

"You think you know everything about me?"

"Now you are speaking like a Nigerian."

"I have to be like you to be with you."

He kissed her tenderly on her lips. She responded eagerly and ran her hands across his shoulders, over his neck, and rested it at the back of his head. He cupped her pert buttocks with his right hand and strummed her back with his left, light caresses that mimicked playing a guitar. He knew how much she loved it.

"If we get into our groove you better expect the firemen to come put out the flames."

"I know how heated it is when we get nasty."

"I was referring to the food." He said laughing.

"What the sweet smelling roses?!" she exclaimed and took on a pouting look "You just ruined the mood."

"Better than having to pay damages for a burnt out condo." He continued laughing.

She walked back to the stove, opened the pot, sniffed the aroma, and smiled.

"I have this soup down pat." She changed the topic.

"You are simply and lovingly too much." He was flowing with her, still leaning on the countertop.

"Everyone says so."

"Like who?"

"Therese."

"Therese?" He feigned ignorance.

"Therese Sciorra."

"Oh!" He went quiet.

"Is that all you'll say?" She walked to one of the lower cupboards, bent down, and brought out a vat of powdered yam flour. She placed it on the top of the island.

"What am I supposed to say?"

"I expect you to ask me how she said it, why she said it, stuff like that."

"Okay, why did she say it?"

"Cos I advised her."

"On what?"

"Life."

"What about life?"

"Like how to live fully and be happy."

"You?"

"What do you mean by you?"

"I don't figure you being all philosophical."

"What if that is the Angela I choose to show you?"

"Didn't realise there was more than one Angela."

"Isn't there more than one Saz?"

Osasu went quiet. His senses were awakening. He could feel that a moment had arrived in their relationship. A change. A transition into new environments. Subtle but real. He adjusted his position and spoke, careful to mask the alertness in his voice by a nonchalant charm.

"Well, there are always a lot of sides to everyone."

"And do I know all your sides?" She had a pot under the faucet and was filling it with water.

He hesitated for a moment before he spoke.

"I try to show you as many sides as I can."

"Not true."

"What?"

"The bathroom earlier on, that was a side of you I had never seen before."

"I was just startled, that's all. I thought I explained."

She put the pot she had filled with water on another burner and started up the heat.

"That is some fear you have, Saz."

"I didn't realise it was you."

"Who else has your key?" She opened the pot of egusi soup, sniffed again, smiled, and turned off the heat.

"You don't believe me?" Osasu was becoming uneasy.

"I believe you are trying to protect me from something you think I shouldn't know"

"Like what?"

"I don't know; that's why I am asking."

Osasu inhaled. He knew he had to seize back control. He walked over to her and held her gingerly.

"It was nothing, mon bebe, just all my martial arts training coming to the fore. I want you to know that if there is something I have to tell you, I will, okay?"

She looked at him, her aquamarine eyes searching his hazelnut brown eyes. She smiled and then nodded. He smiled in return and placed a kiss on her lips.

"So what was it you were telling me about Therese?"

"She has hired me as her SA."

"Like a Special Assistant?"

"Yeap."

"I thought you worked for Andrew and Annabelle Sciorra?"

"For Annabelle. And I was going to be fired"

"Fired?"

"Yeah, she is dead and there was no more need for my services."

"And what changed?" Osasu couldn't believe his luck. He couldn't even begin to imagine what would have happened to his plans if Angela actually stopped working for the Sciorras. All he could imagine was disaster, everything going up in smoke.

"I spoke to her, honestly, like truly connected, and she thought we would both make a great team. I guess the universe intervened."

"Woow, I guess this calls for a toast." He kissed her on the lips and walked off to bring out a bottle of wine. She looked at him as he came back with the bottle of red wine; a 1967 Pinot from the vineyards of Le Chateau Rothschild. He placed it on the counter top and turned to go bring two glasses. She reached over and slapped him playfully on his butt cheeks. It was taut and made a smacking sound. She laughed out loud.

"You will pay for that," he called out to her with a guttural laugh.

Little did she know how well he was planning for her to pay for every second of the extremely valuable time he had spent with her, nurturing her, preparing her for the role he had mapped out for her; a role the good graces of providence had secured for her by the virtue of her timely appointment as special assistant to Therese Sciorra.

If God was not on his side, why else would providence intervene so expediently? He asked himself as he brought the two empty glasses back to the smiling, totally-trusting, perennially-cheerful Angela.

The music that spewed out of the speakers that hung from the high ceilings was hypnotic and fever inducing. It pumped with an infectious rhythm, moving the crowd of worshippers in a chaotic swoon. Some jumped high with arms raised, others screamed in joyous abandon while rotating around the same spot, some actually ran down the centre aisle shouting at the top of their voices, "Glory! Glory! Glory!..."

And right in front of the congregation, in the carpeted space between the front row of seats and the stage on which the choir and the pulpit stood, was Tirin Tirin. He was dressed in a riot of colours: green pants, yellow buttoned-up shirt, black and white striped tie, red jacket, and white shoes. He appeared to be staring forward at the stage, eyes closed in silent meditation, and when the song went into its swinging chorus, Tirin Tirin broke into a dance. It was crazy as it was beautiful, it was comical as it was inspiring, a gyration that was an amalgam of every known and unknown dance form. He was in the spirit and he wanted everyone else to know it. He was thankful for so many things and his dancing was his way of showing of it. The eyes that were not in themselves caught up in their own personal spiritual revelry were glued to him. He did this most Sundays, yet each time was like the first time; an honest attestation in dance of one complicated man's relationship with his God.

Nosa was sitting five rows from the front of the congregation. He was watching the bedlam around him. He was quiet, his Catholic upbringing in conflict with the happenings around him. He was used to the quiet contemplation of his faith and was at crossroads with the careless, riotous abandon that swirled around him. This was a house of the Pentecostal faith and this was his second time sitting in it. The earlier time was a more quiet and reserved midday service; both times he had come upon the invite of the ecstatic Tirin Tirin.

Finally the music came to a sonorous, climatic end and the crowd, mopping up their sweating faces and shouting over and over again, "Hallelujah! Glory! Hallelujah! Glory!..." returned to their seats. Tirin Tirin on his part knelt down before the stage and touched his head to the floor three times, stood up, and, to a resounding applause from the laughing choristers and some members of the congregation, returned to the empty seat beside Nosa.

"God is good, bro!" he quipped between pants as he sat down.

All Nosa could do was smile. When he thought he knew Tirin

Tirin, the little man threw him a curve ball. How can a mouth so profane be so sacred in a different setting?

On the stage, the well-dressed pastor walked to the pulpit, picked up the microphone, and spoke in a deep baritone that was peppered with a forced falsetto.

"People of God, we have not come to His house by our power nor by our might, but by His choosing. Can I hear a hallelujah to that?"

"Hallelujah!" the gaily-dressed congregation responded in excited overtones, Tirin Tirin's response being the loudest, Nosa's the most quiet.

"We have shown our father our infinite love through our songs and our dance, but there is still a lot to do in order to obtain for ourselves his special blessings and anointing. How many of you here today have come to his throne with a receptive spirit?"

Hands flew up in the air, each straining person trying to out-raise the other. Tirin Tirin on his part actually stood up. His arm was raised the highest. The pastor smiled.

"The eyes of the Lord have beheld your willingness and is pleased"

The hands came down and a thick silence descended on the hall. The pastor looked at them intently. Nosa could feel the air of expectation that had gripped the congregation.

"God spoke to me today, he said he is ready to surprise. In fact, he said he is ready to shock, to embarrass some people today. He is going to show some of you this morning that he is the Lord your God and nothing is impossible for him to do," his voice began rising, "He will show to those who have not yet encountered him that he is ready to bless whomever he chooses to bless and curse those who have not sought his mercies. He asks you to dare him. He challenges you to put him to test. He is God!" The last word came out as a sudden shout; some of the congregation jumped up to their feet and raised their hands to the heavens, eyes looking up as though searching for the face of God in the white ceilings. The pastor continued as he walked away from the pulpit and strutted to and fro the length of the stage.

"He laid in my heart the scripture, Isaiah 45, verse 11, 'thus saith the Lord, the Holy One of Israel and his Maker, ask me of the things to come concerning my sons and to the works of my hands, command ye me.'" He stopped and shook his head in marvel and then continued in a low-pitched voice.

"The Lord is asking you today to speak to Him in truth, to ask Him of those things you desire, those things you crave, those things that still confuse you, those fears you have. He is saying you should command Him concerning the works of His hands and He will answer you, He will do that which you are calling out to Him for. If you believe that God is ready to meet you at your point of need today, send out a resounding hallelujah to the heavens above."

"Hallelujah!" the congregation screamed at the top of their voices. Nosa practically held his ears to shut out the headache-causing sound of hundreds of voices shouting as one.

"He is Lord and there is no being greater than Him, whether they be in heaven, on earth, under the earth or even in the seas."

"Baba Olodumare! Action God! Nothing do you!" Tirin Tirin shouted the phrases and abruptly fell silent. There was a smattering of laughter in the church.

Nosa didn't turn towards him but viewed him from the corner of his eye as Tirin Tirin sat there staring at the pastor and mumbling intelligible words.

"He is Jehovah Jireh, our God who provides." the drummer who sat behind the choir responded with a joyful strike on the high hat cymbals and a thud on the bass drums.

"He is Jehovah Shammah! Our Lord who is present." the pastor continued and the drummer with the clash of cymbals and thud of drums concurred.

"He is Jehovah Gmolah! God of recompense."

"Hallelujah!" The lead chorister called into the microphone as the drummer responded and the Pastor swayed, arms spread wide like an eagle, to his own zealous chant.

"He is Jehovah Maccaddeshem! The Lord our sanctifier."

"Jehovah Rapha! The Lord our healer."

"Jehovah Tsidkenu! The Lord our righteousness."

"Jehovah Rohi! The Lord my shepherd." He was stumping his right foot on the floor in synchronicity with the clash of the cymbals and the boom of the drums.

"Jehovah Nissi! The Lord our banner."

"Glory! Hallelujah! Yes! Preach it, Pastor! Say it! Forever! Yes Lord!" The cries rent the hall from all corners, throwing some of the congregation into apoplectic fits. In spite of himself, Nosa could feel the electric current creep on the skin of his forearm.

The pastor fell on his knees and raised both hands high, his black jacket hanging like the cape of a superhero. His voice was choked as tears streamed down his face.

"El Elyon, you are the most high God!" He called out.

"Yes you are, Father!" The congregation responded. The drummer ceased playing and the pianist took over, slow music playing forth, like an instrumental lullaby, suffusing the hall with a celestial cadence that gave even more power to the professions of the wailing pastor. Nosa watched even as he felt the first stirrings in his chest.

"El Roi, you are the God who sees!" The pastor continued in his baleful voice, something Nosa found intriguing, because it sounded to him like the wailing of the pastor seemed to herald the presence of a God that was altogether malevolent instead of unconditionally-loving, like his mother had often told him as she rocked him on her knees as an ultra inquisitive toddler. Even at that moment, Nosa could still see through his questions and feel the rising awareness of a divine presence.

"El Olam, you are the everlasting God!" He called out in a high-pitched voice that reverberated across the hall and slapped most of the congregation to their knees.

"El Shaddai, you are the God Almighty!" The pastor was now visibly crying.

Nosa was watching intently as the church went silent and the lead chorister began singing the classic gospel track "*Hallelujah*"

"Father, it is you who told me to tell them that you are ready for anyone who comes to you with the honest desires of their heart. Your people are ready, father; they are yearning for you. They are on their knees; they are speaking to you."

Nosa felt a nudge on his side, he turned, and it was the already kneeling Tirin Tirin.

"Are you a child of Satan?"

Nosa understood what the question meant. He slid from the chair unto his knees and bowed his head.

"Hear them speak to you, Lord; hear them unburden."

For a moment Nosa didn't know if he was to listen to the words of the pastor as he had been doing earlier or if he was supposed to pray. He kept quiet.

"Some of them do not know how to talk to you, some don't know if they deserve to talk to you, some don't know if you actually hear their prayers; show them, father, that you are Jehovah, you are the Elohim, you are the omniscient, the omnipotent, the omnipresent."

Nosa took in a deep breath and slowly exhaled. He tried to clear his mind and pray. He was at loss as to how to begin.

"Just talk, my Nosa." His mother's voice floated into his subconscious. His heart began pounding, not in fear, but in excitement, like there was a joyous expectation coming that he had no knowledge of.

"Mum..."

"Pray to God not your mother." Tirin Tirin's voice intruded

onto his quiet and drew him back to the present surroundings. Nosa hadn't realised he was praying aloud.

"God is listening to you; He is waiting for your prayers." The pastor's words came flooding from the stage, the surrounding speakers, to his ears.

"Father, I have come into your presence today," Nosa began.

"Correct guy," Tirin Tirin responded.

Nosa shook his head and tried to block Tirin Tirin's words from his ears. He closed his mouth and continued praying in the privacy of his mind.

"I ask for divine mercy for the soul of my father. I beg that you do not condemn him to hell but you restore him to the divine mercy of your grace. I know you say those who take their lives are not deserving of a place in heaven, but you are a God of mercy and of love, please forgive him; he was in so much pain when he took his life."

"Pray people, pray!" The pastor's voice floated outside the confines of his head.

"And help me find Osasu; I do not know where to begin searching for him, but I believe that you will bring him to me, you will make our paths cross."

"He is hearing your words; the heavens are opening up to receive your prayers." The pastor continued as the choir kept singing and the people kept praying; some silently, most boisterously, heads shaking as though in epileptic fits.

"I know my mum is with you in heaven, please keep taking care of her, and thank you for allowing her come talk to me and comfort me in the time of fear and loneliness."

"God is asking you to make a dedication to him right now; He says if you truly want Him to surprise you then you should sow a seed into His vineyard and He will shock you with the abundance of your harvest. He says that no man can expect to reap where he did not sow and it is in planting in the house of the Lord that prayers are answered."

The words crashed into the sanctity of Nosa's praying mind and he was jostled out of his prayers. He opened his eyes and looked up at the stage. The pastor was no longer kneeling but was now walking down the aisle and modulating his voice in a low register that gave it a lulling effect.

"He says if you believe that He is a God of pleasant surprises, you should raise your hands and indicate if you are ready to sow a thousand dollars into his ministry."

Once again Nosa felt a nudge at his side. It was Tirin Tirin.

"Close your eyes and keep praying," he lectured.

Nosa kept his eyes open and turned to look at the Pastor who was a couple of yards away from them. There were several hands up.

"Do not make a pledge that you cannot keep because the good Lord will look at you as a robber, and a man that steals from the house of God is condemned forever."

"Nosa, close your eyes," Tirin Tirin nudged him again.

"God loves a cheerful giver, my people. For those who have raised their hands, the Lord is going to embarrass you with his generosity, you will receive more than you have even requested for, your cup will overflow, you will be lifted high and celebrated, there will be no trace of sadness or tears in your lives, that which you have done today will be counted as favour in the presence of the Lord." For every prayer the Pastor said, there was a resounding amen even by those whose hands were not raised.

The pastor continued, "The ushers will take down your names and contact information and the church offices will expect the redemption of your pledges latest by Wednesday evening. Cheques, cash, credit cards are all accepted in the house of the Lord."

Nosa cringed from the blatant materialism and spiritual larceny that was taking place. How could such a beautiful service have suddenly taken the turn of this charade that passed as

Pentecostal jingoism? He was shocked. This couldn't happen within the confines of the Catholic Church, where one's relationship with God wasn't hinged on how much one paid into the coffers of the church, but on how much piety one exhibited in the upholding of the spiritual and canonical law. He didn't agree with everything the Catholic Church espoused but this was something else; this was what made Jesus, in righteous anger, flog the shit out of the merchants and pretentious zealots of the synagogue in biblical days.

It was surprising how people emigrated with their prejudices, biases, fooleries, stupidities and wisdom intact, Nosa mused to himself. One would have thought that moving to a more highly evolved but not necessarily superior culture will necessitate the dropping of the negative and the taking up of the positive, but the few days he had spent in Canada had thought him the opposite; some people actually rabidly held tight to whatever it was about their old lives in their former domiciles they could find, whether they truly believed in it or not. They craved for any semblance of an identity, and only the passage of time and the improvement of their material and emotional well-being will actually allow them let go of the old and ease the acquiring of the new.

He trained his eyes at the Pastor as he sauntered amongst the faithful, well-tailored, supremely expensive suite hugging his tall, well-coiffed Nigerian frame, the same pastor who had now mutated in his eyes from a lightning rod of evangelical ardour into a hideous cunning strumpet of Shakespearean devilry.

"Nosa don't mind him. God is not a tax collector. Let the mugus raise their hands if they choose to. What concerns agbero with overload?" Tirin Tirin whispered to him.

Nosa looked at him and saw the smile on Tirin Tirin's face.

"We are all here to hustle. If they think by giving what they have or don't have they will get favour from God then good for them; to each his own. All I know is that God has no checkpoints; He is not an egunje olopa. Abeg, fashi the guy and pray your own. It is the message we are here for, not the messenger." There was an honesty in Tirin Tirin's voice that was endearing.

Nosa stifled the laughter that rose in his chest as he regarded the impish fellow. Tirin Tirin was an unearthly enigma without comparison, he said in his mind as he shook his head and closed his eyes. Yes, he will pray in truth and ignore the temptations of the flesh. God is a spirit and the ideologies of the flesh serve only to corrupt the true essence of the spirit.

Even as the ushers took down names and financial pledges from some of the spiritually-charged, mostly African and Caribbean congregation of the Church of the Holy Tabernacle that stood like a huge, white-painted and tinted glass-dotted, traffic jam-causing albatross in the Keele and Finch neigbourhood, Tirin Tirin and Nosa, kneeling side by side, unknown to them, began to forge the beginnings of a deeper and more honest brotherhood.

"I do not care what she says; you had no right to bring her into this house!" Therese shouted the words at the now silent Phillip.

"You have to calm down," Phillip implored.

"Don't tell me what to or what not to do; this is my home. I told you, no one sees my father without my express permission."

"I know you said so, but we have to work together..."

"I will not work with you on anything, trust me, once I confirm the validity of those papers you said my dad gave you, I will come at you with all I have; I advise you to watch your back."

"I don't care what happens to me; it's Andrew I'm worried about. He is wasting away."

"The best medical personnel have seen my father and they advised, in a black-and-white written medical opinion, that he stays at home, he rests until he comes out of his fugue; that is from the best minds in the world, not your busker-looking, hippie-dressing, new-age-preaching, bullshit psychologist."

"And these best minds were introduced to you by Mr. Vinelatter."

"So what if he linked me up with them?"

"There is a pattern; can't you see it?"

"The only pattern I see is you getting too big for your breeches."

"What do I have to gain?"

"You ask yourself that question."

"You are the one accusing me."

"You have a conscience; you want to maintain the status quo, bilk my father for all he is worth, indulge him, corrupt him…"

"Listen to yourself."

"No, you listen to yourself. My mother loved you, she took you into this family like you were her blood; you betrayed her!" The beginning of tears appeared at the edge of her voice. She gripped the French Henri II walnut style desk in the study to steady herself.

"Don't go there, Therese." His voice was calm.

"Are you scared of the truth?"

"You know I am not."

"Then listen to me call you out for what you truly are; an enabling leech who wants my father back on his feet not for the sakes of his well-being, but for the reinstating of the decadence in which my father has run this estate for God knows how long."

"I did my best for Andrew and for this family."

"And what did your best result in?"

"You cannot blame me for…"

"Tell me, what has your best resulted in?"

"Therese, this is not fair."

"And you think my mother hanging from her neck in her wedding dress is fair?"

"Therese, please."

"You think aiding my father in his serial cheating is fair?"

"Therese." It was a plea.

"You think robbing me of a loving mother and turning my life upside down is fair?"

"I do not think we..."

"You think making the Sciorras the laughing stock of high society is fair?"

"No one is..."

"Tell me, what do you think is fair?"

"Heaven knows I tried to manage an already bad situation."

"My father was on the straight and narrow until he met you."

"And who told you that lie?"

"I know more than you give me credit for."

"Mr. Vinelatter told you, right?"

"Why don't you get over Timothy and focus on you?"

"Because whether you want to hear it or not, Mr. Vinelatter is the problem."

"I refuse to discuss Timothy with you."

"Then we have a problem." Phillip said the words as he walked over to one of the leather chairs and sat down.

"Isn't it already obvious?"

"If you want to leave Timothy out of it, fine by me, but do so in the entirety. Remove him from your decision making processes, even if not totally, at least partially, broaden your sources of information, show some independence; you are a Sciorra."

There was silence as she maintained her gaze on him. He returned it. He could feel her thinking. The thought of Andrew safely upstairs in his sprawling bedroom being attended to by Nurse Maria comforted him. He was happy Andrew hadn't witnessed the exchange between him and Therese.

"So, who is this psychologist?" Therese's voice broke into his thoughts.

Timothy walked down the winding staircase into the lower level of the Casa Loma Castle in the high-priced neighbourhood of Davenport and Spadina in midtown Toronto. It was the former residence of a onetime richest man in Canada, Sir Henry Pellatt, and was now a museum and landmark.

He had just taken a lunch break from the meeting of the trusteeships of one of several not-for-profit organisations upon whose boards he sat. He detested this place. It reminded him of the fleeting nature of wealth and how happenstance can lift up the lowly and bring down the mighty. How Sir Henry Pellatt had built such a masterpiece of architecture and go bankrupt in under a decade beat him. He had insisted that the meeting be moved somewhere else but Lady Madeleine Kent, who should instead have been called Lady Macbeth, insisted in the touristy location. To her, where better to hold a meeting that raised funds for the upkeep of Ontario's heritage sites than a heritage site itself. Timothy honestly couldn't care less; his mind was locked in on Nicole and his next course of action.

He sat down at a table at the far corner and looked at the menu that lay on the pressed, crisp table cloth, normal fare, nothing fancy. He glanced through it one more time as he waited for a waiter. Two minutes and no one came. He looked up and noticed the line by the open food counter. The people were holding trays upon which the servers behind the counter placed plates of food. He shook his head again in exasperation. He was starved and needed something in his system to feed his overworked brain. He swallowed his injured pride, stood up, and made his way to the line.

Once there, he smiled politely at the server at the far end and picked up his tray. He quickly scanned the canteens of food behind the show glass. It looked delicious, he confessed under his breath.

"Can I have some beef lasagna, garden salad, and some green tea?"

The server dutifully smiled and began to dish out the food. Timothy held his plastic smile and turned to face the other tourists who stood in line. A tall, blond, lean-muscled, and arrestingly handsome man with an expensive-looking camera hanging from his neck made eye contact with him and smiled. It was suggestive. Timothy regarded him. His effeminate nature was evident. The man walked over to him.

"Hello," the man offered. His voice was also effeminate but with a thick Swedish accent. His smile was contagious.

"Hi," Timothy responded, politely holding his plastic smile.

"From Toronto?" the man continued.

"Yes." He watched as the man moved closer and then stopped a distance away.

"Oh, I'm from Sweden, catching the sights."

"Nice, you travelling alone?" Timothy queried.

"No, with my boyfriend, but he pissed me off, so I am exploring the city myself."

"What a shame."

"Yes, what a shame."

They fell silent. It seemed uneasy and tensed. Then the blond haired man broke it.

"Are you alone?"

"Unfortunately no."

"Wife?"

"No, more like a meeting upstairs, boring as hell."

"I wouldn't mind some company."

Timothy regarded him for a minute. The temptation gripped his guts. He could conveniently place a call upstairs and excuse himself, engage this fine specimen of a man head-on, and feed his homosexual desires, but he knew he couldn't afford to publicly display his bisexuality.

"Company would be great, but work calls."

The server placed the salad on the tray and called out.

"Sir."

Timothy turned to her, smiled wider, picked up the tray, and joined the line that led to the cashier. The blond man walked along side him; he reached into the breast pocket of his jacket and brought out a card holder. He opened it, brought one out, and handed it to Timothy.

"I will be here for the next month. Should you have time to spare, I really could do with the company."

Timothy held the tray in one hand and collected the outstretched card with the other hand. He looked at the card. It read ERIK BROLIN, FOTOGRAF and had his phone and email details. He raised his eyes and stared into the clear blue eyes of the blond man.

"Nice to make your acquaintance, Erik, maybe I could find some time to get to know you better."

"That will be great. Can I get a number to reach you on?"

"I will call you."

Erik nodded and smiled, "See you around then."

"You have a great day." Timothy also nodded, pocketed the card, and walked over to the cashier. The line was moving fast.

He looked in front of him as the cashier punched in the figures and then deftly turned his head and watched Erik walk back to a table on which was a tray of food. Erik sat down and began picking from the plate of food, then abruptly looked up and caught Timothy's eye. He smiled. Timothy managed an embarrassed smile and looked away. He was uneasy. How could the blond man have noticed he swung both ways? What gave him away? He knew how hard he worked on hiding it. No unnecessary familiarity with men, whether tactile or oral. His dressing was always aggressively masculine. He flirted subtly with the most beautiful of women even though it was discrete, since he didn't risk flaunting his infidelities in the presence of Therese. So how could that man have picked him out of the crowd? He looked at himself briefly as he paid, to ascertain if there existed any giveaways on him. His suit was severe enough, the colours of his shirt and tie conservative and sober. He turned and walked over to his table and spied Erik stand up from his, take his tray over to the bin, empty the contents, place the tray on the wooden housing within which the bin was located, and walk towards the staircase. The man was fine, he mumbled to himself as he sat down. Even at that moment, he knew he was going to call him up and sexually devour him with the brutality that only he was capable of. He felt himself stir in his silk boxer shorts.

Once Erik got to the ground floor of the castle, he walked down the grand hall to the far entrance that led to the gardens. He brought out his phone and hurriedly placed a call. There were a couple of rings and then it was picked up from the other end.

"Good news?"

"He collected my card." Erik responded. There was no Swedish accent.

"You think he will call?"

"My bet is that he will."

"Good, let me know if he does."

"Will do."

He hung up the phone and looked at the number he had just called.

It read Phillip.

He deleted it.

11

"Plenty dollar, moway!" Tirin Tirin sang as he walked into the apartment. Nosa turned from the television show he was watching and looked at the dancing Tirin Tirin shut the door behind him. He was wearing his stained construction clothes and holding his huge lunch box. He continued dancing as he made his way into the living room.

"I don hammer!" he sang on.

"Hey, what's the good news?" Nosa called out to him.

"I don win lottery, my bro." He kept dancing.

"What?!" Nosa sprang to his feet, his eyes wide in joyous shock, his boxers crumpled between his legs and riding up the crack of his butt cheeks.

"Troway! Mugu don pay, shout hallelujah!" He dropped the lunch box on the table and took the dancing to another level.

Nosa rounded the couch and approached him.

"How much did you win?"

"Fifty million dalaz!"

"Yes!" Nosa punched the air.

Just then from the buzzing television set the words

rang out,

"...Canada is abuzz with expectation and the frenzied purchasing of tickets for the mega lotto draw which is a record fifty million dollars... the lucky numbers will be announced tomorrow evening..."

Nosa froze in mid-action for a moment, then he thawed and turned to the still dancing and singing Tirin Tirin.

"I don hammer, moway, shout hallelujah, troway!" he sang on.

"How do you know you've won the lottery?" Nosa asked.

"Faith, my friend, faith; speak about the things that are not as though they are." He said the words in a sing song as he kept on dancing to the imaginary music that played in his head, his lithe frame slowly moving to the ground in harmonious circular movements and then rising up again on the pivot of his rotating hips.

"Christ! You are something else!" Nosa exclaimed in irritation. He truly had been happy for the little man. He walked back to the couch and flopped on it.

Tirin Tirin burst out laughing and sat on one of the chairs around the dining table and began taking off his shoes. The apartment was well furnished even though the furniture looked randomly-picked; a miss match of colours and shapes, yet it had a homeliness to it that was inviting.

"Don't bring your bad head to spoil my luck o!" he said laughing.

"Don't talk to me." Nosa retorted, feigning anger.

"See this babe o!" Tirin continued laughing.

"Who is a babe?"

"You are my babe na; why else will you be vexing like that?"

"I have no words for you."

"Oya sorry; no vex." he cajoled as he stood up, walked over to Nosa, and patted him behind the head.

"So what did you prepare for dinner?" Tirin Tirin asked in a false baritone.

"You are out of your mind, trust me." Nosa began to laugh.

"No action for you tonight if you don't feed me." Tirin Tirin sounded serious.

"My God! Where the hell did they pick you out from?"

"I'm serious... no fiki fiki, if no choppy, choppy." Tirin Tirin continued as he walked into the kitchen.

"I always knew you were gay," Nosa countered.

"Thunder faya ya yansh!" Tirin Tirin shouted from the kitchen.

"My lawd! You have been in this country forever and you still sound and talk like a bush rat!"

"See who's talking; so staying true to my culture makes me a bush rat?" He switched to proper English.

"Who told you that is Nigerian culture?"

"Well, for us who were born with omoroguns, we know what it is to be real unlike all you silver-spoon-fed farts who think speaking Queen's English is your passport to heaven."

"You are just a hater, young man," Nosa called out as he turned down the volume of the television.

"Young man? See this guy o; no respect. You no know say I fit born you?"

"For your village!" Nosa attempted to speak in the same colloquial way.

They both burst out laughing. Tirin Tirin walked out of the kitchen and began taking off his clothes.

"Bros, go undress for room, abeg you."

"You never see naked man before? Abeg, fimisile joor." Tirin Tirin said, taking off his heavily stained jean pants.

"Finer looking men; not your scrawny ass."

"See who was calling me gay. Closet freak. I must find you a woman, by fire or by force!" Tirin Tirin mimicked chagrin.

"Thanks, but no thanks. How was work?" Nosa redirected the

flow.

"Same ole, same ole! They want to kill me with work but dem no fit."

"Atom ant; that's what I should call you."

"Were you born when they were showing that cartoon in Nigeria?"

"I am older than you think or you pretend to think," Nosa said watching Tirin Tirin flop on the couch next to him in his white cotton underpants. He shifted to the far right to get away from the tired-looking man.

"Na age we go chop? Abeg, make I see road. Did you call the medical board?" Tirin Tirin asked with a yawn.

"Yeah."

"When do they say you can start wearing a lab coat and carry a stethoscope?"

"After my exams."

"How many?"

"A lot."

"I told you these folks will burst your balls,"

"Passing exams are no problem for me."

"Okay, I will listen to your story one year from now,"

"I am a straight 'A' student, thank you."

"Life is not about 'As,' my friend."

"Here comes the lecture." Nosa rolled his eyes.

"You should hold my hand and let me lead you; all these years count for experience. This is Canada; it has destroyed the dreams of many an immigrant."

"Positive mindset please, no negativity."

"Okay, as you like it." Tirin Tirin leaned back on the couch.

"But I need to work though, can't keep sitting around the house."

"Don't bother yourself, since you want to take exams, just sit at home and play wifey; you will have all the time in the world to read."

"Come on, be serious. How do I get a job?"

"Depends on the kind of job."

"Something to keep me busy for now."

"Well, the job boards are online, Workopolis, Monster, take your pick."

"I have been sending out resumes for two weeks now, no call back."

"Well, it takes time."

"I don't have time."

"Okay, if you have the liver, I could introduce you to the foreman at my site; he could get you something to do."

"Like?"

"Nothing that needs skills or brains."

"Why are you such an oaf?"

"Because you deserve an oaf." Tirin Tirin replied smiling.

"I'm game."

"Seriously?"

"I have to get out there and start meeting people."

"Trust me, the sort of folks you need to meet are not at a construction site."

"Well, the sort of people I want to meet are not where you think the sort of people I should meet are?"

Tirin Tirin fell silent and looked at the television set. Nosa began to randomly flip the channels.

"You know you can talk to me, right?" Tirin Tirin's voice was serious.

"Of course I know, at least in the moments you are sane."

"I am always sane."

"Few and far in between."

"I like you, Nosa, and I want to help you; just be straight with me."

"Thank you, Sir benefactor — if I could call you that, sir."

"What are you looking for, Nosa?" It came straight from

the heart.

Nosa heard the seriousness in his voice. He went quiet for a fleeting moment then he turned to him.

"How do you mean?"

"Dude, I've been around, seen people, new people coming to this country from all over, starting a new life, you can sense something about them when you meet them, some dislocation, some apprehension, but mostly a huge sense of expectation and bewilderment mixed with a huge dose of hope. With you, it's different."

"What are you talking about?"

"You seem focused on something. I don't know what it is, but I glimpse its shadows in your eyes."

"Okay now I need the crazy Tirin Tirin," Nosa said with an uncomfortable laugh.

"Are you running from something or is someone after you?"

"Look, I'm cool, maybe I've overstayed my welcome here..."
"Come on, you are my brother, my own is your own, I just want to help."

"If I need your help, I will let you know."

"I'm sorry about your parents."

Nosa went quiet. He inhaled deeply and exhaled. His past had followed him to Canada. How much did Tirin Tirin know, he found himself silently asking.

"It is none of my business, I just thought you should know that I have your back and you can talk to me."

"You said so before. I have heard you."

"Sorry, just that I hear you talking to yourself or someone in your room and it makes me wonder if you, like sort of need, you know, help, there is a lot of free counselling in this country, it's fully covered."

"Are you saying I am mad or something?"

"No, not mad, just troubled. Life hasn't been kind to you, there is no need pretending otherwise."

"How much do you know about me?" Nosa turned to him.

There was a moment between them. A moment that felt like aeons as Tirin Tirin weighed his choices. He knew he had to tread carefully and not appear obnoxious or intruding or stifling or cantankerous. He exhaled audibly. It was heavy.

"I know enough."

"Like?"

"The obvious of course."

"And?"

"Something I was wondering why you never spoke about."

"Which is?"

Another moment passed. They held each other's gaze.

"Your brother."

Nosa allowed the hot air rush from his mouth; it came out with a barely audible sound, like a gentle rustle of wind racing through autumn leaves.

"What do you know about my brother?

"Just stuff I heard from home, that's all."

Nosa knew it was an honest answer. He knew Tirin Tirin that much.

"You haven't met my brother, right?" Nosa needed to be sure of his conclusions.

"I wish I have, but I have not."

"You asked me earlier on, what it was I was running from, right?"

Tirin Tirin nodded.

"I am not running from anything. I am just searching for my brother."

"Is he here, like in this country?"

"I believe he is." "I had no idea."

Another moment passed on. This time the sound of the ticking clock could be heard and the eyes of the multiple faces that lived behind the framed pictures that dotted the walls stared at them as though desperate to bear witness to the epochal moment.

"Can you help me find my brother?" Nosa asked in a voice that dripped with all the concealed and conflicted festering pain of his achy breaky heart.

Nicole watched the city flash by from the window of the car. The whine of the engine wasn't ingratiating but somewhat comforting. It reminded her of the humanity of the architects of her misfortune. If the detective couldn't operate a well maintained car, then it meant he had weaknesses, lapses in his mental judgement she could exploit if she was patient and fastidiously observant.

She turned and watched him drive. He was now bespectacled, a change in appearance that was magically transforming. A hint of respectability now hung on his person. She could imagine a police officer looking at him and immediately coming to the conclusion that he was as harmless as an overly pampered poodle. What about this man can she exploit? She found herself asking beneath her breath.

"I still haven't got your name."

He smiled and shook his head, but remained silent. She changed tact.

"What is in this for you?"

He still remained silent, smile lingering on his face.

"What are you going to do to me?"

Silence.

"I know you are taking orders from someone, mister, you don't look like a guy who is capable of evil."

This time he laughed and then fell silent. Smile intact. She gave up.

"Please, let me go, I will do anything, anything you want, I've got some money. I could give it to you and simply disappear and you can tell your bosses that I escaped or that a cop pulled you over and I like screamed, so you had to take off and leave me behind, you are a smart man, you can come up with something they'll believe, I am begging you in the name of God just pull over and let us make a deal, I'm sure you have a sister, or cousin like me, someone who..."

"Shut the fuck up for Christ's sake!" he screamed.

The suddenness of his outburst knocked the panic out of Nicole's system. She fell into a deathly silence and with the same suddenness of his scream, she started crying. It started with a whimper, and then, in a space of several seconds, broke out into a full-bodied cry. It shook her shoulders, bowed her head, streaked her face with hot tears, filled her nose with liquefied snot, opened her mouth and let out a guttural wail.

The Private Investigator was not impressed and kept driving. They were now on Highway 401 which had an average speed of a hundred kilometres per hour, and it was moving freely, so chances that anyone will notice her cry was close to nil. He reached over and switched on the car stereo. He scanned the station, found one on the FM frequency playing Diana Krall's version of "Cry Me a River." It was a jazz station. He loved jazz. It calmed his perpetually agitated nerves. He turned it up so loud it drowned out the wailing of Nicole. Then he relaxed back on his seat and kept driving on. Let her cry and give character to the song.

She did give the song character when she launched at him in a hysterical fit, tearing at his face with her long, red-painted fingernails, screaming, at the top of her voice, intelligible words as she attacked him. The abruptness of her action took him by surprise and caused him to swerve the car right into the path of a trailer travelling at high speed, loaded with a drove of bleating cows.

All anyone who was driving down the highway that day heard was the shrieking of wheels against heated asphalt as both cars and several others behind and beside them tried vainly to avoid a fatal multiple car crash.

Nurse Maria and Harriet stood talking as Andrew sat strapped up in the whirlpool. One's shift was ending and the other beginning. It was their usual handover chat.

"... and she was practically screaming at him, I mean I know he works for her father but please, she needs to show him some respect." Nurse Maria spoke in a conspiratorial tone.

"I would rather just focus on Mr. Sciorra and avoid all the other things going on around here," Nurse Harriet contributed.

"But how can you? It is everywhere."

"All I can do is try."

"Even if you close your eyes and ears, you will still see and hear it."

"Thank God I take the night shift. The silence helps."

"I need the drama to keep me alive."

"Then you shouldn't be complaining."

"I wasn't complaining. I was just talking to you, like two friends catching up, you know what that is like, right?" Nurse Maria was getting pissed at her.

"Of course we are just chatting." the sarcasm was obvious.

"Fine," Nurse Maria opened the file in her hands and began looking through it. "So, I administered one unit of Celexa at three hour intervals, the next dose is due for nine o'clock..."

"What?!" Nurse Harriet exclaimed.

"What's what?" Nurse Maria was surprised as she looked up at her.

"We were supposed to discontinue that."

"When?"

"It is in the notes."

"There is nothing like that here." Nurse Maria looked through the file again.

"Not those notes."

"Which notes?"

"The ones Mr. Neri gave us."

"Oh those. Mr. Vinelatter instructed that we ignore them."

"Mr. Neri instructed we ignore Mr. Vinelatter."

"We can't ignore Mr. Vinelatter; Therese insisted on that."

"Not to me."

"Well, I am sticking with what Therese wants."

"I thought a minute ago you were mad at how she was treating Mr. Neri."

"And you didn't want to involve yourself in the politics," Nurse Maria countered.

"We have to do what is right by Mr. Sciorra."

"Yes, by sticking to what the doctors prescribed."

"You and I know Mr. Sciorra does not need Celexa, come on, antidepressants for a case like this? I mean…"

"I will advise you not to pick sides, Harriet."

"We can't in good conscience…"

"I insist we stick to the prescriptions, Nurse Harriet." There was authority in Nurse Maria's voice.

"But there are second opinions, Mr. Neri said…"

"The grass suffers when two elephants fight, Harriet, don't be the grass."

"What if we…"

"Now I am instructing you as your superior, let it go." It was firm.

They fell silent. The purring sound of the whirlpool could be heard. Andrew sat there starring into nothingness, his eyes in a slight squint as though he was listening to the peculiar tone of the silence. The warm water was necessary for maintaining the tone of his flaccid muscles.

Nurse Harriet looked over at the sitting Andrew. She knew his well-being was all that should matter, but then, she was just a nurse and nominal knowledge preached that doctors knew best, yet she knew how wrong they were, especially in the medical science of the mind, which was the last frontier of medical knowledge, a no man's land; no one knew best, all were searching, all were learning. How dare they claim to know it all? She shook her head in regret as to her powerlessness, then she turned to Nurse Maria, who had been staring at her in cold reproach and spoke.

"Yes Ma'am."

A smattering of birds rose in frightened flight from the college of white spruce trees that stood a couple of metres from the Private Investigator. He was shouting at the top of his voice into the phone. His anger was brimming over as he repeatedly wiped the sweat from his face while he looked at the clear blue waters of the Caledon Lake in front of the cottage where he stood.

It was a private lake and the beautifully large cottages that stood on its shores were owned by some of the wealthiest people in Canada. This was a closed community; a retreat for those who valued their privacy and understood the social power of their gargantuan loads of money and their attention-attracting fame.

"I have a good mind to shoot her straight through the head and piss on her Godforsaken bloody face."

"Let's try calm down." Timothy advised from the other end of the phone in a voice that tried to soothe his frayed nerves but instead stoked his rage the more.

"She fucking tried to kill us!"

"I understand."

"No you don't, you didn't see the mayhem, six cars mashed together, dead folks."

"But you guys weren't one of them."

"Thanks to my skills, that's why."

"What about I throw you say an additional twenty, no, thirty-five thousand, will that make things better?"

"What I want is for you to allow me beat the whore into

a pulp."

"You know I can't do that."

"What's the difference? She should have been dead by now."

"No one is going to kill anyone."

"I meant from the accident. I might be pissed the fuck off, but I'm not crazy."

"Fine, I will throw in something more for your troubles; now let's put it behind us and focus on what we have to do."

The Private Investigator closed his eyes as he replayed the scene on Highway 401; Nicole lunging for him, the pain as her finger nails dug canals on his face, he pulling at the steering and swerving to the left, the thunderous blaring of the horns of the approaching trailer, seeing from his side mirrors as it bore down on them, he pushing Nicole back with his right arm as he swerved the steering back to the right, another car blaring its horns, he swerving back to the left, the car going into a spin, the sounds of screaming wheels as brakes tried to grip the road, he hearing the soothing voice of Diana Krall mixed with the screams of Nicole as the world spun around him, he gripping the steering and turning it the opposite direction of the spin, a skill he had learnt at the beginning of his law enforcement career; the car righting itself and facing the road, he looking through the rear view mirror with his heart thumping so loudly in his chest that his ears ached, his eyes bulging in shock as he saw the mayhem behind him, twisted metals, upturned wheels, bodies of cows and two humans strewn around the highway. It hadn't taken him a second before he went into crisis management mode. He engaged the gear and slowly drove on, desperate not to attract attention to his car by over speeding. Nicole was no longer screaming, only Diana Krall was singing as he drove on, pressing gently on the gas pedals as he got further away. He knew he had to get far away from the accident before the cops arrived. He was a former cop; he knew how things with law enforcement worked.

"Where is she?" Timothy asked.

"Sleeping."

"Sleeping?"

"I gave her something to calm down her nerves; she is a wreck."

"Good."

"What do we do next?"

"I am setting up the meeting with the Editor. I will call you when it is done and give you the terms, then we prep her and get the ball rolling."

"I might need another car. I can't risk this one being pulled over, don't know if anyone pointed it out to the cops."

"The news is saying there is no known cause of the accident; the drivers of the trailer and two cars involved are dead."

"Fuck this bitch!"

"Okay, we are not going over that again." Timothy was stern.

"Fine, I'll let it go; as per the car, I can't risk it."

"I'll send one over."

"Good."

"Hang in there."

"I got it."

He hung up the cell phone and turned around. The luxurious spread of the living room stretched out in front of him. This property had been bought less than two months ago under the company name of one of the firms owned by Timothy through a proxy in Alberta. There was no way it could be traced back to him; there was also no way Timothy himself could be traced to the Private Investigator. They both knew that if shit hit the fan, Timothy would cut the rope and allow the Private Investigator drown. He would allow him take the fall and disappear into the normalcy of Canada. He was paying good money for that surety and chances were that that scenario will not play itself out. They both had a successful history of business between them, too many clandestine operations that had never gone bad. Now it was time to let the ball roll and launch Timothy into the stratosphere, the investigator thought to himself as he walked to the well-stocked bar to pour himself a really stiff, fiery drink.

Nosa tried to steady his arms as he pushed the roller across the ceiling. He could feel his muscles burning and his knees trembling. He bit his lower lip in an effort to force himself to concentrate and ignore the burning pain that seemed to radiate from his face and hands. His eyes burned as sweat flowed into them. How in God's name did anyone do this? He moaned to himself. Less than two hours and he already felt like he was in hell. He shook his head to remove the tears that were flowing from the corners of his eyes; salty tears mixed with salty sweat.

The laughter hit him with the force of gale. He turned his head and spied Tirin Tirin standing in the empty doorway, his trademark work clothes as filthy as usual.

"See person o!" Tirin Tirin teased before doubling over in laughter.

Nosa lowered the roller and turned fully to him. He presented a hilarious picture as he stood covered head to toe in white paint. The gloves on his hands had ridden up, exposing his painted wrist, his eyes and lips were uncovered and peeped out like holes in a white mask, his hair looked like it had greyed overnight.

"Very funny," Nosa retorted.

"Ordinary paint na im make you look like ojuju like dis? Chei! See last aje butter o!" Tirin Tirin said as he walked into the large empty room.

Nosa slouched in weariness as he approached. He had actually underestimated how tired he was. There he was about to drop in a dead faint for working for such a short time in the construction site, and there approaching him was the little specimen of man moving as though he was on holidays on a beach with spotless white sands and clear blue waters in the Caribbean. He saw the heavy back-breaking work Tirin Tirin was doing earlier, building the wooden framework and hammering in dry walls, then sanding them into smoothness after laying putty here and there on the uneven parts—that was after having to lift some huge metal pillions earlier in the day.

"Abeg give me dat thing before dem talk say Tirin Tirin don use labourer work kill their pikin." Tirin Tirin was still joking as he reached for the roller which was screwed onto a long, red plastic pole.

Nosa handed it over to him and looked around for a place to sit as he felt his legs about to give up underneath him. He had always prided himself in being fit, but this wasn't for gym addicts, this was for people who had inner strength acquired only from the rigours of true stamina-demanding labour. He truly felt like he had lived his entire life in a cocoon of comfort. This was the real life. There was nowhere to sit, so he sat on the floor, arms spread out behind him, legs stretched out in front of him, head hanging back, mouth open, expelling exhausted breath. Tirin Tirin looked at him and shook his head in pity.

The construction site was in Markham; a new residential development in the Morningside and Markham neighbourhood. Fifty townhouses on land that had previously been a sprawling farm, land that had to bow to the insatiable hunger of a city that expanded as rapidly as the stomach of a child suffering from a debilitating bout of kwashiorkor. It was being built by a construction firm Tirin Tirin had worked with for five years. He was not part of a union. Actually, he refused to be part of a union and worked freelance, which made work unstable for him, but then, he appreciated the freedom that came with working without the encumbrances of union rules, most importantly, it gave him the ability to get his own jobs at cutthroat fees or even at fees that cut the unionised workers owing to the fact that his fees were cheaper and it also allowed him to work as a jack of all trades; masonry, tiling, drywall, painting, plumbing, hardwood and the list went on and on. He prided himself on leading an honest life and earning from legitimate endeavours unlike some of the Nigerians he knew who would rob the system at the drop of a hat to fuel the demands of a life on the fast lane. Age had thought him that only those who ran a long distance race at a steady pace would arrive at the finish line, even if they actually didn't win the race, but then, didn't one have to finish a race to win it?

"My friend, stand up before they fire me for bringing a lazy ass here," Tirin Tirin ordered in a jocular but serious way.

"Don't they have time for break here?"

"You have worked for how many minutes, and you are asking for break. You are a joker. No one will give you work if you carry on like this."

"Okay, let me catch my breath."

"I told a righteous lie to get you this job, even if you must take a break you have to pretend like you are working." Tirin Tirin's voice went into an audible whisper as he looked around to make sure no one was watching.

Nosa exhaled and then struggled to his feet. He stood in an akimbo stance and looked at Tirin Tirin.

"So can you quickly teach me how to do this?"

"I thought you had painted before."

"In fine art class, yes."

"You are truly useless."

"It is hard work."

"I told them you have years of painting experience."

"Yes I do, but not this kind. Give me a brush and a canvas, put me in front of an easel and I will show you wonders."

"Look at this mad man o! Where do you think you are? Wake up, my friend, and smell your stinking yansh."

Nosa started to laugh. Even in the most serious of circumstances, Tirin Tirin just had a way of making the heaviest load feel lighter.

"Okay look at me, pay attention, I will not do this twice." Tirin Tirin winked at him, raised the roller to the ceiling, and started painting.

His strokes were smooth, parallel movements that were so immaculate, he covered more areas in the one minute he was painting than Nosa had done in the last hour.

"Hold it light and don't push hard; let it roll, easy, effortless; let it kiss the ceiling not like a randy goat or a drunken sailor, but like a Casanova, a man that knows that lighter kisses are what build into deeper, wetter kisses; there, there, like that; one hand high up on the pole, the other gripping the bottom end; one leg in front of the other; bend this knee slightly, the other one, extend it; your hip, not too bent; let it rock, like the salsa, back and forth; like the slow grind of the missionary style, the type that coerces out the mighty O; don't raise your head in a total ninety degrees, more like a slow upturn; you don't paint right on top of your head but just right in front, so you look ahead, not simply above; do you feel me?"

"Yes... Monsignor."

"Good. Oya, your turn." He stopped and handed the roller over to Nosa.

Nosa took position and raised the roller to the ceiling.

"Aren't you forgetting something?" Tirin Tirin enquired.

"What?"

"You need more paint on the roller."

"Oh, forgot."

Nosa lowered the roller and dipped it in the trowel that was filled with paint. He rolled it twice and raised it back up. Paint dripped from it to the floor which was covered by transparent tarpaulin.

He began to paint, his mind relaxing and allowing the words of Tirin Tirin assuage him. The days of viva examinations at the bedside of countless patients at the hospital in Nigeria came to the fore. He learnt by hearing and watching not only by reading, rendering the correct answers spontaneously upon hearing the questions from the sadistic consultants that served as medical examiners, and he always performed above average. Those were the days of academic rigors, the time when passing was to him what swimming was to a fish, but this time, he failed woefully.

"Kai, so you mean you didn't hear anything I said?" An exasperated Tirin Tirin asked.

"Practice makes perfect."

"Not here o, they expect you to come prepared. Oya, stop."

Nosa stopped, lowered the brush, and turned to Tirin Tirin. His face showed the depth of his dismay, not just with the demands of the job, but with his own performance. He was used to being good at everything he put his hand to and being a failure was anathema to him.

"You have a stomach ache and a fever; in fact, you have been shitting water-water shit, you know, diarrhoea; you can't carry on and need to go home; they will allow you go and you won't come back again. It's better one of us loses this job than both of us."

"But I need to work."

"There are factories looking for clueless labour."

"And I can like start immediately?"

"Of course. It's daily wages; they hire easily and fire easily."

"Hard work?"

"We will be selective."

Nosa fell silent as though lost in thought.

"By the way, I have some good news."

Nosa's eyes lit up. Tirin Tirin smiled.

"A friend of a friend says he knows someone who knows someone who might know where your brother is."

"Really?"

"Do I look like someone who tells unrighteous lies?" Tirin Tirin was grinning.

Nosa surprised himself by abruptly hugging Tirin Tirin.

"Hey, hey, dude, easy, you are supposed to have diarrhoea."

Nosa disentangled himself and pumped a fist into the air.

"You are the best!"

"Heafee forkoryo, abeg go report yasef to Oga foreman." Tirin Tirin was smiling as he playfully pushed Nosa towards the doorless door.

Pirlo & Sons was the construction company that Tirin Tirin worked for. It was owned by the Bortoluccis; a large family that had arrived in Canada in the early 20s and had vast holdings in real estate and construction stretching across the country. Tirin Tirin was looked at by Silvio Bortolucci, the third son of the family scion, Mario, as not just an employee but as a friend. The little man's charm had worked its magic on the burly man one afternoon when they had found themselves in a series of unfortunate events, two and a half years ago. In an unexplainable fashion, as life evolved, every piece of their lives had fallen in place, like the pieces on the chessboard of the gods.

And as they left the empty room that day, and walked along the plastic sheet covered corridor, Nosa and Tirin Tirin without affirming it to each other, felt the tightening of the screws of the bonds of their friendship and the fires of their trust burn brighter and for a moment they unconsciously held hands, as though satisfying an inert need for a tactile communication of their present state of being, just like two close friends would innocently do, any given day, on the streets of Nigeria.

The first thing that hit Therese when they pulled up in front of the detached, red-brick two storey building in their silver 600 series Mercedes Benz was how immaculate the grounds that surrounded the silent house were kept. It was like looking at the

Chateau de Versailles on a smaller scale. This was horticulture at its finest. Colours clashing together in beautiful harmony, flowers, shrubs combined in patterns that gave shape and character to the compound. There were dahlias and marigolds, zinnias and snapdragons, gardenias and hollyhocks, moss roses and geraniums, plumbagos and carnations, irises and orchids, sunflowers and bleeding hearts, there were more and so much more, colours of the rainbow in breathing plants; it was like the heaven of gardens, a certain stillness that spoke of unshakeable peace. This was the abode of Sibongile Nene and Therese was entering it with a certain foreboding which she really couldn't understand.

She turned and looked at Angela.

"Isn't it beautiful?" She asked as though trying to confirm if the perfection she was viewing was only visible to her eyes.

Angela turned to her and nodded her head. Her smile was wide and her eyes, giddy. She could feel the energy of the place; she was in tune with the vibrations. What unsettled Therese was actually calming her.

Phillip turned around from the front passenger seat. He was smiling. It wasn't a smile of pride or an I-told-you-so kind of self aggrandisement; it was more like I am happy you are here to behold that which I have beheld.

"Wait till you see the inside."

Therese didn't know if she should smile in response to that because she honestly felt queasy about being here in the first place, so uneasy about it that she had requested Angela came with her. But she knew that if she was to allow Sibongile into her father's life, she had to be sure that she was the right person for the job. In Therese's world of the politically correct and high-society pretentious veneer—that plastic mask one had to wear to hide the stark truth of one's humanity—a psychologist was expected to dress the part and act likewise, there was no place for theatrical dressing and alternative living. If you could not speak the language of Freud and Jung, or practise the often discounted act of the electric shock, you could just as well shut up, pack up, leave town, or at most, open up a bar somewhere in the boondocks.

Angela opened the door and stepped out. Phillip and Therese did the same. The uniformed driver remained in the air-conditioned car. They all stood motionless for a minute as though attempting to become part of the glorious whole; the white-washed gravels on the driveway; the fountain that created a cul-de-sac in front of the house; the endless well-coiffed flower beds; well-trimmed, asymmetrically-arresting hedges; and the huge coniferous trees that stood a distance away in parallel lines on the right and left as though protecting the haven of bliss from all external attacks, whether seen or unseen. They stood and they watched and the silence around them was so deep that it drained out the purring of the luxury car before them. There was no wind, no rustle, no movement; just a pleasurable stillness and two of them luxuriated in it while the other one tried to put under her control, her disquiet.

The sound of the huge wooden door opening was what brought them out of the moment. They turned towards it, and there, standing with a broad, welcoming smile, was the delightful Sibongile Bene.

"Sanibonani," she said with a short bow, hands clasped in front of her. She was wearing a spotless white gown and her hair was wrapped in a white turban. There was no jewelry or make up on her but instead of her being plain because of the lack thereof, she glowed with the perfection of her simplicity.

"Welcome to Ubuntu." She beamed.

Phillip looked at Therese expecting her to respond and when he saw her placid look, he hurriedly spoke.

"Thank you."

"Please come in," She continued and then stepped back to

usher the way into the house that loomed invitingly beyond her.

Angela gently nudged Therese and she obediently walked towards the open door, Angela in tow and Phillip taking the rear. They could hear music floating out of the house. It was foreign; a mixture of African musical instruments that exuded the most angelic sounds. If Therese could taste it, she would have called the music sweet. She could hear the sonorous chimes of the *kalangba*, the fluid twang of the lute, the shrill wail of the ivory horn and the intricate melodies of the *sanza*.

"Beautiful," Therese said again as she surrendered to the language of the foreign symphony.

Osasu peered hard at the words that shone from the computer screen. They were in paragraphs and fitted into columns. In certain parts were pictures and pie charts. He licked his lips in apprehension and then clicked on the back button. He needed to be sure. The page appeared and he read the heading again; ANDREW SCIORRA DONATES 100 MILLION DOLLARS TO THE ROYAL CANADIAN MUSEUM.

"Damn!" He dragged it out.

This had been his routine. Grabbing every spare minute to research and research, he was obeying the Boy Scouts motto: "Be prepared." He pulled out the lower drawer and brought out a compact disc. He opened the drive in the computer and inserted the disc. His finger pressed the close button and it slid in. There was a whirring sound and a circle appeared on the computer screen. A window appeared and Osasu copied the link of the page into the window. He pressed enter and a multitude of figures began racing along the screen. Another window popped up and website links began appearing in that window. He smiled and waited for the circle to disappear.

He had bought this software from a Chinese computer hacker he was introduced to by a Russian contact he met in a nightclub at Bathurst and Steeles. The programme had an algorithm that linked a website address to other websites that contained financial information of names on the website. It was expensive software and it worked.

The circle stopped rotating and Osasu clicked on one of the links on the other window. A website popped up; it read: "MERCANTILE BANK OF CANADA." On the page was the name ANDREW SCIORRA. It had an account number and all other information. In the log-in section of the page, were the account number and password; all he had to do was press enter. This had worked before, so he didn't hesitate. He pressed enter and a second and a refresh later, he was in the bank account of Andrew Sciorra.

He sat back on his chair as he looked at the account details. The balance read: five million two hundred and seventy four thousand three hundred and twenty two dollars thirty one cents. This wasn't what he wanted. He needed the big deal. Osasu understood that if he transferred any amount of money from this account, red flags would shoot up. These accounts had account officers who monitored the transactions. If he touched it, the account officer would know that Andrew was indisposed, so naturally would not be accessing his bank account. The new account officers were not only wealth managers, but lifestyle managers; they knew you in and out. He wouldn't take the risk. He logged out of the bank account.

He wanted access to the wired accounts. He wanted to move a huge chunk. One go, one hit; made for life. He had done it before even though the amount of money wasn't this large. He closed his eyes and tried to block out the memories that threatened to flood his mind. They were painful. They were secret. He had kept them hidden since that night, long time ago. That day when all he knew, all he trusted, all he dreamt about, came crashing down. That starry, silent night, when Osasu Eweka died.

12

The Private Investigator sat watching the door of the restaurant. It was the Bistro 999 at Adelaide and University. A high-priced restaurant on the twenty-fourth floor of the Metropolitan Insurance building that attracted ultra successful professionals.

He looked at his military-issue Cabot wristwatch and sighed to himself; thirty five minutes late. He let his eyes rove across the room that was lit by the natural light, which streamed in from the glass walls. His eyes settled on one of the walls. He could see the CN tower rise up majestically in the afternoon air. The tallest freestanding structure in the world; 553 metres with a telecommunication antenna that stretched so high it looked as though it was destined to poke the butt of the heavenlies.

He allowed his mind stray into his past; the days when he led a crack investigative squad in the Toronto Metropolitan Police. Twenty-two years of meritorious service. A career in which he earned all the medals and citations that existed in the force. He was a legend.

The events of that Sunday night seeped into his roving mind; he was off duty, meeting up with friends at a bar in the Danforth and Pape neighbourhood. He could still remember that night, the crisp cold that bit into your skin but did not freeze you, the clean air that made the act of breathing a near-orgasmic action, the near-empty street as the people of Greek town packed up to go home to their already sleeping families. He remembered looking at his wristwatch and commenting to his near-obese friend that he had promised his wife that he would be home before midnight. His friend had told him that it was already five minutes to twelve and that there was no way he could make it across town to his semi-detached house in Etobicoke. He had protested feebly and when they all insisted he stayed, he had grudgingly obliged.

When he had brought out his phone to call her, the same friend had snatched the phone from his hand. The friend had jokingly advised him never to ask for permission but rather, only forgiveness as a sorry-pity story would always get any wife to forgive one. This was to prevent a domestic Armageddon that would result if one did not run straight home after wifey had ordered it in response to the call that explained why one couldn't make it home in time.

So he had put the phone back in his pocket and had continued drinking into the wee hours of the morning. Five hours later, he woke up in a private hospital room at the St. Michael's Hospital on Queen Street east, bandaged from head to toe, aching like pain was the colour red. It had taken him five arduous weeks before he could talk, let alone eat solid food; it was then he was finally told what had taken place that night. His wife had sat by his bed and listened, while the Special Investigative Unit officer and his divisional head had informed him about what had happened.

They had spoken about a family returning from the Opera; father, wife, two daughters, and a boyfriend. They had told him about the accident. Five deaths. Total mayhem. He had no recollection of even getting into his car that early morning. His alcohol count was quadruple the legal limit of 0.08 percent. It was a disaster. His life imploded. He lost everything; his job, his beautiful trophy wife, his house, his good name. All he had left was the bottle. And did he attack it as though he was bent on committing suicide by fatal alcohol intoxication? It was in that state of deep depression and self loathing that Timothy had found him. That was more than five years ago. They had bonded and without his even realising it, Timothy had reinvented him, given him a reason to live, and killed all the good there was left in him.

"Hi." The feminine voice pulled his head around.

He saw her standing right there in front of him. Slender frame in a body-hugging business suit, hair pulled back in such a severe fashion that it made her look like she was wearing a black ski cap. Standing there was the proverbial barracuda, the famous magazine Editor-in-Chief that was notorious for hammering a story with such vengeance that the subject of the story had only three options: resign, confess, or commit suicide. They called her a social crusader, a fighter for the truth, a destroyer of evil, the protector of the people, and the conscience of the Canadian society. She believed all of it and lived it out to the latter.

"You are the gentleman with something for me?" She spoke in a cold tone as she took a seat at the table.

"Good afternoon."

"So, show me what you have."

"Have you had lunch?"

"Don't fuck around with me; show me what you have or I am out of here." She was playing the game her own way.

"I was of the opinion we were here to discuss."

"I do not discuss with bag boys."

The Private Investigator felt his anger surge up from the pit of his stomach. He clenched his butt cheeks and caught it before it rushed up his throat and exploded all over this utterly rude lady that sat in front of him with a smirk on her face.

"I have a good mind to stand up and walk."

"I dare you."

He bit his lower lip and then leaned forward.

"The stories about you are right on the mark."

"You have approximately five seconds to give me what I came here for."

He sat there looking at her and then leaned back on his chair. He was counting in his mind; three, four, five. She sprang up and spun on her feet. He leaned forward in alarm.

"Wait!"

She stopped and turned back. Her frown was genuine and frightening. He was not scared. He pointed to her chair. She did not sit. He exhaled.

"These are our terms. You, a camera man and a sound man, a place of our choosing."

"I need pictures too."

"Three people, that's it."

She went quiet for a moment, then she spoke, "Fine."

"We want an 'all media exposure.'"

"I run a magazine."

"All media or no deal."

Again she went quiet, then she spoke "Fine."

"Unending coverage until the subject does what is right."

"And what will that be?"

"Suicide."

"Come on, I don't guarantee that."

"But you have delivered in the past, haven't you?"

"You think I take pride in that?"

"We really don't care; it is your guarantee that matters."

"Look, I am no Nancy Grace."

"There are a lot of people who will call that a lie."

She kept quiet. He could watch the thought running around behind her eyes.

"I will have to run my backgrounds, make sure the story pans out, make sure everything ties in, before I will go to press. I am not going to be railroaded."

"Trust me, it all pans out."

"It better."

"So, are we game?"

"One question."

"Shoot."

"Why are you doing this?"

He smiled as he looked at her. He put his hands behind his head, leaned back with all the lethargy he could afford, then he spoke.

"How will a bag boy know the answer to that question, madam?"

She was caught out by his response and stood there silently fuming. She hated losing the advantage and surrendering the last laugh.

Nurse Harriet tucked Andrew into bed. He was propped up on the bed, his back resting on expensive eiderdown pillows. He was wearing silk pajamas and had his thinning hair well combed. His skin was sallow, his jaw slack, and his eyes half-open. The expansive bedroom stretched out all around the king-size four-post bed on three sides.

She was singing to him. It was Nat King Cole's "Unforgettable." Phillip had told her that it was Andrew's favourite. She hoped he could hear her in the silence of his locked up mind. She actually believed he heard her. Her eyes played to the picture stands on the bedside table; one of Therese, one of Annabelle. She picked up the picture of Annabelle and looked closely at it. Her features were so delicate and fine, like how one would imagine an angel would look like. Her hair flowed down in its lushness, each strand on fire with its golden glow. Annabelle was smiling with an open honesty that was heart-tugging, when one remembered how she died. She shook her head and laid the picture back on the table and looked around the room. This was the room where Annabelle slept. This was the bed that bore the sanctity of her marriage vows. She could see her taste all around her; the finery of the dark brown window blinds, the light grey walls flushing with the thick, lush, grey rug, the brown leather couches with cream throw pillows that formed a mini living room a short distance away. She quickly tore her eyes from it all as she refused to allow sadness creep into her soul, but it was too late, so she turned her gaze to Andrew.

"You deserve a whack on your head, Mr. Sciorra," she said in the strictest possible tone she could muster. "How dare you treat such a fine lady like trash?"

Andrew stared ahead through his half-open eyes. Spittle dripped down his open mouth as though in response to her question.

"I really don't know what's wrong with you men; your head is all wrapped between your legs. What the hell were you thinking?" she continued. "What did she do to deserve being treated like an afterthought?"

Andrew's head slowly bowed as he fell asleep.

"Now, don't you dare sleep on me, Sir; you still have to take your meds."

She turned and picked up the tray from the trolley that stood a short distance from her. The little cups had five tablets in them, one of which was Celexa. She picked them up with one hand and turned them into a shallow plastic spoon, then she picked a canter of water which had a depressed trough, and just when she was about turning to Andrew, she stopped.

A moment passed with her standing there looking at the medication. Her breath was coming in short gasps. She looked over at Andrew, then exhaled loudly.

"This is not right." It came out with the force of deep conviction.

She placed the canter back on the trolley and marched to the bathroom. In that moment, she decided to stop administering the medication to Andrew, to alter the files to reflect the lie that she had administered them, and to stand firmly on the side of Phillip. Even as she flushed the capsules down the toilet, she still couldn't say, in all honesty, if she was doing it out of pity for Andrew, or silent love for the quiet, sweet, affable Phillip.

For a woman like her, there was no hope in her attracting a man of such calibre; she, a black woman from the dodgy Finch and Driftwood neighbourhood and he, the polished white man of particular pedigree, but then, she reasoned to herself, maybe if she did what was right, then God in his unfathomable mercies could do what was right by her. Miracles did happen, she reasoned to herself, and no sooner did the thought flash across her mind that she put it to rest.

"This isn't about Phillip or Andrew. It is about me." Harriet valiantly convinced herself, shaking her head as she spoke as though the action in itself would force her conflicted mind into believing her profession.

She had a moral compass and she would be damned if she ignored the direction towards which it was leading her. Nurse Harriet audibly chastised herself, every bristling thought captured in a venomous hiss.

The hallway had terrazzo flooring. It had an illustration of the cosmos at the center of which, instead of the normal shining light, was a dazzling man/woman, arms upturned, radiating light to all parts of the sprawling image.

Therese looked at it, taking it in as she walked carefully along. Angela was looking at the paintings on the wall. They were all of different landscapes. Natural. Tranquil. Eternal. At the end of the hallway was a large stained window. It stretched all the way to the high ceilings and let in just enough light to give the house an aura of sanctity.

The exultant Sibongile led the way down the hallway towards the staircase, which had two landings. A contemplative Therese followed; behind her was the mesmerised Angela, and taking the rear was the expectant Phillip.

"Behind the house are our gardens, sport facilities, exercise room, and a mini golf course, and when we get upstairs, I will show you the living quarters of the brothers and sisters in our care." Sibongile spoke in a calm voice.

They had already taken a tour of the first floor of the house, which comprised of the dining rooms, kitchens, consultation rooms, private meeting lounges, administrative offices, laboratories, and other medical facilities. She had also shown her the set of lounges she called, LOVE, HAPPINESS, AND PEACE. She said they were for reflection and meditation; a communal bonding triumvirate.

Therese hadn't asked questions, but simply nodded. She was still thinking, still wondering if Sibongile was the right person for Andrew. She needed to make her mind up before deciding on her next step of action because she had promised Phillip that she would hear Sibongile with an independent mind; a mind that closed the door to the opinions of Timothy before she either allowed this strange-looking psychologist take charge of her father's journey back to full health, or shut the door squarely in the face of her unorthodox medical practises.

They ascended the staircase. Sibongile kept turning back as she recounted stories of past events and supplied more information as to the purpose of the retreat. They got to the first landing and turned left, down a long corridor which had doors on both sides. It looked like a floor in one of the five-star hotels they had been to; beautiful carpeting, ornate lighting, colours painted in a subdued colour that looked light grey under the lighting but was in fact ash. Therese stole a glance at the other part of the corridor; it was the exact replica of the one down which they were walking. She turned back to the team.

"Can we see the rooms?" Therese finally asked.

"Yes, I want to show you an empty room," Sibongile responded.

"I will prefer an occupied one," Therese continued.

"We value the privacy of those in our care."

"I do have to see someone, some patient, you can't be the only one in this entire place." Therese had stopped walking. The others stopped.

"I am not alone here."

"Where is everyone?"

"In these rooms, most of them I mean; they are here."

"And why can't I see them?"

Angela watched on in rising interest. Phillip's discomfort was apparent.

"It is the hour, that's why."

"What hour?"

"Of rest, recovery, reuniting with the wholeness of self."

"And the staff?"

"To care for, you have to be refreshed."

"You mean the whole house is sleeping?"

"Replenishing as we continue on the journey to full recovery."

"So you mean I wouldn't see anyone else but you?"

"You will if you can wait."

"How long?"

"Two hours in human terms."

"Come off it, would you?" Therese said rolling her eyes in exasperation.

"Come off what?"

"You don't have to over-flog your spiritual piousness." she

threw out every word.

"I know; all I have to do is be that which I have been blessed to be."

"Whatever."

Silence rained as the two women looked at each other. Angela shifted her gaze to the door closest to her. She stared at it as though hoping she could see through the doors. Phillip fidgeted for a moment, then he spoke.

"Do you still want to show us the rest of the house?" he asked Sibongile.

"If Miss Sciorra is still interested, I am more than willing," She responded, looking at the frowning Therese.

"I do not have two hours to spare."

"Perhaps we could retire to my office or one of the visitor lounges to talk."

"If I do not see any other person then there won't be a need to talk."

"Would you rather I break the rules to please you?" Sibongile asked.

"I would you did all that is in your power to convince me that you are the right person for my father."

"That is why I suggested we talk."

"I insist on seeing some other souls here."

"Two hours and you will."

Another period of silence ensued. Therese watched Sibongile hold the smile on her face; the peaceful mien that seemed to ooze from her, somehow irritated Therese. She took a deep breath and instantly decided to take a chance and obey her gut instincts.

"I am out of here."

She turned abruptly and headed for the staircase.

"Angela, let's go." She didn't bother calling Phillip. It was his to decide; stay here and step over the line into enemy territory, come with her, and perhaps, there could be a chance for redemption.

Angela hesitated for a minute. She knew what she felt was a deep belief that this was the right place for Andrew. She could feel the healing in the air, the light that seemed to radiate out of everything, the oneness of love that was Sibongile, but then, she also knew who was boss. She managed an apologetic smile to Sibongile, and then hurried after the rapidly descending Therese, her last glance being a plea to Phillip to come along.

Phillip watched them go and turned to Sibongile. He shook his head.

"I am sorry."

"Like I said before, no need to be sorry; God works in mysterious ways."

"I really believed she had changed her mind."

"His ways are not our ways."

Phillip exhaled audibly and looked down the staircase; Angela's back disappeared from view. He turned to Sibongile.

"I better get going."

"Go in peace, my brother."

Phillip smiled, bowed, turned, and walked away briskly.

13

Nosa stood outside the large rectangular building that was dotted with loading docks and sucked in the cool air. He held his knees and bent over in a bid to catch his breath. Right at that moment he felt like he had run a marathon.

He tried to move but the steel-toe boots that hugged his feet felt like they had tonnes of bricks in them. He lifted his right hand to his face and was shocked at the wetness he felt.

"I can't believe I'm crying," he whispered incredulously to himself and willed his tears to cease. Just when he thought he had a grip on his emotions, he burst into tears again.

He wept and wept.

Alone out there on the tarred lot, Nosa let go of every emotion he had bottled inside himself ever since he arrived in Canada nearly two months ago. The strain of beginning a new life was breaking his resolve to find Osasu and unearth the reason behind his self-serving actions. He crouched to stop himself from falling over on his head.

"Why did I come?" he mumbled as he sobbed.

He had never done work as hard as this, never been so far from home without the warm support of abundant money, comfortable accommodation, and loving parents who were with him in flesh or a simple phone call away. Now, here he was in the country of his birth, but not his upbringing. A country that didn't connect with him as home, that didn't recognise his pain, or appreciate his desires. He wasn't Canadian in the least; he was more British or American since he had spent many a wonderful vacation in those countries, and here he was, after over a decade in the country in whose hospital he had stepped into the world, a stranger in his motherland.

This was the third job he had got after the botched experience at the construction site. The first one was at a huge food processing plant, where he had worked in the cold room lifting and stacking huge boxes of chicken into refrigerated trucks. He lasted two days and had to quit when he couldn't stand straight. His back had given out, his arms ached to the very nerve endings, his fingers, toes, and ears were frozen to the very edge of frostbite. He had pretended all was well, not wanting to appear a weakling to Tirin Tirin, but when he overslept his alarm clock and Tirin Tirin's furious shaking of his sleeping body, there was no denying he was spent. So under the insistence of Tirin Tirin, he had quit.

The second job was at a garbage processing plant. It wasn't the fully automated modern plants that had sprung up around the suburban fringes of the city but one of the archaic, manual-labour-intensive set ups that were right in the city. It was large, dingy, and the work was back breaking. He and a team of over twenty men had to manually lift heavy sacks of garbage, open the sacks, and empty the contents into huge metal containers under which were wheels. When they were full, they had to push them over to a huge crane, hook it up to the dangling tether hooks, and guide the operator as he lifted the container into another part of the warehouse where a hall filled with women sorted out the contents and bagged them in bales, which were then arranged into different categories by Nosa and the same team of men for onward sale to people from all parts of the globe in terms of nationalities, who would then ship them out to be sold in the second-hand markets that existed in the cities and towns of the hopefully developing world and the hopelessly underdeveloped world. Nosa had lasted two weeks on the job before he was fired for taking incessant breaks. He just couldn't keep up and deserved the ruthless teasing he got from the ever-jocular Tirin Tirin, who forced him to arm wrestle with him to prove his manhood. He acquiesced and was beaten in the fifteen bouts they had. For the next week, every time Tirin Tirin came back from work, he shouted playfully as he shut the main door of the apartment behind him.

"Now, where is my bitch?"

And when he didn't respond, conveniently ignoring him while purring over a book or watching TV, Tirin Tirin still continued.

"There's my bitch."

Shaking his head in pity and disgust never forced Tirin Tirin to stop, because he always ended his solo dialogue with the words, "Hey gurl, daddy's back!" It came out with the vocal draw of a late-night comedy talk show host in the likes of Jay Leno; actually, more old school, enter Arsenio Hall.

And when he couldn't stay at home any longer, he had gone out to the labour agencies and had submitted himself for work, and once again, in the spirit of before, he had been sent to this auto parts factory where, in brow-beating heat, he was expected to receive hot, new rubber parts from a mechanical arm, dip it into a vat full of coolant, and drop it on a conveyor belt. It wasn't that the part was too heavy; it was not heavy, but it was hot. It wasn't that the coolant was too cold and the smell, pungent; it was cold and extremely pungent, that was why he had to wear a huge pair of rubber gloves and a respirator over his nose and mouth. It was more that the speed at which the mechanical arm delivered the part was so superhumanly fast that even before he could dip the part into the coolant, let alone drop the cooled part on the conveyor belt, the mechanical arm already had another one outstretched for pick up, and whether he was ready to pick it up or not, the forceps, like claws of a mechanical arm, opened and the part fell out. Before he realised it, he was already standing with hot rubber automobile parts all around his trembling, tired feet. He couldn't reach down to pick them up out of fear that he would be buried deep if he wasted one more minute in receiving the parts that were already being offered him by the merciless mechanical arm, but then, another reason was that he really didn't trust the stability of his back. He feared that if he bent down he might not be able to straighten back up. That was how much his back was killing him. It was radiating a deep pain that pushed him to the brink of sheer collapse. A pain he was sure others must have felt before, and complained to him about while he worked as a doctor in Nigeria; one he must have nodded in understanding of but now knew he never truly understood. This was the miserable life on the bottom rungs and he never imagined he would one day experience it.

Nosa hated Canada and its innocuous maple leaf flag at those moments with the very fibre of his being, but he was smart enough not to allow it cloud his appreciation of certain parts of the country, because he knew that the complaints that coursed through his soul as regards the job at the factory were infinitesimal when compared with life at the bottom rungs in Nigeria. Back home, it was a living hell to exist at so low a level. The society had no pity and gave no protection. It milked you and abused you. It neglected you and disenfranchised you. It refused to give you recognition as a human being deserving of respect or appreciate you as a living soul capable of anything other than menial labour. You did as you were told in the most inhumane of conditions with miserly wages as recompense. If you refused, someone else was so very willing to take your place. In a country of very few jobs, what you got was what you took. Nosa had observed this on the sidelines. He had heard drivers complain as he sat in the rear of the air-conditioned luxury cars that zipped him all around Lagos. He had heard of the hellish misery that existed in Lagos and even though he could see some semblance of it, he was innocuous to its real nature or dastardly effect. He was protected from its sharp talons by the pedigree of his family and the depth of their wealth. And when it all changed and he had to leave the land he knew as home, he had fancied that life would not be as hard as it was for the unfortunate in Nigeria. He was heading for Canada; a land of surplus and equal opportunity, a land that called to all beings from all nations, "come to our shores and we will give you hope where you had none, a quality life where you simply existed, a future where you lived only for today." He really did believe he would pick himself up from the disaster that had befallen him and begin to build back again when he boarded the flight that day, several months ago in Nigeria. He really, truly believed that there might be challenges, but nothing he couldn't overcome. He was truly ready. He was psyched in finding Osasu, obtaining closure, and truly beginning the real life he was ordained by God to live. That was the unflagging strength of his conviction.

It was because of this that he had never imagined it to be this hard when he first mulled the thought of how he was to survive when he got to Canada. It sounded so easy then. There was McDonald's at the end of the day or even Wal-Mart he had thought to himself, not considering the fact that his over six-feet-four frame made him stick out like a sore thumb at those jobs and instantly created a discomfort both in him and the customers he was serving; well, it took Tirin Tirin pointing that out to him before he actually realised it.

"See this giant o! You no go go get better job? Agbaya, Oloshi!" he had advised when he first asked what the requirements of getting a job at McDonald's were. And to the question of getting one at Wal-Mart he had said,

"Fuck, dude, don't you think you kinda like huge for this job? This is for the bitches or the man bitches. Fine-ass, tall, strong-looking guy like you gotta have some real job. Unless you actually a sissy in dem man pants," he said waving his left hand in front of his face, other hand placed on right hip, head moving from side to side, hip pushed to the side, voice an octave high into the feminine range.

And when Nosa had tried to explain that he really didn't care what people thought and that all he needed was a job to keep his mind active and his pocket full, Tirin Tirin had surmised with his eyes rolling in disbelief,

"Puhleeezzzz brovaaa! Those jobs will fry your brains. Seriously, bro, you don't even need a brain to flip burgers or stick price tags on some fucking cheap stuff on endless racks. Come on, didn't you say you were a doctor or somfin?"

As far as Nosa was concerned, Tirin Tirin was a living case of an endearing individual with multiple personality disorder, or, in more medical vocabulary, dissociative identity disorder. He just could switch characters with a kiss of his teeth.

Thinking about Tirin Tirin cheered him up, so much so that he stood up, wiped his face clean, looked at his wristwatch, and decided to go to the lunchroom to spend the remaining forty-five minutes of his one hour break. He walked down towards the lit side entrance of the building, sharing his glances between the rows of cars to his right and the deserted bridge that stood over dense foliage about a hundred metres in front of him.

He got to the metal door, opened it, and stepped in. The door swung shut behind him. He was standing in a small holding ante room. He looked up at a camera that was pointed at the door. He smiled into it. There was a buzz and the inner door opened. He gave a thumbs up to the security officer he knew was watching him and walked into the factory.

It was well-lit, yet the steam that billowed at intervals from certain parts of the large hall, idle forklifts, and the blinking red lights gave it the appearance of a war front deserted on the brink of an assault. He walked towards the sign that pointed out the way to the lunch room.

Once there, he made his way to a vacant chair at the far end, avoiding eye contact with the men and women that sat eating and chatting at various parts of the well-lit, spacious room. He sat down and looked at the bank of microwaves at the far end, the refrigerator, the washing sink, the drinking water dispenser, the safety posters, and bric-a-brac that occupied the far wall of the room. This was where they were meant to stretch their tired limbs, fill their empty stomachs, and occupy their idle minds, so that they had enough strength to go hard once again at the slave work; all this for a miserly eleven dollars an hour, but that was for the daily labourer. He heard the full-time staff made twenty-seven dollars an hour, such discrepancy in amount for the same back-breaking work, but then, the labour agency was paid seventeen dollars, they kept six dollars and gave him eleven dollars, still there was a difference of ten dollars. He couldn't understand why there was that difference, especially when the full-time staff also got the additional perk of full benefits. He looked closer at the wall and could see a union flyer. He shook his head. Thank God for unions; if not for them, these capitalist assholes would pay peanuts for gargantuan work and throw one's carcass out on the streets if one dropped in a dead faint at one's work space. He caught himself in time; why was he even thinking about this like it was the place he envisioned himself ending at? He was a doctor. He was well-educated, trained; all these people sitting around him were supposed to come to him for help to fix that which plagued them physiologically, and not him standing side by side with them, slaving at a job that required the better of one hour training in total. This was wrong, he reasoned to himself; a total waste of manpower. He sat there praying for the time to race on to the end of his shift so that he could go back to Tirin Tirin's apartment and attack his books. He needed to sit for those exams, pass them, and get back into the medical field. He needed to start a real life in this country of startling, unfair contrasts, then just as he had flogged himself into rising up from the drudgery he found himself, the thought of Osasu came seeping back into the resolute mind.

He sighed as he remembered the disappointment. It had been more painful because of the amount of dead leads they had run into in search of the person who had the actual address of the 'Osasu' that was rumoured to be his brother, and then one faithful Sunday evening, they finally got the contact to lead them to the right address.

Tirin Tirin and him following the friend of the friend who knew the friend that had told Tirin Tirin of one Osasu he knew that seemed to fit the description Nosa had given him. Nosa remembered his heart beating and his palm sweating as they walked down the corridor to apartment 806 in the Mayfield Terrace buildings on Duncanwoods Drive at the Finch and Islington neighbourhood.

The friend had told them that Osasu was expecting them even though he didn't know who they were, but was acting on the respect he had for the friend who knew a friend who knew the friend that had supplied the tip. So they got to the door on which was a sticker that read, "Jesus Saves." Tirin Tirin had winked at Nosa and whispered,

"E be like say na only you be the only Satan your mama born."

Nosa couldn't manage a smile. He really hadn't told Tirin Tirin all the crimes of his brother, at least, the ones he knew of. Nosa still felt some loyalty to blood; he had been brought up to keep things that related to family within family. A habit he found so difficult to break. So yes, even though Tirin Tirin might have heard whispers of the deeds of Osasu from his contacts in Lagos, Nosa was not going to confirm those stories to him. All he had told Tirin Tirin was that his brother had a misunderstanding with their father and had fled to Canada; a misunderstanding so deep that he had cut off all communication with his family, a cut so severe that he hadn't even heard of the death of their father. So, Nosa wanted to find his brother, break the bad news to him, and try to reconcile with the only member of his nuclear family that was still alive. It wasn't a blatant lie. It wasn't even, in the words of Tirin Tirin, a righteous lie. It was more a partial, convenient truth just enough to get him what he wanted. He truly liked Tirin Tirin but he still wasn't family, at least, not yet, he concluded.

They had knocked on the door and after a short wait, it opened and standing there, in a pair of checkered wool boxer shorts on which was an imprint of a semi-tumescence and dirty white socks, which had a gaping hole on the left one of the pair, was a short, rotund man. He had his hair permed and in a ponytail, a pair of thick bifocals hugging his shiny black face on which close to nose was a large, ripe zit. He smiled and his mouth opened to reveal missing two front teeth.

"Ah my brothers, welcome; come in."

"Osasu man, how bodi?" the friend who was leading them there had said before exchanging a "whatzup" handshake with the specimen of a man.

Nosa felt his jaw drop as he stared at his assumed brother. What a waste of the time he didn't have and the emotions he guarded so jealously. He turned to Tirin Tirin and shook his head in slight anger.

"How I suppose know na?"

Nosa turned and, without excusing himself, walked down the hallway away from the surprised trio. Tirin Tirin smiled in apology to the two men and took off after Nosa, and as he walked hurriedly, he called out to him.

"No be the same mama born three pikin, one na afin, the other one na crippo, the last na im win mister Nigeria?"

Nosa didn't respond and instead pressed the down button when he got to the bank of rickety-looking elevators. Tirin Tirin got to him.

"You no get manners?"

"I described him to you," was Nosa's hurt response.

"And I described him to my friend, don't know what he heard, but trust me, if you gave me your brother's picture, we won't be here; in fact, we will just go to the cops and declare him missing, give a reward of say one bottle of odeku." Tirin Tirin smiled as he tried to make light of the disappointment.

"Not funny," Nosa said as the elevator doors opened and he stepped into it.

"Oya, dey vex!" Tirin Tirin feigned anger as he followed him into the elevator and as the doors closed he said, "Make you no use mess kill me o for dis lift as per say your belle dey worry you with vex."

Even as hard as Nosa tried to keep a straight face, he found himself smiling.

He didn't even realise that as he sat in the lunch room that day, he was actually smiling so very broadly that a Pakistani middle-aged man walked up to him and sat by his side.

"It is nice to see you smiling," he said in a thick accent.

Nosa broke out of his flashback and looked at the man who seemed to have suddenly appeared out of nowhere. Nosa was no longer smiling.

"I did not mean to startle you," the man continued.

"It's okay." Nosa regained his composure.

"I have been watching you for days and I see you keep to yourself; it is good to like one's company, but you need friends to see you through jobs like this."

"Thank you." Nosa attempted being civil.

"You are new, right?"

"Yes, my second week."

"I meant in the country."

"No, over three months."

"Ah, that's new. It takes some of us over a decade to settle into this country, some more, some never even settle; they die of a broken heart from dreams that never came true and regrets that ate the heart out of them, then the sad part is that they still take their corpses back home to bury. You see, you leave your country alive, filled with hope and you return dead, filled with bitterness; the soil you ran away from still had the last laugh."

"You are Pakistani?" Nosa observed.

"Yes... you?"

"I am Nigerian... no Canadian." He always found himself struggling to correctly identify himself, yet he found it particularly exciting being able to positively identify the correct nationalities of people he came across based on their accents and looks.

"Oh, dual nationality, how come you said you have been here for just over three months? It takes like three years to get a citizenship here, that is, if you arrived as a landed immigrant in the first place."

"I was born here."

"Oh you are a repatriate?"

"If you call it that."

"Your parents here?"

"No. they are dead"

"Ah! Sorry to hear that; what Allah gives, he takes. Peace and mercy be upon them."

"Amen."

"Muslim?"

"Christian."

"Ah! We who are of the book are all the same; Muslims, Jews, Christians, slight difference we have, but still the same brothers. It is the Hindus, Buddhists, and all the funny religions you see all over the place, those are the faithless sons of a bitches you should watch out for." His tone was low and conspiratorial, as though he was sharing the most prized information.

Nosa instantly took a dislike to him, but out of politeness he smiled.

"So, judging from your English, you obviously are well-educated; what did you do back in your real home?" there was an emphasis on the word "real."

"I was a doctor." Nosa said with some pride.

"Ah! A colleague!" the Pakistani's face lit up; he smiled at Nosa and then turned to the others and spoke loudly.

"Everybody, meet my Nigerian friend; a doctor from Africa."

They all smiled at him and sent him nods of friendship. Nosa for the first time realised that they were all immigrants sitting in that room; Indians, Chinese, South Americans, various nationalities of the Caribbean, and it went on and on, tired faces staring back at him. Why would the night shifts be given to the immigrants and the more convenient day shifts to the naturally born Canadians who were ironically the full-time unionised workers? Curse the unions, he said under his breath in an apparent volte face; all they did was protect their members and stick it to those who were not of their hallowed charter.

"I am a cardio-thoracic surgeon. Twenty two years of practise in Karachi, big hospital I worked at; senior consultant training medical students, house officers, registrars, the entire thing, but look at me now, working for nothing at a factory, and they call this the Canadian dream," he cursed in Arabic before he fell silent, his eyes flashing in sudden anger.

"How old are you if you don't mind my asking?" Nosa asked him.

"How old do you think?"

"I would say forty-five."

"Ah! Fifty-nine… looking very young, eh? I should marry me say two more wives, but the Canadians, they call our culture primitive. Polygamy, they say, is a crime. What Islam permits they say they forbid; a country of infidels. I wonder what I am doing here, but then, I think of the children and I say, 'okay, I do anything for them, even pack shit from roadside to give them a good life,' yes my children, five of them; one married here to a good Pakistani boy, works at a bank downtown, the other three in university, the last one in high school, two wives, but I call the second one my cousin, one has to be smarter than these Canadians you know. So, tell me, how long did you practise back home?"

"Just finished my house job, would have started residency but I had to come," Nosa tried to match him with personal information revelation but noticed that he came terribly short.

"Ah, so I am your senior colleague, but don't worry, in Canada we are all the same. You see that man?" He pointed at a portly man reading a newspaper in the fore of the room. "He was a judge in his country. He comes from Ecuador; you see how he carries himself, like a big man," he kept pointing at various other people "You see that woman, she was an engineer, one of the biggest in Morocco, built dams and huge drainage, hydro geology was her second degree; and that one, a fine architect in Trinidad, great designs; the other one, an aeronautics engineer from Shanghai, built huge turbines; you see us all here, professionals, but Canada has made us all the same; we do jobs that even retards can do, we pack shit together, so you see, in our misery, we have to come together, give each other encouragement and hope, forget where we are from and the colour of our skin and create something for ourselves. This country only wants us for our children; they don't care about our skills or experience. Look at us; see what Canada wastes and then they have the mouth to say shortage of doctors, but the truth is the professional associations here, they protect their jobs, the fewer the professionals, the higher their value and their pay, so they close the door on us. They say you don't have Canadian experience; how will I get Canadian experience if no one is willing to give me work? They say you have to pass board exams; twenty exams for a man my age? Exams that I myself was conducting back in Pakistan? I say at least my experience should count for something; reduce the exams I have to sit for, maybe two or three, they say no, we don't trust Pakistani medicine; you see how they treat us, yet doctors from South Africa, I mean the white ones, Australia, New Zealand, Britain, they allow them practise immediately they come in here; you see, double standards. It is all about the colour of their skin and not their skill; the bloody racists, what do they want us to do? We can't go back because we have spent so much moving here; the emotional cost of going back to pick up where we left off is too hard to bear, but then, sometimes you are so angry and you want to go back, but you pick up your passport, you dust it up in anger, then you remember your children, so you sit back down, you shake your head, and you put your passport away. But then, you are a young man; I'm sure you have no children. You can always pack up and leave when you get tired of the madness of this country; it is not too late for you to go back, you know, forget the fact that you were born here. What good has it done for you? Aren't you in the same shit hole with us that were born outside this country? It is the first world against the other worlds, plain and simple. A new kind of slavery, the one that you yourself surrenders yourself into, you take your wrists and you show them, you say, 'take me into your promised land,' for a bite of that carrot they dangle before you; voluntary slavery, that is it, and then you come here and your eyes open, and you say, 'what was I thinking?' But then, it is too late; your master is calling and you have to go to the plantation. My junior colleague, do you understand what I am saying?" he asked with a fever building up in his eyes.

Nosa nodded. He could feel the frustration in the man; the deep seethed anger, the all-consuming, depression-causing disappointment one feels when one is neglected or not recognised for one's true worth; the disdain one has for a people or system that allows your skills atrophy just because of some inconsequential technicalities that shouldn't matter in the first place. He looked at the man and could see that the light of hope had been extinguished from his eyes. In its place was a spark of something he could not put a finger on, something he prayed not to witness explode.

"I tell you, if I..." he continued, his face inching closer to Nosa's.

Nosa felt like his private space was being invaded and as he began backing away in the most surreptitious way possible, the buzzer went off; a loud sound that announced the end of the one hour break. It was a welcome intervention. Even though he was empathising with the irate man, Nosa, felt overwhelmed by the information unleashed at one time and the vitriol of his anger.

As they stood up, walking towards the door, each one dragged their feet and stole a look at the clock; a silent plea for time to speed up its slow stroll. Nosa watched them as he joined them. The man was right; they were all slaves, souls sold to the dictum of money, wedded to the idea that there existed freedom in another clime, a proverbial place where you didn't have to work hard to make a living, where the burdens of survival were lesser, where you were rewarded equally for your efforts and protected from the evil of exploitation. That was the lie sold by the west through their films, television shows, and paradise-painting music and its accompanying video.

There was no El Dorado, no land of milk and honey, just different plantations and different paymasters, but one thing remained constant wherever you went, and that was the supremacy of money and the prevalence of greed. And the truth was that you were either being exploited or you were an exploiter. All else pointed to the fact that every soul that trudged the earth was in one way or the other an economic slave.

These were the thoughts that ran through Nosa's head as he walked across the factory floor, which had already come alive with the whine of forklifts and the calls of the supervisors to the workers, and took his place in front of the machine that no sooner had he positioned himself, without notice, had begun handing him the hot automobile parts in that same pace that showed no compassion for the frailty of his normality.

Nicole walked along the shores of the pristine lake and watched the expensive yachts that bobbed on the tepid blue waters. She allowed the froth of the water bath her bare feet and marvelled at the clearness of her toenails. She looked up at the sky and felt the heat of the sun caress her makeup-free face. A bare-chested man waved at her from the deck of the yacht to her left and she waved back. He shouted and allowed the slight breeze carry his voice to her as she walked along.

"Welcome to Caledon!"

"Thank you!" she shouted back and walked on. This was a notoriously private community and any new face was easily noticeable.

She wondered what these uber-rich folks that luxuriated in the lap of untold wealth would think of her when they found out what she had done. She wondered if anyone would understand, let alone forgive her for the betrayal she was being forced to commit. Who would know what these men had threatened to do to her if she didn't co-operate? Who would she tell without putting herself in harm's way? She asked silently as she made her way back to the cottage within which she had spent the last week and a half.

She could see the Private Investigator at the upper balcony watching her approach. He wore a Hawaiian shirt over Bermuda shorts with dark Ray-Ban glasses and presented the picture of a newly rich Silicon Valley investor. She realised she had to play the cards they dealt her to the hilt. The skirmish on the highway was a wakeup call to her. Andrew was already a living cadaver; what more harm could she do to him? And if she couldn't do more harm, why were the men so interested in harming him? She had thought hard and each time she came to the same conclusion that it wasn't Andrew they were after; it was his business. They wanted to destroy him and everything he had, make him so hated in the eyes of the public that he and his would be a pariah in the business and social circles of the people that mattered. So, she had thought further and tried to imagine that it was Annabelle's family that was orchestrating a payback scheme in memory of their dead daughter. She had read about the wealth of Annabelle's parents and she remembered Andrew speaking about it once, so she could imagine them having the financial wherewithal to pull this thing through. She exhaled as she readied herself for the visit that was to take place later that day. She had rehearsed for days for it, she and the Private Investigator going through all the information she had supplied earlier or he had unearthed in his own mysterious and awe-inspiring ways. They had worked on her presentations, polished her enunciation and perfected her elocution, everything that meant something had been covered, even the clothing, the shoes, the type of makeup, the way to smile, the angle of her head, the position of her hands. The Private Investigator had drummed on the word "victim" over and over again.

She understood what it meant to be a victim; she had been that a couple of times in her past and then in some ways, she was a victim of this unfortunate scenario, active participant in some ways, but blameless in a lot of ways, she again convinced herself. After all, she wasn't the one that made a play for Andrew; he was the one that came after her. She never, even for one minute, aspired to take the place of Annabelle or assume the place of authority with Andrew; he was the one who had tried to lift her up in status. Maybe he really loved her to an extent that he was prepared to risk it all for her. Maybe that was what Annabelle found out that pushed her over the edge. In the world of the rich, Nicole had finally understood that normal mortals existed only as pawns.

She got to the porch of the yellow and white painted cottage and turned to look one more time at the lake and feel the gentle wind caress her face. It felt like her last taste of freedom. In hours, she will let go of her identity and relinquish control of her story. Her parents and friends will hear things about her that will shock, annoy, and repulse them. They will call her on end, since the Private Investigator had made sure that she stayed in touch with them all through her stay at the cottage. But she knew that she wouldn't be able to explain to them the reason for her actions or the truth of her story; she would have to take it in her stride, an answer that would say, "I can't talk about it now," "my lawyers insist I make no comments." She would say the normal Gloria Allred bullshit, knowing that the journey might be long and strenuous or quick and relieving; the decision of the duration not being in her hands.

She would do what she had to do not only just because of her having no options, but having the comfort that after it was all over, she had a million dollars nested in an account in the Cayman Islands that the Private Investigator had confirmed to her, in writing and via telephone, was opened in her name in payment for all the pain and suffering she had been through—and those that she would go through.

"Forgive me, Andrew," she whispered to herself as she shut the door behind her and disappeared into the intrigue that was to consume her.

Angela held her tongue and gave her mind time to think. She

knew that Therese was open to her speaking as frankly as she could, but she wasn't sure if Therese would actually welcome the truth, even though the truth in itself was cold and brutal. She turned and threw her gaze out of the open window of the reading room. It was on the second floor of the Sciorra residence. She could see the rolling expanse of a well-mowed lawn that lay beyond the west wing of the house. Therese was the sole heiress of this mind-boggling fortune and if she was to act in her best interests, she owed her the truth in whatever shape or form, irrespective of her perceived feedback.

"I believe she is the right psychologist for Mr. Sciorra," she said, turning back to Therese.

The response was silence.

She kept her eyes on Therese.

"There is something about her that just doesn't rub me in the right way," Therese finally said as she stood up and walked to the sturdy shelf of books that hugged the opposite wall. She got there and scanned the shelves with her questioning eyes.

The reading room was like a nest. The walls were painted burgundy as though the colours were meant to wake you up and force you to read the endless tomes that lay on the six levels of shelves. The chairs were a mixed lot. A cream-coloured leather sectional took up the right part of the room, just underneath the large windows and it was on it Angela sat. A deep well sat on the black leather couch for Andrew; a comfy, grey chaise filled with throw pillows and a large, brown teddy bear for Therese; and a throw-pillow-filled, knitted, white and pink divan for Annabelle. The divan somehow looked sad; it stood alone at the far wall and appeared as though it was in mourning. In the middle of the room was a low center table on which sat a full tea tray, and by the couches were wooden side tables, which shone from incessant polishing. There were no television sets, entertainment centers, or computers. This was a room to read.

Therese pulled out a leather-bound book from the neatly arranged rows of books on the fourth shelf and turned around. Her face looked worried. She sat back on the chaise couch. She opened the book, which had on its cover the words: Interpretation of Dreams; it was written by the father of psychology, Sigmund Freud. She quietly began to read from a page in which a book marker sat. Angela watched her.

"Maybe she doesn't rub you the right way because she is actually focused on the spiritual instead of the medical," Angela tried to bring back the topic they had been discussing.

"The question that plagues me is why she does that," Therese tore her eyes from the opened book and gave them to Angela.

"She is enlightened, that's why."

"You mean that medicine as we know it is not real or what?"

"More like there is a line where we cross from the physical into the spiritual."

"But you agree that there are lots of quacks who exist in that world?"

"There are a lot of quacks who thrive in this world."

"Don't hold brief for her."

"I thought you wanted my honest opinion."

"Yes I do, but…" Her voice disappeared and she looked back at the book.

"I'm listening," Angela helped out.

"There is something not natural about her, like she is putting up a front; impervious to normal emotions is more like it."

"It is not a front."

"How do you know?"

"I recognise the light when I see it."

"The light?"

"Yes. The light of enlightenment."

"Hold up now, I don't want you to go into your new age religion; all I want us to do is logically and rationally discuss this."

"It is not a new age religion; it is the simple truth and the truth has always been here. We are the ones who find it in our own time."

"But what if it complicates things, creates more problems than we already have, pushes my father into an abyss he cannot come out of?" She looked up at Angela. Her eyes showed the confusion in her mind.

"What if the truth is not what you make it out to seem?"

"How do you mean?"

Angela held her breath for a fraction of a second, then she took the dive.

"What if the truth is that you do not trust Phillip?"

Therese did not respond and did not bat an eyelid. She allowed the question sink in. She took her time as she thought about the reasoning behind it and the truth of it. Then she exhaled.

"You might be right." She confessed.

Angela slowly let her breath flow out. She had actually held it in as Therese earlier fell silent. She had taken a gamble on being brutally honest. Now she was glad it looked like it was paying off. She decided to continue.

"So, why don't we work on the relationship you have with Phillip, maybe if we sort that out, you might feel a lot better about Sibongile and her methods." Angela advised.

"I don't even know how to start, I mean, we have like really been cruel to each other, and to be honest, I don't think I can just so easily brush away my suspicions and behave like all is dandy and sweet."

"I'm not suggesting you ignore your suspicions or anything, just saying that you give him a chance to really talk to you, explain his positions, his motivations, stuff like that, even in court we all have a right to a defence."

"Has he been talking to you?"

"It's no secret; we all know."

"Who?"

"The staff."

"What?!"

"You both are doing a really poor job putting it on the down low."

"What do you all know?" Therese was more focused on the fact that the staff was privy to the deteriorating state of her relationship with Phillip. She didn't like the fact that the staff could pick on that dysfunction for their own ulterior motives.

"You are both at loggerheads as to the influence of Mr. Vinelatter in the running of this house and your father's business,"

"But how...?"

"It's everywhere, Therese." She said it in as comforting a tone as possible. It was easier talking to Therese, especially when she had insisted that Angela called her by her first name.

"I make my own decisions."

"I hate to disagree with you, Therese."

"I just listen to Timothy's opinion and weigh it thoroughly before I use it in making my decisions, that's all."

"We all do what we must, but what matters most is how what we do affect all those around us."

"I am doing my best." It came out as a plea.

"The house is divided; people are pitching tents."

"Between who and who?" Therese enquired.

"Timothy and yourself and Mr. Sciorra and Phillip."

"What?!" Therese was stunned

"It is the truth."

Therese fell quiet. She bit on her lower lip as it painfully sank in. People actually thought that she was working against her father. Why would they think that?

"I'm sorry," Angela volunteered. She could see the pain on Therese's face and her heart went out to her; so much so soon on such a shoulder so very unprepared.

"Please don't be." She fell silent after the words.

The silence dragged. One minute. Two. Three. Angela

squirmed silently in discomfort. She exhaled with a controlled rush of air and then spoke.

"I see you are reading Freud." she needed to change the topic and bring some cheer back to the room and brighten the now gloomy mood that had descended on Therese.

Therese looked down at the book as though seeing it for the first time. Her eyes squinted as she struggled to pull herself back into the moment. There was so much to think about. So much to consider, but this wasn't the time and place.

"Yes."

"Trying to interpret some dreams, I see," Angela continued.

"Sort of."

"I always had a knack for that."

Therese turned to her. Her brows were furrowed.

"Seriously?"

Angela nodded and then smiled as though the smile was supposed to make the believing easier.

"Interesting."

"You could try me if you want." She offered while still holding her smile.

Therese held back and deliberated in her calming mind. Should she open the door to her life wider for Angela? Should she confide in her what she had not confided in anyone including Timothy? Even as she thought about it, the answer was even clearer to see, understand, and accept. Therese marvelled at how easy it was to bond with Angela. To meet her and love her. She could hear her mother chirp on the way back from shopping at the trendy Yorkville high-society district, "Ressy, I mean it was incredible; I tell you that girl, Angela, is the best hire I ever made. Talk about an angel from heaven." She remembered her response to her mother, "Isn't that why she was named Angela?" and as usual her mother's razor-sharp wit had come cutting through, "I tell you, Ressy, you got your sense of humour from your father, my God, you couldn't crack a joke to save your life." and then as usual, her darling mother laughed in her crackling way that felt like there was no care left in the world and life was the best thing in all of existence. How could her so-very-happy mother have sunk into so deep a pit that she found no way out of, but through the noose? Her lovely mother who was the only one who called her by the pet name, Ressy. She felt her chest begin contracting in pain and quickly held herself back. Not here, Therese, not here, she chided herself.

"I have been having really strange dreams," it came out like she was speaking in a trance.

"What are they about?"

"They are..." she paused as she fought the last doubts that threatened to hold her back. Then the dam broke and the flood of pain rushed out.

"...about my mother... she appears to me... like every night... standing there just crying... and when I try to talk to her... she never says anything... just watches me with so much sadness... so much pain... I'm so sorry, mummy... I'm so sorry." She broke down in tears. Tears that shook her entire frame and bent her over.

Angela stood up and hurried over to her. She sat next to her and pulled her close in an embrace as she cried into her shoulder.

"It's okay."

"I should have known she was so sad; I should have helped her." She kept on bawling, her hot tears soaking the light purple blouse Angela was wearing.

"It's okay, Therese, it's okay."

"I was just focused on me, just me, me, me, me; what kind of a child am I?" Therese was flogging herself with regrets.

"It will be okay, it will be okay." Was all Angela could say as she allowed her mind wander into the world and attempt a deciphering of the dreams that Therese had so graphically described in the throes of an obviously painful process of recollection.

Therese cried on. Angela comforted her with the same phrase that flowed over and over again in the same soothing tone. The herbal tea in the bone china teapot went cold and the sunrays disappeared from the open window.

14

Phillip walked down the grand staircase and stopped at the marble-floored hallway. He could hear voices floating towards him from the open door of the study that sat several yards away. He hesitated for a moment and then decided to check up on Andrew, who he knew would be in the study at that time of the day.

When he walked in, he saw Timothy standing by Nurse Maria. They were both looking at the seated Andrew, who himself was staring at the depleting light that hung over the garden outside the large windows.

"You think he might need more medication?" Timothy enquired.

"It really is not in my place to write prescriptions, Mr. Vinelatter." Nurse Maria answered, looking up at Timothy.

"But what do you think, like, what is your gut take on it?" He pushed harder.

"I really don't know." She hovered on the thought.

"You said he is not improving, right?"

She nodded.

"Then he needs more medication or a new treatment plan," he continued.

"I think the doctors are the ones to decide."

"I have learnt that you don't give doctors total control over your treatment; you have to research, find out more about your medical condition yourself. Doctors are some of the worst serial killers known to man," he said, looking back at Andrew.

"His doctors are coming in tomorrow; maybe you could come in and ask them to revisit his treatment plans." Nurse Maria offered.

"Yes. I think I would do that," he said, lost in thought.

Phillip walked into the study. He bristled inwardly with a heated conflagration.

"No, you won't!" It carried every ounce of his fury.

Timothy and Nurse Maria turned around in the same movement, like they had rehearsed it. There was shock on their faces.

"Mr. Neri," Nurse Maria gasped.

"Leave us!" Phillip ordered her.

She didn't utter a word as she hurriedly left the room. As she did so, Timothy regained his composure and levelled his sights on the now standing Phillip. Nurse Maria didn't shut the door behind her.

"You've got to back off, you hear me?" Phillip spat the words at him.

"And you have got to grab a hold of yourself," Timothy calmly responded.

"I know what you are up to." Phillip felt his disgust rise like vomit into his mouth. How he despised this specimen of a man, better said, this sly monster, he thought to himself.

"And what am I up to, Nostradamus?" Timothy was now smiling.

"You think you are smart, right?"

"I know what I am." It was cocky.

"You have no right to come here speaking about Mr. Sciorra's treatment plan."

"I am his son-in-law; I have every right."

Phillip's incredulity showed on his face; "Son-in-law, you are really deluded, you know? Don't you have to be married to have a father-in-law?"

"Not everyone operates under your own rules." There was still a smirk.

"How do you mean?" Phillip took a moment before he had uttered those words. He couldn't for a minute underestimate Timothy. He was very well aware of his chameleon nature and his many secrets. Those words threw up red flags.

"There is a lot you do not know, Phillip."

Phillip looked into Timothy's eyes; piercing eyes that had a devious glint to it. As he looked harder and sought to unravel the intent behind the glint in those eyes, Timothy crossed his arms over his chest and smiled broadly in a posture of victory. The seeming truth hit Phillip. He panicked.

"Therese will never do that to Andrew." Phillip wished he could believe his words himself as soon as he uttered it.

"You don't know Therese."

He was right. Therese was changing so fast he couldn't vouch for her. But how would she do such a fundamental thing in secret? How would she deprive her father of his right, especially when she was his only child? The questions came surging through. Does Therese know the real Timothy? Was she aware of his multiple lives?

"If you want a future with the Sciorras, Phillip, I will advise that you find your place and stay there."

"Is that a threat?"

"Take it as you want to."

Phillip once again fell silent. Was there something he didn't know? Had things gone faster than he had anticipated? What was this sleek eel up to? Whatever it was, Phillip knew that his one and only option was to take the war to Timothy and buy himself time to gather enough evidence to confront Therese with. After all, there was something called an annulment. He went for Timothy with added vehemence.

"I don't have time for this; just stay the heck away from Andrew."

"And if I don't?"

"Then you might as well watch your back."

"Is that a threat?" He mimicked Phillip.

"You bet it is and a serious one at that."

Timothy looked at him, then at Andrew, and back to the slowly-panting Phillip.

"Okay, I guess its game on." Timothy's eyes were cold.

Phillip held his gaze, shook his head like the only emotion he had for Timothy was that of lingering pity.

"Leave!" Phillip ordered.

Timothy didn't move or flinch. He stood there looking at Phillip with a smile.

"I said... leave!" Phillip took a step forward, his chest raised, his hands in a fist.

Timothy still did not move, but his eyes played down to Phillip's balled fist and then back to his contorted face. There was a good eight inches between them, Timothy having the upper hand. He could take Phillip down, he decided to himself, but fighting was beneath him. He turned to Andrew.

"We will take care of you, Andrew; I promise you, we will." It was calm and reassuring. He then bent over and planted a kiss on his forehead.

Phillip winced as though stabbed by a knife in his solar plexus. Andrew did not move. His eyes remained fixed at the now nearly-dark garden, and as before, he sat there locked in the vice of an unresponsive mind, his terry cloth robe hiding his withering frame. Timothy straightened up and walked directly towards Phillip. He approached with his eyes fixed at the standing Phillip, daring him to stand in his way or back down.

Phillip did not back down. He stared back and dug in, and just at the last second before inevitable collusion, Timothy changed his course and walked around Phillip towards the door. As he walked, he began to whistle. Phillip could recognise the tune. He knew the song. It was a song Andrew whistled when he needed Phillip to create a scenario as an escape from the confines of the house and Annabelle's company into the embrace of an eagerly-waiting concubine. Phillip was caught off guard. He understood Timothy was sending a message. How on earth did he know the reason behind the whistle? He could feel cold wariness descend on him. He turned around, and instead of Timothy exiting the study, it was Nurse Harriet walking in. It was time for a shift change.

"Good evening, Mr. Neri," she said with a sweet smile. Nothing like seeing Phillip Neri at the beginning of a shift. It somehow made the shift go by quickly and the rigors more bearable.

Phillip did not respond, and instead, turned around and walked back to the seated Andrew. The stakes were increasing. He knew he had to up his game. He laid his hand on Andrew's shoulder, an unspoken reassurance that, come what may, he will remain by his side.

Nurse Harriet stood at the door and wondered why Phillip's mood was sour. It was very unlike him to not acknowledge or return her smile. Had she done anything wrong? She wondered. She was caught up in her thoughts when a flustered Nurse Maria walked to her and stood by her side. She also laid her eyes at the sight of Phillip standing beside Andrew, hand on shoulder in bonding. She wondered inwardly if she was in trouble with Phillip or if he was discerning enough to know that she had kept her own counsel and kept Timothy at bay. There was no way to know how he would react because Phillip stood by Andrew's side and they both stared out that window for the next two hours. It was silent, yet filled with unspoken fears and indescribable apprehension.

Nurse Maria had stayed with Nurse Harriet until Phillip finally left the study. It was only then that they both entered into the study with the uniformed male orderly who came in for three hours in the morning and evening to help with moving Andrew, up and down the staircase and around the house, to begin preparing him for his sleeping rituals.

Nosa sat in the library at the Albion and Kipling intersection. It was quiet and conducive to the mental demands of studying for the medical board exams. There were two floors and he was on the upper floor. It was the unofficially designated floor that seemed to house the more serious-minded individuals, people who had an axe to grind with one examination or the other. Interestingly enough, they were mostly immigrants, reading to prove themselves qualified to join the several Canadian professional associations and guilds that had slammed the glorified gates in their faces with the excuse that their qualifications were not necessarily recognised in Canada and had to be upgraded by passing additional exams or in some worst scenario, altogether thrown out.

Nosa fought to keep his mind on the pages before him. It was essentially a revision, so he had devoured the pages like a Russian gulped down ice-cold vodka. It was once said by his anaesthesiology lecturer at the University College Hospital at Ibadan, that he had a photographic and auditory memory. All he had to do was see or hear to remember.

He had been sitting on the same chair for the last six hours. Non-stop reading. He had registered for the examinations, the part one exams of the Medical Council of Canada Qualifying Examinations, which comprised of four tests; the first three of which were multiple choice questions which candidates had three and a half hours to answer, while the last comprised short answer questions that candidates had four hours to answer.

A week before he sat at the library that day, Nosa had taken an evaluation test. It was an online test, which was a compulsory requisite for foreign trained medical doctors who wanted to practise in Canada and it tested the candidates' knowledge of the primary areas of medicine. Both examinations were expensive, draining his purse of the funds he had brought over from Nigeria and as he had predicted, Nosa had passed it in his first sitting.

Tirin Tirin had taken him out to a bar to celebrate his success. While he drank a bottle of Smirnoff ice, Tirin Tirin had bravely handled, alone, a bottle of whiskey. Nosa had watched him as he downed shot after shot, talking and laughing to boot. After he passed the half mark of the bottle and carried on in his quest to empty the whole thing, Nosa had intervened in a concerned voice.

"Don't you think you've had enough?"

"Enough of happiness?"

"No."

"Enough of celebrating your flogging-that-exam-silly?" Tirin Tirin punctuated his sentence with a belch, before continuing, "Excuse my mannerlessness." A loud guffaw followed this.

"I am talking about the whiskey."

"Why? Don't you realise that we need to keep the economy booming? This is my contribution to starting the fire under the yansh of this goddamn economy." He filled his glass, stood up, and raised his glass. The bar was filled with other people. They were huddled around their tables talking, while some sat relaxed, drinking and watching an ice hockey match that was showing on the four large screen televisions that were tacked to the walls.

"To the economy!"

"To the economy!" Half of the other drinkers responded and

raised their glasses. The others couldn't be bothered.

Tirin Tirin drowned the glass and uttered a loud cry as he sat down.

"Ah! Hot! Jesus, you are good!"

"Your concept of sin is intriguing."

"Why?"

"Here you are getting drunk and you are thanking Jesus."

"But the good Bible says that in all things, we must give thanks—to God." Tirin Tirin said as though confused as to why Nosa was bothered about him in the first place.

"You are drunk, man!" Nosa reminded him.

"No, I am not." It came out with conviction.

"Yes, you are."

Tirin Tirin stood up, stepped away from the table, stretched his hand sideways, and began working in a straight line, one foot after the other. It was one of the tests the police gave drivers to find out if they had been driving under the influence of alcohol.

"One, two, three, four, five, six, seven, eight..." he counted as he walked.

Some of the people at the bar looked towards him and started counting along with him.

"...nine, ten, eleven, twelve, thirteen, fourteen..." they chorused to his counts.

Nosa watched them and shook his head. The world of the drunk and the near-drunk was something that intrigued him. Why would anyone willingly surrender control of their faculties to the unpredictable dictates of the intoxicating liquid?

"...fifteen, sixteen, seventeen, eighteen, nineteen, twenty!" They all broke out in cheers as Tirin Tirin got all the way to the tinted glass door. He turned around and gave a bow and when the applause continued, he gave another bow. No sooner had he straightened up than he began bouncing around in a boxer's pose. He punched the air rapidly. His footwork was intricate. Mohammed Ali materialised right there.

"...I am the king of the world! I float like a butterfly; I sting like a bee!" He taunted an imaginary opponent. A flurry of punches followed and the opponent crashed on the canvas. He stood over the fallen man and smiled. Nosa watched him. The bar laughed.

Blacks, Whites, Latinos, some Asians, and Indians united in the gospel of the bottle.

"...that is from Tirin Tirin to you, with all my love, signed, sealed, and delivered."

He spoke adorably to the empty floor, then looked around and raised his arms in victory. The bar cheered and finally turned back to their drinks and the unfolding ice hockey match which was as usual showing the Toronto Maple Leafs being trashed as thoroughly as Tirin Tirin's imaginary opponent by the Detroit Red Devils.

Tirin Tirin walked back to the table and flopped on his seat. He was not panting neither had he broken out in a sweat. Nosa watched him and even though he was concerned about his sobriety, he found himself smiling.

"You see, the sin is actually in getting drunk and not in drinking; our God is a merciful and understanding God."

"You mean to tell me you are not drunk?"

"Do you have a breathalyser?" he countered.

"I don't and for the records, you are drunk."

"Me? Drunk? One bottle of whiskey will shack me? You never see something. A mi, Shayo Brotha, my friends at Iyana Abegi, our favourite drinking spot back in Surulere, which was and will forever be at Sixty Ogunlana drive, go and ask and they will tell you, either in Yoruba or English — 'Tirin Tirin at age fourteen, in one sitting will finish a carton of Star lager beer and top it with one extra bottle, just to calm the soul and Tirin Tirin will stand up, eyes clear as day and go tap a game of football before he will return home, brush his teeth and sit down to wack a plate of poundo.' You know what they called me back then?" he asked Nosa.

"Tirin Tirin or whatever your real name was back then."

"No... you are wrong... they called me 'One Carton and One.'"

"Meaning?"

"You mean you didn't hear my story?"

"You were blabbing."

"Ah, you are the one that is drunk; one bottle of Smirnoff and you can't hear perfect elocution, Queen's English in perfection, and you call it blabbering. Ogun fire your head!" He laughed and poured himself another shot of whiskey.

"You have to stop."

"You have to shut up!"

"Easy." Nosa was shocked at the intensity of the reprimand.

"While elders eat kola nut straight from the husks, children cry for it to be dipped in honey." Tirin Tirin assumed a fatherly tone.

"And I am the child?"

"No, you are the woman."

"Woman?"

"Aren't you the one with a bottle of Smirnoff?"

And before Nosa could respond, Tirin Tirin stood up and raised his glass high in the air. A comical smile plastered on his face.

"To the women in our midst!" he called out in a toast.

"To the women in our midst!" came the response from fewer of the bar enthusiasts.

Tirin Tirin laughed loud, patted Nosa on the shoulder, and sat down.

"When are we doing our next exams?" Tirin Tirin asked as he switched from his jocularity to a serious mien.

Nosa smiled to himself as he remembered the events in the bar. He turned to the next page in the textbook in front of him.

He had two more weeks to the exams and he was already feeling good about it. The unpleasant memories of the hard work he had done, which in his opinion were menial although most Canadians will look at it as just another job, kept him going. From where he came from, certain jobs were for the uneducated and hopeless, but here in Canada, there was dignity of labour; it didn't matter what you did, all that mattered was that it earned you an honest living and provided a reasonable quality of life, everything else was vanity. Yes, he confessed to himself, vanity was one of the things that kept him mentally unprepared to take the route of hard menial labour. One didn't unlearn the birthright and grooming of a king overnight. These things took time and Nosa had decided to spend it acquiring the required skills and educational qualifications to become that which he had been so meticulously trained for. Even though it was bleeding out his pocket, he had calculated that he could rely on the generosity of Tirin Tirin as regards room and board with feeding to boot, and in six months, he would be through with the exams and ready to mount the throne of a medical doctor. Yet even as he sat there in the library and revised at his peculiar lightning speed of scholarly learning and retention, he inwardly fought to keep at bay the encroaching thoughts of Osasu.

He had decided that night after his horrible experience at the automobile parts factory that he was going to focus on changing his lot and would shelf, for the time being his pursuit of Osasu and his gnawing need for closure. Strangely, with his decision to focus on what mattered and ignoring the need for explanations and quasi vengeance, he no longer heard the calming and comforting voice of his mother.

Osasu sat in the room and waited. It was very bare; just two chairs and a table. The walls were painted a shocking white, the window shuttered, and the floor so spotlessly clean Osasu could swear that a germaphobe, or in more medically correct terms, a mysophobe, cleaned it.

He looked at the jewelled face of his wristwatch. Tiny diamonds embedded in a black dial glittered back. In that same instant, it announced the time. 8:14 p.m. Osasu sighed; he had been waiting for the better of two hours. He looked over at the white door on the far wall. It wasn't the door he had been ushered through. That door led to a place he knew not. All he was concerned with was the man who would come through it.

Finally, the door opened and a tall, lanky Indian man came through. He was in his late fifties and was a living legend. Osasu stood up in respect. All he got was a smile as the only acknowledgement of his presence. The man was known simply as Safe. A nom de guerre that was indicative of his expertise with the cracking of safes. There was no safe that had survived the magic of his fingers or the scrutiny of his eyes. Sometimes, he didn't even need to see the safe to crack it. His genius even extended to proxies.

"I hear you have been in search of me." His voice was hoarse.

"Yes. It has been a long wait."

"Others have waited longer."

"I appreciate your seeing me."

"You are here because The Shah referred you."

The Safe was notoriously secretive. It was harder to see him than it was obtaining an audience with the Pope. He had a reputation of never having been arrested for as little an infraction as a traffic offence. He was cleaner than the floor of the room they sat in. Osasu had met The Shah when he visited Nigeria to close an oil deal. At the time, he needed enforcers for a journey into the notorious Urhobo enclave of Okparavero Waterside in Warri in Delta state. Osasu had organised the enforcers and ensured his safety. There were friends of friends who owed him and paid him back by ensuring The Shah's safety in the militant enclave. The Shah never forgot him. So, when Osasu heard about the expertise of the Safe and how difficult it was to get an audience with him, he had placed a call to The Shah at his offices in Istanbul and five months later, he was sitting right there in the spotless room with the enigma.

"I am honoured."

"So, how can I help you?"

"I have a job and I was hoping you will be willing to help me out with it."

"You know my rates?"

"Yes, I was told."

"And the conditions?"

Osasu nodded. He remembered the intense search he went through before he was allowed into the car that took him away from the mall where the first meeting took place. Then he remembered the additional search at the semi detached house he was taken to from where he was bundled into another car that took him on the most roundabout journey he had ever been through. Finally, after an hour and fifty minutes, they had arrived in the huge warehouse complex, in which this room existed.

"Fine, so what is this job?"

"A safe."

"Of course it is a safe, if not you won't be here. Now which safe is this?" His voice showed a slight irritation.

"It is owned by a very wealthy man; I believe it is in his study. It is a Traum."

"I have cracked Traums before."

"This one was custom-built, believed to be impregnable."

"I have cracked custom-built and supposedly impregnable Traum safes before." There wasn't an iota of pride in his voice. It was a statement of fact.

"That is very reassuring."

"I believe you have a picture?"

Osasu shook his head.

"Then, you have the safe itself?"

Again Osasu shook his head.

"How do you intend I know what we are dealing with?"

"I have a serial number."

"A serial number?"

"Yes, and I was hoping with the serial number, you will have a picture of it in your archives."

"And how did you come about this serial number?"

Osasu kept quiet for a moment. He didn't need to tell Safe about his software with the algorithm that pulled that which a lot of knowing people believed could not be pulled out of the highly secure databases within which they had been hidden.

"I have my ways."

Safe fell silent. He closed his eyes. He looked as though he was talking to his mind. His eyes were moving behind the closed eyelids.

"What is the serial number?" he asked without opening his eyes.

"FSA1249733KSA," he ratted offhand.

Safe was quiet. His eyes were still closed. Osasu was watching him.

"I know that series."

"Thank God!" it came out with genuine relief.

"The lock mechanism is the same."

"It is supposed to be customised."

"Yes, it will be but that is for the thickness of the panels, fire, and explosive resistance, stuff like that, the lock series is the same."

"So can you break it?"

"I can help you break it. What are you looking at as per time?"

"Three months tops," Osasu said.

He was banking on getting Angela around to be ready to do his bidding by that time. Osasu at that moment felt the time was right to take Angela to the next stage. He had softened her enough with the cunning of his mind and the vitality of his body, now the time had come to mould her into that which he wanted her to be. Yes. Three months was enough, he mused to himself.

"Okay. I will build the device. I don't know how you intend to get it to the safe, but once you do, all you will need to do is stick it to the door and follow the instructions I will give you and you will have your safe divulge its secrets to you." After the last words, he opened his eyes. He smiled as though boasting, "See how good I am?"

"What are the chances that there will be proof the safe has been broken into?"

"Physically, there will be no proof, in fact, you could gain as much access as you wish, but as long as you wear gloves and leave no prints, you will be good, and then if you don't take anything out of the safe and leave the contents as you met it, no one will ever know."

"Are you sure?"

"I take that as an insult."

"I'm sorry," Osasu offered quickly.

"Is there anything else?" he asked ignoring the apology.

"That's all."

Safe stood up. It was brisk as though he wanted to get as far away from Osasu and as quickly as he could possibly manage.

"We see in three months. My people will see you out." With those words, he turned around, walked to the mysterious door, opened it, and disappeared into the catacombs of the warehouse complex.

Osasu heaved a sigh of relief and waited as he had been advised by the men who brought him there. They had said they would come when they were ready. Osasu just prayed their being ready didn't mean another two-hour wait.

The Private Investigator looked at his wristwatch for the twelfth time in five minutes. Half an hour left before the dice will roll, he observed and lay his head on the headrest of the couch. He willed himself to breath more easily. Shallow breathes let out at short intervals always calmed ragged nerves. They had worked before, while he was still a cop and they will work now.

He was dressed in a black suit and white Thomas Pink shirt. His tie was black and narrow. He cut the picture of Tommy Lee Jones in the Men in Black movie franchise. The only missing piece was the sunglasses, which was in a leather pouch that hung from his black belt. Timothy expected him to perform beyond reproach and he had no intention of letting him down. Just then, there was a sound behind him. He sat up and turned around. It was Nicole. She had come down the staircase and was standing there with her hands crossed in front of her, like a young Catholic girl ready for her first holy communion.

"You look beautiful."

"Thank you." Nicole responded.

She was dressed in a dark blue skirt suit. The white silk blouse she wore under the jacket, unfurled over the lapel of the jacket in a flowery pattern. Her makeup was very faint and her hair was packed in pig tails. This wasn't her style. She had dressed out of a script, a script that was given to the Private Investigator and then handed down to her. The goal was to make her look virginal. An innocent girl from Sasketchewan and a worldly, wealthy man. Beauty and the beast. Innocence and Worldliness. Good and Evil.

Nicole walked over to the couch and sat at the opposite end from the Private Investigator. They both latched onto the comforting ambience of silence. Time ticked on.

"Is it too late to change my mind?" Nicole finally broke the chord of silence that bonded them together.

"Don't even think about it." It was curt, yet the unspoken threat lingered on.

Another bout of silence descended. This time it was pregnant with heavy thoughts. The Private Investigator was alert. He was listening to every sound, both the ones that came from the various parts of the house and those that emanated from Nicole. Hers were mostly sighs and her incessant shifting of her sitting position on the couch in a bid to find the most comfortable position for her aching heart. He had counted six sighs that had escaped from her. It was already getting on his nerves.

"Just relax, okay, before you know it, it will be done."

"I have a conscience."

"So do I."

"Is that a joke?"

"I can't hear you laughing."

She held her tongue. It was evident that talking with him was only going to make her feel worse, she observed. What was the point of finding comfort from a soul whose main preoccupation was causing discomfort? After all, one could not give what one did not have.

"We have rehearsed this, you have it down, everything, every word, so all you have to do is be, just be you, that's all."

"Be me?"

"Yes, it's as easy as that."

"If I am to be me, I won't be here; what you are saying is that I should be the bitch who drove the knife into Andrew."

"Same thing."

"You think I'm a bitch?"

"Yes, I do."

She caught her breath in shock and it came out as a gasp.

"This is not the time to psychoanalyse yourself, just gather your wits and do what we agreed to do, okay?"

Just then the bell chimed and they both turned towards the front door. The Private Investigator stood up, straightened his jacket, and walked towards it. Nicole pulled her knees together and placed her left hand on it and then her right hand above her left. This was how she had rehearsed her seating position would be, under his demanding tutelage. She knew in her thumping heart that it was now too late to turn back.

The door opened and he flashed a smile and as usual the Editor didn't return it. So, he stepped aside to give her access to the house. She walked in and the two men standing behind did the same thing. They were carrying huge bags. He shut the door and walked over to them as they stood at the foyer looking around.

"This way please," he announced as he led them towards the living room where Nicole was sitting quietly.

"I hope it wasn't too hard finding this place; the exit from the main road is pretty hidden."

"Your directions sufficed." She was in no mood for small talk as she followed behind him. She really didn't like the men who used women or any victim for that matter in achieving their own ulterior goals. She knew that was what was at play here and she detested the fact that she was playing ball. But then, if not her, they were still going to get someone else to break the story. And apart from doing what was right for the victims she met in the course of things like this, she knew that a great story was all that mattered. It created a following, it sold magazines, and it was good for her brand. She was not going to be sentimental about this. She was going to approach it with cold detachment and milk it for all its worth. The file the Private Investigator had given her was a treasure trove but hearing from the victim herself was what turned lead into gold.

Nicole saw the Private Investigator walk into the living room and spied the severe face of the Editor walk in after him. She felt a constriction in her chest upon seeing her. There was a meanness that seemed to radiate out of her very person. She held her breath and awaited the onslaught that was to begin. The Editor, on the other hand, laid her eyes on Nicole the minute she walked into the room. There she sat, germane in her pig tails, eyes showing fright as though not comprehending the upheaval around her, licking her lower lip in a betrayal of her apprehension, right foot tapping the air as though her bladder was about to burst and only that repeated action somehow stemmed the flow. She looked at the lady who was the vortex around which the whole debacle was to play out and smiled.

"You must be Nicole?" She walked straight to her, with her hand outstretched.

Nicole didn't expect the smile that came forth; the transformation she beheld was intriguing. How could that face which was so severe the minute before, so much so that it looked like the scowl of an alabaster ghoul, dissolve in such a smile that somehow spread genuine care and deep compassion? She also didn't expect the handshake; all she knew was what the Private Investigator had drilled into her head, all the nightmarish situations that could unfold, and ways to handle them. They were living nightmares in which the principal antagonist was this smiling lady who was approaching her with an outstretched hand of friendship. Nicole struggled to her feet and received the handshake.

"My pleasure," was all she could utter as they shook hands.

"Before we begin, I want you to know that this is all about standing up for you, telling your story, and seeking redress."

"Thank you." Her warmth was so touching that after muttering those words, Nicole looked down at the floor to prevent the Editor from seeing her smile of relief.

The Editor misrepresented her action for that of sorrow and stretched her arms wide in preparation for a comforting hug.

"Oh! Come here, it will be okay, alright?" she said, hugging her.

And as the Private Investigator had drilled her, she forced herself to cry. He said it was called affective memory and came from the Stanilavski system of method acting in which an actor was to call on the memory of the details of similar events in their past, in order to bring out the emotions that was required for the performance of the character. So, she called on her memory of things that had made her cry in the past. They were many. They were still fresh. They were exceedingly painful.

Nicole burst into tears. And they were so genuine that the Private Investigator began to fear that she might suffer a total emotional breakdown and throw their plans in disarray.

The Editor, moved by her tears, hugged her tighter. Even though a story was a story she thought to herself, the human element was the core, the heartbeat, the essence for the tireless search of it. It was what made the story catch on. It was what made people care. As she stood there hugging Nicole, she mentally scrapped the interview she had mapped out to perform and began planning out a new approach. In this approach, she was going to focus on vulnerability and innocence, the lack of hope and the predatory actions of people who thought that their wealth was an excuse to be callous. She decided right there, to bring out the two sides of the story and focus on the action of one man on the lives and destinies of two women. She stroked Nicole's hair and whispered warm words of comfort into her ears even as the Private Investigator and the other two men watched.

The knock on the door was light but audible. Therese raised her head from her soft, large eiderdown pillows and looked at the door. She stayed motionless in that position wondering if she had heard correctly. The knock sounded again. She looked at her jewelled digital illumined clock on her bedside table. It read 3.15 a.m. The knock sounded again.

"Who's there?"

"It's me, Tim." His voice wafted through the darkness of the room.

"Oh Tim." It came out with a groan.

"Are you okay?" he asked, concern in his voice.

"I was fast asleep." She lay back on the bed.

"Sorry, I can't hear you."

"Come in!" She spoke louder.

"I tried, the door is locked."

It came flooding back. Her tears of deep sadness. Angela sitting by her in comfort. The frightening and confusing dreams of her sleeping moments spilling out of her tortured mind. The warm, languid bath surrounded by lit perfumed candles and the incense Angela had given her. She lying on her bed, naked and relaxed. The music of Vangelis relaxing her every nerve. She didn't remember the moment she slept or if she had actually dreamt.

"Therese, open the door," Timothy pleaded.

Therese really couldn't remember locking the door, but she still sat up, switched on her bedside lamp, and dragged herself out of the bed. She didn't bother putting on any clothes and walked naked across the plush carpeting to the door. There was a key in the lock. She turned it with her right hand and did the same to the door knob with her left. Then she stepped back and watched Timothy walk into the room. He was dressed in a suit and his tie was missing. He looked at her with bemused eyes and enveloped her in a hug.

"Are you okay?" he asked again with affected sweetness.

"Just sleepy," she returned his hug, oblivious of her nudity.

"So sorry for waking you up; I just had this feeling that you were mighty sad and I came to be with you."

"You are so sweet," Therese said, smiling.

Timothy carried her in one fluid movement. He gently kicked the door shut with the heel of his well-polished, black, ankle-length dress boots and walked back to the bed with the smiling Therese in his cupped arms. Once at the bed, he lay her down and smiled at her supine form.

"You are so beautiful, my love," he said with eyes that gazed deeply at her.

"Am I beautiful or am I naked?" She was fully awake now.

"Beautifully naked," he replied as he began to take off his jacket.

"Did you come to keep me company or to make love to me?" She was smiling. The sadness of the earlier hours was fast receding.

"I came to do to you whatever you wish me to."

"I want you to just hold me close and talk to me."

He was taking off his shoes and then his pants. She watched him. He took off his shirt and then his undershirt and finally his silk black boxer shorts. He stood there naked. His body was toned and his arousal was visible. She looked down at his enlargement.

"I will try," he said.

She tapped the space beside her.

"Come to mummy."

Timothy laughed, knelt on her side of the bed and flipped over her. He landed on his back on the other side. She turned on her side and placed her head on his hairy chest. He wrapped his right arm around her and slowly started stroking her head. They stayed in that position for the better of five minutes. No words. Timothy could hear her breathing becoming shallow.

"Are you awake?" He finally broke the silence.

"Yeah."

"What you doing?"

"Thinking?"

"About what?"

"Everything."

"Everything?"

"Yeah, everything."

The words disappeared and the quiet descended. Timothy looked up at the ceiling and on it he traced the map of his plans.

He wondered right at that moment how the meeting between the Editor and Nicole was panning out. The Private Investigator had told him that it was going to take all night. The plan had actually been for it to wrap up by midnight, but somehow, the Editor was delving deeper and covering more grounds. The longer the meeting took, the more uneasy Timothy had become. Something in his gut kept eating at him. He saw it as an omen, a warning that a spanner was about to be thrown into the wheel of progress. It was in the bid of his need to control the pieces and put himself at a vantage point to oversee everything that was taking place that he had come over to the Sciorra residence. He felt better knowing that he was right by her side and would have first hand information if Phillip was about to make a play. He didn't know what Phillip knew, but he was ready to pre-empt and presuppose in order to be one step ahead of him. He sighed and stroked Therese's head lovingly.

"I was trying to reach you earlier today."

"I'm sorry I forgot to return your calls."

"Where were you?" he gently prodded.

"Around."

"With who?"

"Angela."

"Where?" His possessive streak was rearing its ugly head in spite of his herculean effort of holding it beneath his calm surface.

"Here."

"On this bed?"

"You wish," she chuckled.

"Where?" He was bent on unearthing information. He could use everything and anything towards protecting his mission and at the same time maintaining control.

"Around the house; she is my P.A, you would expect that we would spend time together," she observed.

"I know, but you realise you didn't actually run her appointment by me."

"It was nothing, didn't think it would be something you would be interested in."

"We promised to share everything, Therese."

"I know and I am sorry."

"Too many apologies suggest a behavioural pattern."

"I really don't want a lecture, Tim, just hold me."

"I am holding you, love, just concerned about you that's all."

"Thank you."

He allowed a detente to ensue. He lay there stewing in the thoughts that swam around in his head. He couldn't deny the fact that there was now a petulance that was emerging in Therese's behaviour; a certain growing independence and courage that hung around her like a halo around the head of Mary, Mother of God. He could see it in the way she carried herself. The lift of her shoulder, the angle at which she cocked her head when he spoke to her, the sense of disengagement of her speech over the phone, her frequent delay in picking or returning his calls. A transformation was occurring in her very core. He wondered as to the identity of the source from where she was drawing her strength and who it was that was feeding her seeds of knowledge. He knew the person didn't speak to her over her cell phone or the house phones because he had them bugged and could listen to every conversation she had. So, it had to be someone she spoke to in person. It couldn't be another man because he was paying good money to have her followed. So, it had to be the only two people who had direct and unfettered access to her, and who could in their own unique way have some influence over her. It had to be Phillip or Angela. He knew it wasn't Phillip because of the enmity he had already sown between them, so that left Angela. The innocent, sweet-looking lady with the cheerful smile and quick laughter would have to be the source of the change. He decided that he had to do something about her.

"You know, it's not healthy to have people who remind you so very much of your mother around you."

"How do you mean?"

"You need to properly heal, Therese."

"I know and I am working hard at it," she mumbled from his chest.

"Not with Angela around you."

Her brow furrowed in surprise as the words hit her. How could Timothy think ill of Angela? She immediately wondered. In the deepest recess of her memory, the earliest recollection she had of Timothy was him oozing out such control that the one thing she instantly felt with him was being protected. She remembered feeling that with Timothy she could walk on the surface of the sun and yet not dematerialise into floating ashes. He had so much control of himself and all that was around him, so much purpose and focus, a sparkling intellect, and uncanny discerning powers. He analysed people with dizzying speed and knew precisely when and how he was to relate with the vast amount of people that crossed his path. She had trusted him then and if she was to be honest with herself, she still trusted him now. But then, she couldn't ignore the suggestions of Phillip; they were persistent and burdensome. She knew how much she had fought them from barging into her mind. She had barricaded the windows of her overwhelmed mind with excuses and justifications, fought his reasoning and suspicions with counter accusations, but she was not stupid and could see that Phillip was making some valid, salient points. But how did anyone expect her to believe that the man she loved was working against her? The thought was so preposterous that she found herself getting angry with a molten fury at the temerity of the accusers. What would he want from her? He was already stupendously wealthy in his own right. He had women flinging themselves at him with lust-filled abandon like snowballs in a snow fight. The name, Vinelatter, itself opened over half as many doors as Sciorra did. Her parents loved him and took him in like the son they never had. So, what would he gain by working against her? It didn't make any sense to her. It came across as the paranoia of a hypochondriac. This was Timothy, the man she was going to spend the rest of her life with, a notion she was living out by faith as a result of the fact that he hadn't actually proposed to her. But that was then, the time when love was like the very life-preserving breath she took, and Timothy had existed beyond the questioning reaches of reproach, and this was now, a time of discovery of both the evolving world around her and the truth of her own diverse experiences and long ignored fears, doubts, regrets, and desires.

She knew she didn't trust Timothy any less than she did before, but she was now giving herself a chance to look through her own maturing eyes at the mysterious world that was pulling at her from all directions. How would she be worthy of inheritance if she couldn't prove to herself that she was deserving of trust, respect, and loyalty? She was certain that her father had built the Sciorra Empire through those three qualities and so much more. She knew that before these unfortunate months, she had simply existed as the girlfriend of one of the most eligible bachelors in the upper-class society of North America, which was in addition to her also being practically the most eligible spinster, not just because of her beauty or education, but because she was a heiress of a mind-boggling fortune. But these were not of her making. It was not a product of the works of her hands or genius of her mind. That was meant to matter was 'your core, your training, your experience, your own skills and attributes, your wisdom, your character, your integrity, and not what you stood to inherit or whom you chose to love.' This was why she had chosen to shut Timothy out of her most private thoughts and decisions and walk alone along the sometimes frightening and mystifying road to self-enlightenment and growth.

"Angela is helping me heal," she said with a quiet firmness.

There was a finality to it. Timothy took note and relaxed. He wouldn't press it. Even as he lay there and allowed his mind sail back to the shores of Lake Caledon, he made a mental note. Angela was now in his cross hairs.

15

Nicole took in a deep breath and looked away. She laid her eyes on the Private Investigator and silently pleaded with him for direction. This had taken longer than she was told and far deeper than she had expected. She had to give it to the Editor. The lady with the reptilian snarl knew her job. She plucked follow up questions from the air that were in themselves incisive as they were revealing. Nicole begged with her eyes for permission from the Private Investigator. He nodded. She exhaled in relief and turned to the Editor and the intimate glare of the camera that stood a short distance from her.

"Yes, he did," Nicole responded.

"He told you in passing or over time?" the Editor burrowed deeper.

"Overtime."

"For the records, I will repeat what you have said and you will confirm; is that okay?" she asked, looking at the notes on her lap.

She had already scribbled on over forty-eight pages. The

amount of information she was mining from this sad, tortured, and broken soul was enormous. She proceeded to read from the open page of her note pad.

"You said that Mr. Andrew Sciorra told you over time, which means on several occasions, that he was going to divorce his wife, Annabelle, and marry you. Can you confirm this?" She looked up at Nicole.

Nicole nodded in response.

"I will need you to say a yes or a no, sweetheart." the Editor said with a warm, supporting smile.

"Yes."

"And you have evidence of this?"

"Only some cards and letters he sent me on which he addressed, 'my darling wife' and the ones he signed, 'your darling husband.'"

"But you said he told you he was going to divorce his wife and marry you."

"Yes, he did, he told me, but I have no evidence of him telling me, I didn't record him saying it to me. I was saying that the only evidence I have of him having said that to me are those cards and letters that addressed me as his wife and him as my husband."

"But you aren't his wife."

"Mr. Sciorra chose to address me like that; I guess it was his way of comforting me and stopping my complaints."

"Your complaints?" The Editor pounced on that.

"Yes. I told him I wanted to end the relationship."

"Why did you want to end it?" She was already scribbling on the notepad.

"I couldn't live a lie any longer. I felt bad. I mean, I have never dreamt of myself being the other woman and there I was wasting my youth with a married man."

"But you said you loved Mr. Sciorra?"

"Yes, I did."

"So why the change of heart?" Her eyes were now narrow, puzzled slits.

"Mr. Sciorra had other women."

"Other women. Like how many?"

"To my best recollection, I know he had over fifteen."

"And how did you come by this?"

"I saw texts on his phone from them and also, word goes around."

"Were they all as young as you are?"

"Some."

"And can you state how old you are?"

"Twenty-one."

"And the others, were they older than you were?"

"Two were."

"I want to ask you a question and I want you to think carefully before you answer, because as you have said you have no physical proof of your information, so it will be in the interest of the truth that your response is true, you understand?"

Nicole nodded. Her palms were clammy, her toes tingling.

"Were any of Mr. Sciorra's other female sexual partners younger than you were?"

"Yes, they were."

"How many?"

"Five."

"Was any of them younger than sixteen?"

Nicole fell dead quiet. Her heart began to thump in her chest. She closed her eyes in order to hide her panic and steel the chaos in her mind. Everyone was watching her. The Private Investigator was impressed. Her hesitation rang true and that was important to get the Editor enraged with the behaviour of Andrew Sciorra and cause her to genuinely empathise with the plight of Nicole. Finally, Nicole opened her eyes. She turned and looked at the Private Investigator. She was awaiting his permission as they had agreed. The Editor looked at the silent exchange. She was seized by a just rage.

"The questions are for Nicole and Nicole alone!"

Nicole and the Private Investigator turned to her in the same instant. Her voice did not mask her anger. The man recording the sound had reduced it a little when her bark crashed into his ears.

"She is answering your questions," the Private Investigator said in a calm, reassuring voice. She was not deceived.

"But you are guiding her."

"No, I am not."

"I'm not blind!"

"She does not know you, and when you attack her, like you have obviously been doing, she looks to me in confusion. Nicole is barely twenty-one; she needs me for strength that is all."

"Cut the cameras and sound."

The cameraman and sound man did as he was told. The Editor stood up and dropped her notepad on her earlier occupied seat. She was angry and she was not afraid to show it. She walked straight to the Private Investigator.

"Look, mister, I don't know who you are and I don't care either, I came here to get a story from a girl who has been so horribly exploited and abused, and I will not allow you orchestrate the conduct of this interview or control the quality or quantity of information I am going to get from her."

"We brought you here; you should be grateful for that."

"You need me just as much."

"We have fall-backs, so don't get carried away."

"No one will touch this story with the level of attention it deserves or run it the way I would through all media as you requested; you take this story to your so-called fall-backs and this story will come out as tabloid fodder."

The Private Investigator fell silent. He knew she was right. She glared at him. Nicole and the other two men watched on. Nicole was taken by her. Her self confidence was impressive. Her courage was awe-inspiring. This was a woman's woman and Nicole couldn't help but wonder what her own life would have been like if she had gone off to college like her parents wanted her to. She wondered if it was too late to put her seemingly wasted life back on track. She was just twenty-one and there were ways to go. Decades stretched forth in front of her with uncertainty but also with hope. Would she one day be like this self-assured woman or will she wallow in pity as to the life she once lived, or the life she was condemning herself to? After all, she reasoned to herself, whatever happened to Monica Lewinsky of the Bill Clinton fame? He starved off impeachment, won re-election and was still loved the world over but who under the forgiving heavens could testify to the outcome of Monica Lewinsky? What did she gain for kissing and telling? The million dollars waiting for her was enough to start over again, to build the blocks of her life in a new environment. She had decided to change her name, go to college, and take chances. She was too deep in this to now back out. If she was going to do this, she might as well do it in such an honest fashion, that she could actually be the poster child for the socially redeemed.

She looked at the two people glaring at each other, like two enraged, bloodthirsty roosters in a cock fight. She intervened. Her voice so tiny it appeared shrill.

"I will answer the questions."

The Editor and the Private Investigator turned to her. Her face was set in deadpan mode. There was a moment as they all regarded her. She smiled and nodded.

"I am ready."

"Fine, but you will promise me not to look over at this man here for support as he calls it. This is your story. I don't know why he is helping you out; that is really none of my business. I am concerned with the truth, discovering it, getting it to the people, and holding people accountable for their action, so I need to know that what you are doing is out of your volition, that you are not being coerced or blackmailed to do this. I had checked out the contents of the files that were given to me by your wing man here, and because they pan out is the sole reason why I am here tonight. So please, if you truly want to go through with this, you have to focus on me; I am your friend as far as this is concerned. I am the one that will stay with you through thick and thin until Andrew Sciorra pays for the way he treated you. Are we clear?"

Nicole nodded.

"Good," the Editor said as she walked back to her seat, picked up the notepad, and sat down. "Roll camera and sound."

She waited for a minute as she read through her notes and the camera and sound man got their equipments rolling, then she looked up at Nicole.

"So, I will ask you the question again. Were any of the ladies that Andrew Sciorra had sex with younger than sixteen?"

Nicole exhaled audibly and clashed her now trembling, sweaty palms together and spoke with a voice that came out as rushed. It was like it was burning her mouth and she needed to quickly get rid of the words.

"Yes, they were."

"Like he was having sex with girls who were not legally of the age of consent?"

"Yes."

"Are you certain of this?"

"He brought two of them to his chateau once."

"Two of them?"

"Yes, two of them, like a threesome."

"A threesome?"

"Yes."

"And you witnessed this?"

She hesitated for a moment. A positive response might implicate her. A negative response might colour her as a lie. She decided to go for the latter. The truth be damned.

"Yes."

"You were right there, like, you participated?"

"He told me to record it."

"Wooow," It came out in a daze. "Like on film?"

"Yes... he gave me a Panasonic camera."

"And do you have the recording?" The Editor was dumbfounded. This had to be true, she thought to herself. Why else would this innocent flower implicate herself?

"No. He collected it as soon as we were done."

"And do you know what he was going to do with it?"

"He said something about showing it to friends." She mentally read from the script the Private Investigator had given her.

"And do you know any of these friends?"

"No."

"So, he had you film him having sex with two underage girls and he went on to distribute and exhibit the footage with some friends; is that what you are saying?"

"Yes, ma'am." It was said respectfully.

"You know that is a crime?"

Nicole hesitated for the sakes of creating an effect. She had rehearsed this moment with the Private Investigator over and over again. Accentuating further, she nodded and bowed her head in shame.

"Why didn't you report it to the police?"

"To survive in that world, you had to know when to shut your mouth and look the other way."

"And if you had reported it, what would have happened to you?"

"I won't be sitting here with you."

"How do you mean by that?"

"Andrew Sciorra did not become the wealthiest man in Canada by playing nice." The Private Investigator had insisted during their rehearsals that she dropped this line at a moment she herself could discern was a point where it would have the greatest emotional and psychological effect.

"So, your life was in danger?"

"He didn't threaten me or anything like that."

"Then why did you insinuate that you won't be sitting here if you had reported to the police?"

Nicole paused for a double heartbeat and then she looked up.

"Because Andrew will do anything to survive... he was unpredictable when he had his back to the wall. I couldn't risk it."

"So, you mean you didn't agree with the essence or nature of the act?"

"No, I didn't."

"And why did you do it then?"

The Private Investigator watched Nicole. They had talked about this in the mock up sessions. He had gently told her at the time to count up to ten before she responded. This was the point where the audience would start to empathise with her. This was the moment she could get the sympathy of a blind, selfish world. Nicole looked away but not to the direction of the Private Investigator. She remembered his direction.

"It was very difficult to bite the hand that was feeding me. The truth is that I was depending on him for my very survival, and at the time, all I could think of was indulging his fantasies and guaranteeing my position with him and... and... I was in love with him."

There was a moment of deep reflection on her response by the Editor. The Private Investigator held his breath. Bite the hook, bitch! He muttered in his pensive mind.

"I have a lot of respect for your courage in coming out to do this, Nicole, and I know this is painful for you. If you need a break to catch your breath, drink something, ease off some tension, please let me know, you understand me?"

Nicole nodded and wiped a slight tear that she had willed to slide down her rosy cheeks that now looked pale from the excess application of water resistant foundation. The Editor looked over at the Private Investigator.

"Can she get a handkerchief or something?" The Editor looked at the Private Investigator with something akin to disgust. Where was chivalry? The words were silent but angry.

He walked towards Nicole and brought out a well-pressed handkerchief from the inner breast pocket of his well-tailored jacket. He handed it to her and whispered.

"You are doing great."

She collected the handkerchief and dabbed lightly at her pretentious tear, then she looked up at him and smiled. She was loving it. An idea was forming in her mind. After this has all blown over, she would go south west to the Mecca of entertainment, settle her aching heart in the mirage that is Hollywood, and try her hands in the make-believe world of the unforgiving silver screen. These days notoriety was rewarded with celebrity and the accompanying material success. The Editor looked at her with a malaise that felt so very much like a feverish bout of pity.

"Are you okay?" she enquired.

"Yes."

"Do you want to continue?"

Nicole dabbed her dry eyes one more time and then nodded. The Private Investigator tapped her on her shoulder and walked back to his position of silent connivance. The Editor looked at her notepad, reined in her troubled thoughts, and continued.

"'Where was it that you filmed a threesome involving Andrew Sciorra and two under-aged girls?"

"In Montreal, he was there for a meeting and I went with him."

"You understand how serious this allegation is?"

"Yes, I do."

"And you are sticking to it."

"Yes, I am." She closed her eyes after she made that statement. She couldn't believe that she, who Andrew trusted with so much fervor, had now been forced and bribed into doing him in. She prayed silently that he never recovered from his state of mental gridlock, so that he would never get to witness the depth and scope of her betrayal.

"Okay," The Editor scribbled in her notepad and continued, "We will go back a bit; so, as regards Andrew Sciorra's relationship with his wife, did he tell you his marriage was troubled?"

"Yes."

"Can you remember how he described it?"

"Well, he used like swear words when he referred to his wife and cursed generally when he talked about the marriage. He really wasn't happy."

"Swear words like what?"

"Well, he called his wife… a cunt… a slut… a spoilt bitch who only knew how to blow through cash and didn't have any brains to see her through a normal day."

"He said that?"

"Yes and more." She was acting flawlessly according to script.

"More?"

"Yes."

"I would not ask what other disgusting words he used to address his wife, but instead, I want to know, how you took it, like how it affected you when you heard him speak about her in such terms?"

Nicole held her own counsel for a moment. This was a curveball. They hadn't rehearsed this. She couldn't look to the Private Investigator for direction so she had to dig deep and find a path that would lead her towards the light. She searched briefly, found an opening in the dark of reasoning, and stepped out of her quagmire.

"To be honest, I believed him."

"That she was all those things he said she was?"

"Yes… back in Regina, I know women like that… my aunt is

actually worse than he described, so it wasn't strange to me to hear him describe his wife in those terms."

The Editor nodded in spite of herself. What Nicole said was true. She also knew women who were worse than the uncouth description of his wife by Andrew but her ultra-feminist, rigid backbone was lout to bend in public admission of that, so she decided to change the direction of her questions.

"So, I presume your willingness to come out to talk about this is admission of the fact that you have changed your opinion about Andrew Sciorra and his actions?"

"Yes, I have." It came out with a remorseful undertone.

"And why have you changed your opinion?" Her eyes were questioning.

"The death of his wife, Annabelle."

"Do you blame him for that?"

"Yes, I do and I blame myself."

"I understand your blaming yourself, but why do you blame him?"

"Because of the phone call."

The Private Investigator beamed with pride. Nicole was good. Now, he could understand why Andrew was besotted with her and had made her his numero uno undercover sexual and emotional escape. There sitting next to him, was not just a twenty-one year old concubine of the wealthy, but a natural western geisha. The Editor's voice sounded high above his thoughts.

"Phone call... how do you mean?"

"The day she died... Andrew got a call from her."

"And?"

"He was angry, really mad; he cussed her out, accused her of infidelity, and told her that he was going to leave her."

"And how did you hear this?'

"He put the phone on speaker... he wanted me to listen in."

The Editor's eyes opened in disbelief and no sooner had they done that than they closed in narrow gashes as she fought to control her bubbling rage. How could he?! She screamed in her mind. How much she hated the human species of the masculine kind. Clare, her partner, would never treat her like that. She wondered how people could look at homosexuality as the greatest sin and vilify her lesbian partner and herself, but keep sealed, hypocritical lips in the face of the callousness of some heterosexual men. She held her breath for a second and then let out a hiss, like that of queen cobra about to strike.

"And you listened?"

"What was I supposed to do?"

"That was another woman like you that was being treated like an animal, I mean, he put her on speaker so you could hear him mistreat his wife; what kind of a man does that and what kind of a woman listens to another woman being treated like that?!"

"A woman that uses her body and feminine charm to survive, a woman that has been given a chance to escape a life of near-poverty and wanted to do anything to change the lot of her family and herself, a woman that is not as smart, as angry, as well-connected, as well-paid and celebrated as you are. That is the kind of woman that would listen and even watch another woman treated like shit, but would keep her lips shut even though her bruised and damaged heart cries out in pain." Nicole spoke with a dramatic cadence that had a ring of truth to it.

Her response caught the Editor unprepared. She was shocked at the amount of honest hurt that resonated from Nicole's voice and words. She was from a different world. A world of power game in high places, a world of influence peddling and fame measuring, a world of name dropping and gutsy tirades, a world of fine speeches and scholarly accolades, a world insulated from the true existence of pain, want, and neglect. The Editor felt chastised.

"I am sorry."

"It is okay. I understand," Nicole responded.

"So, what else did you overhear?"

"His wife was crying and begging him not to leave her and the more she cried and begged, the angrier he became, he screamed at her and threatened to shame her in the eyes of the world and she said to him that if he left her, she would kill herself..."

"She said that?" The Editor leaned forward in rising interest.

"Yes."

"And what did he say?"

"He said she should go ahead, kill herself, and save him the pain of her existence."

"My God!" The Editor's hand flew to her mouth and her notepad fell to the floor.

The Private Investigator rubbed his hands together in childish delight. This was unravelling even better than he and Timothy had expected. The legendary barracuda was melting into putty in Nicole's hands. They would mould her into something that, even in enlightened hindsight, she would not recognise.

"I can't believe he said that." The Editor mumbled the words in a daze.

"I thought he was saying it because he was mad at her, but what he said after she had said she was really serious about killing herself shocked me."

"What did he say?" she asked in dread.

"He said he would kill her himself if she didn't have the guts for once in her life to do what she said she would do and prove with her death that she was capable of an independent thought and action."

"What in the name of Jesus?" It was a whisper.

"You should have seen his face when he said it." Nicole added that, remembering at the nick of time to drive in the nail at every opportunity as the Private Investigator had repeatedly insisted.

"I don't know what to say."

"Now, you understand why I am here doing this."

The Editor nodded. Nicole sat there looking at her, willing her to ask more questions. The professional in the Editor allowed her sense the willingness of Nicole to reveal more, so once again, she bit the dangling hook. "I just want to go back and tie in some loose ends; I know you said you were invited to the Sciorra residence and was going to be held against your wishes to try to nurse Andrew Sciorra, I know you have filmed under-aged sex, you witnessed a phone call, and all, but what I don't understand is this... why will Andrew think his wife was ... you know ... the words you used?" The Editor couldn't even manage to utter the hurtful words.

"Because he suspected that she was cheating on him."

"Cheating on him... my Lord!... the nerve of that man!... even if she was, wasn't he cheating on her with you?" she couldn't help but express her outrage at the unfairness of it.

"It's a man's world."

The Editor shook her head in anger, bent down, and picked up the note pad. She kept shaking her head and panting audibly in anger as she scribbled on the notepad. When she was done documenting the words of Nicole and her own commentary, she looked up.

"So, did he have an actual proof of her infidelity?"

"Yes."

"What was it?"

"Therese."

"Therese?"

Nicole nodded.

"What about Therese?"

"She is not Andrew Sciorra's child."

"What?!" Shock ricocheted around the room as the Editor exclaimed.

The Private Investigator smiled as he watched the reaction of the otherwise well-put-together editor. Nicole had performed incredibly well. She had been convincing in an effortless way. The reaction of the Editor and her crew who had lapped like thirsty dogs at the fountain of her stories were in themselves informative of the strength of her stellar performance. The story would grow legs and run and when the legs were tired, it would grow wheels and then wings; it would fly to places unknown and light the fire of the reaction Timothy so desperately needed. Sometimes evil didn't live in the dark; it was itself the bearer of the flaming torch.

He brought out his cell phone and typed out a text. It read only three words that were pregnant with meaning, both for the sender and the receiver; "Coupe De Grace!"

16

Nosa sat on the high stool in the kitchen and watched Tirin Tirin chopping carrots on a wooden slab. He had on an apron and with a straight back, he presented the picture of a professional chef.

"...And they were all there from every place; China, Brazil, Ghana, Mexico, India..."

"Thank God you mentioned India; trust me, man, those guys are going to take over this country. Look everywhere, Indians; taxi, Indian man is the driver; corner store, Indian; government officer at the city hall, Indian; police man, Indian; real estate broker, Indian; they are climbing up the ladder, they even have members of parliament, ministers... soon and very soon, mark my words, we will have an Indian Prime Minister or an Indian Governor-General and when that happens, we are finished!" Tirin Tirin threw his hands up in the air in mock alarm.

"... and what is bad with an Indian Prime Minister?" Nosa enquired.

"What is wrong with kini? Don't you know the Indians are

like five billion people? And they move in hordes, like those ragos, you know—sheep— in the north in Nigeria. If you give them that job, then they would move like just ten million of their people here as charity for their home country. Imagine ten million Indians added to the thirty million Canadians; that is like hell as a residential district in heaven, madness, it will be so bad that if you cannot sing and dance..." He started singing and dancing like an Indian Bollywood star, one hand hanging over his head with the knife pointed high and the other pointing sideways at his hip, mimicking a popular song from a famous Indian movie, "... desi numbari o me desi numbari/me ni ka nu, na na ku di, me ni ka nu ona me nana ku de/yo yo, yo yo/ yo, yo, yo, yo, yo, yo" He finished with a flourish and returned to his carrot cutting with a renewed vehemence.

"You are racist!"

"Me, racist? Nah! An unmarried polygamist, yes! A spiritual pragmatist, yes! But racist, Naahhh! Do you know how many Indian babes I have given pleasurable happiness to or how much curry I use in my cooking?"

"I was talking about my exams and you have taken the gist somewhere else."

"Was I supposed to first take permission?"

"Constructive contributions, that's what is welcomed."

"You and your plenty English."

"Don't think I don't know you are capable of same things you just hide under the cover of this your clownish self, but I know you; you are an educated, well-brought-up mind."

Tirin Tirin stopped cutting his carrots and turned to Nosa. He looked annoyed. His nose flared as though Nosa had touched a raw, hidden nerve. Then he broke out in a swagger that appeared drunken but was actually the ritualised zig zag movements of the people known as Area boys, who terrorise the streets of Lagos.

"Ahhh... ma rogo o!... ami ti condemned... forgotten broda

of no known mother... government pikin number one!... the dustbin is my provider ... the motor park is my arena!... I am redeemed by my holy hustle!... ahhhhh!... you, who was mistakenly born in Nigeria... no near my side o!... Many wounding is the attention that I am giving... e ma so pe... you were not warned!" It came out with a guttural drawl, knife-drawing threatening circles in the air, and no sooner had he finished than he burst out laughing. "See how e dey fear; liverless dokita of an aje burra persuasion." with that flourish, Tirin Tirin turned to his carrots and continued his methodical chopping "So, what were you saying before you were so rudely interrupted?" he asked the mesmerized Nosa.

"We should like get you on TV. I'm sure Comedy Central can make big bucks from you, you'll make people laugh like mad, and get doctors coming to check your head."

"My friend, what were you saying before you were rudely interrupted?" he repeated again with playful chagrin.

"Now he goes serious; okay, I was telling you about my exams."

"I'm listening."

"So, the people there were like from every nation on earth, everyone chasing the jewel of the Nile..."

"Wasn't that a film with that brief looking guy... what's his name again?"

"Danny Devito."

"Yeah, the midget!"

"You are not taller than he is."

"I will pretend like I didn't hear that insult. Now, respect your old age and tell me more about your exams." He said the words in grandeur, like a self-serving king pardoning a formerly condemned, yet still rebellious convict.

Nosa looked at him as he finished the carrots and starting slicing a ball of cabbage.

He found himself smiling as he watched the diminutive man.

"There were like over three thousand of us there; that is a large group of out-of-work doctors, and this is just in Toronto. Imagine the amount in Vancouver, Calgary, Edmonton, Ottawa, all these people fighting for two hundred open positions every year. I mean, it is madness; how on earth can anyone explain the reason Canada would allow this continue?"

"Don't lose your shirt over it; the way they think, if you don't like it then go back to your country, and you know they don't include medical doctors amongst skills they need in the independent class application?"

"Why would they allow the folks return to their countries? I mean, what use is that? They are here already; that is what matters even if Canada didn't ask for the skills. So, if a lady migrates here based on her skills being sought-after and her husband is a doctor, what do they expect her to do? Leave him back in their country or have him become a house husband in order for the family to move on with life? I mean, didn't I hear over the news yesterday that Canada has a chronic shortage of doctors?" Nosa was getting worked up.

"Look at me; don't you think I should be doing something better than breaking my back in construction?"

"Don't change the topic."

"It's true; I came here with a degree from the University of Ibadan, a bachelor's in Civil Engineering. I tried, trust me, to get in, but no, they shut the door in my face, so what did I do? I went for the closest thing to what I studied that didn't have the wall of China built around it, construction," Tirin Tirin lectured on.

"So what are you suggesting?" Nosa was lost.

"These three thousand folks you talked about must face reality. There is no way in hell that Canada will give all of them jobs as doctors, so they could go to like Nunavut and freeze their asses off; chances are they will have a better chance of being doctors there than in the mad rush of Toronto or the other major cities. They could also go back to school, take up nursing or something. They already have medical knowledge, so that shouldn't be sweat for them, and if three to four years is too much stress for them, then they could do the EMT course or PSW stuff; that is short and work is abundant."

"EMT, PSW, what's that?"

"EMTs are the guys who work for the ambulances, the guys who keep you alive before real doctors take over; PSWs are personal support workers, they take care of..."

"Of course I knew who they were, just wanted to know if you know what you are talking about."

"Your problem is that you have no respect for your elders," Tirin Tirin said smiling "You behave like all these spoilt Canadian kids who were born and brought up in this anything-goes society."

"Maybe I am trying to make up for all the time I've been out."

"Don't try me o! Forget my size. If you mess up, I bulala you!"

Nosa laughed loud. Tirin Tirin never failed to pump the bright light of humour into his dark, dreary days.

"But seriously, do you think it's fair the way these people are being treated?"

"Nothing is fair in this world we live in, my guy; that's one of the shit you have to bear with when you up and move into another person's country. They set the rules, they play the music. Either you obey those rules or dance to the music or you do return-to-sender, thank you very much."

"Canada is calling for immigrants from every corner of the world..."

"Don't become a madman because of these people; do your own thing and let them do theirs because to be honest, Nigeria doesn't treat immigrants there any better."

"Oh, you are very wrong!" Nosa came down from the stool.

"How?" Tirin Tirin stopped cutting the cabbage and turned to him.

"Look at the expatriates from the US, UK, even Canada, we treat them like kings and queens, even the ones from the Middle East, from India, and China, we welcome them with open arms."

"What about the ones from Ghana, Cameroun, Benin Republic, and Niger, how do we treat them?"

"We treat them..."

"As second or even fifth class citizens, we make them cobblers, mobile tailors, gate men, washer men, cooks, house boys, and maids and the ones from Niger we are content to see them begging on our streets; is that what you call treating all people fairly?"

"I really..." Nosa was stumbling in his thoughts.

"Let's don't try to ask of the Canadians more than what we are or were willing to give to other strangers in our own countries. We are here out of their generosity, and as they want to use us to better their economy, we must learn how to use them to better our own personal economies. It has to be mutually beneficial. No harm done to either party, just living in a new society with our eyes open, ready to do what is necessary, to bend our backs to get what we want. You know how a male prisoner uses his ass to survive in jail?"

"You can't be serious?"

"As Machiavelli said, 'the end justifies the means.' So, Nosa, as a friend, my advice to you is that you should focus on you, pass those exams, take your chances, meanwhile, let us see how we can get you a PSW job to keep you busy as you study for your next exams." Tirin Tirn said solemnly.

Nosa stood there and watched Tirin Tirin wrap up his sermon. The little man turned around and faced his slicing while Nosa stood there pondering the honest words he had just heard from the most delightfully contradictory human being he had ever met.

Angela opened the door of her room and stepped out onto the polished Jatoba hardwood hallway. It was the day of the traditional quarterly family lunch that took place on Saturday at the Di Canio family residence. It normally was raucous and even more so, when any one of their multiple relatives were invited. Today their guests were the Bortoluccis.

Even as she descended the staircase, which had the same hardwood running down its several flights, she thought about the conflicted thoughts in her head. She knew that a time would come when she would have to confront her inner doubts and proudly step out into the light of public opinion and say with courage, 'this is me, take me as I am or move on.' She was tired of hiding in the shadows of pretence. Annabelle's death had been the one incident that began prying open the securely shut doors behind which lurked her true inner self. She was tired of pretending to be an average Catholic content with the dictates of the church, even though not necessarily obeying them. What would her family say if they knew of her true, more modern, and yet, very ancient spiritual views? What would they say if they knew that their own bubbly, severely obedient daughter looked at salvation, Jesus, Mary, and God in a far different light than they did? And what would Osaz—as she called Osasu—say when he found out that she was not all about raunchy sex, unbridled fun, and dove-eyed love? Would he embrace the deeper side of her, the side of her that vibrated with a pure truth? That part of her that, even though enlightened, still found itself addicted to the dictates of her flesh? And what would he understand of the depth of her love? This love that she had that was all at once sudden as it was consuming, burning her very enthrals with the fiery flames of adulation and breathless desire. This love that was awakening as it was revealing, leading her on as though she were caught in a dark tunnel and her love for him was the faraway speck of light that urged her to carry on.

This love that questioned and questioned but was yet patient enough to wait silently for answers, believing in the kernel of truth that lay in the core of the relationship they shared. This love that was inhumanely tolerant, yet courageous enough to venture into realms unknown, in search of the fresh experiences that would broaden the scope of her existence and give her love a language that held no prejudices and believed no lies.

What would her family say if they really knew her for what she was; an Italian bred in the ovens of Italian hood, forged in its flames to be that which every good well brought Italian girl of her ilk should be, but yet, now walking across the aisle of her religion and race to embrace foreign ideals of which she would normally be forbidden? What would they say if they knew that she was on the edge of revealing her true self and damning the gates of hell, the maelstrom that will come? Would they advise her to keep her counsel and wait for another day as she had always done, believing that all these like all things would pass and she would find her way back to her Italian hood to live out her life as unremarkably as she had been brought up to? Would they tell her that there was no point fighting a fight, the victory of which was doomed from the onset? Would they be like those who preached that only Catholicism had 'the light' and miscegenation was not of God? She knew her family, she knew of their beliefs, she knew they would stand up as one against her and fight her to the very last breath she drew, yet she was at the verge of drawing the battle line, standing in their face and revealing the truth of her, but first, she needed to know that Osasu would stand by her, fight the currents of the fast-moving river when it rushed ashore, struggle through the thickets of strife that she knew will populate her world, together, side by side, back to back. She knew that before she revealed herself to the family she had always known, she needed to reveal herself to the man she was getting to know even deeper as the days unfurled.

With her clouded mind and worried heart, she walked into the rambunctious family that sat talking in loud voices around the large dining table.

"There she is!" her father called out, smiling at her with love from his position at the head of the table.

Angela smiled in return, eager to shield the rawness of her thoughts from the eyes that all turned to her. Her mother stood up from the table and walked over to her. Her overly dramatic, fawning mother as they all knew her to be, eager to babysit even her oldest nephew who, though was forty-one, was still her very own 'Baby Giorgio' as she called him while playfully pinching his now tanned and lean, albeit once rosy and chubby, cheeks. Her mother hugged her, like it was the first time she had laid her bespectacled eyes on her even though she had last seen her only an hour and a half ago.

"Il mio amore," her mother said in Italian that came out as though it was choked with tears.

Angela hugged her mother obediently, sensibly playing the part. They kissed on both cheeks, disengaged, and turned to the table.

"Isn't my baby so beautiful?" her mother said, addressing the extended family.

"More beautiful than you were at her age." Her father teased.

"You have, my darling husband, always been so ugly, so very hideous in your looks and barbaric in your nature, that I married you as a favour to God."

The table thundered in laughter. The chandelier that hung from the high ceilings over the table seemed to sway with the force of the joy that exploded from the seated people around the table. Angela looked at her laughing family and even though she believed she was socially evolved compared to these souls that shared the same love with her, she couldn't deny her long suffering love for her.

"Okay, once again you win! I give up." He raised his arms up in mock surrender, "Now, would you allow the better version of you come sit with her family?"

Angela's mother laughed and led Angela to the other side of the table, she drew out a chair and watched her sit down, then walked back to her position next to her husband and placed a kiss on the lips. The table burst out in applause. Such was the genial love that was the living core of their extended family.

"So, Silvio, continue your story about this man... how do you say his name again?" Her father asked Silvio Bortulucci, who was seated a couple of seats away from him.

"Tirin Tirin,"

"Yes... Tirin... Tirin," he repeated the words as though it were a telephone ringing.

"A dear friend he is, trust me; funny like nothing you have ever seen, tiny like a leprechaun but as powerful as an ox. So, we are at this site looking at this burst mains, water spurting everywhere, trying to figure out how to shut it off because of the water pressure, then Tirin Tirin looks at me, he says, 'Oga Italo, I have a wonderful idea,' I turned to him, 'Tell me quick,' because I was frantic. He says, 'Why don't we pray about it?' I say, 'Pray about it?' he said, 'Yes, pray' and right there, he fell on his knees in all this water and raises his hands high up to the skies..." Silvio raised his hands, "...And he begins saying this prayer in some crazy language, it lasts like one minute, we were all watching this madness and when he was done, I asked him, 'What the hell did your prayer do?' He said, 'Oga Italo, relax, I serve a living God,' then he brings out his cell phone and places a call, now remember water is still spilling everywhere" Silvio mimics the phone call, "'Hello, I want to report a burst water mains, yes, very bad, it's flooding everywhere, yes I will give you the address, you have a five minutes response time, right? Good, okay here is the address...'" Silvio starts laughing as they all listen to him around the table, "So, after giving them the address, he hangs up and stands there smiling at himself, and I say, 'So what was that all about?' and he looks at me and says, 'I just fixed the problem; we will shut it off from the pumping station and a team will come over and fix the pipe itself,' I look at him and I said, 'Why did you need to kneel down and do all that prayer bullshit, when you could have just made the call?' and he looked at me and appeared surprised and then said, 'Because I was divinely inspired,' and I said, 'Bull shit,' and he asked me, 'Oga Italo, why didn't you call yourself?' and I thought for a minute and wondered why I hadn't thought about it, so I replied, 'I was confused, that's why' and he said, 'You see, you were confused because you were not divinely inspired, but I was divinely inspired that is why I was not confused. So first, I thanked God for the divine inspiration as we must all do when we are divinely inspired, after that, I made the call and here we are about to get the water mains fixed and work continues; Oga Italo, isn't God great?' Silvio finished his story to the already giggling crowd.

"You sure this is a real guy?" One of Angela's cousins asked with a smile.

"Oo as real as you get. I can actually give him a call and if he is not busy, he can drop by," he said earnestly.

"Hey, we have food and extra chairs; invite him over." Angela's father said in building excitement.

Silvio brought out his cell phone, placed the call and put it on speaker.

"Oga Italo." The call was answered. It was Tirin Tirin's voice. It was a whisper.

"Hey bro, it's me, Silvio."

"I know it's you, that's why I said, 'Oga Italo.'"

"Oh yeah, I missed that. So, what you up to?"

"Babysitting."

"Nice one, bro; whose child?"

"My roommate."

"Oh your roommate has a child?"

"No, sir." Tirin Tirin said it with a dramatic flair and then fell silent.

"You're babysitting your roommate?" Silvio sounded confused.

"Yeah, he is a grown-up man but sometimes he like retrogresses into this fetal state and when I see him like that, I have no choice but nurse him back to his real biological and mental state."

Every one around the table looked at each other. One of the Bortoluccis pointed to his head and rolled his finger before silently uttering the word "nuts."

"Interesting... Well, I was wondering if you could come over to this get together; I want you to meet some people."

"Really?"

"Yeah, they are family."

"Where?"

"Woodbridge."

"How many people there?"

"Say..." he did a visual head count, "... say eighteen."

"Hmmm... my boss calls me on a Saturday afternoon... out of the blue... not a work call but says he wants to check up on me... I call him 'Oga Italo' and he does not recognise that name... I say okay, maybe he didn't hear it... then he says he is inviting me to see his Italian family... eighteen people... out in Woodbridge... first time he has ever invited me anywhere that is not work..."

Everyone looked at each other incredulously as Tirin Tirin spoke on.

"... So, I say to myself... hmmm... why would Oga Italo do that which is not in his nature?... What is his goal?... I add everything together and I say to myself... the mafia call themselves family and the illuminati call themselves family... and I decide... this is not Oga Italo that is calling me but a Mafiosi or Illuminati... sorry you have the wrong number… good bye." And the line went dead. The two last phrases had been said in a jocular soprano.

There was silence for a moment and then in unison everyone burst out laughing. It was deep. It was honest. It was intoxicating. They laughed and laughed and laughed. Angela laughed along with them, even as she made a mental note to ask Osasu if he knew any character called Tirin Tirin. She knew he had to be Nigerian, because she knew Nigerians called Italians, Italos and Master, Oga, so chances was that a character like this must be known in the Nigerian community. But then, she caught herself even in the bout of her side-hurting laughter, Osasu might not know the joker of a fella since he rabidly avoided Nigerians as though they carried the plague. And as she laughed on, she asked herself, why in the first place does Osasu abhor and avoid Nigerians so much? And as the besotted lover she was, she filed the question in her mental in-tray, knowing that she had enough patience to wait for the manifestation of its answer. Still she and her family, both nuclear and extended, laughed on under the now clinking chandeliers that hung above their well-dressed and hilariously-infectious selves.

"Osasu!"

His name raced out of the looming darkness. The voice was hoarse and angry. It had a threatening ring to it that echoed with the very essence of evil.

He ran as fast as he could. The voice chased him. He jumped over the shape of a tree trunk that lay prone in his path. He landed on his feet in an unnatural angle and winced in pain as he nearly twisted his ankle. He was panting. Loud, dry, and fast paced. He knew he couldn't stop to catch his breath. The voice was too close. He ran.

"Osasu!" Now it came from somewhere to his left, very close to him; he swerved right to get away from it. He could have sworn he smelt the breath. It stank like the flatulence of a tortoise. He couldn't see through the mist that swirled in the darkness, yet he ran blindly into it. His arms were stretched out in front of him tearing at the cold leafy things that flogged his face and bare chest without mercy. He felt like crying, but crying will take too much effort, it will sap his flagging energy; he couldn't risk that, so he bottled his teary urge and ran a little faster.

"Osasu!!" This time it came out louder. It was filled with accusations and contempt. He felt his outstretched arms touch the vestige of the voice. It was slithering over an unseen surface like the phlegm of a hobo on the window of a restaurant that catered only to the bourgeoisie and the elitist pretenders.

He recoiled in deep irritation, but he couldn't afford the feeling as it obscured his attention, so he pushed it aside and tried to wish his tired legs to run faster. He had instinctively turned left after feeling the malignant molten mass that seemed to hang in the air in front of him. Yet, even now he could see that the darkness had become more impregnable, as though it was jealously guarding a secret it was wont to give up. He had no time to dwell on the change he had noticed from the suburbs of his mind, so he ran faster.

"Osasu!!" This time it exploded all around him; a suffocating high-pitched wail that seemed to suck out the very breath out of his rapidly constricting chest.

He fell to his knees and grabbed his chest with both hands. He had never felt this kind of pain before. It hurt so bad his ears and eyes lost their lives. Then when he felt he had reached the very edge of his threshold for pain, he willed his last once of strength and screamed with the very essence of his being.

"Noooooooo!!"

He sprang awake from his bed.

For a moment, he lost all sense of bearing and all he could feel was the cool sweat he was bathed in. Where am I? He asked himself in his disoriented mind and after a few seconds, he slowly began to see the silhouettes around him. The Bose flat screen TV on the wall, the open door to his walk-in closet, the highly-prized painting of a naked woman by Jibola Fagbamiye that hung on the adjacent home.

"Thank God," he whispered as the familiarity of his room slowly quietened his pounding heart.

The chopper's blade flogged and cut through the air in the same movement as it screamed under the rising sun. The runway of the small municipal airport at Buttonville in Markham was nearly deserted. There were four men standing a short distance from the helicopter as its blades churned and it rose up into the rolling winds. They watched it as it rose higher and higher and then banked forward and fly towards the sun, climbing the white-streaked blue sky.

Behind the throttle, sporting dark Ferragamo sunglasses, was Timothy Vinelatter and sitting at the front passenger seat was Therese Sciorra. They were flying to Ottawa to observe the Remembrance Day ceremonies from on high. Therese had refused to go; Timothy had insisted. She was dressed very conservatively in honour of the day; he didn't think it poor taste to be garishly dressed.

They were both seated in a helicopter and Timothy had announced that he was going to fly it all the way to Ottawa, refuel, and return back later in the evening. Therese wasn't at peace with his plan, but she trusted him; he had a full pilot's license on different aircrafts and had piloted his private jet to Europe and the Middle East a couple of times. It was more of the helicopter she wasn't sure about. It looked so frail and could have passed for an oversized toy plane in one of the super Toys "R" Us shops.

It headed in full speed towards the horizon and Therese looked out of the window at the tiny dots and winding broad lines that were houses and roads. She imagined for one moment if this was the same sight the Angels had as they looked down from their heavenly perches. The view was changing rapidly as the plane flew further, from the red and grey roof tops and broad pencil strokes to rolling greenery and thick, wide swathes of bushy green that looked like a thousand broccolis bunched together in a heads up position. Still, the helicopter flew further and she could see the Highway 401 snaking through distant towns that looked scanty when compared to the crammed developments of the Greater Toronto Area. They flew in silence for what seemed like an eternity. This was the kind of period when she tried to enforce her need for respect from Timothy. She was here against her will but had come on the trip because Timothy tried to build Mount Vesuvius from a termitarium. She had come for the sakes of peace and was not going to utter one word to him throughout the journey. If he insisted on staying in the kitchen, she was going to turn up the heat. The helicopter kept clunking towards the horizon and they kept feeding the bitter silence that hung between them.

After a while, Therese looked down again and strained harder as she tried to see if she could identify the towns from that height.

"Cobourg?" No, they must have passed that already.

"Trenton?" It couldn't be; where was the canal?

"Belleville?" She wasn't too sure; where was the Moira River?

"Kingston?" It could be but it should look bigger if it was.

"Gananoque?" If it was, then she should be seeing the Thousand Islands Parkway.

And just as she was about taking her eyes off the scattered formations before her, she saw the St. Lawrence River and smiled. The helicopter banked to the right and flew closer to the river. She kept her eyes glued to its approaching blueness. If Timothy wanted to scare her with this kamikaze dive, she wasn't going to give him the satisfaction of hearing her scream in fear, she said to herself and steeled her nerves by grabbing tight to the armrests of her chair. She closed her eyes tight and clenched her teeth. Her stomach felt queasy, like a million nightingales were doing the tango. She began counting down from hundred. Ninety-nine, ninety-eight, ninety-seven, ninety-six, ninety-five, and just as she was about to say the next number the chopper came out of its dive and settled. She felt the smoothness of the ride, no sudden bumps, no trembling, just an effortless cut through the air to the chorus of clapping, rotating blades. Since she was satisfied that all was well and the impending danger averted, she exhaled and opened her eyes and the sight that greeted her took her breath away.

There sprawled out before her, where five yachts. They stood bobbing on the placid waters of the St. Lawrence River. On each of the yachts were a number of men holding up alphabets cut from galvanised aluminum sheets. It took her less than a minute to read each alphabet, join them together in a coherent whole, and read it out in a flowing sentence.

WOULD YOU MARRY ME THERESE?

She looked at it again and read it one more time. Her heart leapt in her chest, a lurching action that was of joy and also in the same instant of incomprehension. She was giddy with excitement, and yet so faint that she feared that a sudden movement on her part would cause the helicopter to fall out of the skies and hurtle down uncontrollably towards the inviting waters. She was gripped in the strangulating vice of bad luck. In the recent past, every good thing that happened to her seemed to be so promptly followed by something irrevocably bad. So why will this be different? She found herself asking.

"Therese," Timothy's voice knocked on her pulsating ear.

She willed all her power to quell her fright and turn her head.

He was looking at her with a smile on his face. His eyes were covered by the sunglasses and as though hearing the question in Therese's head, he removed his sunglasses. The helicopter hovered high over the yachts and Therese looked with sweet bedazzlement at the hunk of a man she had spent a couple of years of her life. Every iota of anger, irritation, loathing, doubt, fear fizzled like ashes being blown away in the air, circling high and high into the firmaments above.

"Therese, would you give my life a meaning, colour my heart with joy and make me the man I was created to be... Baby love, would you marry me?"

She silently looked at him. There was no movement. The chopper blades kept applauding. And then slowly, her lower lips starting trembling and hot tears made their way happily down her cheeks. Therese was awestruck and it took all she could do to manage a nod. Timothy smiled, reached into his pocket while he balanced the throttle with the other hand and brought out a tiny, black leather box. He opened it with his thumb and forefinger before stretching his arm out and showing her the contents of the box.

She sat there staring at the most beautiful diamond ring she had ever seen. It was huge. Like a mountain of glittering glass winking up at her. This was the rock on which their future would be based. A symbol of a love that was so very much deeper. She had waited for this day. She had dreamt dreams and imagined visions but never had this scenario unfolded in her mind. With hesitant hands but one that exulted in her changing fortunes, she reached out and collected the box from Timothy's outstretched hands. It looked and felt like a benevolent collecting the sacrament of Holy Communion from the outstretched fingers of His Holiness the Czar of the Vatican.

Therese sat there as the helicopter slowly descended on one of the helipads on the second largest island in the archipelago. Her heart was about bursting. Her pulse quickened with infinite possibilities. And on the throttle expertly guiding the helicopter to touchdown, was the silently jubilant Timothy. His grin was sly and the glitter in his eyes mirrored the deceit in his heart.

The wedding was another stroke towards his devious plan to steal from under the noses of the seeing. In his books, the son-in-law of a King with one child, if he played his cards well, had the high probability of being a future King himself, especially if that son-in-law was Timothy Vinelatter.

17

Nurse Harriet turned from the page of the book she was reading and looked over at the sleeping Andrew. She watched his relaxed face and listened attentively to the hum of his breath. It sounded normal. As she was about turning to her book, her eyes roved up to his eyes and she noticed that there was a stream of tears flowing down the corner of his eye. It ran down in a river, down to the pillow on which his head lay.

"Mr. Sciorra," she called him in a low voice.

There was no response.

"Mr. Sciorra," she called, a little louder.

Once again there was no response.

She could see he was breathing in a normal fashion. His chest rose and fell in an even rhythm. She was not alarmed. She was worried.

She placed the book on the side table and pulled out a couple of tissues from the silver tissue box, then she stood up and walked to the bedside of Andrew. Once there, she stood by him for a while, looking down at his sleeping form. He looked so peaceful but the tears that were flowing and soaking the pillow showed he was deeply troubled.

She knelt down by the bedside and began speaking in a soft voice. It sounded like a mother reading a bedside story to her tucked-in child. It was calming.

"Mr. Sciorra... this is Harriet... I am here by your side... do not cry... please, do not cry... what is happening to you will pass, believe me, it will pass... I want you to know that there are a lot of people out here who are pulling for you... a lot of people praying and believing you will get well... you have to be strong, Mr. Sciorra... you have to fight... fight real hard... your daughter, Therese... she is so lonely... so alone... She needs her father, Mr. Sciorra... she needs you... you have to forgive yourself, Sir... you have to let the past go... we love you and we want you back... everyone of us... everyone of us... try and sleep.... forget about everything and just sleep... tomorrow you will feel better." She finished speaking as she cleaned the tears from his otherwise peaceful-looking face.

Nurse Harriet didn't realise that all the while she had been speaking to Andrew as he lay on the bed in his tortured sleep, Phillip had been standing at the doorway watching her.

"Andrew is lucky to have you by his side," he said as he walked into the room.

She was startled and turned around and when she saw Phillip, she held her face in embarrassment and remorse.

"I'm so sorry, Mr. Neri." It came out as an audible whisper.

"You shouldn't be sorry; I should be the one apologising for not knocking," he said as he stopped at the foot of the bed.

"You didn't need..." She attempted to speak as she stood up.

"Yes, I did need to knock; I need to show you and Andrew respect." Phillip wasn't allowing her act the subservient part. "So, I say I'm sorry."

Her smile opened up like a lotus flower in full bloom. She could feel the pleasantness of his person right at the pit of her stomach. Her giddy smile met his subdued smile and from the periphery of her tunnel vision, she could see the reflection of the fireworks that were exploding.

She walked over to him like an automaton and before he could make sense of her intention or unexpected action, she encapsulated him in a hug. Phillip was shocked for a second. He had never imagined she would breach his personal space. This isn't how the relationship between an employer and an employee should play out, he thought to himself. He hired her so he could rightfully call her his employee even though his hiring authority came from the Sciorras. In the seconds that followed that second of initial shock, Phillip found himself naturally giving into the warmth of her large heart as he returned her hug.

"Thank you so much," she whispered.
"Why are you thanking me?" he asked.
"For being you."
"I am always me."
"That is exactly what is so beautiful about you."

He didn't know what to say. Her voice had changed. He would have lied to himself if he didn't in all honesty acknowledge the truth of her intent he could hear in it. Nurse Harriet was not just an employee who admired her boss for all the positives he brought to his functioning on the job, instead she was a woman who had developed a soft spot for her male boss and that soft spot wasn't in the least platonic. He took a deep breath in as he wrapped his head around the stunning reality and gently extricated himself from the hug. She stood there for a moment, sensing the change in the mood of the room and knowing that Phillip had somehow felt the inner yearnings of her preening heart. This time around, she didn't apologise or stand there in catatonic awe, but instead, quietly walked over to her chair and sat down. Phillip stood there and consciously kept his eyes on the sleeping Andrew.

"How is he?" Phillip finally asked.

"He is the same." It was a subdued response.

"Same?"

"Yes, like he was yesterday and the day before and the day before that; the same since the day I got here," Nurse Harriet could feel the sadness creep from her toes up through her legs, her pelvis, her torso and coagulate at the base of her throat. She was mourning the tragic end of a relationship that never started. It was not *even* a still birth; it was an abortion. She closed her eyes and clenched her hands to stifle the pain.

Phillip turned to her and saw her sitting there, her face contorted in an unsightly frown. He knew at that instant that she had felt the true reason why he abruptly ended their earlier hug. He felt sorry for hurting her, but he knew the expectations of his position. He understood that he couldn't encourage her on a fruitless adventure, a desire that could not be met and even as he stood there watching her, he unconsciously allowed himself pull down the drawbridge over the moat that surrounded his heart. It had been a long time since the death of his partner, Haykuhi, who had died in a car accident twelve years ago. Although he had sworn never to care about anyone so intimately again as he dedicated his heart as an altar to her memory, he found himself questioning the lingering interest he had shown to Nurse Harriet but had up to that moment passed off as an appreciation of everything that was different from the caustic nature of Nurse Maria. He actually heard his voice before he realised he was already speaking to Nurse Harriet.

"What do you do when you get off work in the morning?" Nurse Harriet wasn't expecting the question as she battled her emotions so she remained silent.

"Harriet?" It came out very endearing.

She felt it at the same time as she heard it; the layering of affection that was spread across her name like peanut butter on a toasted slice of bread. She slowly turned to him.

"Yes?"

"I was asking what you normally did when you got off work."

"Me?" She was confused.

"Yes, you... Harriet." He was smiling.

"I usually go home, get breakfast, and watch some shows I have recorded and then I go to sleep."

"Well, I know you care a lot about Andrew and you know I care a lot about him too, we also know that he doesn't have too many friends here, so I was thinking that since we both are on the same team, it would be smart to get to know each other better; what do you think?" She had lost her words as the wind of hope gave life to her sails. She nodded.

"So, why don't we do breakfast and catch up."

Once again, she nodded. Once again, he smiled.

"I guess it's good morning then."

"Good morning, Mr. Neri." She finally gave voice to her words.

"It's Phillip." He corrected her in a gesture that drew lower his drawn bridge.

"Good morning, Phillip," she said in a whisper.

"Take care of Andrew... and of yourself." With that, he turned around and walked out of the bedroom. He shut the door behind him in a bid to shut off the sound of his beating heart, hoping by God that she didn't hear it.

What the hell are you doing, Phillip? He screamed inwardly at himself as he hurried down the hallway towards the winding staircase, fleeing from a certain truth he had finally found the courage of confronting.

The heat was sweltering, undulating waves of burning energy raining down on the Lagos landscape from an unforgiving sun. People went about the normal aspirations—both desired and undesired, with a certain magnanimity that spoke to the degree of fortitude to which they had accepted the luxury in few cases and the drudgery in most cases—of their daily lives.

The bank stood majestic in the oasis of wealth in the vast desert of deprivation and decay. There were uniformed guards at the gate who exuded boredom and lackadaisical disposition to their monotonous jobs of opening the gate to vehicular traffic and the brutal or courteous control of the entry and egress of people, depending on their ability to colour their day with a courteous greeting or an errant naira note.

There was a huge fountain in front of the bank, sitting securely within the walled compound. It was painted white and made up of an eagle on a pedestal beneath whose talons were the words GUARDIAN BANK OF NIGERIA. The water from the fountain sprayed up in parallel spurts and flowed back down the drain in the marbled floor to be recycled back for its aquatic display. Ironically, the houses that bordered the houses on the left, right, and behind didn't have running water, so they had private boreholes pumping their water from the deep wells that sat in their backyards. This was Victoria Island, the once exclusive government reserved residential area that had morphed into a ridiculously priced business district dotted with doubly obscenely priced residential mansions, a haven for the kleptocrats, morally-jaundiced bureaucrats, and unrepentantly-greedy and self-serving business men. This was the best part of Nigeria morphing daily into the worst part of the country. This was the symbol of promise that had become a tombstone of its potential.

In a lavishly furnished office in the top-most floor of the glass-walled bank, seated on two leather chairs, were the Managing Director of the Bank and the family lawyer of the Ewekas. While the latter was leaning forward in earnest engagement, the former was leaning back, relaxed, and listening with megalomaniac aplomb.

"What I heard is that the account is in your bank and also that she had a safe deposit box here." The lawyer spoke in all seriousness.

"What if it's not true?"

"Then I will pack my bags and leave your bank, simple as that, I will not disturb you again with my requests."

"Like I said before, I really cannot help you."

"Why would you say that, Kola?"

"Because it is the truth."

"It is not the truth."

"So, are you going to tell me what is true or not?"

"I am your friend, Kola, if you..."

"This is business."

"Fine. Can't you just go through your records and confirm the information I am giving you?"

"You know this involves probate issues?"

"I know it does, but that route is too cumbersome. I don't want to waste my time going through the messed up courts. If you confirm it's there, then I will have reason to bear the pain of the probate process; I need the confirmation before I even bother." The plea of the conscientious lawyer to the financially-cold banker was evident in his tone.

"But even if I did that, I wouldn't be able to tell you either a yes or a no."

"Why is that?"

"Personal accounts are highly confidential."

"Come on. Kola. This is me, why are you talking like you are dealing with a stranger?"

"This is the bank. When I am in this office, it's strictly business."

"Okay, if you won't do it for me, do it for Ibude Eweka; he was your friend."

"Well, the account you are asking for is not in his name, right?"

"It is in his wife's name."

"There you go. Even if Ibude was sitting in the same seat you are on right now, I will tell him the same thing. I can't reveal confidential bank details to individuals who are not the owners of the accounts, joint signatories, possessing a legal, notarised power of attorney documentation, or empowered by the law of the land to possess the information."

"So if I go through probate, you will give me access to this account if it exists?"

"Why won't I?"

"You know you are a prick, right?"

"Well, we are living in a very dubious world, my friend, my clients are happy to have a banker like me, and I'm sure you will too if you did open an account in this bank like I have been asking you to for ages."

"Oh, is this about that?"

"No, even if you did open an account now, I wouldn't give you the information."

"Kola the money, na wa for you o!" The lawyer leaned back on his chair in exasperation.

"Gani the law, na so we see am," he replied laughing.

"I just really want to do something for Ibude's son." The lawyer spoke his thoughts aloud and then yawned in admission of the hopelessness of it all.

"Does he know about this account you are talking about?"

"No."

"Why?"

"What is the point in raising his hopes?"

The banker did not respond as he ruminated on the wisdom of the statement. Then not being able to find an adequate response, he decided to ask a question.

"What of the elder son?"

"Osasu?"

"Yeah, that one."

"No word, like he just disappeared."

The banker again thought about the response for a moment

and then sighed loudly. It was deep and carried across the wariness of his contemplative mind.

"May God save us from sons like him."

"Amen," the lawyer contributed in honest agreement.

The two men sat there in silence, thinking about their late friend, Ibude Eweka, and the unfair cards life had dealt him.

The lady with the fiery red hair kept her gaze fixed on Tirin Tirin and Nosa. She wasn't going to give any ground to their demands.

"Ma'am, believe me; it is not too late to come to your senses?" Tirin Tirin said with all seriousness.

"Are you serious?" She was gobsmacked.

"If I wasn't serious, I will be laughing, trust me," Tirin Tirin continued with a dead-pan expression.

"You can't come in here and insult me?" She was furious.

"Why would I insult you? Wouldn't I be out of my mind to do that when I know I need your help?" He countered with a mystified look.

"Precisely what I was thinking," She concurred.

"Exactly. That is why I said it really is not too late to come to your senses."

"There you go again!" she threw her arms up in the air. She was incensed.

"Ma'am, please don't be mad at me; I am just trying to communicate with you."

"You are pissing me off!"

"Look, if you help us, we will just leave and your day won't be ruined."

"Okay, I think that's what I will do, since you want to waste your money, then be my guest. What's his name?" She rolled her chair to the computer and began typing on the keyboard.

"Nosa Eweka."

"Sorry Ma'am, it is Nosakhare Eweka." Nosa butted in.

"Bros, the computer no go fit carry dat name o, na error e go soon hala." Tirin Tirin said laughing.

"How do you spell that?" she asked.

"N-O-S-A-K-H-A-R-E and the last name is E-W-E-K-A." Nosa spelt it out.

"Great, so what day are you good for the exams?" She asked.

"Today will be best."

"Today?"

"Yes, I'm very well-prepared."

She typed and then printed out a document. She handed it over to Nosa.

"Thank you, Ma'am," he said as he collected it.

"You pay in the next office."

"God bless your sweet heart and your lovely red hair," Tirin Tirin said with a broad smile.

"Can you please leave?" She didn't find it funny.

Nosa kicked him on the foot and headed to the door. Tirin Tirin bowed to the lady who rolled her eyes in response and hurried after Nosa. When he got to him, he whispered.

"That's how you deal with the Oyinbo people; you start creating a scene or you get under their skin, they will quickly give you what you want and send you on your way."

"One day they will call the cops on you."

"For what crime?"

"Being a public nuisance."

"Dem never born that Olopa." Tirin Tirin fired back immediately with playful chagrin.

"Whatever. Me, I'm going to revise for the exams. You can go wait in the lobby or the car or go home."

"See this ungrateful goat!" he exclaimed as they walked into the other office.

"Lower your voice." Nosa pleaded.

"Why? Do you see any sign that says no noisemaking here?"

Tirin Tirin argued and pinched Nosa on his buttocks "That's for not saying thank you."

Nosa pushed his hand away as they walked into the office. Their playfulness was infectious and instantly brought a smile to the middle-aged woman who sat behind the cashier's booth. Nosa got there and proceeded to pay for the examinations. Just then, Tirin Tirin's phone began ringing. He took out his cell phone and the ring tone exploded into the hearing of the occupants of the room. They were intrigued.

"Tirin Tirin, gbosa! eh, gbosa! eh, eh, gbosa! Tirin Tirin, gbosa! eh..." the ring tone continued. He looked at the caller ID, it read SILVIO.

"... gbosa! eh, eh, gbosa, eh..." he picked the phone and cut off the sound of the ring tone which had actually been recorded in his voice singing the song.

"Oga Italo, I remain loyal!" he said into the phone.

"Hey dude, you hung up on me two weeks ago."

"Was that you?"

"Of course it was."

"I thought it was a Mafiosi or Illuminati; I don't want anything to do with folks like that, man."

"What the fuck will they want from you, dude?"

"Oh, don't look at me like the ordinary construction guy you see; I got hidden value and mystical people or people who operate underground know it."

"You one crazy motherfucker, man," Silvio said laughing.

"Tirin Tirin at your service, licence to love and laughter, 006, before Bond, I was. My name is Tirin, Tirin Tirin." he finished mimicking the verbal flow of James Bond.

"Damn men, you should have come over to my cousin's and make them shit and piss their pants."

"Thank you very much; I'm not into those kinds of fetishes."

"Fuck you, man. Who the fuck was talking to you about shit

like that?"

"You know one can never be too sure about folks like you, sir." Tirin Tirin said with a courteous tone.

"I love you, man; you fucking funny. Check this out, I want you to come over for the next lunch we are having, three months from now, no excuses. Are you game?"

"Definitely, can I bring a friend?"

"Fuck yeah. I hope he is as funny as you are?"

"He is a bore, but I will be twice as funny to make up for him."

Silvio erupted in a loud round of laughter at the other end of the phone; Tirin Tirin took the phone away from his ear to save his ear drums. Nosa finished paying the fees, thanked the middle-aged, perpetually-smiling lady and walked over to Tirin Tirin.

"Done," he said with relieved finality.

They both turned and walked out of the office. Tirin Tirin put the phone back to his ear when he heard Silvio's voice.

"You crack me up, man. So, are we game?"

"Definitely, who am I to say no to the boss?"

"Cut the boss crap, man; my dad is the boss, not me."

"If you say so."

"So, how is the new site? I haven't been there in a month or so."

They continued talking as Tirin Tirin made his way to the car. He had decided to go home and catch some sleep and then come back to pick Nosa up when he was done with his exams. These were the exams that would open the world of Personal Support Workers to Nosa and allow him work at night and read for the second part of his medical exams during the day. He had taken the day off work to ensure he got to sit these exams. He had also pulled in favours from a friend of his who was already a personal support worker to give Nosa a three-day practical crash course. Then Nosa had read the entire syllabus in two days and now in under a week, he was ready for the exams. The kid was extremely bright, Tirin Tirin conceded. With the right guidance, Canada could be so much more favourable to him than it had been to Tirin Tirin, he had often told Nosa.

Tirin Tirin hung up the phone as he got into the car. He thought to himself, as he slotted his key into the ignition, about the irony of life. He remembered picking up Nosa from the airport that day several months ago and as arranged with his relative in Nigeria, he figured it was just a couple of weeks stay until Nosa found his footing, but now, here they were totally bonded as brothers. Life was truly a box of chocolates, he surmised to himself and as he eased out of the parking lot, he remembered his promise to hook up Nosa with a lady. He couldn't understand how the young man had gone without sex in months; he could understand beating the beef to ease the tension in the twin balls, but then, that was for folks locked up in detention or folks that were so ugly their own mothers cried when they saw them. But for folks like him and Nosa, fine men with finer bodies, the valley of pleasure that rested between the soft thighs of the beings of feminine persuasion was where their destiny lay; it was where bliss resided, the tomb of Tutankhamen, the proverbial El Dorado, the fountain of life, the Garden of Eden, Paradise. He had to get someone for Nosa; he had to help him spill *but not sow* his wild oats.

The Editor placed the phone back on the receiver and leaned back on her swivel leather chair. The whole story was even bigger than she had ever imagined, she told herself. It was career and life changing, something that had the potential of bringing down a great dynasty of untold wealth and immense power. Is this something she wanted to pull the magazine into? Was she ready to take whatever fallout resulted from this? Was she willing to give the other networks that were coming with her on this the assurance that everything about these accusations was the gospel truth and not just the vengeful machinations of a vengeful lover or an angry family bent on taking their pound of flesh for the untimely demise of their flesh and blood? She knew the story needed to be told, not because it was riveting but because it revealed so much of what unbridled power could do. The cankerworm it festered in the fabric of society. It would shine the light on the need for checks and balances, speed brakes, and social handcuffs that protected the poor and vulnerable from the rich and predatory. It could be the beginning of a new era; an era that heralded social responsibility and accountability for the rich and poor alike. The thoughts danced around her head like a pod of dolphins breaking through the rolling surface of a calm ocean in joyful abandon. They splashed and splashed, gathering momentum and leaping higher with rising crescendo. She looked up at the ceiling and all she could see were unrestrained possibilities. Her research team had scoured through the documents and evidences the Private Investigator had provided on behalf of Nicole. The letters, the cards, the pictures, they had confirmed the dates she had supplied. The locations had cross checked. They had pulled up her phone log and each outgoing and incoming that was associated with Andrew was scrutinised. The accommodations they had stayed in as they had their world wide trysts. The bank accounts and the wire payments were revelatory of a financially rewarding relationship. Andrew Sciorra was paying Nicole big bucks to hold his hand, warm his bed, listen to his whining, and generally be there for him.

She sighed to herself and sat back up. To cover all angles, she needed to speak to Therese and give her an opportunity to defend herself before she was excoriated in the unforgiving court of public justice. The information about her not being the biological child of Andrew Sciorra, but instead, a bastard who was the result of an illicit affair by her late mother was in the plainest terms, massive. It was like the news of the Titanic sinking into the cold embrace of the Atlantic after the fatal kiss of the iceberg. It would reverberate through the corridors of the people that mattered and change many a calculation. Therese needed to speak to it before she lost the chance and initiative. She reached for the phone, picked it up, and pressed a button. There was a buzz and her secretary's voice came on.

"Do you need anything, Ma'am?" the voice sounded.

"Yes, can you get me on to Therese Sciorra?"

"Definitely, one minute."

The phone went numb. The Editor took in a deep breath in preparation and slowly exhaled. She needed to calm her nerves.

"Her Personal Assistant is on the line, Ma'am, can I place her through?"

"Yes, thank you."

"Hi, this is the Editor-in-Chief of *The Quill*; I understand that I am speaking to the Personal Assistant of Miss Therese Sciorra."

"Yes you are. I am Angela Di Canio."

"Nice of you to take this call."

"You are welcome; what can I do for you?"

"I was wondering if I could speak with Miss Sciorra about a story we are working on that unfortunately concerns her."

Angela heard the word "unfortunately" and her antennas started buzzing.

"When you say unfortunately, can I know how you mean?"

"I would love to tell you, dear, but it happens to be for the ears of Miss Sciorra alone." It was icily crisp.

"I understand, let me see what I can do as regards fitting you into her very tight schedule."

"You will be doing just the right thing if you can manage to get her to meet me at the soonest possible time." She kept up her coldness.

"Most definitely, how about two weeks to this date on the Tuesday by one, lunch perhaps?" Angela asked.

"What about tomorrow, dear?" It dripped with sarcasm.

"Miss Sciorra will be leaving for an extended vacation and won't be available."

"I advise you to make her available, look up our numbers, and have her call me. Am I understood?" her haughtiness rang in every word.

"Miss Sciorra will call you at her earliest convenience; is there anything else I can do for you, madam?" Angela professionally held her tongue as she proceeded to dismiss her. She didn't care if she was the head of the biggest magazine in all of Canada. To Angela, she was just one of the hacks that were looking to drive one more nail into Annabelle's casket and if she could help herself she would deny everyone of them access to Therese, Andrew, or anyone that was associated with the Sciorras.

"That will be all and by the way, next time you address me, you will be well-advised to use Ma'am and not madam."

"Good day, madam," Angela retorted and hung up the phone.

The Editor sat there with the phone in her hand. Her fury bubbled to the surface and she slammed the hand piece back on its base. The table shook. She screamed loudly to give an escape to the rage that had built up so suddenly in her. Her voice ran around the floor in which her office sat. The souls who laboured at their work places pretended like they heard nothing. It was the second of many screams to come. They knew their boss and they also unanimously agreed that the only way of surviving in her world was to politely ignore her quirks and unquestionably obey or satisfy her whims and caprices. There were no half measures when it came to dealing with her. You were either good or evil. In or out. A friend or an enemy. She existed in realms of extremes and only the seemingly or pretentious extremist could roll through its band waves. Ironically, she was the one who defined the word. So you had to give her the reins and allow her take the lead, if not, you got out of her way or found another job to avoid your being chewed up, spat out, and promptly forgotten.

The Editor was now prancing around her office in blood red haze. Her anger was the singular focus. She, who she said was a champion that fought for the defenceless against the oppressor, didn't have an inkling of the fact that she was a full-bodied, complete tyrant in her own right. The one who fought against the trappings of vanity was herself trapped in its seductive embrace, with the sad commentary being that she didn't even realise it.

She raged on in her thoughts: How dare she? How dare a common Personal Assistant speak to her that way? She would show her. She would give her a taste of her power. She would change her world for the worse. She would destroy the very foundation upon which she existed.

"I'm okay, Mom, you got to believe me." Nicole spoke into the phone as she lay on the sectional sofa in the living room.

"We want to come down and see you," her mother insisted over the phone.

"I'm like up to my neck in work, mom, you guys can't come down now."

"What work?"

"What sort of question is that, Mom?"

"What kind of work keeps you away from your family for so long?"

"Modelling, mom, I told you it's crazy busy."

"We never see your pictures or you in front of magazines..."

"Come on, Mom, I sent you pictures and a magazine..."

"That was like years ago, Nicole."

"My bad, I should send you more stuff I've done."

"I don't want to see your work; I want to see you. We love you Nicole and we miss you."

"I love you too, Mom, all of you; soon, I will come over and spend time with you."

"I don't want you to promise anything, cos the pain of you breaking them is too much."

"Okay, just know that I am trying to get out of all this modelling, singing, and acting stuff, saving enough to go back to school, start again, just like you always wanted me to." Nicole said in a soulful voice.

"Really?"

"Yes, mom."

"Oh my God!" She screamed in delight.

"I'm thrilled you are happy, mom."

"I'm overjoyed; your dad is going to be so proud of you when I tell him."

"I know he will but I also want you to know that you might hear a lot of stuff about me in the news, stuff that you won't like."

"Are you in trouble?"

"No, just that I am trying to turn a new page, get on with a new life, but I have to close the page on my old one."

"What are you talking about?"

Just then, the front door opened and Nicole could hear voices in the doorway.

"Mom, can I call you back?" she whispered.

"Are you okay?"

"Yeah, just need to call you back." She continued whispering.

"You're scaring me, Nicole."

"I'm okay, Mom, I'm at work and need to go."

"Okay, love, take care of you and please call. I love you."

"Love you too." She hung up the phone and sat up. She adjusted her top to cover the cleavage and looked up just in time to see the Private Investigator walk in with a grey-haired man in his late fifties.

"Oh, you are up." The Private Investigator said as soon as he saw her.

"Hi." She responded, looking instead at the man in suit.

"This is Mel Rubinstein; he is an attorney and will be handling your case."

Nicole frowned in confusion. She looked up at the Private Investigator and asked him silent questions through her perplexed eyes.

"My pleasure," the grey-haired attorney said and stretched out his hand for a handshake.

Nicole tore her eyes from the Private Investigator and briefly shook the hand of the lawyer before quickly removing her hand and looking once again at the Private Investigator.

"I am told you will like to press charges against Miss Therese Sciorra for assault, kidnap, illegal confinement, and threat to life and property."

She wheeled about and stared at him. Her eyes were open wide in numbing shock.

"Mel, give Nicole and I a moment, would you? The family room is just around the staircase over there."

He nodded and walked towards the direction to which the Private Investigator had just pointed. Once they heard the door shut behind him, Nicole burst out, speaking in lightning fast speed.

"What the hell is going on? No one bleeding told me about any charges I was pressing against Therese or me meeting any lawyer."

"I told you that you will do as we say; no questions."

"That was for the interview with the magazine and the television crap."

"You think we are paying you a million bucks just for that?"

"Yes, that was the deal."

"I tell you the deal, you hear me?"

"I am not filing any charges against Therese."

"You have no choice in this matter."

"Is that what you think?"

"That is what I know."

Nicole sat there glaring up at him. She felt cornered, like a rat encountering a wall and hearing the growl of a hungry cat on its tail. A wave of defiance was swelling inside her, she could feel it spreading, rushing, giving purpose to her resolve.

"Now, I am going to get Mel and you are going to listen to everything he has to say; all you have to do is nod. He really doesn't need your input. We have briefed him. So promise me you will be just as cooperative as you were for the interview."

"Fuck you!" Nicole spat out at him.

She didn't see the balled fist that slammed into her face. The force was so much that she felt her cheekbone crack just in the instant that the blinding light of pain flashed across her and darkness washed over her. She went limp and collapsed on the couch.

The Private Investigator stood over her and smiled to himself with savage satisfaction. He had been waiting to do that for a *very* long time. He could taste it at the tip of his tongue. Blood. This was what he excelled at, inflicting unbearable pain. She would come around and shape up, he thought to himself. There would be many of that coming her way if she decides to develop a mind of her own, he told himself as he turned and walked over to the family room to meet up with Mel Rubinstein, a lawyer who was neck deep in the legal sewers of the Canadian justice system. The saying was that if Mel couldn't fix your case, no one else could, and if Mel represented you, no one fucked with you. He played under and above the law, but never by it. He was the pitbull. And the courts, back rooms, and police stations where his dog fighting rings. He knew how to aim for the jugular, he understood what it meant to bite down, hold tight, don't let go. He was an expert at going for the kill. The Sciorras had no idea of the earthquake that was about to hit them.

As he opened the door, he sighed, and said in his unfeeling

mind.

"Thank God I am on the side of Timothy." He knew with an unwavering certainty that no one stood a chance out-plotting or outsmarting the evil genius of no mean repute.

18

Therese walked out of the screen door that opened from the large sitting room into the lush garden behind the house. She walked towards her father who was sitting on his motorised wheelchair, staring at the rising sun.

She got to him and kissed him on the crown of his head before she walked over to the gazebo that stood a couple of steps away and brought over one of the chairs that sat under it. She placed it beside her father and sat down on it.

Therese didn't utter a word. She simply allowed the silence embrace them. The gold radiated over the horizon and sent red hues into the blue heavens. It was like a painting from one of the masters, Leonardo Da Vinci, Michelangelo, Van Gogh or Matisse materialising before their very eyes. The sounds of the morning gave ambience to it, rushing from the ravine that occupied the depths at the edge of the property, into her ears, and over her head. From birds of various breeds, flying from far-flung corners of the world with chirpings that told of stories of their journeys from the wondrous yonder, to the insects that harmonise with their high decibels and low registers, a commentary of the diverse character of Mother Nature. This was the world of the Sciorras; the world that was simple in as many ways as it was complex, was endearing in as many ways as it was repulsive. There, sitting with her father in the presence of the beauty of life, healing from the pain of the loss of her Annabelle by the sweet balm of the love of Timothy, Therese felt at home.

Nurse Maria who was sitting some paces away and working on her knitting kept stealing furtive glances at her. In her eyes was the burning fire of curiosity. She had noticed the huge diamond ring on her finger and was dying to find out how it came about.

"Isn't that sun so beautiful?" she asked in a whisper.

As usual, Andrew just stared forth in serenity of his troubling quiet.

She reached over and covered his right hand with her left hand. The diamond ring caught the glory of the rising sun, and dazzled in the fullness of its brilliance.

"Daddy, I hope you can hear me?" she said with her eyes on the rising sun. "Your baby is very happy, daddy," she continued in a barely audible whisper.

She massaged his hand very gently and turned to look at him.

"Timothy and I are engaged, Daddy; we are going to get married," she announced to the locked up mind in a controlled glee.

Just then, Timothy stepped out of the sitting room and walked towards them. Nurse Maria looked up at him and quickly looked away. She had learnt to steer way clear of him, in order not to incur the wrath of Phillip, and per chance, jeopardise her position in the house. He did not look at her, although he knew she was there. He had already decided on the hospice to dump Andrew in when he finally ascended the throne of the Sciorra Empire.

"Daddy, you must walk me down the aisle, so please get well for me," she pleaded.

Timothy arrived at her side, bent down, and kissed her on the lips.

"How is the old man doing?" he asked as soon as he straightened up.

"He is doing so much better."

"Really?" Timothy frowned in concern. It couldn't be. It shouldn't be, his mind screamed in panic as it searched for meaning in the sudden news.

"I'm speaking by faith." She replied without looking at Timothy and leaving her eyes staring lovingly at her father. There she was totally forgiving and bearing no ill will towards the man that she had often blamed for her mother's death, the man that her mother's family who had kept their distance ever since the funeral blamed for everything evil under the sun. If only she had looked up into the eyes of Timothy as he hovered over her and Andrew like an eagle with talons unleashed, hungry eyes zeroing in with focused attention and ravenous hunger on an unknowing prey.

"For a minute, I was so glad; don't worry, hon, I am with you in faith," he professed as he kissed her on her cheek and slowly massaged Andrew's shoulder. His face was in a wry smile. It mocked the very soul of his empty words and ridiculed the unconditional love that oozed out of Therese.

He stood there caught up in his own self adulation and didn't feel the eyes of Nurse Maria as it burned into him. She was not smiling.

Angela looked over at Osasu as he did his one hundredth push up. He was sweating and his agitated muscles bulged with raw energy. She was thinking as she gazed at him and when he stood up panting in exhaustion, she spoke.

"Therese Sciorra is getting married soon."

"Really?" Osasu asked in genuine surprise. His mind went into alert mode as he began factoring all the ways the news could or would affect his plans.

"Yes, she showed me the ring Timothy gave her, talk about huge, that thing is huge." There was no excitement in her voice.

"Why do I feel like you are not happy for her?"

"Maybe I'm not too thrilled with Timothy."

"Why?"

"I told you, there is something about him that is not like right."

"You still insist on that?"

"I have a thing for things like this; I pick them up like I have antennae."

"I see." Osasu said in ironic attestation of understanding. Strange she could pick up the nature of a man without good intentions who existed ways away from her world, yet for the man who shared her bed, she drew a blank. Love did not only blind the eyes; it also dulled the brains, he surmised to himself.

"Maybe you are a little bit envious or should I say jealous your new best friend is about to dump you for her new best friend."

"Jealous? Why? I am happy that she is happy and I want her to remain happy, that's why I look closely and watch continuously and I don't like what I see that's all." She said and decided at the nick of time not to tell him about the phone call from the Editor of *The Quill* and how she had refused to pass her message on to Therese. She had promised herself to try her utmost best to keep business and pleasure separate.

Angela sat there and struggled with the thought that had plagued her for days. She knew that she had received a boost of energy and courage when Therese showed her the ring. It wasn't jealousy or envy that had gripped her, but an affirmative realisation, something like anointed bulbs going off in her head, each one signifying that the time had come for her to step out of the Angela Di Canio as conceived, birthed, and moulded by her parents and extended family to the Angela that she was, created by her and for her.

"I was wondering if you would like to meet my parents," she blurted it out.

Osasu stood there and stared at her speechlessly. Her question had blindsided him and knocked the air out of him. Parents? He heard it reverberate around his emotional and mental hemispheres. This was not the plan. When you met your girlfriend's parents, you complicated issues and you created tracks in the sands of your deceit. He couldn't meet her parents, not now, not ever he silently swore to himself.

Then it hit him. How could he still make himself the center of her world and keep stringing her on, if he did not acquiesce to her offer which she had veiled as a question? He knew all too well that when women got to the worrying age or mental, socially-burdensome frame of mind that thought marriage, they were often very quick to toss in the baggage of time any man they deemed deadwood or barren land. They wanted to plant wise and invest wiser. Their time was money and frugality was the watch word.

He knew he couldn't afford to be seen as a basket in which water was being poured into by Angela. A wasted effort where loss needed to cut short and bleeding stopped. He knew he had to keep the illusion going until he got what he had so patiently and laboriously worked for. This was an all or nothing game and he gambled only to win.

He stared back at her and searched for a way out, but as her eyes bore into him in search of an answer, all he could think of was smile.

He smiled sweetly and she smiled back lovingly.

Nosa pulled out the clothes from the woven raffia basket and began pushing them in a haphazard fashion into the washing machine in the laundry room that existed in the basement of the building. Tirin Tirin was at another machine putting some whites into it with a careful deliberation that bordered on adulation of the very act in itself.

The machines were old models and had a junk look to them even though they worked perfectly. The room buzzed with activity as mothers struggled with crying babies, other with toddlers who couldn't keep still and kept sprinting around the room, girls clad in tight bum shorts and tops showing their midriffs chatted over the cell phones while they went about their laundry, women who worked like in a trance as they mechanically folded the clothes they had just brought out of the dryers, and the young men who seemed to look at doing laundry as a lengthy prison sentence with added hard labour. The fluorescent tubes that hung in parallel lines glowed down with an audible whine that sounded like a cricket that had lost its voice. It illumined the faces of the occupants of the room and all it revealed were the faces that told stories of hard, unforgiving work, a life that revolved from pay cheque to pay cheque, a sink in which was heaped plates of unresolved issues, emotional baggage that could bend the strongest knees, lives that were revolved so much around the now that they couldn't dare think about the later. This was Saturday morning in the tenements and it rang with the music of the at-the-edge human story.

Tirin Tirin looked over at Nosa and saw how he was heaping in the clothes. He left his load half way and dashed over to him.

"What are you doing, bro?" he asked in alarm.

"What does it look like?" Nosa responded. He hated the chore called laundry.

"You have to sort through them, check the pockets, do it with respect for the clothes. It's not fair to just push them in like that," Tirin Tirin said in a dramatic drawl that dragged on each third word.

"Do yours and I'll do mine." Nosa attempted to continue.

"Wait, let me show you." Tirin Tirin gently pried the shirt from Nosa's hands and slowly began going through the breast pockets. "You have to check to make sure there are no documents you forgot and don't want to lose, you check for loose change, money, a condom, things that you will weep over when you discover your hurried folly." He spoke with his over exaggerated sequence of checking through the shirt.

Nosa stood there watching him as he pulled out the clothes that Nosa had earlier put into the washer. These were the times that Tirin Tirin was so much of a pain in the butt that all he wanted to do was crap him out like a nauseating turd.

"Carefully, you check, you find nothing, you keep on this stack, you find something, you keep the something on the top of the machine and you keep the dress on the same stack. It is your property; treat it like it is yours."

"Okay, lesson taken, now let me continue."

"Wait, patience is a virtue, my young man, you have to watch, oh o, what is this?" Tirin Tirin said as he brought a business card out of the trouser pocket of one of the trousers he had been slowly going through. He looked at the card and read it "MARSHA STEVENS, ATTORNEY'S AT LAW"

"Let me see that," Nosa said reaching for the card.

Tirin Tirin handed it to him and just when Nosa was about to collect it, he pulled his hand back.

"Behave yourself." Nosa shook his head wearily.

"So, you are now a gigolo?" Tirin Tirin was smiling.

"Come on, man, behave."

"See me dey pity you say you never fire woman since you land Canada, I no know say as I waka enter work, u dey do kurukere moves, enter backyard go dey nack babe."

"Backyard? Christ. You are so native."

"U wan tell me say you no know backyard?"

"Give me the card."

"Who be the babe?"

"What babe?"

"You carry secret pass FBI, I swear."

"Stop keeping me waiting."

"Answer my question; where you find this babe from?"

"I don't even know who you are referring to."

"So the card carry im sef waka enter your kputu?"

"My God. You speak like you never left Nigeria." Nosa laughed.

"Sharap dia; you wan change topic. Answer the question; na where you find the babe?

"If I read the card, I will tell you."

"Tell me first."

"How will I tell you if I don't even know whose card it is?"

"Shebi you be bini man, use your zuguzuguness."

"You are one messed up—" He reached for the card that Tirin Tirin had raised up beside his head.

"Morrafucker?" Tirin Tirin interjected.

"I never called you—"

"Confess your sins!" Tirin Tirin challenged him.

"Shove it." Nosa feigned anger and turned around.

"Ah, na me you dey yarn Americana for? Shove it!" Tirin Tirin mimicked the speech of Nosa on the last phrase, "Omomo, abeg take your thing before you start to cry." he called out to him.

Nosa stopped, turned around, he couldn't hide his smile. He reached out and collected the card from Tirin Tirin's outstretched hand.

"Undercover freak," Tirin Tirin whispered.

Nosa jabbed him playfully on the chest and Tirin Tirin stepped back and began feigning a boxer ducking punches. Nosa stepped back hurriedly and once a couple of yards away from him, he began reading the printed words on the card. As he read it, his brow furrowed; he couldn't remember who had given him the card or where he had picked it up from. Tirin Tirin stopped his feigning, picked up the trouser, and began going through the other pocket while keeping his curious eyes on Nosa. Nosa's puzzled expression finally gave voice to Tirin Tirin's thoughts.

"You didn't tell me you had a court case," Tirin Tirin observed.

Nosa's face finally lit up in recognition and then morphed into a smile. "I had totally forgotten about her."

"Who is *her*?" Tirin Tirin asked, curiosity dripping from him like a cow in heat.

"She is a lawyer I met in the plane on my way here."

"So?" He stopped going through the clothes.

"So nothing. I just met her on the plane."

"And why did she give you her card?"

"I remember her saying something about me calling her if I need her help."

"And?"

"And what?" Nosa was getting flustered.

"And you don't need her help?" It was sarcastic.

"She is a lawyer; what will I need a lawyer for?"

"Can't you read where her office is?"

Nosa took another look at the card.

"Twenty-five Bay Street." he read out.

"That is like Bay and Front, man, don't you know money, power, connections when you see it?"

"I don't need a lawyer."

"A lawyer has connections; can't you see what you need, even more than your qualifications, exams and all the bullshit you are doing, is someone who can open the right doors for you?"

"But she is…"

"She is worth a try, come on, or are they doing you from your village?"

"You've started again." Nosa had had it with Tirin Tirin teasing him as it concerned the wickedly spiritual.

"You know you Edo people and your godfatherism and godmotherism of witchcraft."

"Please let's get this laundry done and get out of here."

"Get out of where?" Tirin Tirin looked like he was spoiling for a fight and in one quick movement he snatched the card from Nosa.

He brought out his cell phone, looked at the card, and began punching numbers into the phone. Nosa looked at him with his eyes rapidly opening in alarm.

"What are you doing?"

"What does it look like?"

"Are you crazy?"

"You are the one that is mad. You think I will watch you throw away your destiny?"

"Hey man, you can't do that."

Nosa hurried over to him and tried to grab the phone. Tirin Tirin shoved him away with one hand and he staggered with the sheer power of the little man. The other occupants of the room kept about their business even though they could observe the two men's drama from the corner of their eyes. The byword of survival in the tenements was to always mind your business. It was see no evil, hear no evil, report no evil.

"If you don't want me to do it, you can go hug a transformer." Tirin Tirin said laughing as he finished dialing. He lifted the phone and listened to it ringing. It rang thrice.

"Hello." Answered the voice on the other side.

Tirin Tirin did not say anything but pointed the phone at Nosa.

"Hello," Marsha said again.

Nosa rolled his eyes in vexation and collected the phone from the now smiling Tirin Tirin, he put it to his ears, and spoke.

"Hi, can I please speak with Marsha Stevens?"

"Speaking. Who is this?" she continued.

"It's Nosa, I met you in the plane a couple of months ago, the black guy, from Nigeria, you had..."

"Oh my, yeah, I was wondering whatever happened to you; nice to hear from you." She sounded genuinely happy.

Nosa couldn't help himself as he allowed his face melt into a beaming smile. Tirin Tirin was watching him and when he saw the smile, he playfully took a bow in self-congratulations. He made this call happen and he would take the glory whether given or not.

"Actually, I just came across your card and thought to call."

"Bless your soul, you should have called a long time ago; how have you been keeping?" she asked.

"So so."

"Just so so?"

"Well trying to re-qualify as a doctor here."

"Oh that's beautiful, good on you."

"Thank you."

"And have you been working by any chance?"

"Yeah, some odd jobs here and there, you know, nothing really big."

"Oh, I know how dispiriting that can be."

"Yeah, I just actually finished a little course and now would start looking for something more stable and in my field."

"Oh interesting, what was the course?"

"Uhm, it's the personal support worker program, so I can..."

"Oh I know what a PSW is; do you have any leads on places to apply?"

"Yeah, the normal nine yards sort of..."

"Oh my God, this is surreal... I can't believe it."

"What is it?" There was concern in his voice.

Tirin Tirin heard the change in tone and looked over at Nosa, his eyes betraying the concern that had enveloped him.

"Yesterday, a very good friend of mine, actually someone I look up to called me, and we were talking, you know, about this and that, catching up on stuff and she told me about needing to expand this beautiful business she has going for her and guess what?

"I have no idea."

"She is looking for PSW's... Can you beat that?... she tells me about it yesterday and you call me out of the blues today... that is the hand of God if you ask me."

Nosa closed his eyes as calmness flowed over him. Tirin Tirin was watching closely and he could see the peaceful demeanour that descended on Nosa. His senses piqued.

"You know what, I'll give you her number and you call her and you tell her I sent you, okay?"

"Yes, I will do that."

"You have a pen or I will text her number to you, is that a cell phone you called me on?" An excited Marsha asked him.

"Yes."

"Perfect! Her name is Sibongile Bene and she is the loveliest, nicest person you will ever meet, trust me, that woman will practically change your life."

And with those words, Nosa's life took an unexpected turn.

Phillip drove up to the imposing gate of the Sciorras' residence. It had a giant S in pure silver welded into its wrought iron framework. The uniformed guard whose head was visible in the plexiglass window looked at his black Jaguar XJS in recognition and opened the electronically-controlled gate. Phillip drove in and as was his habit, he stopped beside the window of the guard house. It opened and the guard's battle-hardened face appeared. He smiled in response to Phillip's already beaming smile.

"How are you doing this morning, Pierre?" Phillip enquired.

"Perfectly well, Mr. Neri." Pierre responded, warmed by the knowledge that Phillip knew every staff of the sprawling compound by name. He even knew the names of their wives and children. Pierre had worked with people over the years, during his time in the army and as a bodyguard for hire; people who were arseholes with a capital A; people who didn't view you as a human being even though you were ready to lay down your life for their safety; to these people, paying you handsomely was enough balm from their nonexistent conscience. He had now been with the Sciorras for five years and had experienced their joyful highs and painful lows. If there was a family he could die for with a smile, it was the Sciorras, if there was a person who he could brave the devastating effects of a nuclear bomb for, it was Phillip Neri.

"We should go grab a drink sometime soon," Phillip offered.

"That will be great, Mr. Neri." He accepted

"What will it take to make you call me Phillip?"

"Nothing, sir." Pierre smiled.

"We will see," Phillip challenged, saluted him, accepted the mirrored response from Pierre, and slowly drove into the compound.

As he navigated the long drive way that led up to the stately mansion, he allowed his mind wander to the breakfast he had earlier with Nurse Harriet. It was like harsh day and balmy night; like the howl of the sirocco and the whistle of the evening breeze; like the looming boredom of a starless night and the dazzling splendour of the northern lights. The difference between the prim-and-properly-dressed, ebony-skinned, politely-smiling, rule-following, impressionable-diligent, pleasantly-disposed Nurse Harriet and the jeans-wearing, lusciously curvaceous, happily-smiling, quick-to-laughter, effortlessly-confident, open-minded, crazily-funny, spiritually-aware, and deeply-insightful Harriet was as starkly contrast as white was with black.

He had surprised her by taking her to the popular celebrity breakfast hang out, Marcelo's, and they had eaten the morning special of baguettes, scrambled eggs, maple covered English biscuits, and steamed "free range" milk. And even though they had planned to spend no more than an hour, since she needed the replenishment of her delayed sleep, they had unconsciously found themselves talking and laughing over mugs of hot chocolate two and a half hours later. He had not really intended to connect with her on the multiple levels he found himself doing so effortlessly. Since before the semi-official date, he had pummelled himself into accepting that the modus operandi was going to be strictly business. He was grossly mistaken in all aspects, both in the spirit and letter of the delightful and refreshing indulgence in the haute cuisine of the territorial French.

As his car pulled up into the parking lot at the east side of the building, which stood beside the tennis courts, he saw Timothy walk towards his silver Buggati. Timothy on his part had on a smug smile and upon seeing Phillip called out to him without changing direction in a voice that was bursting at its edges with sarcasm.

"Hey Phillip, didn't think you'd still be hanging around here."

Phillip opened his door, picked up his slim attaché case and stepped out of the car. He was going to trade fire for fire. He refused to be intimidated by this bullish lout.

"I will be here a lot longer after you have been kicked out." It came out matter-of-factly. He made sure he ended it with a sardonic smile to counter the still smug-looking Timothy.

Timothy stopped and turned to Phillip.

"Seems like you have not yet heard the good news, my friend, or should I say, enemy; someone soon is going to be known as Mrs. Sciorra-Vinelatter and once that happens, you and all who you, I repeat, all who you care about or those who give a flying fuck about you, will be history. Now make sure you mark my words."

He turned and now laughing, walked briskly to his car. He was leaving later on that evening for Europe with Therese, a two-week vacation into the hedonistic heart of the continent of decadent royalty, borderless bohemia, fine-tuned culture, and divergent tastes. But before he boarded the Sciorra private Gulfstream V jet later that night, Timothy was focused on satisfying a deep craving that consumed him since a chance meeting at the Casa Loma basement eatery one afternoon several weeks ago. He got into his car, ignited it, engaged it, backed out of his parking space, and zoomed towards the gate with an ear-splitting screech. Phillip stood there and watched the Bugatti disappear around the winding driveway. He shook his head in deep incomprehension before he walked to the massive building and opened the huge, vintage wooden door that had been shipped from the Viking capital of York, with the story of it having been the door into one of King Haldan's throne rooms. It had been purchased at an antiquities auction in London, restored, and now protected the entrance into the inner enclaves of the Sciorras.

He walked into the foyer and rested his eyes on the large portrait of the Sciorra family that greeted anyone who stepped into the building. Andrew, Annabelle, and Therese, smiling in warmth and love at a time so far away in the past, when all seemed good and the future held immense hope. A time he knew was peopled with lies, deceit, and pain. He walked on through the foyer into the marbled hallway and just as he was about to head to Andrew's study to pay his normal morning visit, Therese ran down the spiral grand staircase. She wasn't running in fright or anger but in spirited joy. Phillip felt it in the air; the changed mood, the brightly-lit happiness, the wind of hope. And as soon as she stepped onto the hallway, his eyes flew to her right hand and beheld the dazzling stone. His breath halted for a moment as he took it all in, Therese on her way to a desecrated altar to seal her future in an accursed union with a soul who was itself an apostate. The omen hung heavily in the air and a funeral mode descended on him. Timothy was right. The beginning of the end had come. He stood there and watched Therese walk with spritely steps to him and surprise him with a kiss on his cheek and in a voice that rang with cheerful charm say to him.

"Morning, Philly."

And hearing his disembodied voice from an out-of-body experience, he answered as though in a hypnotic trance.

"Morning, Therese."

"You look like you just saw a ghost; it's me, Therese. I need to grab a bite and then we are going to sit down and talk over a lot of stuff. You want to have breakfast with me?" She continued, her voice overflowing with infectious joy.

Even though he couldn't swallow another morsel lest his stomach explode, Phillip found himself nodding. He was like a zombie. And even in the frozen state of his mind, he still could recognise the lady standing in front of him. A lady whose smile shown like a thousand ecstatic suns, whose voice sang out pleasingly loud and saintly clear, whose playfulness was virginal and whose charm was altruistic. This was the Therese he once knew, the Therese that he watched grow up, the Therese that always called him Philly and never Phillip; the former being a term of endearment, something shared between them and no one else. She was back. She was here. And yet about to go to a place he feared from which there would be no return.

"What will you have? I want to go to the kitchen and make breakfast myself... oh, yes! Let's make breakfast together; remember like the old days, me throwing the eggs to you, you catching them and cracking them open over the pan in that deft movement, like Ned Kelly gunning them down in the outback, pow! pow! pow!" She mimicked a pistol with both hands, "Bonny and Clyde, come on, let's go do it." She practically pulled him as she skipped in front of him.

He followed her and was stunned when he felt the tears mist up his eyes. He felt the love swell in his chest. The love he used to feel even though he could not claim to hold that kind of relationship with her. The love that was akin to that, which a father feels as he watches his daughter grow up. And with that love came the fear, with that fear came the desire to do all that was possible to keep the one you love safe from the dangers, both seen and unseen of this treacherous world.

But what could he do to stop the impending doom? He found himself asking in the riot of his mind. He saw it in the eyes of Timothy. He recognised it. It was there in its fullness of being; proud and unpretentious. He saw it. And it was Evil.

Just then, his phone beeped loudly. He had programmed that beep for a certain person, a beep that was supposed to wake him up from the deepest of slumbers and summon him from the most unmanageable chaos. His senses automatically focused and the cloud that beguiled his mind instantly cleared. It felt as though some invincible hand, maybe one of the divine varieties, had put a copious amount of smelling salts under his nose. He was alive, every nerve buzzing with bioelectricity. He reached into his pocket with his left hand and brought it out, since his right hand was being held by the giggling Therese who was saying something he really couldn't hear; it seemed to echo from a place so very far away. He looked at the screen of the phone and on it was the word, beeping in urgency, the word that was in itself a name, the name that was in itself Erik.

He clicked on it, a movement that was smoothly choreographed with the motion of them bursting through the swinging doors of the kitchen into the multiple sense-arousing aromas invoked by a hand possessing of exacting culinary skills.

A line of nine words appeared.

Nine words that in themselves fanned to life the dying embers of hope, nine words that in that fleeting moment provided Phillip with an escape from the future to which they had all been earlier condemned to.

The words which lined in front of one another in docility, yet possessing of immense powers were, "TIMOTHY IS ON HIS WAY, WE ARE A GO."

19

Andrew sat there in the loneliness of his world. His eyes were dull, but yet alive. A light flickered deep in the shadows of his pupils. It wasn't a reflection of the morning light that streamed in from the window of the study or Nurse Maria's knitting needles that in itself was also catching the sunrays that illuminated the room. It was the slow unlatching of the bolt that held locked in his memories. It was the light of an awakening of his consciousness.

As he sat there, his frail frame hidden in his thick grey flannel robe, the first memory slipped into his semi-consciousness. It was about the day of the death of Annabelle. It started with a warm buzz; the sound of something vibrating. It was persistent. His eyes opened and through the fog of his sleep, he saw his cell phone dancing on the bedside table. It moved round and round in a circle and then stopped when the buzz ended. It lay motionless beside his quiet pager—two tools of instant communication, his umbilical cords to the demanding world—lying loyally together.

He closed his eyes and just as he was about drifting back to sleep, the buzz started again. He held his eyelids shut and waited for the phone to fall quiet. He counted and it buzzed. He counted and still it buzzed. Finally exasperated, he reached over and picked up the phone. He didn't want to look at the caller display since he knew who it was. The phone had rung all through the evening that came before the night that just passed and had now started again.

He had been tempted to switch off the phone or put it on silent to kill the irritating buzz, but he had never done that since the day he first acquired a cell phone and had no intention of starting that day. There were certain rules he lived by, one of which was always being reachable—at least within his human powers. He would let the phone ring. He would not let Annabelle run his life. He would not give in to her hounding.

That day, he lay on the well-slept-in bed in the bedroom of Nicole, which was in the condominium he had bought for her in downtown Toronto. He was naked and was alone on the bed. The sound of running water could be heard drifting from the en-suite bathroom. He closed his eyes once again and right at that moment, the phone started up again. He lifted it up and looked at the display. Annabelle blinked at him. He was right. It had been her. Over fifty calls in a day. A mind fixated so much on him that it practically wilted his spirit. The love he once had shrivelled as the seconds ticked away. Sometimes he swore to himself that he despised her with a perfect hatred but just when he decided to begin his plans for disengagement, he laid his eyes on her in a chance meeting around their sprawling residence and was startled by the rush of deep emotions that flooded him.

At those times, he realised and was reminded once again that the fire of his love for her might burn hot, flicker, wane, but its embers never died. He knew that breaking the bond binding them together was a feat that existed in the realm of the impossible. He was someone that picked his battles. He fought only those that he could win. The final break might not be possible, but frequent escapes to the privacy of his several hidden residences for his carnal dalliances with a plethora of women was something he would not deny himself, whether Annabelle liked it or not. As the thoughts swirled in his mind that day, the door of the washroom opened and a naked Nicole walked out, smiled at him, and walked to the bed.

"Someone's awake," Nicole said.

"Someone's lovely," he replied with a refreshed smile.

"You know me and my morning showers."

"Makes you smell delicious."

"Enough to eat?"

"Enough to devour."

"If I wasn't this sore, I would surrender."

"We could lube it up."

"I don't want to give you a heart attack."

"I'm fitter than all those young guns you give what is mine to."

"There is no one but you, Andy, and you know that."

"So you say."

"And you don't believe?"

"Well, an eye in love is blind."

"I will never take your love for granted, Andy?"

"Promise?"

"I promise never to do anything that would hurt you," she said with an earnest seriousness before she leaned forward and kissed him.

Once again, the cell phone began to buzz on his chest. Nicole looked down at it.

"Ignore it; she'll tire and stop."

"It's not Annabelle," she said, looking at the call display.

"Really?" he asked in surprise.

"Yeah, it says, 'Ibude.'" She hesitated as she pronounced the last word.

"Oh." He picked up the buzzing cell phone from his chest and looked at the name that was flashing on the screen. She was right. He picked the call. She rolled over and lay on her back for an instant before rolling to her side to watch Andrew on the phone.

"Hello, Mister Nigeria," he said with a fond smile.

"Hi, Andrew." Ibude's voice was heavy.

"Are you okay?" Andrew picked up the gloom in his voice.

"Disaster." The word dropped with despair.

Andrew sat up. His face suddenly moulded into a frown. Nicole looked at him in worry. She gestured to him in silent words that said.

"What's wrong?"

"I'll tell you later." He gestured back with silent words.

She settled back and watched him as he listened to the voice at the other end of the phone.

"I've lost everything," Ibude said with solemnity.

"How do you mean?" There was genuine concern in Andrew's voice.

"My son... my son..." His voice trailed off.

"What about your son?"

"He took it all... he has destroyed me." Ibude managed the last word and broke down into deep sobs.

Andrew was lost for words. He could hear the borderless pain in the sobs that floated across the yawning distance. He remembered meeting Ibude at the World Economic Summit at Davos in Switzerland. They had both been sequestered in a high-level meeting which was set up for a group of twenty super successful businessmen from North America and Africa. It was about private socio-economic development initiatives in Africa and Ibude had made a brilliant presentation.

They were drawn to each other like a wandering fly to a fly

trap. Andrew remembered the mentally engaging days and socially relaxing nights they spent in the posh restaurants that dot the glittering districts in several capital cities around the world and the leisurely weekends spent on private yachts and country golf courses. Theirs were a meeting of like minds. Two incredibly smart, business-savvy, and socially-graceful men meeting to forge a new relationship, one that was based on mutual respect, like-minded opinions, and unified vision. It wasn't a public show of affection or one that paid lip service to a different form of cooperation than what normally obtains. It was instead hidden from public view, built cautiously, yet diligently in an arena that was as individual as it was collective. Two men with a belief that their destinies were tied; therefore, the need to work together was a duty they were bound to perform.

"I'm sorry," Andrew said finally as he struggled to make sense of what Ibude had said. He knew Ibude had two sons but he had never met them. He also knew he was a widower and a man who loved his family with a nurturing and protective fierceness. In all their meetings Ibude had exuded filial love and Andrew had presumed that it was the central theme of his family, a reciprocal feeling that bonded the Eweka family together. So, he was thrown off balance now that Ibude had just told him about his son destroying his fortune. It was at that moment the thought came back, but before he could pull it together, Ibude spoke.

"I need help."

"You haven't lost everything."

"How do you mean?" There was a ring of confusion to his voice.

"Remember Aqua terra 550?"

There was silence. It lasted for a minute and was punctured by a sigh from Ibude. And as though in obeisance to the helpless sigh, Nicole's eyes finally shut as she drifted off to sleep.

"I can't remember."

"The oil prospecting block in Venezuela."

"Oh, yes, I remember, but Chavez cancelled that."

"Yes he did, but just three days ago, I was speaking to Ambassador Guardiola at the Venezuelan embassy; he said he could do something about it."

"And you believe him?"

"I believe me."

"What?"

"I am going to chase that lot; it's ours and I don't care what that communist hothead thinks. We paid good money for it, so he has no right to seize from the rich and give to the poor."

"It's gone; don't waste your time."

"Are you telling me that you are going to allow the millions of dollars you invested in that oil lot just go to the dogs like that?"

"Andrew, this is not the time for political shenanigans or economic crusades. Chavez has never given back anything he seized, so I can't wait for any pipe dream, or some litigation that will take forever; I need money right now, not tomorrow, not the next, now!" Ibude's voice echoed with desperation.

"You are serious about this." It was a whisper.

"I have been calling you for the last hour; do you think by any chance I will do that for some April fool's joke?"

"I'm sorry, I didn't mean to make light of it; how much do you need?" Andrew asked.

Nicole's eyes flung open. She was frowning, her protective instincts bursting at the seams, like a hen whose chick was being circled by a soaring eagle.

"I need to keep the banks away."

"How much do you need?" Andrew's tone was calm.

"Three million dollars."

"I will wire it to you in three hours."

"Thank you."

"You're welcome."

"Once I get it sorted out and the banks don't swoop on my

assets, I will get the money back to you." Ibude promised in a voice that breathed relief.

"No, look at it as a gift."

Nicole sat up; her eyes were crisscrossed in fury. She clenched her teeth to prevent herself from shouting.

"Andrew, please don't do this."

"I insist; now you go rest, clear your mind. We will sort this out," Andrew reassured him. Nicole crossed her arms over her chest and silently fumed.

"You saved my life."

"It's just money; if you lose it, you can always make more."

"Not in my world; without you giving me this money, my only way out will be to die."

"Don't say stuff like that; only cowards quit."

"I cannot scrounge, no, I cannot live like a beggar."

"Okay, stop all this talk and go to bed or go watch some TV or something. I told you that I will handle it. Now, I'll hang up and call you when it's done. Take care of you, okay? Stay easy, Mister Nigeria," he said with a chuckle and hung up.

"Three million dollars as a gift?" Nicole exploded.

Andrew placed the phone back on the bedside table and leaned back on the headboard of the all white queen-size bed. The gloom of Ibude had also descended on him.

"Andy, what is wrong with you?" She said with ironic incredulity.

Andrew turned to her and stared at her infuriated eyes. For an instant, a wave of irritation and ingratiating disgust swept over him. Annabelle would have urged him to give more, would have pushed him to help, and here was Nicole, mad at his generosity. Her greed seeped from every pore of her smooth skin. Was it youth that made her so selfish or was it simply her nature?

"I told you not to concern yourself with my business." It came out matter-of-factly.

"Are you shutting me out?"

"You were never in." he felt an urge to hurt her deeply, a desire to unmask her and have her peep into the rot in her soul. She was shocked.

"Andy?"

"Yes."

"How can you speak to me like that?" Her eyes had suddenly gone misty.

He stared at the first tear as it slid down her right cheek. This girl was either the greatest actress he had come across or the most naïve angel on earth. One minute she was all about his money and the luxuries he could provide and the next minute she was ready to go to bat for him, take a bullet, fight a bull, walk over hot coals, and swallow a vial poison. Was he wrong to have judged her protectiveness of him, her desire not to allow cheats get to his money, as greed or hard-heartedness? Another tear dropped as she stared at him silently.

"When would you start learning how to take my jokes?" He leaned towards her.

"It's not fair." She pleaded in an already weeping voice.

"I will show you what is fair," He gently kissed her on the lips.

"Andy, stop."

"Sssshhhh." He gently pushed her back on the bed and slid over her, his lips covering hers and willing her into total submission.

They kissed tenderly and in seconds allowed the heat of their passion take charge. Andrew felt his cells come awake. His pores dilated and blood pumped into spongy tissues. His muscles hardened and throbbed and just when he manoeuvred into position, Nicole gently pried her lips away from his.

"Wait." It was like a low moan.

"Why?"

"I don't want your phone to kill the fun."

"My phone?"

"It rang all night and threw me off."

"Just ignore it." He attempted to kiss her again. She turned her head away.

"Put it off."

"You know I can't."

"Okay, put it on silent." She was whispering.

"I can't miss my calls."

"You don't even answer it when it rings."

"I need to know it rang."

"There is something called voice mail, Andy."

He kept grinding his torso on her washboard stomach and gently kneading her perky breasts, the tip of his fingers alternately caressing her hardened nipples.

"Come on, don't ruin the moment."

"I need to enjoy it just as much as you."

"I will make it fast; we will be done before it rings again." He was impatient, hurriedly trying to pry open her legs, which were clenched together, with his knee.

"I want it to last, Andy." She clenched tighter.

He stopped and stared down at her. Why were these women so insistent on changing the well-laid-down rules of his life? Why did he have to pay so much to eat his indiscretions and still have his integrity?

"Please." It came out as a plea laced with the touching tone of pity.

Her face was like a lost kitten crying for help. She looked so vulnerable, so defenceless, so young, so naïve, like a prepubescent caught at the dusk of innocence. Just the way he truly liked it. He felt his resistance wane.

"Just this once and never again," he said as he reached over, picked up the phone, and pressed the button that instantly silenced it. He placed it back on the table and turned to her. His eyes were hungry and his nose slightly flared in rising ardour.

"Fuck me, daddy," she cooed in the most childlike voice she could muster.

Andrew felt himself fall over the edge and drop into a swirl of raging lust and as he proceeded to make hot, sweaty love to her, he remembered Ibude and the dilemma that confronted him; he was tempted to do as he had promised, but the strong arms of lust held him securely in its grip. He decided to give into the urgings of his hormones and made a mental note to call Phillip and have him wire the money to Ibude. For now his entire being craved for release and he was going to give it that which it desired.

His body yearned to connect in totality with the lusciousness that was Nicole, so he drew a dark blind over the fermenting thoughts of Annabelle, Ibude, and all the big and small things that usually plagued his mind and totally zeroed in on Nicole. She was the only lady he knew who did this to him, who aroused him by the mere sound of her sultry voice, whose body—whether clothed or not—set him on fire. He knew he stood on the verge of love with her, and it was a love that was focused on much more than her body, a love that was at peace with the ease of her company, that blended effortlessly with the vitality of her youth, that was like an eternal fire that perfected his imperfections and imbued him with the mindset of the boy he once was. It was a love that he really couldn't define. A love he really did not want to define since it came loaded with infinite complications. He didn't want to think about the strangeness of his love for her because right at that moment all he wanted to do was ravish her completely and worship at the temple of feminine bod.

As he slid down to her erect nipple, he could never have imagined that a phone call was going to come barging into their sensual reverie and change his idyllic paradise of a life into a chaotic, miserable hell in which all was still and silent and only pain that defies description was the consciousness that exists.

As he sank into her moist eagerness, he could never have imagined that because he was going to be abruptly shocked into deafening silence in a couple of hours, he would not make the call to Phillip. And since he did not call, there would not be any money wired to Ibude. And because Ibude would call repeatedly in the ensuing days and not be able to get through to him, since Phillip shut his phone, he would feel so shamefully abandoned and miserably hopeless that the only solace he would think of will be the peace that comes with death. A death that came in the form of a car filled with pungent, poisonous exhaust fumes.

Even as he sat on his well-padded couch in the study that day, trapped in the slow unfolding of his mental recollection, Andrew's eyes slowly came into focus from darkness to a pin of light that appeared to glow from a distance. He strained with all his might and focused on the tiny white spot and it grew; slowly, very so slowly. He also began to feel the presence of his surroundings. He could sense another person in the room with him, so he tried to turn, but there was no movement, just the little consciousness that was blossoming in his mind, rolling around in listless vacuum. He focused on the white spot, but it was now static. It wasn't moving; neither backwards nor forwards. It just stood there, like a distant star in the night sky, so far and yet so close. In a feeling of dismay, he returned to focusing on turning to face the other presence.

He tried, he tried, and he tried, and just when he was about giving up, he felt his finger move. It wasn't his finger but what felt like a finger, something that felt like a natural extension of him. He tried again; it was a short trial, as he had cut it short because dollops of exhaustion rained down on him, a feeling of weariness so heavy that all he wanted to do was take his focus away from the speck of light that stood so far away in the distance and just surrender to the lull of the darkness of the surrounding calm.

And just when he decided to surrender to the darkness, more memories began to ignite. It began with the sound of his beeper going off as he ploughed sensually into Nicole. He remembered ignoring its insistent beeps. He remembered listening to the voice message on his cell phone, the sound of Phillip's voice in panic and horror and as he tried to remember the words Phillip uttered, a memory crashed into his awakening consciousness and abruptly extinguished the earlier memories. It was actually a picture of a yellow body bag being lifted on a stretcher into a waiting ambulance. The word screamed at him through the undefined darkness, Annabelle!

And just as his re-awakening had begun, so did it vanish. One minute he was here. The next he was gone. The speck of light receded at a dizzying pace until it disappeared altogether. And it was as though an unknown force sucked into extinction his rising awareness of his surroundings. Like the gravitational pull of a black hole sucking into its abyss, defenceless stars. The flickering light in his pupils had disappeared and only the steadily breathing husk of his person remained.

Andrew sat there locked up in a vortex, like he had been for days. This time around, tiny beads of sweat were on his forehead, and if Nurse Maria had looked up from her knitting, she would have noticed that he had moved his right hand, and now instead of it resting on the arm rest, it was now resting on his knee.

As miracles happen, Nurse Maria raised her head and looked over at Andrew. He looked okay, she muttered to herself, and as she was turning her eyes back to her knitting, she stumbled on the right arm rest of the couch. She squeezed her face in bewilderment; she squinted her eyes to see better. She was not seeing things, she confirmed.

"Mr. Sciorra, did you just move your hand?" she asked with a hint of confusion.

Andrew sat there unresponsive as the real reality swarm

around the vortex of his subsumed reality with the electric verve of life.

20

The year hurtled on to the yellowing leaves and semi-chilly winds of autumn as it shed itself of the warmth and carefree giddiness of summer. The cold hand of death switched off the eternal switch of life and ended the existence on the earthly plane of many a soul. The beaming gaze of hope and nonexistent prejudices of unconditional love welcomed with open arms, the unseeing eyes who announce their entrance to a complicated world with a cry that gladdens even the hardened heart. Drops of deep joy and even deeper sorrow fell like raindrops on the heads of all those who people the earth, yet the beacon of hope shone for all whose eyes were focused on the horizon of tomorrow.

Sibongile continually nurtured the broken souls she led with love on a healing journey. The lawyer battled without end in his burdened mind under the blazing Nigerian sun, the temptation to submit to the doubts and excuses of the rigors of battle and the desire to unearth lost treasures and pay back an old friendship with an unflagging loyalty. Marsha celebrated a reunion with the charming soul she met on her journey back home, and regretting her inaction at the airport a long time ago, promised to extend without fail a hand of help to ease the burden of resettlement that she knew the promising soul would face. The enigma known as Safe sat late into endless nights fashioning that which he believed will open the cache of indescribable treasures and cement his name in the halls of infamous lore. Erik waited in a hastily-booked penthouse for the arrival of a soul most vile as he strove with a singular mind to rectify a deed so evil. Pierre peopled each day of his militarised life with a conviction and acceptance that it might be his last. Mel sunk into the legal cesspool of traps and counter-traps as he marshalled the forces of untruth for an unprecedented attack on the citadel of the Sciorras. Nicole surrendered to the grip of the Private Investigator who held her without mercy as she accepted the dictum that a coward lives to fight again. The Private Investigator allowed the beast in him rear its ugly head as the thirst for blood existed to him as recompense for the frugal morality of his earlier life. The Editor's temper flared and her ego bristled as she fleshed out her story and struggled to hold true to the line that separated the professionalism of her mind with the vanity of her soul. Silvio looked forward to introducing to his private world, the social gem of a character he had befriended in his public world. Nurse Harriet and Nurse Maria stood at opposite ends of a duty to care; the former treasuring a glimpse into the heart and life of a man she admired, not daring to wish for much in order not to be grossly disappointed while resolving to do what was right and keep her peace, the latter searching with urgency for stories that consolidated her fame as the only one of those who lived at the outskirts of the life of the fortunate who had an entry into the lives of the extremely fortunate. Tirin Tirin kept being his ebullient self even when life threw balls at him that spoke the languages of fortune and misfortune, he held the hand of a brother he had found and marched with unfailing courage into a future unseen. Angela stood at the edge of her conflicted character and wondered how far her plunge would take her, if she decided to jump into the abyss of her true self and flee the world of that which she had pretended to be. Osasu kept his gaze at the future, fighting hard not to look back at the ruinous path of destruction that littered his past; he fought nightmares and held onto the schemes of his heart, holding at bay a demanding love even as he dreamt of the fortunes that lay ahead for him. Timothy pursued the dark with drunken abandon, he craved power and controlled his pawns, that which was fake he sold for real, and mortgaged the hope of all for his monstrous dreams. Phillip held his tongue and bottled his emotions, he made silent vows that spoke of his loyalty, he pushed his mind to scheme and plan as he built barricades to save the ones he loved. Therese sailed into the future with a heart brimming with love. She held nothing against her father and threw caution to the wind, the urge to be her own person faded into the past as once again she placed Timothy on the highest pedestal, his love she counted as a gift to treasure.

Different souls existing in a world of competing aspirations as days turn into weeks and the future marries the past, and when time will mature like the grapes in a vineyard, which hang ready for plucking, and memories will coalesce into an abiding understanding, the wheels of that which have happened will spin into that which will happen and the end of this story will become the beginning of yet another story.

THE STORY CONTINUES IN 'BY YOUR OWN HANDS' (BOOK TWO IN 'THE HANDS TRILOGY.')

ACKNOWLEDGEMENTS

To all the Angels who walk the earth as living souls, selfless beings who have crossed my path as I embarked on the journey of writing this novel, you know who you are, for being the bridges that enabled me cross life's stormy waters, the footstools that helped me climb over the looming obstacles and the ceaselessly flowing fountains that quenched my thirst. Words are not enough to express my deep appreciation and pure gratitude. Without you none of this would have happened. I say in full genuflection; thank you.

ABOUT THE AUTHOR

A multi award-winning screenwriter, poet and playwright and a graduate of the celebrated Theatre Arts department of the University of Ibadan, Jude Idada extensively writes, produces, and directs critically acclaimed plays, documentaries and feature films.

He lives in Toronto, Canada and Lagos, Nigeria.

www.judeidada.com

Other Books by Jude Idada

Short stories
A Box of Chocolates

Poetry
Exotica Celestica

Drama
Oduduwa – King of the Edos

Made in the USA
Charleston, SC
15 February 2015